ESCAPE

FROM THE

SHADOWS

C L Tustin

Copyright © 2021 by C L Tustin

Cover design by Creative Covers

ISBN 978-1-8382139-1-6 (paperback)

ISBN 978-1-8382139-0-9 (ebook)

Published by Cebalrai

For Sarah

With love

(thanks for all the nagging…!)

Cx

24th December 1969...

NATALIA TRAVESS LOOKED into the mirror and saw a stranger staring back at her.

Her hair was a mess from where she had pulled it in her frustration, her mascara was smeared across her ghostlike face after she had wiped away the tears, and she could still see the shock in her blue eyes reflecting back at her.

Why did it hurt so much this time? She knew he had cheated on her many times, knew he lied to her more than he ever told the truth, so why did this time hurt so much?

She had found her breaking point. He had finally pushed her too far. In her house. In her *bed*. No, he could not frighten or charm her into staying this time.

This time, she was taking their little girl and going.

Natalia hurriedly stuffed some clothes for her daughter into a bag and rushed the sleepy child from her room, shaking all the way down the stairs. *Car keys.* She needed the keys, but hers were in the bedroom—*that* room, where he was with that tart. She would take *his* car—his beloved Bentley—and that gave her a momentary stab of pleasure amongst all the anguish.

Natalia was still shaking as she put her daughter on the back seat and shoved the bag in next to her. The little girl yawned. "It's ok, *malyshka,*" she soothed. "We are going to stay at Aunty Fenella's and see the horses."

The child smiled, yawned again and lay back against the big seats, looking impossibly small in the huge car.

Natalia hesitated, suddenly doubting her strength to do this; doubting if she could actually leave him. She could suddenly hear her best friend's words in her head, pleading with her to get out of her bad marriage, where he cheated and lied and she was sometimes too scared to move. She had argued with Fenella that he had never touched her, never touched their child, but her friend had responded that it was only a matter of time and she deserved so much better. They *both* deserved so much better than Jack Travess and his temper.

Natalia slammed the Bentley into reverse. She was not used to driving his car and she ground the gears, causing them to scream just like she had wanted to.

Halfway up the gravel drive, she remembered to turn on the headlights. It was cold; it was dark. It was also Christmas Eve, and it was this last thought that provoked the tears that began to flow again, partially blinding her.

"Mama." A small voice made itself heard above the grinding of the gears and the roar of the engine. "Mama, why are you sad?"

Natalia jumped; she had momentarily forgotten her daughter was there. "Mama is not sad, *malyshka* she has a cold. Go to sleep. We will be at Aunty Fenella's soon."

She swung the Bentley onto the road and slid on the ice that had started to form. She switched the lights onto full beam and slowed down, thinking. She wished she could *stop* thinking. She had been nothing more than a girl— a beautiful girl, a prima ballerina, the youngest ever with the Royal Ballet—when she had met him. Jack Travess: singer, star—and absolutely gorgeous. She had fallen hard, believing him when he'd said he loved her, and within three months, she was pregnant and he married her. Her life had felt complete.

Their daughter, her little Anastasia, was born a year to the day they had first met.

"So romantic," Jack had said, whilst his mistress was waiting in the car outside the hospital. It seemed such a long time ago.

Natalia could not help the sob that escaped her, and her foot pressed harder on the accelerator. She needed her friends. She needed sanctuary.

Her thoughts drifted again; she had been so lonely in the beginning, but his bandmates had befriended her, sympathising with all her woes. Two of them were married already and the third was getting divorced, but they had all, at some stage, begged her to leave him; begged her not to let her daughter grow up in that toxic house.

Natalia swerved suddenly—ice again—and she reflexively slowed down.

She remembered the first time she had realised her husband was a philanderer. Back then, she had excused him; he was a rock star with girls throwing themselves at him all the time, and it was not his fault that he was tempted, that he was weak. But, deep down, she knew it was. It was his fault and no-one else's. Natalia clung to that, clung to the belief that her daughter deserved a happy home, and she accelerated again. She knew that if she did not get there soon, she would eventually weaken and would find herself crawling back to him.

Tormenting herself, she recollected all the names he had called her, all the awful things he had said and how he behaved so perfectly when others were around. His act was so polished, he deserved an Oscar.

She pressed her foot down harder, angry now.

Suddenly, Natalia was at the crossroads. She slammed on the brake, and the car skidded. It slid as she desperately tried to get it back under control, but to no avail; it slammed into a tree, an awful crunching filling the silent air.

Her head hit the steering wheel hard as the car came to rest from the impact. She heard a little girl crying. She tried to speak. She knew no more.

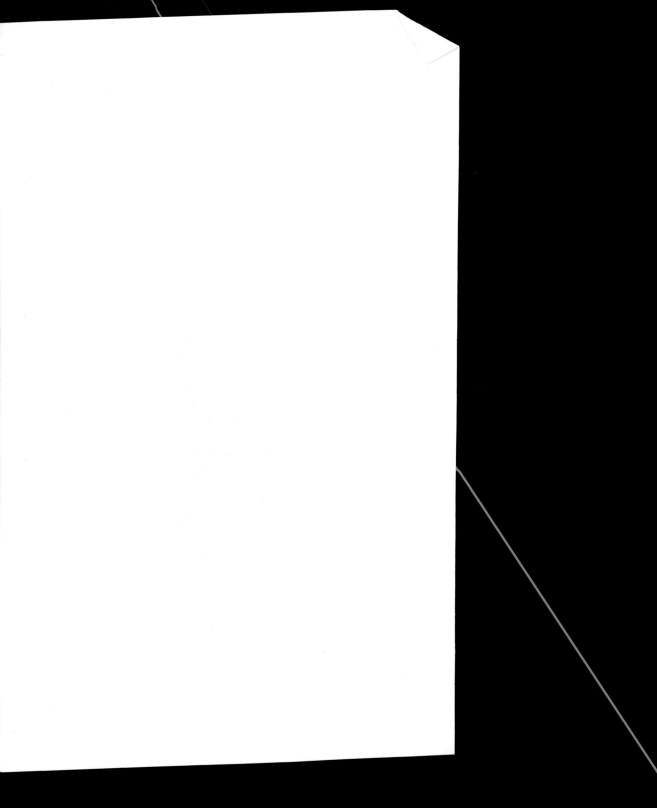

Chapter 1

23rd December 1989

THE E-TYPE JAGUAR in British racing green wound its way up the long gravel driveway and pulled to a halt outside Starbrook Manor in Hertfordshire; a rambling Jacobean extravaganza smothered in Christmas lights. It looked to the driver like someone had run riot in Selfridge's Christmas department and then stopped by Harrods for good measure. The huge open double doors were flanked by enormous Christmas trees that were both lavishly decorated with glimmering white and blue lights. The whole thing was way over the top. Piers Talbot tore his eyes away and focused on the doors.

She was waiting for him. "Piers!" Joy sounded clear in her musical voice as she ran forward to yank open the driver's door.

Piers climbed effortlessly out of the car and grasped the hands held out to him, lifting them to his lips to kiss them. He was over six feet tall and towered over the glowing, dark-haired woman who gazed up into his deep blue eyes.

"I am so pleased to see you!" Anastasia Travess threw her arms up and around him, grateful not to see any new scars or bruising on his face.

He held his beloved friend close and said into hair that always smelled of Chanel, "You have no idea how glad I am to be back.

9

And to have some time off. I've missed you."

Anastasia stepped out of his embrace as her boyfriend coughed discreetly from behind her. She laughed and turned, saying playfully, "Don't worry. I haven't forgotten you, Bryan."

Piers nodded to him and held out his hand. Bryan Darnell was not quite as tall as the lean, black-haired man now shaking his hand. "Congratulations," began Piers. "I like your new single. It's doing well, by all accounts."

Anastasia went back into the house, calling out as she went, "Leave your luggage by the door, Piers. Someone will take it to your room."

As Bryan made to follow her, Piers put a hand out to stop him. "I've been hearing rumours," he said darkly. "*Blonde* rumours."

Bryan raised one dark eyebrow that contrasted with his ruthlessly bleached hair.

Piers continued. "I'm not saying they're true, but if they are and Anastasia is left unhappy, you and me won't be friendly anymore." His tone was silky smooth, but the eyes were as sharp as shards of ice.

Bryan put up his hands in a defensive gesture and stammered, "You know how much she means to me."

Ignoring him, Piers brushed past and stepped into the entranceway.

Anastasia's father Jack Travess, ageing singing legend of the rock band Retribution, was not due until the following day, and so it was a somewhat thankful threesome that sat down to dinner. Anastasia observed Piers carefully, picking up on the slightly chilly atmosphere. "What's up, handsome? Are you tired?" she asked.

He laughed. "No, sweetheart. I'm just miffed about South America."

"South America? Is that where you've been this time?" Bryan was keen to embrace any subject not related to the rumours about his infidelity.

Piers nodded.

"Trouble?" Bryan asked, intrigued. He had never quite

managed to work out exactly *what* Piers Talbot did for Her Majesty's Government.

"Local issues," Piers replied evasively. "I had to call on a bit of assistance to smooth things over." He took a drink, and his eyes, alive with mischief, met Anastasia's. Hers were an even deeper blue than his own, and they had those little devils dancing in them that he loved. "Anyway, work is work. I'm so looking forward to the party tomorrow night and then a real Christmas with all the trimmings." He had decided not to tell Anastasia who her father had invited as a surprise, primarily as it suited his purposes not to forewarn her. She needed to make up her own mind on this one.

"Bryan is going to sing for us tomorrow, and, of course, there will be salsa music." Knowing Piers so well, Anastasia knew when to change subjects, when to push topics and, most importantly, when to stop.

"Ah, sweetheart! Salsa music and you? Words I've longed to hear." Piers grinned at her and reached across the table for her hand.

Bryan watched this flirtation with narrowed eyes. Two years ago, he had been so consumed with jealousy over the chemistry between the two of them that he had unwisely picked a fight with Piers; something he was lucky he lived to regret. Bryan knew that Piers' and Anastasia's relationship was the most important one in both their lives. Throughout his relationship with Anastasia that had been made painfully clear to him. To keep Anastasia, whom he loved passionately, he accepted that Piers' presence was non-negotiable, and that would not change because of his feelings. But be that as it may, it didn't mean he liked it.

"Where's Suzanna?" Piers asked casually, letting go of Anastasia's hand to reach for his glass.

"She'll be here soon. The film she's working on had to re-shoot some scenes, and they couldn't manage without her. She is the best make-up artist in the business, after all."

As if on cue, a doorbell clanged in the distance and Anastasia half-rose from the table, listening. A few moments later, a slender young woman with long honey blonde hair came through the doors. They all rose to greet the new arrival.

"Suzanna!" Anastasia reached her first and briefly embraced her. "Did you get everything finished?"

Suzanna smiled at her friend, her green eyes holding a sweet, kind expression. "Yes, all done, so now I'm free until the New Year." She returned the embrace warmly.

"Look who made it home!" Anastasia's pleasure was obvious as Piers came around the table to join them.

"Hi, Suzanna. Nice to see you again." Piers smiled down at her, and, as always, Suzanna felt that slight shiver run down her spine.

Then she was facing Bryan Darnell, her heart skipping a beat and unable to help a faint blush from stealing across her face as he leant over to kiss her cheek. "Glad to see you," he said. "Have you eaten?" He grinned at her expression, appreciating her evident admiration.

"Yes, darling," began Anastasia. "Do you want something to eat? What can I get you to drink?"

Suzanna settled herself at the table and replied, "Some soup and a coffee would be nice, please."

Anastasia rang a bell and repeated Suzanna's request before changing her seat to move next to Piers. Bryan had been expecting this. It was always the same; as soon as Piers Talbot was home, he was the centre of her attention. Bryan sighed, sat back down beside Suzanna and engaged her in light-hearted conversation.

As soon as Suzanna had finished eating, the four moved into one of the manor's drawing rooms.

"This place is far too big! What *was* your father thinking when he bought it?" Bryan asked.

"Well, I think it was a tax swindle, to be honest. Original owns it." Original was the record label fronting Retribution's music. "My father just pays rent to his own company."

Bryan laughed. "That I understand," he said, tightening his hold on Anastasia and hoping they would soon go to bed.

Once in the drawing room Anastasia poured them all drinks as Piers switched on the radio. Within five minutes, they were all dancing in the middle of the room, all four singing along and making a reasonable harmony.

Suzanna yawned suddenly. "I'm really sorry, but I'm exhausted and I think it's time I called it a night. Goodnight, people." She bestowed kisses on them all before heading to her room.

Bryan sat down and watched Anastasia; she knew how to move, and he really wanted to take her to bed. He stood up and said abruptly, "Let's go up, too, Stasia. You've got a lot to do tomorrow, what with the party and that."

Anastasia turned around to face him, and she could feel his frustration. "Well, you go up if you want." She saw his eyes flicker up and down her figure and she added, "It's ok, he's not here, so you can sleep in my room." She laughed at his expression.

Bryan moved forward and jerked her roughly into his arms. "Don't be long," he said, kissing her and holding her close.

Slightly breathless, Anastasia replied, "I'll be up when I'm ready." She turned her back on him to carry on dancing with a now smug-looking Piers.

Bryan walked out of the room, resisting the urge to look back. He knew, of course, that she would not come to bed until Piers decided he wanted to.

Piers waited for the door to close, then he caught Anastasia in his arms and, as the music was now a slow number, they danced closely together. "Have you been down The Star recently? Everyone doing ok?"

The Star was their London haunt, where they had been regulars for years.

"Last week, actually. They're having a Christmas do tomorrow, and they were most disappointed you wouldn't be there."

Piers smiled down at her. "I'll make a point to call in on New Year's Eve. It's been months since we had a night out there."

"To be honest, I'd rather be there tomorrow, or with Fenella and Rick," she sighed.

Piers let her go and indicated to the sofa. "Now it's just us, we can catch up. There'll be too much going on after tonight, and I've missed you."

"I've missed you, too," she said, and, impulsively, she hugged him.

He loved feeling her close and he knew he was running a huge risk. Piers had decided recently that he was going to tell her the truth; he was going to tell her how much she meant to him and that he had loved her for such a long time. But then his older brother Guy had dropped the bombshell that their father had been given months to live, and he'd told him that if he wanted to build bridges, Piers needed to do it soon. To make matters worse, his father was coming to spend Christmas with his old friend, Anastasia's father, and he was bringing his youngest son, her ex, with him. Piers knew they had unfinished business, that Mark and Anastasia had issues to deal with. He knew he had to put his own wants on hold to make things right with his father.

"How are Rick and Fenella? Why aren't they coming here for Christmas?" He was exceptionally fond of Anastasia's godparents, who treated him like a son.

"I'm not sure. I think my father had words with Fenella, and you know Rick wouldn't like that."

"He'd better not have upset her." Piers was not a fan of Anastasia's father; many times, he had wanted to deck him for the way he treated her.

"Well, Johnny is going to them, so I won't see any of them, but at least I've got you." She settled herself against him, snuggling into his shoulder. Somehow, no matter what was going on around them, he always made her feel safe.

Johnny Fielding and Rick Lascelles were her father's bandmates. Retribution's fourth member, Frankie Beaumont, had died over ten years ago.

"Oh, guess what?" she said, sounding excited.

"What, sweetheart?" He smiled at her.

"I'm having a proper birthday bash in February." She paused, her face glowing. "And I'm going to sing live with Johnny and Rick and a couple of boys signed to Original!"

Piers returned her wide smile. "I can't believe you're finally going to do it! How long did it take you to talk Rick round?"

She grinned. "Actually, just once to suggest it and then once to beg. He's a sucker for this." She opened her blue eyes wide, an expression of innocent pleading on her face at total variance with her normal provocative look.

Piers laughed. "Sweetheart, we're all a sucker for that." He was conscious of an almost overwhelming desire to kiss her. Maintaining control, he asked about Fenella's horses; she owned stables and had competed at the Olympics before marrying Rick. Always happy to talk about her godmother, Anastasia filled him in on the gossip, and the moment passed.

They were still talking when Piers realised it was gone midnight and he suddenly felt really sleepy. "That's me," he said, stretching. "I need my bed. Where have you put me?"

Anastasia stood up reluctantly; she liked having him all to herself. "I'll show you." She caught the look on his face. "And no, it's not near me and Bryan. You really pissed him off last time, scoring his performance out of ten. You *are* bad!" she said good-naturedly.

"Tough if he can't take a joke." Privately, Piers was glad; he had no desire to listen to and be tormented by Anastasia and Bryan's bedroom antics. He followed her up the stairs, which gave him ample opportunity to admire her from behind—she was so shapely—but he stopped himself, firmly acknowledging that that particular line of thought was not going to help. He had made his decision, and, for now, mending his family had to come first. He would have to accept the consequences.

She stopped along the corridor and opened his door. "I'll see you in the morning."

He leant down and kissed her cheek. "Are you going to be ok tomorrow? What with the anniversary and everything?"

She nodded. "Yes, there'll be plenty to distract me, and I prefer to think about Mama on her birthday." She returned his kiss. "Sleep well, handsome."

She smiled and he slipped inside the room, gently closing the door behind him.

Chapter 2

24th December 1989

ANASTASIA LOOKED OUT at the rain. She had been four when the car accident had happened, twenty years ago to the day, but she could never forget trying to wake her dead mother and not understanding what was going on and being so scared.

She traced a pattern on the window with her finger, drawing little people in the mist created by her hot breath, and considered how Christmas was often no fun. Her father never discussed Natalia with her; never took any responsibility. Anastasia remembered very little of her mother, only recalling the warmth of her kiss and the intriguing accent in which she'd spoken. But she remembered the harsh words, the distress, the crying. And she would always blame *him* for what had happened, her precious memories sullied by violence.

As she reflected on the past, Anastasia knew that she had never felt loved by her father. Instead, a truce of sorts had developed over the years, although her striking resemblance to her mother antagonised his temper and led to the impasse being punctuated by massive rows. She hated rows and the anger she experienced from him, and she had grown up in fear.

Fiercely independent and loyal to those she loved, she trusted very few people. She trusted Piers, though. She trusted him with her life.

Following a vicious, unprovoked attack years ago Anastasia was prone to experiencing panic attacks, for which she had developed her own method to control the rising anguish. Being shouted at was the one thing she hated most; the one thing guaranteed to trigger that awful numbness before she began to drown in fear. Particularly when the raised voice belonged to her father.

Her meandering thoughts were disturbed by Suzanna's clear, sweet voice.

"Stasia! Anastasia, your father's here!"

Anastasia moved to the top of the sweeping staircase to see her friend greeting Jack Travess home. He was a couple of inches shorter than his official biography claimed, with years of hard living etched across his unnaturally tanned face, but he was still a handsome man. Jack had been away in America for three months, but Anastasia had not missed him.

She came down the stairs to meet him, wondering what sort of mood he would be in. He held her close briefly, but she knew it always pained him to see her because she was the spitting image of her mother; a constant reminder of the guilt he could not admit.

Jack kissed her cheek, murmuring, "Dearest Anastasia."

His daughter feigned pleasure at seeing him, avoiding a confrontation. She never actively sought confrontation, especially given her father's volatile nature. "I was beginning to think you wouldn't make it home in time," she said, trying not to reveal the lost hope behind her words. It was always her hope for him to be absent.

"I'll always come home for Christmas." He flicked her cheek carelessly and held back self-indulgent tears. The part of 'grieving widower' was one he played very well.

Walking to his study, he called out, "Are you going to sing for me at tonight's party?"

Anastasia followed him, frowning. "I prefer to dance with Piers."

He smiled, but it did not reach his eyes. "You shouldn't hide your voice. You know you can have a recording contract any time you want."

Anastasia laughed, knowing full well that the moment she agreed he would change his mind; *something* would stop it, just like all her other dreams. "No, thank you. I'm quite happy where I am with Rick." Then, giving in to her own devil, she added, "Why don't *you* sing this year? We haven't heard you for ages." She knew *that* would push a button.

A look of pain passed momentarily across his lined face, swiftly replaced by annoyance, and he gave her a dark look. He responded sharply, "You know I don't sing anymore. I'm far too old to be a rock star these days. I'll leave that to the likes of Bryan. I suppose he's here?"

Jack raised his black brows to question his daughter, but he already knew the answer. He had never approved of any of her boyfriends. There was only one person he wanted her to be with, and that, he hoped, was about to happen.

"By the way, we're expecting two more guests from New Zealand," Jack said smoothly. "They're coming to spend Christmas with us. I hope you'll be welcoming."

"Who?" Anastasia narrowed her eyes. "And why didn't you let me know earlier?"

"Because I wanted it to be a surprise, a Christmas treat for you." Her father smiled smugly; he was enjoying winding her up before he dropped his bombshell. "Our old friend Joseph Talbot and Mark."

Anastasia faltered; she had never expected to see *him* again. Her mind immediately began to drift at the mention of his name, and she was grateful when Suzanna stepped into the breach. "Is Piers' father coming?" She did not understand why this should so unsettle her friend.

Jack Travess kept a sharp eye on his daughter's face. "Yes, he's a very old friend of mine, but we haven't seen him in years. One of his sons is a long-lost friend of Anastasia's."

Suzanna guessed what was coming, much from Jack's almost victorious tone than anything else: after staring angrily at her father, Anastasia abruptly left the room.

Noting Suzanna's concerned expression, Jack elaborated. "Mark was once besotted with her, years ago. I'm hoping he still is, despite the trouble they caused. He's the only one I would ever let her marry."

Suzanna was staggered. As if Anastasia would let *her father* dictate anything? She knew how angry his scheming would make her friend, especially trying to force her hand on a clearly sensitive subject. "Bryan is devoted to her, Jack. Perhaps you should give him a chance? He's very nice when you get to know him."

"So, you've got a crush on him too Suzy?" was Jack's shrewd response, laughing at her.

Conflicting emotions fighting to get the better of her, Anastasia ran back up the staircase. Anger that her father continued to interfere in her life and fear of his motives were at the forefront, but she also felt anxiety over Mark's expectations.

She had enjoyed a fling with Mark years ago, when she was only seventeen. She knew now that, back then, she had been utterly out of control. Their brief affair had ended when his older brother Giles had caught them in flagrante and fetched her father. In retaliation, they had stolen Giles' brand new Porsche and crashed it. Not her finest hour.

She had got over Mark fast, but it had taken far longer to get over the verbal and physical tirade her father had delivered. She wondered how Mark would feel seeing her again after all these years, especially as he had never made even the slightest attempt to get in touch.

At the top of the stairs, Anastasia stopped to take a deep breath and gripped the bannister hard, her nails beginning to dig into her palms. A door opened behind her and Piers stepped out.

"What's wrong, Stasia?" He immediately recognised the signs of a brewing panic attack.

She turned and then smiled reluctantly. "Piers. How can I see you and not smile?"

"Because the look in your eye suggests you've heard Mark's coming with Dad."

Of course Piers would have known. She wasn't annoyed; he would have avoided the topic entirely to spare her feelings. "I know, I know—I'm overreacting," she sighed, reading his expression. "I guess it had to happen one day."

"Be thankful Giles isn't tagging along." Piers said cryptically and then instantly regretted his words as he saw her shiver and pale. Feeling guilty, he raised a hand to her cheek and murmured, "Still our secret, sweetheart."

After a moment, Anastasia stood on her tiptoes and kissed his cheek. "I don't doubt it," she said and then wandered away.

AFTER HALF AN hour of quiet reflection, Anastasia made her way to the huge ballroom at the rear of her country home to join Bryan. Her boyfriend was sitting on the stage, idly swinging his long legs whilst supposedly helping with the sound check for the party. He suited his rugged good looks and very short, aggressively blond hair, and he had a pair of the most mischievous hazel eyes imaginable.

Anastasia sighed; she knew she had to do something about the rumours she kept hearing. Anastasia was not stupid; she knew Bryan had a roving eye, and she had caught him out on several lies over the two or so years they had been together. But the lies seemed to have multiplied these past few months, and he was getting careless. Anastasia just wanted to end it; she knew they were not right for each other and she knew she did not love him, despite believing him when he said he loved her. She was not terribly concerned that he was cheating on her, either; if she was being honest with herself, it would not break her heart to leave him, but she would miss the sex.

Bryan looked up to see her walking towards him and felt the familiar surge of almost overwhelming desire towards her. Although not tall enough to be a model, he thought Anastasia had a body that belonged in a centrefold, and he was completely bewitched by her, irrespective of his infidelity. He wondered again why she would not move in with him; did she now know about his dalliances? Had Piers told her of his suspicions while the two of them had been alone? Perhaps it was something more? Bryan had felt her gradually drawing away from their relationship for some time, almost from the moment he had told her that he loved her, and he could not shake the feeling he was second best to a phantom; her true love.

He helped her up onto the stage next to him and kissed her hard before asking, "Do you know what I want to do to you?"

Anastasia laughed and, with provocative eyes, replied, "What you always want to do?"

"You're such a temptation, my darling, darling little devil," he said mischievously, grasping her tightly and forgetting there were also others in the room.

"A couple of potential song lyrics for you there." She knew that would annoy him, undermining his feelings with characteristically dismissive humour.

"I mean it, Anastasia. You know I adore you. The things that go through my head when I look into those eyes ..."

"But here is not the place to tell me," she said firmly as she dropped down from the stage, walking away before he took the conversation any further.

Bryan frowned. There it was again—that tiny rejection that felt like a knife to his ego. He made to follow her, his mind immediately drawn to thoughts of losing her, and was just in time to hear a voice calling out, "Hello Anastasia."

Anastasia stopped and stared at the arrivals. Here was the moment she had never expected or wanted. There, at the front door, was Mark Talbot. She had forgotten just how striking he had been, and the years had only enhanced the hard, moody face which now broke into a smile as she walked slowly down the corridor to face him.

Tall and well built, with finely cut black hair, at first glance Mark was the spitting image of his older brother Piers. But, unlike Piers, he had a pair of icy grey eyes which his smile could not reach. "Is it really you?" he asked as she stood before him.

"Why not come here and see for yourself?"

Suddenly she was hugging him tightly, and they held each other before the moment passed and a slightly embarrassed Anastasia pulled free. "It's been a long time," she said self-consciously, shocked by how much she had enjoyed the feel of his arms around her again.

Mark had the grace to look uncomfortable as he replied, "I know."

Giving herself a mental shake, Anastasia turned to Mark's father, Joseph; he was a good six inches shorter than his sons and had the look of a once powerful man gone to seed. As she hugged him, too, she could not help but notice the grey tinge to his pallor. "I'm so pleased to see you again!"

"Darling girl," Joseph began. "You look *sensational*. We've *all* missed you. The house was never the same without you."

"Quieter though without the fights and arguments, I'd imagine," she interjected, before things got too uncomfortable.

Joseph Talbot smiled ruefully, running a hand through his snowy hair. "Yes, I miss Piers, too. Is he here?"

"He's about somewhere; probably in the kitchen, eating. He got here yesterday."

"Such slander, sweetheart!" called a powerful voice, as Piers strolled into the hallway, laughing. He nodded to his father and said, "Dad," and Joseph Talbot looked at his son with undisguised pride. Piers smiled wickedly at Mark's darkened face. He was not going to show how inconvenient this reunion was; he would keep it friendly for appearance's sake. "Little brother."

Anastasia glanced at Mark's irritated face and decided to intervene before the iciness set in. "Let me show you to your room, Mark. Once you're settled in, you can talk to Piers as much as you like." Taking him by the hand, she led Mark away.

Too occupied with the prospect of antagonism between the two brothers, she was oblivious to the evil looks Bryan was giving her and this newcomer. Wanton flirting with Piers he would tolerate; another man intruding, he would not.

Piers followed Mark and Anastasia upstairs and along the corridor to one of the guest rooms. Anastasia turned and smiled at Mark, his expression softening as he smiled back. "I'm sure you'll be comfortable in here." She glanced at Piers and added, "Now I'll leave the two of you to catch up." With a deep breath, she turned her back on them and left.

Mark barely waited for the door to close before he erupted. "I've got nothing to say to you." He glared at his older brother, any pretence of coolness now having vanished.

Piers shrugged. "Whatever."

As his older brother made to leave, Mark hesitated and then put out a hand. "No, please. I have to know."

There was anguish in those grey eyes.

Piers tilted his head; he had no intention of making this easy. He was seething that his plans were about to be trashed. "Know what?"

The charged silence hung heavy before Mark eventually managed, "You and Anastasia. How long has it been going on?"

Even though he had known this question was coming, Piers was annoyed. "For Christ's sake, Mark! Grow up!"

Mark's hot temper leapt to the fore. "You expect me to believe there has never been anything between you and her?" He took a hasty step towards his now furious older brother. Mark's suspicions had consumed him for years, fed by endless rumour and innuendo, and now they threatened to overwhelm him.

"What the fuck, Mark? What. The. *Fuck?*" Piers was contemptuous. "There is nothing romantic between us. If you don't believe me, then I suggest you speak to Anastasia, if you dare to have that conversation with her. Because you're sure as hell not having it with me."

Piers turned on his heel and stormed out of the room. There was no way he would give any hope to Mark.

Mark let his brother leave, instead focusing on taking deep

breaths with which to calm himself. That was the closest he had come to losing his temper in years. He did not know what to think. Mark had spent the last seven years believing that his brother had taken his place with the girl he loved. And who was this Bryan, the popstar boyfriend she now had? Where did he fit in to all this?

As Mark made to follow Piers out of the door, he walked straight into Bryan Darnell.

"Ah, hello. Mark, isn't it?" Bryan offered his hand, determined not to provoke a situation unless he needed to.

Mark fixed unsmiling eyes on his rival's face. "Anastasia's current boyfriend, I believe."

Bryan felt the unspoken threat and curled his lip. "That's correct."

A very unpleasant sneer appeared on Mark's face. "Not if I have anything to do with it. Watch your back."

BRYAN FOUND PIERS outside, smoking a Cuban cigar. Throwing caution to the wind, Bryan snarled at him. "What the hell's your brother's problem?" he raged. "Keep him away from my girl or he'll be sorry."

Piers took a long drag on his cigar. "That's not very friendly, Bryan. Please remember who you're talking to."

"Who does he think he is, trying to stir up trouble for me and Stasia …"

Piers cut across him, more amused than anything. "If you want to smack my brother, go ahead. You'll save me the trouble."

Bryan glared at him, disbelief on his face.

"At this moment in time, Bryan, I couldn't care less. But"— and here his laughter died, leaving only an explicit threat—"But, you will let Anastasia make up her own mind and if you think giving Mark a black eye will mean something to Anastasia, you clearly don't know her." Piers took another long drag on his cigar, eyeing Bryan with a knowing look, before ending with, "Mark was her first love, Bryan. That's always a hard act to follow."

Chapter 3

Anastasia busied herself in the library, finalising the guest list for the party. It always amused and sometimes exasperated her how much credit she got for organising Original's functions. All she did, in her opinion, was to pick the right party planning company in plenty of time and give orders to people. Still, she reasoned, they were very well paid for making her life easy.

As she resumed her review of the names before her, Piers walked in.

Anastasia looked up and smiled. "Hello, handsome," she said, immediately thrown by the frustration on his face. She stood up and moved towards him, asking, "What's wrong?"

Piers hesitated for a split-second before relenting. "Mark thinks you and I are sleeping together, and Bryan wants to smack Mark in the mouth. That's what's wrong, Stasia—the men you attract."

Her eyes opened wide, and she looked offended. Recognising how unfair his hasty choice of words had been, Piers softened his tone. "Sorry, sweetheart. I shouldn't take it out on you." He moved closer to her and wrapped his arms around her.

"It's ok. Maybe you've got a point." Her voice was muffled by his jumper.

"Just because I have a point doesn't mean I should make it," he said. "And I don't want to ruin all your hard work tonight. I'll make an appearance after dinner, and I'll even play nicely with

Mark. Then I want to spend some time catching up with Dad."

Anastasia appreciated his need to rebuild a relationship with his father; although she was not sure she would have been so forgiving, especially after all this time. "I know your dad will love spending time with you."

Piers kissed her cheek. "How do you feel seeing Mark again?"

She shrugged. "I don't know."

Piers watched her anxiously. "He has always loved you, you know." That cost him something to admit.

"Has he?" Anastasia was instinctively defensive, even without meaning to be. She broke his embrace and backed away. "Then why the silence for all these years? And now? To just turn up unannounced? Time doesn't stand still." She sighed impatiently. "I've got to do something about Bryan, though. I know what he's been up to. And I know I don't love him."

"Then you know what you have to do." Relief flooded through Piers that she was unconcerned her boyfriend had been cheating on her. "Let him go, Stasia."

"I know that, but . . ." She could not continue. "Why didn't we just do what we planned all those years ago? Do you remember?" She seized his jumper and looked up into his blue eyes.

Piers smiled regretfully. "Yes, I remember. Our Caribbean island. Tell you what. If we're both single at fifty, then I'll take you there."

Anastasia could not help chuckling. "Sounds perfect."

Piers reached for her again, hugging her before offering some wise words of advice that cost him dear.

"Just see how things go tonight. See how Mark behaves and then you'll know what you really want. Courage, sweetheart; that's something you've never lacked. *Courage.*"

She smiled wistfully. "What would I do without you?"

"If you need me, I'll come running, but you owe this to Mark. And to yourself. This is unfinished business. Give it a chance—just one chance—for your own sake. I know how much he once meant to you. First loves are difficult to shake."

The words stung.

Anastasia looked puzzled and opened her mouth to reply, but she heard the door and saw Suzanna. "Hi, Suzanna. Am I needed?"

"Yes, Stasia. Time to get ready if you want me to do your make-up." Suzanna smiled nervously, acutely aware that she had walked in on something.

Relieved to escape the conversation, Anastasia turned to Piers and said, "I'll see you in a bit. Try not to reek of cigar smoke at dinner!" She winked at him mischievously, highlighting that she had noticed the scent she so disliked, and then she was gone, leaving him alone to think.

As the door closed, Piers thought to himself, *Why the fuck did you have to come here, Mark?*

Mark could not have given his brother an answer to his question.

He was not sure why, after all these years, he was now seeking Anastasia out. All Mark knew was that when his father had offered him the opportunity to see her again, there had been no hesitation. His brother Giles offered many well-reasoned objections as to why he should stay away, reasons to stay in Paris with him, but they had been meaningless in the face of such temptation. He was honest enough to admit he still had strong feelings for Anastasia, and as soon as he saw her again, he knew he wanted her back.

More confusing still was that Mark had been led to believe that Piers had taken his place in both Anastasia's heart and her bed and yet still she had a boyfriend. Why the need for secrecy? Mark dismissed Bryan Darnell as irrelevant, but he could not dismiss Piers. He had always felt inadequate next to him; always felt in his shadow. Piers had been the wild child, loved by family and always surrounded by friends, no matter how bad his behaviour had been. No matter what Piers seemed to do or what he got involved in, he always came out of it looking good, achieving exactly what he wanted.

But one thing Mark was confident of about his brother was that Piers had never lied. Sure, he had wound Mark up, pushed his buttons, but he had never lied.

Mark sighed and finished dressing for dinner. He would see how Anastasia reacted to him; try to act as if he was in control, his mind not in turmoil. As Mark checked his reflection in the mirror, he reminded himself that he was no longer beholden to anyone.

Neither his father nor his brothers could not stop him now. He was free.

Suzanna stepped back from her friend to cast a critical eye over her work. Satisfied, she allowed her curiosity free rein. "How many brothers does Piers actually have? I've never really thought to ask."

Checking her reflection in the mirror, Anastasia replied, laughing, "Far too many! His dad's been married twice."

"No sisters?" Suzanna started packing her brushes away.

"No." Anastasia sighed. "But I think Joseph Talbot always wanted a daughter." She recalled how he had always welcomed her into his homes; how he had always been so kind.

"Well, don't keep me in suspense. How many brothers does he have?" Suzanna wanted to know.

Rolling her eyes, Anastasia told her. "Well, there are two from Joseph's first marriage—twins, I think. Both out in New Zealand now." She paused and then counted on her fingers. "Matthew was the eldest full brother."

"*Was?*" Suzanna queried her use of the past tense.

"Yes. I didn't really know him, but he was very clever. A psychologist or psychiatrist; I can never remember which. All very sad."

"What happened?" Suzanna sat down next to her.

"An overdose, I think. He and his girlfriend partied too hard, which I always thought was weird because he didn't seem the type. He sent me a book for my library, which was kind but unexpected. I don't think the family has ever recovered from his death," Anastasia paused. "Like I said I never really knew him. Then there's Guy—he was always fun—and then Giles." Her face darkened. "Always hated me. Don't know why." She shrugged and then, in a brighter tone, said, "Then Piers and, finally, Mark, the youngest."

"Do they all look alike?" Suzanna had been struck by Mark's uncanny resemblance to his brother.

Anastasia thought for a few moments, seeing each one in her head as she recalled. "There is a similarity, yes. They all have black hair, and they're all quite tall. Do you think Mark looks so very much like Piers?"

"Spitting image," Suzanna replied, before adding, "Except for the eyes."

Anastasia shook her head. "No, Piers is far better looking than all of them. But don't tell him I said that—he's vain enough!" She laughed.

Suzanna observed her friend, scrutinising her eyes carefully. "Stasia ..." she began tentatively.

Anastasia smiled. "I know you want to warn me to be careful. To think before I do anything stupid."

Suzanna blushed. "I would never tell you what to do, but I am worried."

"Please don't. Mark and I were a long time ago, in a different life. I won't be cheating on Bryan." Anastasia had seen the concern in her friend's eyes and knew that was for him.

But Suzanna surprised her with, "Promise me you'll be fair to yourself?"

"No matter where that may take me, Suzanna?"

"Yes. Be true to your own feelings, not those of everyone around you."

Suzanna's perception, as always, was acute, and Anastasia could only smile warmly at her in response, grateful for her support.

Mark hesitated on the landing. He had heard her voice; light and musical. She sounded happy.

Taking a chance, he knocked on the door and walked in. He could not help a sharp intake of breath as he drank in the sight he had dreamed of for so long before managing to say, "Are you ladies ready to go down for dinner?" His heart was now pounding, his instinct to just kiss her.

"Suzanna's ready." Anastasia felt her hands shake ever so slightly under Mark's very intense expression. "I'm waiting for Bryan."

Although disappointed, Mark promptly held out his arm and escorted Suzanna down to the opulent dining room. They chatted politely about music and the weather, with Suzanna dying to enquire about his past relationship with her friend. But although Mark was friendly enough, there was no welcoming smile, his chilling eyes frightened her, and she felt his coldness. Suddenly she thought that Anastasia might have been right; the resemblance between the two brothers now seemed less obvious.

Talking to Mark and despite her friend's insistent denial, Suzanna could clearly see how this was going to play out. Anastasia would be tempted by the return of her former lover and Bryan would be cast aside. He deserved better than that.

Suzanna had liked Bryan from the moment she had met him at a party over two years ago. She longed to be close to him, wanting to drown in his tempestuous eyes, but instead she was made to watch with envy while her friend captivated him without even trying. Now he was Anastasia's devoted slave. How she wished that Bryan was at her feet. She felt sure she was better suited to his temperament than her fiery friend, and she was sure she could make him happy.

But Suzanna knew the only chance she would get to be with him was when Anastasia finally set him free.

Anastasia tapped her long metallic blue fingernails and sighed impatiently. Bryan knew how much she hated to be kept waiting, let alone when she had guests. Resigning herself to probably being late for dinner, she left her own room to walk the short distance to the guest apartments. So strong was his desire to control his daughter's choices that her father would not allow them to share a room in his house.

As she reached Bryan's door, she thought she heard a female voice and, puzzled, she listened carefully. Her eyes flashed as suspicion darted through her mind, and she noticed that the door was not shut properly. She pushed it gently, and it opened noiselessly.

Anastasia was staggered, affronted by what met her eyes: Bryan and one of the other guests—a blonde guest—naked together on the bed. Oblivious, they did not notice the outraged figure in the doorway. Reeling from the shock and insult, Anastasia kept her head and withdrew silently.

She felt slightly sick, but here was the shove she needed; she would do what Piers wanted. Mark would get his chance.

Twenty minutes of polite, if uninteresting, conversation passed between Suzanna and Mark while he waited expectantly for Anastasia to appear. His patience diminished, Mark politely excused himself, slipped out of sight and ran back up the stairs to Anastasia's room.

Knocking loudly, he called out, "Anastasia, it's me, Mark. We're all waiting for you."

He heard feet pad softly towards him and the door swung open. The faintest flicker of a smile formed on Anastasia's lips before she turned away quickly from him, unsure of what to say.

Her melancholy did not go unnoticed. "Anastasia, are you all right?"

She had been thinking bitterly about men; about wasted time; about Piers and their relationship; two very different summers so long ago. Bryan was forgotten. She faced him, and the concern in Mark's eyes softened his face. She took one step forward, wanting to ask why he had come to look for her, and why it was so important to Piers that she give him a chance.

Mark moved hesitantly towards her. "Is something wrong?"

Anastasia felt her heart begin to thump violently. With Piers keeping things between them platonic and Bryan having behaved so appalling in her own house, why not see where things might lead? And most importantly, it would piss Bryan off. "I saw Bryan with some blonde. I'm sure you can guess the rest." Her voice was hard, emotionless.

Mark was genuinely shocked. "Did they see you?"

She shook her head. "No. He only had eyes for her." Anastasia shrugged her shoulders. "I've been expecting it, if I'm honest. I've always known he was wild, and he's always resented that he never had all of me."

"That's no excuse, baby." His old name for her slipped out with ease, and they were both surprised by his sudden use of it.

Anastasia stared at him. "I haven't heard that in years." She smiled, thinking back to a time when everything had been so simple.

Mark moved to kiss her and stopped himself. *Not yet*, he told himself. "I'm so sorry," he said. "He never deserved you."

"No. Neither of you did," she said pointedly, closing the door in his face and leaving him with a chill in his heart.

Chapter 4

JACK TRAVESS AND his dinner guests sat down to a delectable meal in the huge, lavish dining room decorated in homage to Tsarist Russia which led directly from the ballroom where the main party was due to take place.

Anastasia's father signalled his continuing disapproval of her choices by interfering with the seating arrangement; Bryan was now next to the peroxide blonde he knew intimately. Bryan spent the whole meal watching Mark watching Piers and Anastasia and gaining satisfaction from the annoyance on his face. Piers and Anastasia flirted quite happily, with Piers leaning in to whisper comments in her ear that made her laugh out loud.

As the diners began to move to join the guests already in the ballroom, Anastasia stood by the doors, directing them towards the bars and wishing them a wonderful night. Piers stood behind her, one hand resting protectively on her shoulder.

Bryan stopped on his way past and leaned in to kiss her, unaware of what Anastasia had seen earlier. "I'm on first, darling. I'll be singing for you."

"Sweet," Anastasia remarked, her tone sarcastic.

Mark was one of the last to leave the dining room. "Going to dance with me, baby?"

Remembering how inept a dancer he was, Anastasia laughed but agreed. She tapped Piers' hand, and he let her go.

Anastasia grasped Mark's hand, her deep blue eyes dancing

devilishly. "Shall I teach you a few moves? See if we can make you into a dancer?"

Mark gripped her hand tightly and smiled. "Can't hurt to try."

Together, they entered the ballroom as Bryan's powerful voice boomed out.

With the lights in his eyes, Bryan did not notice Mark and Anastasia dancing together while he sang his set. Once finished, he left the stage to rapturous applause, and the disco began to belt out a stream of classic dance and Christmas favourites. Bryan made his way through an admiring group of girls to get to a bar. He leant back and looked for her, spotting his beautiful girlfriend in blue dancing with a tall black-haired man, something he had expected. Downing his drink in one, he made his way to her side.

As he approached, Bryan saw that Anastasia was laughing animatedly and he tapped what he thought was Piers' shoulder, saying, "I'm cutting in."

Anastasia looked up at him. "No, you're not."

Mark turned his head to smile mockingly at him.

Fury leapt in Bryan's eyes as he moved to try and get between them.

Anastasia spoke sharply. "Cause a scene and I'll have you chucked out. Why don't you run along and find a peroxide to play with?" Her eyes told him she knew, and suddenly fury was replaced by fear that he was about to lose everything. "I will talk to you at the end of the night, Bryan, and not before."

Mark pulled Anastasia into his arms and watched Bryan smugly over the top of her head as he backed away, hatred etched in his eyes.

After a few more songs, Mark was fed up of dancing. He knew the sooner he spoke with Anastasia, the better, and he couldn't begin to fully enjoy himself until he had put his mind at rest. He slowed his steps and said into her ear, "Can we talk now, please? It would mean a lot to me."

Anastasia nodded, her heart hammering, unsure of what he wanted to say and fearing what she might.

They threaded their way across the ballroom and out into the corridor, where Anastasia opened the door to the library. "No-one should disturb us in here," she said.

A small fire was blazing steadily in the grate and two table lamps were already on, casting shadows over the book-lined walls.

Anastasia leant against the dark red leather settee set in the middle of the room, her back towards the fireplace. "Well, Mark, what do you need to say?"

He stood before her, his mind a complete blank. All those carefully rehearsed speeches suddenly gone, he was dumbstruck.

Realising he was lost for words, Anastasia started the conversation she did not want to have. "Where have you been all these years, Mark? Why did I never hear a word from you?"

His brain jerked into action. "I've been in Paris with Giles for the most part."

In the shadows, he did not see the fear flickering in her eyes. "I've never been to Paris," she managed, an unpleasant feeling rising to her throat.

"I've been working in PR for a while and then I went to New Zealand for about six months with Dad, to see my half-brothers. We came home a few days ago."

"Didn't know how to use a telephone?" She raised one eyebrow.

"After, you know, after we got caught together, Dad moved me to Paris and kept an eye on my post. I was banned from contacting you." It sounded lame even to him. "But you didn't exactly make an effort, either," he countered, annoyed by her just observation.

She laughed, but it was not a pleasant sound. "Afterwards my dad beat me, I was too scared. And then … oh, it doesn't matter. Neither of us made any effort."

Mark stared at her, unsure he had heard her correctly, but she held up a hand before he could clarify. "I don't want to discuss my father, Mark. That's definitely none of your business."

Mark did not know how to respond. *Her father hit her?* He

hesitated, then stated, "There's been no-one I've loved quite like you."

Anastasia cut across him ruthlessly. "You hardly expect me to believe you've been living like a monk?"

Mark had the good grace to blush before countering, "You've not exactly been celibate yourself."

Anastasia smiled ruefully. "Didn't anyone ever teach you it's not gentlemanly to discuss a woman's sex life?"

"I think we're beyond being coy around one another, Anastasia. What about Piers?" He pursued his obsession stubbornly.

"I don't understand you," she stammered, unsure what he was asking.

"Just tell me the truth. You and Piers." He needed to know, but he did not know if he would like the answer.

Anastasia's eyes opened wide. "Me and Piers? We're just friends."

"But I was told …" Her reaction made Mark suddenly very unsure and wary.

"Do you expect me to believe that Piers told you we've been shagging? Because whatever cock-eyed opinion you have of your brother, you know he is not, and has never been, a liar."

"It wasn't him." Mark's voice suddenly trailed away, puzzlement across his face and concern in those icy, grey eyes.

"What is this, Mark?"

The conversation was not going as well as Mark had hoped. "I just need the truth, baby. I deserve that much, at least."

Anastasia looked him up and down and said, "Very well. Let me tell you this once and for all, and it really is very simple." She folded her arms defiantly. "Piers and I have never had sex. *Never.* Forget what you've been told, Mark, and if you still don't believe me, that's your choice."

Mark's icy eyes melted and he suddenly reached for her, kissing her passionately. Anastasia was stunned by his hunger, and she was equally stunned by how much she liked it. Finally releasing her, he managed, "I'm so sorry, truly I am. It was easier to believe rumours and try to hate you than to face the truth. I should have acted, I should have risked it all."

She stayed in his arms; this was the closeness she longed for from Piers. "And where does that leave things with your brother?"

"I know I need to make things right with him, and I hope he will accept my apology. I have missed him, I suppose." He spoke grudgingly, but his eyes were filled with tenderness.

"Shall I fetch him?" Anastasia asked. Was this why Piers wanted her to let Mark in? Was this the only way he could repair his family? She did not necessarily like what that meant for her, but she would do anything for Piers. She owed him her life.

"What about Bryan?" Mark left the words hanging; he did not want to spoil things now.

"Leave Bryan to me. I don't want any scenes here, but our relationship is over. And it has been for a while." She thought for a moment. "Luckily, he's given me all the ammunition I need to keep your name out of this."

"Put my name right in the middle," Mark breathed in her ear. "I love you."

A few minutes later, Anastasia was trying to find where Piers was closeted with his father. She hated to interrupt them, but she believed making things right with Mark was important to Piers and it would make his father very happy. A bartender was able to tell her where he had been sending drinks and she crossed the floor, declining offers from friends and colleagues to join them.

As she approached the study, Anastasia saw the door was ajar. She paused, listening to the voices, undecided whether to wait a few moments or walk straight in.

She could hear Joseph Talbot from within, and he sounded anxious. "And you swear there is nothing romantic between you? I don't want you upsetting your brother over this."

Piers answered his father, his tone harsh. "Anastasia and I are friends. *Best* friends. And there's never been anything more to it than that." He paused as her heart screamed. Then he said, "I just want her to be happy."

She pulled back into the shadows, desperately trying to stay in control. Each time he came home, she prayed it would be the time where Piers declared his love for her in the way that she loved him. Each time, she had been disappointed, and it looked as though this Christmas would be no different.

As she composed herself, Anastasia saw Bryan running towards her, which was the last thing she needed right now. A desire to hurt him as much as she had just been hurt welled within her, but Bryan already looked on edge.

"Stasia!" he cried out, coming to a halt right before her and gripping her upper arms tightly. "Please, Stasia. Let's talk. We can sort this out."

"I told you, I will talk to you at the end of the night, Bryan. If you don't want to wait, then go home. I'm not bothered." Her words had a venom to them he had never heard before. She gasped as his hold tightened. "Get off me!" she snapped, forcing him to let her go.

"Stasia!" he pleaded, his eyes wide with pain and fear.

"Go back to your little playmate and enjoy her smiles. I have something to do for Piers." She knocked loudly on the study door.

Bryan backed away. Confronting Piers would not help him. "Ok, ok. Have it your way. Where do you want me waiting at the end of the night?"

As the door opened, she replied coldly, "In my library," and she stepped into her father's study, brushing past Piers.

"Problem, Bryan?" Piers asked, his deep voice filled with menace.

Bryan threw up his hands, and Piers shut the door in his face.

"I'm so sorry to disturb you," Anastasia apologised stiffly, rattled by her encounter with Bryan.

"Not at all. You're always welcome, my dear." Joseph Talbot was seated comfortably, a glass of brandy in his hand. He smiled warmly at her.

"Mark would like to speak with you, Piers." She could sense the sudden pleasure in the room, and that hurt even more.

Piers cut straight to the point. "Is he going to apologise?"

She looked up at him. "Yes."

"Excellent!" Piers' face broke into a broad smile.

Joseph stood up. "But are you going to accept it?" He watched his son's face.

"Yes, Dad. It's been a long time coming. I'll be back in a bit." Taking Anastasia by the hand, he pulled her after him into the corridor. "Before we go, what have you told him?"

She drew her hand away; touching him now made her want to cry. "The truth. That we've never slept together, despite what he has been told."

"Anything else I need to know?" Piers wanted to be sure, something was wrong.

She faltered "No."

Chapter 5

Waiting impatiently in the library, Mark had no idea what he was going to say to Piers. He wanted to resolve the bad blood between them, as much for Anastasia as for himself, but he was not sure of the best way to broach the subject.

He was also still trying to figure out why he had been fed misinformation from someone he trusted. He was not entirely sure how to interpret Anastasia's relationship with his brother; they were obviously close, and he knew that she had moved him into her Belgravia home all those years ago and, to his knowledge, Piers was still there. Mark found it nearly impossible to accept that any man could be so close to Anastasia without having an ulterior motive.

He heard the door creak open as Anastasia returned, with Piers a few paces behind her. She crossed the room to stand beside the fireplace and waited in anticipation, blocking out her own feelings as best she could.

Piers and Mark faced each other, an awkward silence filling the room. Anastasia thought about moving things along when Mark suddenly said, "I'm sorry," and his brother pulled him into a one-armed hug, silencing him.

"I know, little brother. I know." They broke apart; close proximity was not something either of them felt entirely comfortable with.

Anastasia moved forward. "I hope this means you are both

going to play nicely from now on?"

Piers laughed and took a step back from Mark to face her. "For you, sweetheart, I'll try."

As much as Mark wanted to repair the fractured relationship with his sibling, he was still wary, still jealous of his brother, and he did not need Piers intruding now. "Perhaps we can catch up properly tomorrow?" he asked. "I know you'll want to get back to Dad."

"That would be excellent. I've got some great Cuban cigars we can share, and I'm sure Stasia's father can spare a few tumblers of the best brandy in his cellar." He clapped his brother on the shoulder, knowing he could go back to their dad and tell him that the family rift was finally healing, which would delight him. But judging by the lipstick on Mark's face, he also knew that the cost had been high.

Piers kissed Anastasia on the cheek and whispered, "Be good." He searched her eyes anxiously, knowing instinctively that something was wrong. He left them alone, regardless; after all, he had no choice.

Now alone again, Mark faced Anastasia, the shadows cast by the fire dancing on the walls, his eyes, so full of the passion she longed for from his brother, fixed on hers. "Do you want to go back to the party yet?" He ran a finger down her face and felt her quiver.

She stepped closer to him, needing to be loved. "We really should. They'll miss me."

But that did not stop him from leaning in closer and kissing her.

A short time later, they returned to the ballroom and, as Mark went to get drinks, Anastasia saw Piers dancing with some of the girls from Original. She forced herself to smile, shoving his words out of her head, and walked over to him, testing her resolve to keep him at arm's length emotionally.

"Sweetheart!" he called out, moving to dance with her, his other partners forgotten.

Anastasia felt the thrill of knowing she was the one he wanted to spend time with. Her resolve crumbled; she loved him. "Have you finished with your dad?" she asked. "All mended?"

He leant closer so she could hear him. "I hope everything's sorted. He's not too good at the moment, but then he is dying, so that's to be expected."

He sounded blasé, but she knew otherwise. She could sense his pain and confliction.

The DJ began playing one of their favourite songs, and Piers started singing the words to her. "Oh, don't! That's dreadful!" She laughed, knowing he wanted to be distracted.

"Why don't you sing it to me, then?" He took her hands and pulled her closer, gazing into her blue eyes. She obliged.

Having returned from the bar, Mark found himself next to Suzanna while he was looking for Anastasia. She saw his scowl as he asked, "Have you seen Anastasia?"

She pointed to the dance floor. "That's where you will always find her at parties. And if he's home, that's *who* she'll be dancing with. Wait till they start to salsa; it's quite something." Suzanna watched his eyes narrow and read annoyance on his face, and she moved away. She did not like Mark at all.

Mark stood by the dance floor, trying to catch Anastasia's eye, but he soon realised it was hopeless; she was totally absorbed in dancing, totally oblivious of everything except for Piers. Then, just as he was about to try and join her, the music changed, and salsa rhythms filled the air. He watched, fascinated; both Anastasia and Piers were excellent, entirely in sync, and he knew there was no way he could compete with that.

He would soon have to make it clear he did not approve of his future wife dancing that sexily with another man, let alone his own brother.

Anastasia spent the rest of the night on the dance floor, mainly with Piers, but also with her many friends and associates from Original. She loved to dance; it made her feel free, and it was also the only thing she felt she shared with her mother. Mark joined her occasionally, but he had to accept that trying to hold her attention when she was having this much fun was impossible, something else that would need to change.

Gradually, people drifted away, some to their rooms at Starbrook and others leaving for their homes, and Anastasia knew the time had come to make her decision clear to Bryan. Feeling a chill, she borrowed Piers' suit jacket and reluctantly left the last few guests talking by the doors as she made her way to meet him.

Bryan was waiting for her in the library, where he had been pacing up and down for half an hour, his temper flaring. Then, suddenly, there she was, standing in the doorway, watching him, wrapped in deep blue and wearing someone else's suit jacket.

"Anastasia." He moved towards her, arms outstretched.

"Can we make this short, Bryan? I'm really tired."

Not the words he had hoped to hear. "I don't understand, Stasia. What's happened?"

She gave a crack of rude laughter. "Really, Bryan? *Really?*" Bryan just looked at her, his eyes tormented. "Ok, play dumb for all I care. I saw you this evening with that peroxide bint."

He found his voice. "What? Talking to her? There's no need for you to be jealous."

"Very funny, Bryan. No, in your room before dinner. I was standing in the doorway. I saw you."

Bryan's face was now ashen. "Stasia, please—it was nothing ..."

She sliced across him. "I am neither blind nor stupid. I've ignored a lot of warning signs, but not anymore. We're finished."

She would have left it there, but he reached out to stop her.

"You never loved me, did you?" His anguish was painful.

Anastasia faced him squarely, hating herself for letting things get this far, for not stopping it sooner. "No, Bryan. I never did."

He could not believe what she was saying. "This is because *he's* walked back into your life, isn't it?" He was angry now, humiliated, hurt.

"Whatever you think, I didn't know he was coming here. But, unlike you, I won't hide the truth; when I saw Mark, I was tempted. What would you rather I did? Lie to you?"

"Yes!" he said, gripping her arms hard. "I love you more than anything, Stasia. I really do."

"Then why can't you keep your hands out of the cookie jar?"

Her words felt like a slap, but he had an answer ready. "Because I never had all of you, did I? Something's there I cannot reach. Someone else always comes first, and I needed more."

"Oh." She gave a wry smile. "So, this is all *my* fault?" She put her hands either side of his face and made him look into her eyes. He could not bear what he saw there, but he could not look away either. "I know I should have ended this months ago, but we did have fun. There were some good times. But it's over."

Bryan felt tears forming. "If this is what you really want, then I'll go—but I won't give up."

"Bryan, please, for your own sake, find someone who will be what you need." She moved away, and with one last look over her shoulder, Anastasia left him.

She walked slowly back towards the deserted ballroom to find that Suzanna had waited for her friend.

"How did it go?" Suzanna's green eyes were anxious, but Anastasia was not sure who that anxiety was for.

"Better than I thought." She paused to consider. "It wasn't pleasant, but I was honest with him."

Suzanna gripped her friend's hands. "Are you sure it's worth leaving someone who truly loves you for someone you haven't seen in years?"

Anastasia frowned. "That's not what's happening, Suzanna. And Bryan cheated on *me*. I saw him."

Suzanna sighed; she was neither surprised by her revelation nor fooled by her friend's denial. "I thought he was."

"Then why didn't you say anything?" Anastasia demanded.

"I wasn't sure. I'd heard rumours, and I caught him out on a couple of lies. But I didn't want to interfere in your business."

"Well, I guess it doesn't really matter now. I don't know about you, but I'm really tired. Time to call it a night."

Chapter 6

25th December 1989

CHRISTMAS MORNING DAWNED damp and foggy, but Anastasia had been awake for hours. She had taken a shower and was sitting in bed wrapped in a black silk dressing gown, listening to the radio, when she heard a soft knock at her door.

"Come in," she called, wondering who else would be up so early after what had been a riotous party, and Mark walked in, fully dressed in a long-sleeved top and black jeans.

"Merry Christmas, baby." He smiled, allowing his eyes to feast on his heart's desire.

"Come in and shut the door. What are you doing up so early?"

Mark did as he was told and replied, "Couldn't sleep. It is Christmas, after all."

"Idiot!" She laughed. "You're twenty-six, not six."

He pointed to the bed. "Can I sit down?"

Anastasia nodded and threw back the covers. "You can get in if you like."

Mark hesitated, but she smiled and held out her hand. Kicking off his shoes, he sat next to her and then tentatively kissed her, which felt more awkward than he had anticipated.

Anastasia looked deeply into his eyes, now warm and tender, and sighed, tempted as she had been all those years ago. She could hear Piers' words in her head, but she was still not sure this was what she wanted.

As she looked into his eyes, Mark handed her a flat blue box wrapped with a white ribbon. "Happy Christmas, my love."

"But I don't have anything for you. I didn't know I'd be seeing you," she protested.

He pushed the box into her hands and smiled. "Being with you again is a present in itself. You're all I ever wanted, Anastasia."

Anastasia leant forwards, her lips tantalisingly close, and whispered, "Thank you."

Mark reached out to pull her into his arms, knowing he wanted her so desperately but determined not to rush anything; this time, he would do everything right. "Open it."

Anastasia did as he asked and gasped as she saw the blindingly blue sapphire bracelet within. "Oh, it's gorgeous!" she exclaimed, stunned.

"Almost as blue as your eyes." He kissed her cheek. "Why don't you get dressed, baby? We could go for a walk or have breakfast; make the most of everyone still being asleep." He specifically meant Piers.

"Yes, I'd like that. I'll see you downstairs in about ten minutes."

Mark kissed both her hands and then, still gazing at her, he left the room.

Christmas Day passed by very pleasantly; there was an atmosphere of joviality throughout the manor that had often been missing. Anastasia felt happy, actually glad it was Christmas. She had her best friends close by, everyone was getting along well, and there were no arguments. And there was Mark, who so obviously wanted to adore her.

They ate Christmas dinner at 1pm, and when they had finished, Piers rose from the table and said to Mark, "Fancy that cigar?" He had endured his fill of watching his brother and Anastasia cosying up to one another and, although still willing to keep things civil for his father's sake, he could take no more.

Mark grinned, absolutely smitten and oblivious for the

moment to any looming difficulties. "Yes, why not?" He leaned over to Anastasia beside him. "You don't mind, do you, baby?"

She shook her head, smiling. "Of course not."

He pulled her to her feet, and she spoke to the table in general. "I'm going to lie down. I'll see you all later." She waved a hand languidly before moving away from the table.

Anastasia had eaten a vast amount at dinner and was feeling sleepy when she entered her library. The fire flickered, and she switched on a table lamp before settling down on the red leather settee. She listened to the comforting ticking of the grandfather clock. The clock struck six, Anastasia looked up and smiled, it was actually only half past three but this clock had a mind of its own. Sighing happily, she slipped into the embrace of sleep.

PIERS AND MARK spent less an hour together. They had been civil, but it had felt uncomfortable enough for them both to realise that there were still problems between them.

Piers was hopeful his brother had finally accepted he had not slept with Anastasia, that they were not conducting some sort of illicit affair behind everyone's backs, not that it was any of Mark's business, anyway.

Mark was reluctant to believe that Piers did not want her, and he could not accept he had been lied to by his other brother, Giles. He had watched distrustfully how they had flirted on Christmas Eve, how she lit up when they danced, how she sang to him and how sultry she was around him on that dancefloor.

He would not tolerate that kind of behaviour, and he would need to make that quite clear.

As they were leaving the conservatory to join the others, Piers suddenly asked, "Do you remember that time when I put worms in your spaghetti bolognese?"

Mark's face broke into a broad smile at the memory and he burst out laughing. The brothers were still laughing when they re-joined the others and Joseph Talbot smiled appreciatively, delighted to see his two youngest sons enjoying each other's company again.

Mark gave his father a hug and then made his way to the library, slowly pushing open the heavy door. Anastasia was reading on the red leather settee, and she looked up, startled, as he entered.

"Mark!" She placed a hand over her heart. "You made me jump!"

He leant over the back of the settee and kissed her. "Sorry, baby. I missed you."

"Come round here, then." She indicated for him to sit beside her.

As he moved, Mark noticed the shadows flickering and turned his head sharply to look at the grandfather clock as it struck one. Then, as he sat down, it struck twelve, and Mark jumped. "What's it doing?"

"What it wants," she replied. "Perhaps you should do the same." Her voice was low, and her eyes were sultry enough for him to drown in. She needed to know how much he wanted her; if he could make her feel again. She needed to be loved. "You can lock the door, if you want."

Mark's eyes, no longer icy, devoured her, and as he kissed her, he pulled her deftly into his arms, feeling her heart pound against his chest.

PIERS HESITATED IN the corridor. Anastasia had been gone a long time, and he had wanted to say goodnight to her. He also wanted to tell her that he was leaving with his father tomorrow morning. He had finally decided to reconcile with Guy, who he had missed most of all.

He heard a door click open and stepped back into the shadows as he watched Mark standing in the doorway to the library. Mark leant forward and kissed someone before heading for the stairs.

A few seconds later, Anastasia came out of the library, and Piers moved forward to intercept her. He smiled ruefully when he noticed that her shirt buttons were done up incorrectly. "That's a dead giveaway, sweetheart."

She glanced down and then blushed profusely.

Piers held his hands up. "I'm not judging. I just want you to be happy."

Anastasia bit her lip as his earlier words to his father echoed.

He smiled sadly at her and walked slowly away.

As Anastasia watched him go, her longing for something more from Piers resurfaced, and she buried it as deep as she could. Her greatest fear was that, one day, he would come to her and tell her that he had found someone; that he was in love. She knew it would kill her.

And although she expected any man in her life to accept her relationship with Piers, she knew no woman in her right mind would ever accept her as a part of his.

Fighting the anguish, Anastasia undid and redid her buttons and went to bed alone.

Chapter 7

26th December 1989

AT 10AM ON Boxing Day, Suzanna stood waiting for her driver in the entrance hall, looking forward to seeing her family. As she waited patiently, a navy blue suitcase next to her and a brand new Chanel bag over her shoulder, Suzanna reflected on Christmas. It had been quite eventful, with her best friend of five years dumping her long-term boyfriend and an old flame walking back into her life. Although Suzanna knew that no-one was more fiercely independent than Anastasia, she still worried about her and did not understand how her friend's mind worked; she only knew she loved her and that life was much more fun with Anastasia in it.

"Going somewhere?"

Suzanna started, startled by a deep voice from behind her. "Piers, you made me jump!"

"Sorry." He grinned and put down his own suitcase. Seeing Suzanna glancing at his luggage, he commented, "Yes. Me, too."

Always slightly overawed by him, Suzanna managed, "I'm going to my sister's. She was working yesterday, so it's 'Christmas Day: Take Two' for me."

"I'm going with my dad to visit my brother Guy. Are you meeting us in London for New Year's Eve?"

Suzanna knew that by 'us', he meant Anastasia. "Yes, I should be at The Cathedral for the party."

Piers was only half-listening, his attention caught by the front doors opening as Anastasia strode in. She was well wrapped up, and her face glowed pink from the crisp air. "Hello, sweetheart," Piers said, leaning down to kiss her. "Enjoy your walk?"

Anastasia nodded. "Yes, it's gorgeous out there." Then, noticing the suitcases littering the hallway, she remarked, "Are you leaving me already?"

"Afraid so," Suzanna said. "I'm going to Jane's, but I will be in London in time for New Year's Eve." Spotting her driver pulling up outside, she gave her friend a squeeze.

"Give Jane my love and tell her she needs to come out with us soon. It's been too long."

Anastasia waved her friend a cheery goodbye and watched as her car wound its way along the gravel driveway, leaving her with Piers. She turned to him and said, "I wish you weren't going."

He hugged her. "It's a family rapprochement all round, Guy invited me."

"I am happy for you"—her voice was muffled by his heavy woollen overcoat—"but I will miss you."

"I promise I'll be back with you on New Year's Eve." He let her go and held her blue gaze.

Anastasia clutched his coat anxiously, not wanting him to go. "Promise?"

"I promise." He smiled and, with sudden insight, asked, "What's scaring you, sweetheart?"

"You know what."

"Then don't let it. You don't have to tell Mark anything. The past is dead. It *has* to be. Enjoy the present and look to the future."

Impulsively, Anastasia threw her arms around him. "That's why I love you."

And she meant it.

There was a cough; another driver was waiting. Piers addressed him. "Won't be long. I just need to get my dad."

Piers forced himself to release her and turned to go, only to find Joseph Talbot and Jack Travess ambling amicably towards them, each bearing a small suitcase.

"Father?" Anastasia was puzzled. "Are you going, too?"

Her father smiled wistfully. "Yes, I'm going to stay at Guy's for a couple of days and then on to Rick and Fenella's. I'll be seeing the New Year in with them."

"Oh." She looked cross; this was news to her. "Well, give them my love."

Her father kissed her cheek, on account of having an audience, and she was left facing Joseph Talbot. He clasped her hands, genuine affection in his eyes. "Anastasia, thank you for helping to patch up things up between my boys. You have made this a very special Christmas."

"You're welcome, Joseph. Take care of yourself." She wondered whether Mark was going, too, half hoping he was.

As if he had read her mind, Joseph laughed at her. "Don't worry, young Mark's staying put." He paused and then added in a lower voice, "I'm really hoping the pair of you will make me even happier."

And then they were all gone. Anastasia waited until she could no longer see the lights of their car in the distance, a single tear tracing mournfully down her face.

Suddenly feeling confused and very alone in the huge house, Anastasia made her way to the library, always her sanctuary. As she walked slowly, oblivious to her surroundings, she pondered if she really wanted to be totally alone with Mark. So many years had passed since their fling, and now he was a virtual stranger. Everyone seemed to want them to rekindle their romance, pushing her along, but, in truth, she felt helpless.

She paused, lost in her own head, her hand resting on the door handle, when she felt someone behind her. Reacting automatically, Anastasia swung around, her eyes on fire, her fight instinct kicking in to knock him off his feet.

Both bemused and concerned, Mark looked up at her. "*Bloody hell*, baby! Where did you learn to react like that?"

Anastasia sighed, now calm and under control, and offered him her hand, hauling him to his feet. "Sorry, but you shouldn't sneak up on people."

Mark stood before her, slightly dishevelled. "I didn't sneak up on you. You were in a world of your own."

"I said sorry," she snapped, marching into the library. "What more do you want?"

Hesitantly, Mark followed her, now wary of her sudden aggression. He stood in the doorway. "Baby?" he said tentatively. "What's wrong?"

Anastasia saw the concern in his eyes and knew he deserved some sort of explanation. She bit her lip, really not wanting to talk about it, but Mark crossed to her in two swift strides, holding her close.

"I'm sorry, Mark. I was miles away." *Years away*, she thought, seeing images that still terrified her.

He held her tighter and kissed her head. "It was very impressive, if a little embarrassing, to be taken out like that." He was trying to inject some levity, but letting her go, he realised she was crying.

"Piers taught me," she said, wiping her eyes on her sleeve. "He wanted me to be able to defend myself if he wasn't there to do it."

Mark grinned. "Well, he must be a good teacher." Then he frowned, fixing on her last words, suddenly seeing fear behind her eyes. "Why did he want you to be able to defend yourself?"

Anastasia felt her heart begin to pound, panic rising within her, and she dug her nails into the palms of her hands, fighting for control.

Mark did not press her, patiently waiting for her to speak.

Eventually, as she turned away from his gaze, Anastasia said blandly, "I was attacked, and my elbow was dislocated. I have a metal plate there now, and I have a scar across my back from the knife."

She faced the grandfather clock, concentrating on the comforting sounds of its ticking. Silence hung over them, save for the ticking which was now synchronised to her heartbeat, making the silence bearable. Anastasia could feel Mark's eyes boring into her, could feel his shock reverberate over her, and she dug those nails deep into her palms again as she fought off the memories.

Then he was in front of her, eyes filled with anger, demanding to be let in. "Who did it?"

Unable to bear it, Anastasia pushed him away. "It's in the past, Mark. It's over. Finished. Leave it."

Her eyes warned him not to force the issue. "Ok, baby. Whatever you need. Just know that I love you."

Anastasia smiled at him gratefully and, going against her own wishes, gave him more. "It was years ago. 1984." Her liquid blue eyes held his, and Anastasia carried on, aware he deserved a little more if they were going to make this work. "It doesn't define who I am, but it made me shut down. Made me wary."

Mark said nothing, sensing there was something else she wanted to say.

Anastasia delivered her final words on the subject. "Piers saved my life."

Tears spilled down her face, unchecked, as she battled that awful choking sensation, remembering the terror and the fear.

Suddenly, Mark understood, and he was kissing away her tears, mentally noting just how much he had wronged his brother and hating Piers for it. "Let's go to London now."

"Now?" Anastasia was surprised but had no objections.

"We need to be there for New Year's Eve, anyway. We can take my car."

"Ok, but can we stay at my house in Belgravia?" She wanted the comfort of familiar surroundings.

"Whatever you prefer, baby."

Mark was rewarded by a genuine smile. "Yes. Yes, I'd like that."

About an hour later, they were speeding along the motorway towards London in Mark's dark grey Mercedes. He was trying to keep the atmosphere light with silly jokes and amusing anecdotes, but he was not having much success. Anastasia had barely said a word since leaving the manor, lost in her own thoughts, processing memories and re-filing them safely away. When the Mercedes finally arrived in Belgravia, the sky was darkening with the promise of rain coming soon, the crisp blue skies of the morning having vanished.

After parking outside her house, Mark carried their luggage up to the door which Anastasia had left ajar for him while she switched on the lights and made sure that there was some food in the house. About half an hour later, they were sitting on the settee with some soft music playing in the background.

Mark stared at Anastasia; he had no idea what was wrong. "Is everything all right, baby? You've hardly said a word since we left Hertfordshire."

She looked a little vacant, but pulling herself together, she replied, "Just organising my head." Anastasia eyed him thoughtfully. "Where is this going, Mark? Me and you. Are we together? It's all a bit overwhelming. Everyone else seems to have decided what we're doing before we've had chance to take a breath."

Mark was taken aback; in his head, things were perfectly clear. "I just want everything to be right, like it was. Like it should be."

"But it *can't* be like it was!" she exclaimed. "I haven't seen you in over *seven* years, Mark. We've both changed. People don't stay the same. You don't even know what my job is!" There was definitely an accusation in her words, his failure to even try to get in touch clearly still needling her.

Mark opened his mouth, but no words came out. She was right.

Anastasia stood up and moved to the nearby sideboard. "You look like you need a drink." She set about pouring them both a generous measure of brandy.

Mark took the glass and put it down. "I'm sorry, Anastasia. You're right, I don't know everything, but I still know you."

"No, Mark. You might think you do, but ..."

"But nothing, Stasia. You were sixteen when I fell in love with you, but you're not so different now. Just seeing you again, I know that. I didn't know what to do to make you happy back then, but I know now. At least I realised I had to do something before someone else did." He meant Piers.

She cut across him pleased to indulge in the past. "You certainly took your time, Mark Talbot, not till that party. Poor Piers with all those girls!"

Mark grinned. "I should be thanking Piers, if he hadn't caused a fight I would never have needed to get you out of the way,"

"He did not!" she interrupted indignantly, defending Piers was instinctive.

Mark held her eyes not sure he liked her leaping so swiftly to his brother's defence. "Well it certainly looked like it to me; no-one else caused that."

Realising he was jealous Anastasia smiled provocatively. "We did have fun. But it was a long time ago, and it didn't exactly end well."

"It was Giles' fault that we took his prized Porsche."

"*We* took it?" she protested. "I think you'll find *you* took it and then abducted me."

Mark shrugged but could not help looking pleased with himself. His brother Giles, five years older and his mentor, had caught the pair of them together and had told their fathers, but Mark had taken his own revenge by stealing his brand new Porsche, bright red and delivered only the week before. Then he and Anastasia had had a wild night of illicit passion and a car crash in the rain. The best time of his life so far.

"Unforeseen consequences, though." She shuddered involuntarily.

"Yes." Mark sighed. "I've never seen anyone *that* angry. Your father terrified me."

"If you ask me, he only reacted how everyone would expect an outraged father to react. You took it all too literally." And the tinge of bitterness was back in her voice; she remembered how her father had punished her, in ways he would never do in front of witnesses.

Mark had the oddest feeling this was not going his way. "What do you want out of this? Out of me coming back into your life? Tell me what you need."

"I honestly don't know. We've both changed over the years. What are you expecting from me?" There was an edge of aggression to her voice; if she was going to do this, she needed him to spell it out.

Mark's brow creased. "I'm not expecting anything. I *hope* to have you permanently back in my life, in the place you've always belonged." He traced the line of her face with one finger. "I love you, Anastasia. I always have, and I always will. Let me back in; give me that chance to prove it to you. Give me a chance to win you back."

Anastasia felt her heart flutter. She was flattered. She found his intensity attractive—so different to Bryan—but, at the back of her mind, she was still unsure whether a relationship was the right thing to pursue.

If only she knew why it seemed so important to Piers; why he had asked her to try.

Chapter 8

THE NEXT MORNING over breakfast, Mark asked, "So, are you working for your father? In the music business or running his clubs?"

Looking thoughtful, Anastasia put down her toast. "I work for Rick at Original, their record company. I was a temp there for a while and now I work in his office as one of his assistants. I love it. I also write articles for magazines, mainly freelance. I do have a project on at the moment, though." She grinned self-consciously. "I've been helping Johnny to write his autobiography. Ghost-writing."

Mark was puzzled. "Johnny? Not your dad's band member, Johnny Fielding?" He sounded shaken.

"Yes." Anastasia was intrigued by his reaction. "It's *so* interesting. Johnny's great. My father doesn't know I've been working with him, of course."

"But Johnny Fielding is notorious!" he protested, unable to quite put his thoughts into coherent words.

"I've known Johnny all my life," she said dismissively. "The drugs, the rumours, the women, his divorces—I already know most of it. His life story doesn't faze me. In fact, I know more about him and Rick—even Frankie, and he's *dead*—than my own father."

"I didn't mean that …" He broke off, a spark of anger flaring in his icy eyes.

"Oh, come off it, Mark! Johnny wouldn't lay a finger on me; he treats me like a daughter." She was scornful of his irrational fears.

"So, why doesn't your father know?" he countered.

"Because he wouldn't want me to know all the stuff Retribution used to get up to before he married Mama." *Let alone after*, she thought bitterly. She laughed at the look on his face. "You honestly need to meet Johnny; he's lovely. Fenella's my favourite, though. Rick and Fenella Lascelles are my godparents, and I just adore them. It was Fenella who taught me to ride."

Mark knew that Rick Lascelles had been the drummer in Jack Travess' band and he had married Fenella Adams, a former Olympian. "Didn't you spend a summer with them recently?"

"How do you know that?" She was surprised, given they had not been in contact for so long and Piers would not have told him anything without her permission.

"I occasionally tormented myself by finding out what you were doing."

Even to him, that sounded wrong.

Anastasia raised her eyebrows. "Well, yes, I've spent several summers with them. The summer before last, I worked as a stable hand for Fenella, exercised her horses. I loved it." She paused and fixed her narrowed blue eyes on his. "What else did you find out?"

Backtracking, Mark tried to explain. "I wasn't stalking you or anything. Sometimes I missed you so much, I just had to know. Of course, I found out all about Bryan. Had to know what I was up against."

Unsure whether to be flattered or not, she commented, "Ok, we'll leave that there, but I'm not sure I like it." Scrunching her nose, she abruptly changed the subject. "Anyway, you really need to meet all three of them. They mean so much to me."

"Yes, I don't think I've actually met any of them."

"I hope Johnny likes you. He wasn't keen on Bryan *at all*."

"Really?" Johnny suddenly had Mark's approval.

Anastasia grinned. "He said Bryan might be able to sing a tune but he would never be a rock god. Wonder what he'll say about you?" Still chuckling, she carried on eating her toast.

A few days later, Anastasia was listening to the radio as she waited for Mark to finish dressing. Glancing at her watch, she called out impatiently, "Do hurry up, Mark! It's only the local pub." She could not believe how long he was taking.

"Never hurts to look good," Mark said, coming into the room and doing up his coat. "Where are we going?"

"The Star; it's my local. It attracted the high and low life of London during the sixties."

"I think my dad used to hang out there," Mark commented.

"Well, my father and his bandmates certainly did!"

Mark slung his arm around her shoulder to hold her close. "Is this a research trip, then? For Johnny Fielding's autobiography?"

"No, I just like drinking there." She laughed, her eyes full of mischief.

It did not take long to walk to the pub, and as Mark held the door open, he could see it was quite busy. Anastasia took off her gloves and unzipped her leather jacket, looking around for a table not too close to the bar. Mark glanced around and liked what he saw: cosy, comfortable, and a seemingly welcoming atmosphere. He also could not fail to notice the signed photographs of Anastasia's father, and what he presumed were other music stars, lining the walls.

Anastasia pointed to a table. "You sit down and I'll get the drinks. I want to say hello to the bar staff." She was gone before he could reply.

Mark shrugged off his coat and sat down, keeping his eye on Anastasia. He watched her indulgently as she leant over the bar, laughing and talking to the staff. So intent was he that Mark did not notice a very blond man with some friends in the opposite corner of the pub, and Anastasia was blissfully unaware that someone else was watching her, too. She was soon back carrying a pint of lager and a scotch for herself.

"Cheers." Mark took a long drink. Anastasia took his free hand and leant towards him, and as they talked, neither of them noticed that Bryan Darnell was watching them.

Mark soon realised he could not keep up with Anastasia. "I'll get you another, baby, but that's it for me." Her drinking was another item added to his growing list of things to change about her.

"Lightweight!" She laughed. "But I don't suppose you've ever had to keep up with Piers on a night out?"

Mark shook his head, silently acknowledging again how much more he had to learn about her and resenting yet another reference to his brother. "Thankfully, that's true. I'll be back soon." He made his way over to the bar.

"Hello, gorgeous!" His voice was right in her ear as Bryan Darnell leant over her.

Anastasia looked up, at first startled and then annoyed. "What the hell are you doing here, Bryan?" Her eyes flickered anxiously to the bar; to Mark.

Bryan sat in Mark's empty seat. "I rang the manor and the staff told me you were in London. I knew you'd turn up here, it's your favourite pub." He reached for her hand.

"Go away, Bryan," she hissed, snatching her hand away.

"What's wrong? Is he so insecure he can't bear for you to talk to an old friend?" Bryan sneered, enhancing his good looks.

"What do you want?" Anastasia demanded again unable to help her eyes flicking to the bar.

"You know what I want. *You*." Bryan stood up as Mark crossed the pub towards them, carrying two drinks.

"Nice to see you both." Laughing, Bryan blew a kiss at Anastasia before lounging back to his companions.

Much to her annoyance, Anastasia felt her hands shaking and a stab of fear at the brutal look in Mark's glacial eyes.

"What the *fuck* did he want?" he demanded as he sat down.

Acutely aware that Bryan was watching her, Anastasia took

Mark's hand and squeezed it tightly. "To take the piss, that's all. Ignore him, please."

Mark resisted the urge to look over his shoulder and stare Bryan down. Instead, he leant towards Anastasia and kissed her deeply.

His point made, Bryan watched for a moment before standing up abruptly. Nodding to his friends, he left the pub.

Chapter 9

MARK GROANED. HIS head felt like it was filled with bees, all buzzing at once. He managed to sit up, but he dared not open his eyes; the effort felt like too much. Taking several deep breaths, he fought the unpleasant feeling behind his eyes and forced them open.

He could see a strip of light between the curtains, and he put out a hand to feel for Anastasia next to him in the bed. She was not there. He could see her clothes from last night strewn over the floor, but no Anastasia. A wave of nausea swept over him and Mark placed his head in his hands, trying to remember. His mouth was dry, and he needed water.

Gingerly, he sat on the edge of the bed. Standing up did not seem like the best idea, but the thought of a cool shower was tempting. Wondering if he dare open the curtains, Mark shuffled to the bathroom and rummaged for painkillers. After downing a handful and a glass of water and fighting the urge to throw the whole lot back up, he braced himself and took a shower.

About half an hour later, he was dressed, the pain in his head having eased enough for him to tackle the stairs. Negotiating each step with care, he made it safely to the bottom. He could hear someone in the kitchen and the sound of a kettle boiling.

He tried to speak but ended up coughing violently, like a smoker with their first cigarette.

"Morning."

Mark frowned; that was not Anastasia's voice. He went into the kitchen and found Suzanna standing by the sink, piling plates into the dishwasher. "Suzanna?" he managed, not quite comprehending. "Where's Anastasia?"

Suzanna grinned at him. "You look awful! Do you want a black coffee?"

Mark felt dizzy. "What time is it?"

She checked her watch. "Half past eleven."

Mark winced. "Coffee would be great, thanks. I think I need to sit down." He made his way slowly to the living room and sank thankfully into a comfortable chair, where he held his pounding head in his hands.

As Suzanna approached him amid a strong scent of Arabica beans, Mark asked, "When did you get here? I didn't hear you arrive." He took the coffee gratefully.

Suzanna sat opposite him and, taking pity on him, answered, "I got here at eleven. Piers got here around the same time. Anastasia said she was up before eight. Apparently you tried to keep up with her and some of the rugby boys last night. Think it's fair to say you failed."

Half-memories floated before Mark's eyes: Anastasia's rugby playing friends joining them, a lock-in, and far, far too much lager. Then he realised what Suzanna had just told him. "Before *eight*? She was up before eight?" They could not have left The Star much before two in the morning.

Suzanna grinned sympathetically at him. "And had a full fry up, by the look of the kitchen."

Mark groaned. Just the thought of food, let alone fried food, made his stomach churn. He suddenly fastened onto another piece of Suzanna's information. "Piers is here?"

"Yes. He and Stasia decided to go to The Star. He said he hadn't been in since last Easter, so he wanted to say hello to everyone."

"They're down the pub?" Mark queried. "Dear God, Suzanna! I don't think I'll ever drink again."

Suzanna's smile widened further. "The trick is not to compete, you don't have to you know. I never do."

"Wise words. I wish I'd heard them last night." He finished his coffee.

"Are you going to join them?" Suzanna asked with a hint of mischief in her green eyes.

"No," said Mark. "Absolutely not. I'm going to lie down for a couple more hours and never, ever drink again."

"I'll remind you of that later tonight. It's New Year's Eve, remember?"

Mark groaned.

Suzanna found the whole thing most amusing, but there was something she thought he should know. "Mark?"

He looked up.

There was anxiety in her eyes. "You do know Bryan will be there tonight?"

Mark let her words sink in slowly. "Really?" He somehow managed to sound disinterested. "I don't think he'll be a problem but thank you for letting me know."

"Piers will be there, anyway," added Suzanna blithely, missing the ice that darted back into Mark's grey eyes. "Bryan would never cause trouble under his nose."

Puzzled, Mark pressed her. "Did anything happen between those two?"

Suzanna looked at him, seeming to shiver at a memory. "Piers wasn't around when Bryan fell at Stasia's feet." Her lips twitched into a bitter smile and she gave away more than she intended. "When he came back, Bryan misunderstood and provoked a confrontation."

"I can't blame Bryan for that," Mark commented fairly.

"Yes, well. It still doesn't justify your brother putting Bryan in hospital." Suzanna held Mark's eyes and saw the shock and revulsion there. She regretted her words, as they were not, strictly speaking, true; she and Anastasia had only taken Bryan to hospital as a precaution.

Mark thought her words over. Piers obviously had not changed, and yet he was still everybody's favourite. Feeling a little better as the painkillers and coffee started to kick in, Mark stood. "Are you bringing anyone tonight, Suzanna?"

"No." She sighed. "My friend Simon has gone to Scotland to see his family. I met him down The Star. He's one of the rugby mob."

Mark had not pictured Suzanna's type as one of those hard-drinking, loud-and-lairy rugby players he had met last night and he was surprised.

"It doesn't matter," she added, standing up and moving back towards the kitchen for another coffee. "It's nothing serious."

Mark smiled consolingly. "You never know, you might meet someone tonight to take your mind off him." Giving a huge yawn and not noticing the blush now spreading across her face, he finished with, "Thank you for the coffee. Back to bed for me."

It was about three in the afternoon when Mark got up again, feeling considerably better, if still a little delicate. He could hear voices clashing happily and lots of laughter as he made his way back downstairs.

"Mark!" Anastasia crossed the room to join him as he entered. "Are you feeling better?" She kissed his cheek, wanting Piers to take note.

Taking her in his arms, Mark caught his brother's amused eye.

Piers called out. "Never mind Mark, you survived ready to do it all over again tonight."

Mark shuddered at the thought. "I hear you two have started already." He could smell alcohol on Anastasia's breath and he did not approve.

"Just a couple whilst catching up with some mates," Piers replied.

"I don't know how you can. I can't even remember getting into bed." Mark shook his head, half in disapproval and half in envy.

"So you don't remember anything you said to me on the way home?" Anastasia was teasing him.

"No," Mark replied slowly, trying to make his brain work. "What did I say?"

She spoke close to his ear, the feel of her so near making his heart pound as well as his head. "Wonderful things," she purred, and she kissed him.

Piers cleared his throat; he had no desire to witness any physical interaction between her and his brother. "Before I forget, Guy has invited me, you and Mark to his birthday do next weekend," he said. "First time I'll have been to one his parties. Should be good."

Anastasia looked around, distracted. "I haven't seen Guy properly in years. I think I last bumped into him in a club somewhere. Isn't he married now?"

"Yes," Piers replied. "I met Lily and my nieces for the first time this week. She's lovely, Stasia; you'll like her. God knows what she sees in Guy!"

She pulled away from Mark, curious to hear more. "Is there a dress code or anything? Will there be loads of people?"

Piers frowned, trying to recall. "He has a huge house so I expect there will be plenty of guests but I can't remember any specifics except for the date and place."

"Did you have fun at Guy's?" Mark asked, wondering what his brother had found to do there.

Piers grinned; he knew what Mark was thinking. "Actually, I did. It surprised me, too. Like I said, Lily's great, and Guy and I played snooker and enjoyed a couple of glasses of his finest scotch. In fact, he pretty much has the best of everything." He silently recalled the twinge he had felt seeing Guy and Lily happily married; something he thought he would never have.

"So why didn't you stay longer?" Mark asked pointedly.

"I wasn't going to miss out on a party with you lot."

Anastasia sat on the arm of the sofa next to him. "Kick back before you kick off?"

"No, sweetheart. Kick back and then go to work." He held her eyes, seeing dismay there. "I'll be able to fit in Guy's do, but then I think they want me back."

"But you've hardly been home this time!" She placed a hand on his shoulder, distressed.

Suzanna was watching Mark's face closely, slightly alarmed by the look she saw there.

"They might not need me for long, but I won't know until I see them tomorrow morning."

"Tomorrow? You're going to turn up at work with a hangover?" Mark was sceptical.

Piers fixed his eyes on Mark's face; he did not like his tone. "They're bloody lucky I'm turning up at all."

Anastasia glanced curiously from one brother to the other. Where was this antagonism coming from? The telephone rang out and she jumped up to answer it, still feeling Piers' eyes staring at Mark.

The others sat in awkward silence, listening as she spoke.

"Hello!... Oh, yes, that would be great. I'll certainly be coming … Yes, let me check and I'll call you back soon. Thank you; love you. Bye!" Anastasia replaced the receiver and then faced them, smiling broadly. "That was Fenella! We're all invited to her and Rick's tomorrow for dinner, and we can stay over, too. Who's coming with me?"

"Lovely," Suzanna replied quickly. "Do you think we can go riding? It was great last time. I really enjoyed it."

"Of course. Have you got your stuff? Fenella has loads of spare gear if you don't."

Piers stood up and stretched. "If you can wait till I come back from the office, count me in. When you ring Fenella, ask her if that gelding is ready yet; the bay one she wanted me to try out."

Mark had remained silent. "Do I get a say?"

Anastasia looked at him. "Sorry, don't you want to go?"

"I may have made other plans." He sounded petulant.

"Have you?" Piers' voice cut through the air like a knife. Mark shook his head, a mulish look to his mouth. "Well then, what's your problem?"

Slightly worried, Anastasia tried to diffuse what was fast becoming a situation. "There's no problem. We're going out tonight and we're all going to Fenella's tomorrow." She stood in between them and said to Mark, "I hope you'll get on. It's important to me that you like them."

With one final look at Piers, Mark pulled her into a hug. "Of course, I'll like them, baby. Them loving you is more than good enough for me."

Piers held Mark's gaze for a moment. "Good that's settled. I'm going for a shower," and he left the room.

Chapter 10

Bryan stopped just outside The Cathedral, an exclusive haunt located down a side street in Soho. Its neon sign easily visible from a distance, he could see the queue was already massive; full of hopefuls desperate for a chance to rub shoulders with a rock star or the latest soap opera diva. He ran a hand through his now dark blond hair and hoped very much that he was still on the VIP list. Bryan brushed past a group of scantily clad girls who giggled as they recognised him and called out suggestions for his entertainment. He looked a little grim as he approached the bouncers—he was not in the mood, he had come for one reason only—and he was thankful when they just waved him on in.

He immediately started looking for Anastasia. As he made his way towards one of the bars, he could hear whispers; could see the faux sympathetic looks and hear people murmuring to him, "So sorry to hear you've split up," and "Such a shame. And at Christmas, too." Bryan knew some of them were genuine, but most were just happy to see him humiliated. He wanted a drink. *Several* drinks.

"Bryan!" a voice called out.

Bryan looked up, still with that dark look in his hazel eyes, and was thankful to see a friend, Theo Cavendish, smiling and waving at him. At least Theo would understand.

"How are you? Where's Stasia?" Theo asked blithely. He obviously had not heard.

"She has a new man, Theo. I expect they'll be here soon." He caught the bartender's eye and ordered several drinks.

Theo frowned. "What happened?" Then, seeing Bryan was disinclined to answer him, he asked cautiously, "Has Piers finally made a move?"

Bryan downed one, two, three shots in quick succession and, laughing bitterly, replied, "I could have taken that, but no. His brother got there first."

Theo was dumbfounded. "His *brother*? Which one?"

Bryan downed another. "His youngest, Mark. The git." Bryan carried on drinking.

Theo's eyes clouded and he repeated the name, tapping into a memory from long ago that still rankled. "Mark? The bloke she had a fling with when we split up over me going to Europe?"

Bryan eyed him speculatively. "You hate him, too?"

Theo sighed. "It was a long time ago, and it was my fault, anyway. As soon as I got back, I turned up in Belgravia with roses and champagne and ..." He broke off, grinning. "God, that was a good night!"

Bryan gazed at him with hostility and ordered more drinks.

"Steady on," Theo cautioned. "I didn't know you belonged to the Piers Talbot School of How To Get Hammered."

Bryan shrugged and carried on drinking. "You in for the duration?"

"No," Theo replied slowly, counting how many glasses were now empty. "No, I'm off shortly to a do at the Ritz with my wife."

"Oh, aren't we superior? Must be fun being a member of the aristocracy, your ladyship," Bryan responded sarcastically.

Theo laughed. "You're such a knob, Darnell. Anyway, I only came in to see Piers. I'm fancying a night out with him and Stasia soon."

"I don't expect her new man will let her out of his sight. And if he's got any sense, he'll get her to kick Piers into touch," Bryan remarked cryptically.

"Yeah, right. As if *that* will ever happen." Theo held Bryan's slightly out of focus gaze and they both knew he was right.

Bryan shrugged. "I'll get out of your way, mate. She won't come over to you if I'm around. Catch you soon."

He tried to move away, now unsteady on his feet, and Theo stopped him. "Word to the wise. Ease up on the sauce. If you do anything stupid and jeopardise your album release, Rick will *not* be happy. And you know more than most not to piss off Rick Lascelles!" Unsure if Bryan had heard him, he watched his now inebriated friend wander off.

AS THEY ENTERED The Cathedral, Anastasia suddenly gave a squeal of joy. Grabbing Piers by the hand, she dragged him over to a man with dark red hair who stood by the bar.

Mark stopped, surprised and annoyed, and Suzanna walked into the back of him. "Who is that, and why does he have his hands on my girlfriend?" he demanded.

Suzanna anxiously sought out her friend and she saw Theo Cavendish with an arm around Anastasia and shaking Piers' hand. She laughed, relieved. "That's Theo Cavendish, the photographer. He's a close friend. Come on, let's get to our table before we lose it."

Mark reluctantly followed her, keeping an eye on Anastasia and a check on his temper.

AFTER A WARM embrace, Theo kissed Anastasia on the cheek and said, "Hey, angel! I hear you've dumped Bryan."

She slapped his arm and demanded, "How do you always know everything? Are you in for the night?"

He laughed. "No, I only popped in briefly to see you and Piers. I'm off with Alice to a posh private do at the Ritz. And I know about you and Bryan because I've just spoken to him," he explained, a grin on his tanned face and a gleam of mischief in his vivid blue eyes. Then Theo turned to Piers and slapped him on the back. "Welcome home, mate. Always good to have my drinking buddy in town."

Piers laughed. Neither he nor Anastasia noticed Mark glaring at them from across the room, but Piers left Anastasia to catch up with Theo while he joined his brother and Suzanna. As he approached, he could see Suzanna looking a little anxious and then he noted the look in Mark's glacial eyes as he glanced towards Theo. Unable to resist, he decided to stoke his brother's jealousy.

"He's a close friend of ours," he said nonchalantly. "And just another of Stasia's exes." He paused as Suzanna passed him a drink and smiled gratefully at her. "Thank you. You know me so well."

He downed his scotch in one and then held out his hand to her. "Come on, Suzanna. You owe me a dance," he said, and he led her away, smirking.

"BEST THING YOU could have done, letting Bryan go. It really was unfair of you Stasia to keep stringing him along."

Theo could always be counted on to say it like it was, even if she did not want to hear it. "I didn't treat him badly!" she retorted. "He cheated on me!"

"That's hardly surprising, given his eye for the ladies, but *why* did he do it, Stasia?"

She glared at him. "I don't know why I was so pleased to see you. Sometimes you can be a real dickhead, Theo."

Theo laughed. "That's as may be, but I'm an honest one. Like it or not, we both know why he'd cheat."

He held her eyes and saw anguish there and then he leant down to kiss her cheek. "Tell Piers I'll call him."

"Don't you want to meet his brother?" She knew that would sting.

Theo made an odd face and replied, "I really don't want to meet the reason we split up, Stasia."

"That was your fault; you didn't listen. You jumped to conclusions and thought I was moving Mark into Belgravia, not Piers."

He smiled and said, "But you were looking for an excuse, weren't you, angel?"

She flushed and bit her lip. "Maybe." She grinned at him. "No matter how sharp your tongue, you know I still adore you, Theo. Give my love to Alice. I don't know how she puts up with you!"

"I'm just lucky, I guess. Try to see sense soon, Anastasia." He smiled and then disappeared into the crowd.

Anastasia looked around, trying to spot Mark, and saw Piers dancing with an extremely uncomfortable looking Suzanna. Anastasia laughed to herself. Suzanna was never relaxed around him—she had no idea why—and he seemed to overwhelm her.

She made her way across the club, skirting around people and exchanging greetings with many of them, thinking about that last row with Theo all those years ago. She had told him about helping a friend, but he had assumed it was Mark—after all, he and Piers did look alike—and lost his temper, accusing her of two-timing him and moving Mark in to carry on their fling. She had tried to explain that they were two different people—so *different*, she thought with an ironic twist of her lips—but Theo would not listen. She had shrugged and told him that without trust, their relationship was over. Once Theo had realised his mistake, he had been mortified, but Anastasia had known she did not want to be with him anymore, she wanted someone else. Since then, Theo had proved himself to be a loyal and honest friend, always there if she needed him, and he and Piers got on like a house on fire, which made her very happy. As she approached Mark, she could see the ice in his eyes and, with a little shiver, she knew that he would hate Theo without even giving him a chance.

She leant down and kissed him, trying to pre-empt any outburst. "Want to dance?" she asked, sliding her hand across his back and giving him her most seductive smile.

He hesitated, wanting to reprimand her for flirting with another man. "No, thanks; it's not really my thing. Sit with me; tell me about your friend." He looked over at the bar, but Theo was long gone. "Why didn't you bring him over?"

"He was late for another do. He only stopped by to catch up with Piers." That was pretty much true, she reasoned.

"Who is he?" Mark asked again, trying very hard to keep the conversation light, pleasant.

She sat down next to him and spoke close to his ear, the noise around them making any conversation difficult. "The Honourable Theo Cavendish. He's a very successful photographer. Does a lot of stuff for Rick at Original."

Mark moved his head so he could look into her troubled eyes. "How long have you known him?" He wanted her to tell him he was an ex; to shrug it off because it no longer mattered.

Anastasia hesitated. "I've known him since I was seventeen. We shared an office when I was a temp at Original, and I used to help him sometimes on his shoots. We've been friends for years." For some reason, she feared telling him the full extent of their history.

"Piers told me he was your ex." Mark's voice was cold, brittle. Why was she trying to hide it? Was this another one she liked to keep on a string?

Unable to hold his gaze and wishing Piers had kept his mouth shut, she responded, "It was so long ago. We were young and stupid." She tried to laugh it off.

"So were we." Mark was not at all happy with her attitude.

Now she was annoyed. Why should she be scared of him? "Yes, we were, but that was different." Taking control, she kissed him, knowing exactly how to distract him.

As Piers and Suzanna left the dancefloor, Piers could see them, Anastasia now sitting on Mark's lap with his arms wrapped around her. He coughed as they approached and Anastasia tried to pull free, but Mark would not let her stand up. He eyed his brother with resentment, sure that Piers had only told him about Theo to wind him up.

"Has Theo gone?" Piers pointedly asked Anastasia.

She gave him an odd look, like she was pleading with him to stop, and replied casually, "Yes, off to the Ritz. He always did move in the top echelon. He said he'd call you."

"Anyone want another drink?" he asked, aware that Mark

was glaring at him as he went off to the bar.

When Piers returned, he tried very hard not to provoke his brother, but that was easier said than done. Despite knowing that he was upsetting Anastasia, Piers could not help but respond to each of Mark's little digs. Eventually, she cracked.

Anastasia stood before the pair of them, evidently unhappy. "Are you two deliberately trying to ruin my New Year's Eve?"

Mark shrugged a shoulder and turned his head away so he could no longer see those blazing blue eyes, but he could feel them.

Piers held up his hands. "I'm sorry, sweetheart."

Just as she was about to demand an explanation, Suzanna appeared beside her and tapped her arm. "Stasia, can I borrow you for a minute?"

Anastasia cried out, exasperated, "Is this a bloody conspiracy?" and followed her friend to find out what she wanted. Once they had cleared the crowd, Anastasia reached out and stopped Suzanna. "What's going on? Why do you need me?"

Suzanna was looking troubled. "It's Bryan. They want to throw him out."

Sighing, Anastasia relented.

They arrived at the manager's office, where two bouncers were trying to reason with an obviously drunk and obstreperous Bryan.

Anastasia banged the door open, right on the edge of losing her temper. "Jesus Christ! What's going on?"

One of the bouncers tried to justify having sent for her. "He's had a skin full, Miss Travess. And he's been trying to pick a fight. We pulled him in here before he got a kicking."

Wanting to smack him herself, she replied, "Thanks, I'll sort it."

They both looked at her, concerned. "You sure?"

She nodded impatiently. "Yes. He's not going to touch me."

"Ok, Miss Travess, if you say so."

As they reluctantly left, she asked them, "Could you ask my driver to come round, please? We'll send him home." Then Anastasia faced Bryan. "Why?" she asked him.

He was leaning against the desk, looking lost and militant;

an odd combination. His eyes managed to focus on her face as he reached out for her. "I love you," he blurted out.

"Please, Bryan. We've been over this."

"You can't tell me how to feel!" He was angry and he stood up straight.

She sighed. "You're right; I can't tell you how to feel, but I can tell you how *I* feel. I don't love you, Bryan. I don't."

He stared at her and then, taking Anastasia by surprise, he grabbed her and kissed her hard. She stayed passive, knowing it meant nothing. He let her go, and she slapped him. That seemed to sober him up.

Anastasia turned to Suzanna. "Can you go in the car with him, please? Just push him in through his front door and come back."

Suzanna was torn. She wanted to help Bryan, but she was concerned about how to handle him in this state.

Seeing her apprehension, Anastasia tried to reassure her. "You'll be ok; he's just had too much to drink. He won't hurt you."

Catching her words, Bryan said, "I would never hurt either of you. No man should ever hit a woman." He nodded, he knew he was right.

"I'll help you get him in the car." Seeing her friend still hesitating, Anastasia pointed out the obvious. "If we leave him, he'll either start a fight here or outside in the street and then he will get hurt."

They each took an arm and led an unresisting Bryan towards the back exit, where the car was waiting. As Anastasia shoved him in, he said, "I'm sorry."

She cut him off. "It's ok, I understand. Once you're sober enough to think things through, you'll realise you don't need me. You need someone who loves you." She hoped her words would eventually sink in.

He observed her sadly, then, yawning, he settled himself on the back seat.

Suzanna turned to her friend, looking worried. "I don't want to do this."

"Please, Suzanna. He'll probably fall asleep as soon as he's home. My driver will make sure you're all right." She glanced at him expectantly.

"Of course. She'll be quite safe, Miss Travess," he replied from the driving seat.

Suzanna gave Anastasia another anxious look and then reluctantly got into the car.

Chapter 11

MARK GLOWERED AT his brother, but Piers was unimpressed. "What is your problem, little brother? You know all you're doing is pissing Stasia off, don't you?"

"Why won't you leave her alone?" Mark snapped at him.

"Whoa! Where's that come from? I thought we'd sorted all this at Christmas."

"Whenever you're around, she hangs off your every word. And don't forget that our family seems to have a habit of brothers stealing each other's girlfriends."

"If you're referring to Matthew and Angela," Piers cut across him, "that was because Giles is a sadistic, controlling bastard and Angela finally saw sense."

"You are deliberately trying to sabotage our relationship! Why don't you keep your hands to yourself?"

Feeling the anger beginning to rise, Piers answered him. "Fuck you, Mark! I've been friends with Anastasia for years. When I was kicked out of home, she offered me a place to crash or I would otherwise have been out on the streets. Nobody else stood by me, and certainly none of my *loving* brothers!" His blue eyes were ablaze.

Disregarding the warning signs, Mark said scathingly, "It's time you found your own place then, isn't it? Especially now you're some big shot for the government."

Somehow resisting the urge to strangle his petulant brother,

Piers spoke in a chilling voice. "That's not your call."

Mark glared at him, his eyes overflowing with jealousy and suspicion.

"You want to make her choose?" Piers stood up and leant over his brother. "Because let me tell you, that's a battle you won't win."

He walked away before they came to blows, but, as he left, Piers feared that if Anastasia really did love Mark, if Mark somehow managed to force him out of her life, then he would lose everything.

And it was all his own fault.

ANASTASIA'S DRIVER HELPED Bryan into his Primrose Hill home as Suzanna hovered nervously nearby.

Bryan collapsed thankfully onto his sofa. "Want a drink?"

She shook her head. "The driver needs to get back."

"*Please*." He fixed the hazel eyes that tormented her dreams on her face. "Please stay. Talk to me. I could use a friend."

She hesitated, and the driver coughed discreetly to gain her attention. "I could come back for you in an hour or so?"

Suzanna was unsure, but Bryan's pleading look won her over. "It's ok; go back to Anastasia. I can get a taxi."

The driver nodded and returned to the car.

"Come and sit down, Suzanna." Bryan rubbed a hand across his face, trying to focus. He could still feel the sting where Anastasia had slapped him. Suzanna was very pretty, he had often noticed that, and she had a sweet temperament so different to her fiery friend; his ex-girlfriend. *My* ex-*girlfriend*, he thought ruefully. He had known that was coming for months.

His thoughts confused, he took Suzanna's hand as she sat next to him in awkward silence. She did not know what to say; her heart was racing and her voice was frozen. She felt him run a finger down her cheek and she trembled. Then, suddenly, he was kissing her and she could not resist; this was what she had wanted since she had first met him. His voice was saying what she needed to hear, and before she knew it, Suzanna was being led to his bedroom.

ANASTASIA HAD GONE straight to the bar and downed a double scotch. Only then did she feel able to find out exactly why Mark and Piers were behaving like a couple of five-year-olds and maybe, just maybe, this entire night out would not be a complete disaster.

She found Mark sitting at their table, looking annoyed and nursing a pint glass. There was no sign of his brother.

"Where the fuck have you been?" Mark demanded as soon as he saw her, an ugly look on his face.

She blinked—she had taken enough for one night—and replied in a voice that chilled his soul, "Who the hell do you think you're talking to?"

Mark did not reply.

"For your information, they needed me to help sort out a troublemaker. Is it ok that I help my father's staff in his club?" Her eyes were on fire, and she was now in no mood to be conciliatory.

Mark shrugged and finished his pint.

Anastasia looked around and then stared hard at the dance floor. "Where's Piers?"

Mark was suddenly on his feet and gripping her upper arm. "Why do you care? You're not his keeper!"

She held his angry, resentful grey eyes for a moment. "Get your hand off me or I'll put you on your arse again." It was a low blow and she knew it, but she was angry.

Mark released her instantly, knowing he had gone too far. "I was worried."

"Where is your brother?" Anastasia asked again.

"Took himself off in a huff," Mark said sulkily.

She laughed derisively at him. "No, he didn't." Her eyes appraised his guilty expression shrewdly. "What did you say to him?"

Mark could not hold her gaze. "If you must know, I told him he was getting in our way and asked him to leave us alone, keep his hands to himself."

As soon as he had spoken, he knew he had made an awful mistake.

Her eyes could not hide her wrath. In a level voice that was disturbingly calm, Anastasia asked, "You told my best friend to go?"

Mark's gaze faltered before her ire, but he believed he was justified and would not back down.

"You want me to choose?" Anastasia said angrily. "Fine. I'm going to look for him. You can stay here or go home alone, I don't really care." She turned on her heel, oblivious to his shouts.

Retrieving her coat, Anastasia found her driver, and even the news that Suzanna had stayed with Bryan did not deflect her from trying to find Piers.

Anastasia had no luck in tracking Piers down and, after an hour or so, knew it could take all night. Her night ruined, she simply asked her driver to take her home.

Mark had left all the lights on, and she looked into her bedroom to see him passed out, fully dressed, on the bed. Not wanting to wake him and have another argument, she grabbed her long silk nightdress and dressing gown and crept back downstairs, turning the lights off as she went.

Anastasia got changed downstairs and sat on one of the sofas, watching the clock. She did not know where Piers was, and the information that her driver had left Suzanna with Bryan was disquieting. Anastasia was beginning to feel drowsy when she suddenly heard a key in the lock and she jumped to her feet, holding her breath. She heard footsteps and was relieved to see Piers standing in the doorway. Unable to hide her anxiety, she said, "Where did you bugger off to?"

He started, not expecting her to be home, let alone waiting up for him. Not knowing what to say, he stayed quiet.

Anastasia moved towards him. "I know what Mark said to you. I'm sorry."

Piers shrugged. "He said it, not you. You don't need to apologise."

"Why did you leave?"

He walked past her to sit down on one of the sofas.

She followed him. "You two were bickering all night, before we even left here. What's going on?"

Piers ran his hand through his hair. "My little brother still seems to have a problem with me, so I left before I hit him."

Anastasia sat next to him, taking his hand. "Then that's his problem, not yours."

Piers held her eyes. "He's my brother. I did what I thought was best for everyone."

"Where did you go?" she asked again.

"To Retro. I found Johnny there with a load of his mates. It was fun, actually."

She smiled ruefully. "Well, I'm glad one of us had a good time."

He raised his eyebrows in an unspoken question.

"I was called away to deal with a drunk Bryan. He kissed me."

"Does Mark know?"

She shook her head. "No point in telling him; Bryan was drunk. Suzanna was there."

Piers understood. "Where is Suzanna now?"

She shrugged. "I asked her to get Bryan safely home and then come back, but my driver told me she decided to stay with him."

"Oh." Piers' lips twitched. "Do you think she might …?"

"Oh, God no, she wouldn't. Would she?" But Anastasia knew the answer.

"Yes, she would." Piers confirmed her thoughts.

"Well, then maybe *two* of us had a good night." She was perplexed by the thought of her friend and her ex ending up together.

"Where's Mark?" His voice was now emotionless.

"Upstairs, passed out. I'm sleeping down here."

Piers frowned at her. "Why would you do that?"

"I didn't like the way he spoke to me earlier. I could do with some space. When you go up, can you chuck me down a blanket, please?"

He reached over to the other sofa and pulled a huge fleecy throw across them. "Use this," he said. "Are we waiting up for Suzanna?"

She rested her head on his shoulder, yawning. "She'll be embarrassed if we do,"

"Want to bet what time she sneaks back in?" He grinned down at her. "I'm going four o'clock."

Anastasia yawned again. "I'll go four thirty."

And settling down to wait, she fell asleep.

THEY WERE BOTH wrong. Around six in the morning, Piers suddenly woke up, his face buried in a pile of brunette hair. He could smell Chanel, and from that, he knew Anastasia was asleep in his arms. He moved his face carefully and blinked several times, the darkness relieved only by the light of the lamp. His arms were wrapped around her, and somehow they had ended up lying down on the sofa. She felt soft in his hold, the silk of her dressing gown under his hands, the perfume in her hair, the way her body fitted perfectly against his; if he was not careful, he would lose his head. He suddenly realised that if Mark walked in on them like this, he would flip out. But he did not want to let her go.

Anastasia began to stir, murmuring something he did not catch, and opened her eyes. "Piers?" She thought she was still dreaming.

"We must have fallen asleep. Did we miss Suzanna coming home?"

"I don't know." She yawned. "Maybe."

He reluctantly moved his hands so she could sit up.

"Did you drink much last night?" she asked.

Piers sat up next to her and stretched. "No," he replied. "Didn't feel like it."

"Same here. I guess I was just really tired." She stood up, yawning again as she re-tied her dressing gown. "I'll nip up to her room and see if she's back. Otherwise, I might scare the hell out of Bryan by fetching her."

Piers sat on the sofa, thinking longingly of his bed. But, he reasoned, he was awake, and if he got up now, he could get his appointment dealt with, and they could all be at Fenella's for lunch.

Anastasia came back into the room. "She's not here. Shall I ring him?"

"Don't be a spoilsport," Piers told her. "Leave them alone. She's wanted this for ages."

She sat back down next to him. "You old romantic, you."

He grinned. "Guilty as charged—and less of the old! I'm only four years older than you. Do you want any breakfast?"

"It's almost five, actually, and yeah, I'm starving. Do you want a hand?"

"Oh, I see." He was laughing now. "I'm cooking you breakfast?"

She looked surprised he was asking. "Of course. You're such a good cook and I wouldn't know one end of a frying pan from the other. Take pity on a poor girl." And without realising it, she held his hand.

Giving in as he always did, he pulled Anastasia to her feet and led her into the kitchen.

Chapter 12

1ˢᵗ January 1990

MARK CAME DOWNSTAIRS at nine. He was not in a good mood, and he had a hangover. He found Anastasia still not dressed and curled up on the sofa, reading. The remains of what looked like a full English breakfast lay discarded on a tray on the floor beside her.

She looked up as he stood before her. "Morning," she said coldly, still annoyed with his behaviour from last night.

Realising he could not defend himself, Mark knelt down beside her and said contritely, "I'm sorry I behaved like a knob."

"You need to dial back on the jealousy, Mark," she said in a carefully measured voice. "You have to trust me, or this will not work. Piers means the world to me, and I won't let *anyone* try to ruin that. If you can't accept him—or my other friends—as a part of my life, if you can't trust me, then we have to end this now."

"I do trust you," he said, moving to sit beside her and pulling her into his arms. "But I also know other men fancy you just as much as I do. I guess I'm still finding that hard to deal with. But let me show you how much I want you. Come to bed. Come on—before we go to your friends." He began to stroke her back and then, seeing a flicker of response in those beautiful blue eyes, he lifted her up into his arms and carried her upstairs to bed.

ABOUT AN HOUR later, Mark came back downstairs, leaving Anastasia to get dressed ready to go to Fenella's. As he switched on the television, he heard the front door open and a shifty looking Suzanna entered the room.

She started. "Oh—morning, Mark."

"Are you just getting in?" he asked, raising a black eyebrow and trying not to smile.

She nodded. "Where's Stasia?"

"Just getting up. Go up to her, if you like. I know she'll be pleased to see you."

"Thanks," Suzanna murmured, not sure she liked him giving her permission; she did live there, after all.

She made her way up to her friend's room and knocked before calling out, "Stasia? It's me. Can I come in?"

Anastasia opened the door, looked Suzanna over carefully and then commented dryly, "My driver said you'd made a new friend."

Suzanna blushed vividly and hesitated in the doorway.

"Do come in. I hope it was what you wanted?" Anastasia was laughing.

Relieved by her reaction, Suzanna grinned sheepishly and replied, "Everything I dreamed of." She threw her arms around her friend. "He's asked me to spend some time with him, so if you won't be too cross, I won't be coming to Fenella's." She seemed anxious, seeking approval.

"You do whatever makes you happiest but remind him I'm a crack shot if he upsets you!" Anastasia was genuinely pleased for her, hopeful that this could be just what Bryan needed to get his act together and be content with only one woman.

"I know exactly what he's like," said Suzanna, eminently sensible. "I haven't spent two years seeing how he operates not to be fully aware."

"Good, but you know that was with me. I was never going to be what he needed." She held Suzanna's anxious green eyes and embraced her. "But I think you could be, darling."

Suzanna dashed a few tears away. "I thought you might be angry."

"No, of course not. I just want you to be sure Bryan is what you want. If you are, then grab it with both hands. Don't wait and miss out, like I have." Anastasia turned away, thinking of Piers, knowing she blew it years ago.

Suzanna wanted to say something, wanted to ask her who it was she needed to be with, but challenging Anastasia had never been something she was able to do. She remained silent.

Pulling herself together, Anastasia said brightly, "I'll let Fenella know there's been a change of plans. She loves a romance, so she'll understand. I'm just waiting for Piers to get back and then we'll be off."

Picking up her bag, she went back downstairs, leaving Suzanna to pack her things for a few nights at Bryan's. As she walked down the stairs, Anastasia thought she knew what was coming; Suzanna would move in with Bryan. It would be strange without her friend; she had lived there for nearly five years and had always been a comforting presence. Sighing, she put her bag down at the bottom of the staircase and went back into the main room.

Anastasia stopped and stared as she saw Piers sitting at the table, his back to his brother, and Mark with a mulish look on his face. Wanting to bang their heads together, she called out, "Everything ok?"

Piers looked up and smiled. "Yeah, fine. I was able to swing enough time off for Guy's do and then I'm off again. Short visit this time, I'm afraid." He stood up and moved towards her, keeping a wary eye on his brother's face.

"Suzanna's back, but she's not coming with us to Fenella's." She held his gaze.

"Ah, things went well, then? Good for her."

"So," Anastasia said, including Mark in the conversation. "How are we getting to Fenella's? There's no way you can drive, Mark; you'll be way over the limit. I'm ok, and I suspect Piers is, too, but his car won't fit the three of us." She paused, waiting for some comment from either of them.

"He's not driving my Merc," was Mark's response.

"Well, I will, then." Anastasia could not believe how childish he was being. "But you do realise Piers is a much better driver than me? If your car means anything to you, you'd be better off letting him take the wheel."

Mark looked at her and gave in. "Ok, whatever you want." He stood up. "I'll get my bag and be back in five."

He stalked away petulantly. He had a call to make, anyway. One he had been putting off.

Mark hesitated. He had promised to call at Christmas, but so much had happened that it had slipped his mind. He picked up the receiver, sure his brother would not be that bothered, but he knew Giles would disapprove of him starting things back up again with Anastasia. He had disapproved most emphatically when Mark had confided his feelings and intentions towards Anastasia to him. He paused before dialling, considering whether Giles had deliberately lied to him about Piers' relationship with her. No, he was sure that Giles had been mistaken; that he had genuinely wanted to protect his baby brother from being disappointed. Mark dialled the number and waited.

"Giles Talbot speaking."

"Hey, big brother! Happy New Year!" Mark tried to inject brightness and confidence into his voice.

"Did you forget your own phone number?" Giles asked caustically.

Mark flinched. "Sorry, but things have been a bit hectic here. You know how Christmas can be."

"How are you? How did it go?" Giles would not say her name.

Mark took a deep breath; he could not tell Giles the exact truth. "Excellent. Anastasia and I are together." His words were greeted by silence. "Giles, I know you think I'm deluded, but I really do love her."

Giles sighed. "I know you do, Mark; I know you do." Although concerned Anastasia would tell Mark what had happened that summer, Giles knew he could turn this situation to his advantage and finally get what he wanted. He could not afford to alienate another brother, the only potential ally in his schemes. "I'm pleased for you."

"Really?"

Giles knew he had to regain ground, find out exactly what she had told him. "Mark, I *am* pleased, truly I am. I only ever wanted you to be happy." He knew which strings to pull, which buttons to press.

"Well, I am." Mark sounded defiant. "We're going to visit Anastasia's godparents now. Hope I make a good impression."

"You'll be fine. How's her dad?"

"I'm not sure I like him." Mark broke off; something was not quite right there, and Mark despised the fact he had hit his daughter.

"Keep on his good side. Never a bad idea to keep your girlfriend's dad on side." Giles tried to be jovial.

"I'm going to ask Anastasia to come to Paris for a visit." Mark was rebelling; he knew Giles would not like that. But this was his ultimate goal; to get her to move in with him, to get her away from all those bad influences she seemed to delight in surrounding herself with.

Giles was taken aback. "Don't rush things. Move too fast and you'll scare her away." This was inadvertent good advice, as it did not come from a place of sincerity; Giles merely had no desire to ever see her again.

"Yeah, yeah, you're right." Mark brushed his words aside. "Ok, well, I've got to go. Take care and speak soon." Mark had heard Anastasia calling for him.

"You, too. I'll be in touch." Giles put the telephone down, wondering which move to make next.

Chapter 13

Anastasia could not wait to get out of the car; it had been a nightmare journey. Neither Piers nor Mark had said a single word throughout the entire trip, and the tension in the air had given her a headache.

Grateful to be free of their sullenness, she rushed forward to greet her godparents. Rick Lascelles was at the door and was surprised to be hugged quite so enthusiastically. "I'm so glad to see you!" Anastasia murmured in relief as he kissed her cheek. She then moved to her godmother Fenella, a tall, shapely woman with an air of calm and control. Her blonde hair was swept up, and her chilly persona disguised a warm and loving heart.

Fenella embraced Anastasia, saying, "Hello, darling. Where's Suzanna?"

"She sends her apologies, but she's a little distracted by her new bloke. I'll fill you in, I promise."

"Yes, there's a lot we need to discuss, isn't there?" As she let Anastasia go, Fenella looked towards Mark.

Anastasia coloured slightly; she usually told Fenella everything. "Later, I swear."

Fenella smiled warmly as Piers strolled towards her. He leant down to kiss her. "You're looking as lovely as ever, Fenella."

She laughed and then scrutinised his face, flicking her eyes anxiously over him.

Knowing what she was doing, Piers grinned and said, "No

new injuries."

Fenella looked relieved—she had always had great affection for him—and replied, "I still like to see for myself." She patted his cheek indulgently.

Piers turned to her husband, and they shook hands. "Nice to see you, Rick." His attention was caught by Mark, standing aloof and looking moody. "My brother, Mark," Piers said dismissively, waving him forward.

Mark solemnly shook his hand. Rick was the same height as him, with very dark brown hair and a pair of hazel eyes that Mark could feel were sizing him up. Mark smiled and turned to Fenella. "A pleasure to meet you both," he said warmly. "I have heard so many wonderful things about you."

Fenella laughed and, nodding her head towards Piers, remarked, "You look a lot alike," which pleased neither brother. Then she asked, "And how long are you visiting Anastasia?"

Mark blinked and frowned at Anastasia, annoyed that she had not explained.

As Anastasia faltered under his gaze, Johnny Fielding moved silently into the doorway, watching Piers very carefully.

Stammering slightly, she tried to laugh the sudden awkwardness off by saying, "Mark's my boyfriend, Fenella."

Piers' face was totally impassive, but Johnny noted the flicker of resentment held there and knew that trouble was brewing.

Rick looked surprised and glanced at his wife, who said smoothly, "Well, it's lovely to meet you. Do come in; lunch is ready." She began leading her guests towards the huge rustic kitchen.

Rick ushered Anastasia in before him and then she caught sight of Johnny. "Hello, *malyshka*," he said, winking at her.

Rick pushed her past him and Mark made to follow, but he was stopped by Rick. "This is Johnny Fielding, reprobate and troublemaker."

Mark found himself facing a languid man, perhaps a little too thin, with the greenest eyes he had ever seen.

Johnny laughed at his best friend, responding, "He loves me really."

"No, I don't," Rick replied, a gleam in his eyes. "I just can't get rid of you."

Johnny slapped Mark on the back. "So, you're Bryan's replacement? You'd better treat her properly; she's a special girl." He walked off after Rick, leaving Mark to stare at him in disbelief.

When Mark got to the kitchen, he saw a giant wooden table laden with plates of sandwiches, quiches, salad and a huge platter of cold meats. Fenella was filling the largest teapot he had ever seen, and a percolator was bubbling away in the corner. He could see Johnny had pulled Piers to one side, and he allowed his paranoia to believe that they were discussing him.

Fenella smiled at him and said, "You might as well tuck in. It's just a cold collation, I'm afraid, but I'm doing chicken chasseur for dinner."

"It looks amazing, as always," said Anastasia, and she began to pile up her plate.

Piers finished his conversation with Johnny and moved to join her.

"Get in before your brother," Rick advised Mark. "I've never seen anyone eat so much, but you probably know that better than me."

Mark smiled, but it did not reach his eyes.

Anastasia looked up from pouring out some coffees and asked, "Where's my father? I thought he was here?"

Rick and Fenella exchanged glances, and Johnny answered her. "He's gone out for a ride."

Anastasia held his eyes and then, looking displeased, remarked, "I see."

After most of the food had been eaten, Piers noticed Jack Travess walking back towards the kitchen, an arm slung around one of Fenella's grooms. Piers watched in disgust as he saw Jack kiss her, his hands wandering. *For God's sake*, Piers thought; she looked the same age as his daughter. He turned his back on the unpleasant sight and realised that Anastasia had seen it, too. Her face darkened and her lip curled disdainfully as her father wandered into the kitchen to join them.

Jack Travess stopped in the doorway and said, "Stasia, you're earlier than we expected." This seemed to annoy him.

"We're actually on time," she corrected him. "How was the ground? Not too hard?" Anastasia knew full well that the only riding he had done that morning did not involve a horse. She did not care if she made him angry; she had Piers with her.

Jack held his daughter's accusing eyes and lied, "Not too bad. Have you left me any food? I seem to have worked up quite an appetite."

Anastasia gave him a filthy look and then abruptly left the room. Fenella hesitated for a second and then followed her. The atmosphere in the kitchen was heavy until Mark unwittingly stepped up. "Hello, Mr. Travess. How was my dad when you last saw him?"

Jack bestowed a warm smile on Mark and blanked Piers completely. "Jack, please. I keep telling you, it's Jack. Your father was doing quite well. Enjoying spoiling his granddaughters, so Guy said."

Piers wanted to follow Anastasia but decided he was better off leaving her with Fenella. He knew Anastasia valued her godmother, viewing her as the only mother figure she had ever really known, and he would not intrude on that. He poured himself another cup of tea and rummaged in the cupboards, looking for cake.

Fenella followed Anastasia to the conservatory; it was always quiet in there and looked out over a wild back garden which, at the moment, was bare and muddy. Anastasia was looking up at the sky when Fenella approached her tentatively. "Darling? Are you ok?"

Anastasia turned around and gave her a sad smile. "Yes. I know what he's like, but I don't like seeing it."

"None of us do." Fenella held out her hand. "Come and sit with me; tell me what's happened. Where's Suzanna and where is Bryan?"

Anastasia sat beside her and replied, "Suzanna and Bryan are together." She saw the shock pass over Fenella's face.

"*Bryan* is Suzanna's new man?" Fenella was genuinely staggered. She was fully aware that Suzanna had always been besotted with Bryan, but she would have bet on Anastasia turning up saying *she* was engaged to him before expecting this news.

"It's ok, really. I'm fine with it." Anastasia tried to reassure Fenella. "I caught him cheating on me on Christmas Eve." She broke off, unsure how much to tell her godmother.

"The pig! He always did think a lot of himself." Fenella considered for a moment. "But what's Mark got to do with this? Where did he come from?"

Briefly filling her in, Anastasia left out anything Piers had said and finished with, "So last night, I got Suzanna to take a very drunk Bryan home, and apparently she stayed. Just like that. He wasn't broken-hearted for long, was he?" Although she turned that remark into a joke, Anastasia was conscious of feeling a slight annoyance. Was she that easy to get over?

"Well," Fenella began, after thinking things through, "I would never have believed it. What does Piers think about you hooking up with his brother?"

Anastasia shrugged. "He's all for it, it seems. In fact, Piers was the one who suggested it." She came close to telling Fenella about Mark and his jealousy and how he sometimes scared her, but an uncharacteristic embarrassment held her at bay.

Fenella sighed; she would dearly have loved to give Anastasia some sound advice, but she knew it would not go down well. "Darling, your father will probably leave tomorrow, off on his travels again, so, for your sake, don't antagonise him."

"I don't!" Anastasia cut across her hotly. "It's not *my* fault he's a selfish, lying, womanising ..." She stopped upon seeing the look on her godmother's face. "All right. I'll try to stay out of his way. But only because this is your house." She stood up. "Anyway, I'm craving ginger cake. Have you got any?"

Anastasia hurried back to the kitchen. When she got there, her father, Rick and Mark were absent, and she saw Piers had found and eaten most of a Victoria sponge.

"No ginger cake?" she asked, reaching over to take the last piece away from him.

Johnny laughed. "You're the only one he'd let do that," he said, and Piers scowled at him.

She sat next to Johnny and enquired, "Where are the others?"

"Jack's taken your boyfriend on a tour of the stables." He broke off momentarily as Piers made a derisive noise. "And Rick's got stuff to do."

Anastasia ate her cake, licking the buttercream off her fingers before speaking again. "Are you still up for this performance at my party, Johnny?"

He nodded, smiling at her. "Sure. In fact, we could go now and I'll run you through the songs." He could tell she was nervous; what had seemed a brilliant idea several months ago was now looming, too close for comfort.

Anastasia rose and washed her hands. "Ok. What about Rick?"

"We'll stick a CD on and you can sing. We'll do a full run-through before you go back to London." He stood before her and rested his hand on her shoulder. "You can do this, *malyshka*. Practice is the key."

She smiled at him gratefully, not wanting to admit that the thought of singing live in front of people, even those she knew, was beginning to make her feel sick.

Piers got up too. "Want an unbiased audience, sweetheart?"

"Hardly unbiased, Piers, but why not?" After all, she knew *he* would never tell her she was rubbish.

Chapter 14

MARK FOUND CONVERSATION with Jack Travess very wearisome; he liked to talk about himself and reminisce about the times he had spent with Joseph Talbot, but Mark had heard all those stories from his own father and knew the truth. He tried several times to get Jack to talk about his daughter, to get a feeling for what their relationship really was, but he was left more confused than ever. Protestations of undying devotion to a daughter he rarely saw, interspersed with barely veiled criticisms of her life, her choices, and even her looks, did not sit well with Mark, only confirming his belief that she needed to leave with him; to live in Paris away from all this toxicity, away from Piers.

As they walked slowly back towards the main house, Mark cut across another of Jack's rambling tales and said, "Mr. Travess—Jack—I want to ask your permission to propose to your daughter."

Jack stopped in his tracks and stared at him and then he smiled and shook Mark's hand. "Of course. Of course! Your father will be so happy! I know we were hard on you both in the past, but I knew you'd come good in the end."

Mark did not know what to say and decided it was best if he left Jack's response unchallenged. "I won't be asking her just yet. I need to make some arrangements for a house near Paris."

Jack blinked. "Paris? You want to take her away?"

Mark nodded. "I think it's for the best all round. Remove her from the worst influences in her life. You will always be welcome to stay, of course."

"Yes, I understand. Get her away from your damn brother! And make me a grandfather soon!" Jack laughed and then added, "I'll be leaving tomorrow for the South of France. I spend quite a bit of time over there, so trips to Paris will always be convenient."

Yes, thought Mark, smiling wryly but making no comment, *convenient*. That epitomised Jack's relationship with Anastasia; at his convenience.

Just before they reached the house, a young woman about Anastasia's age with short blonde hair came running towards them. She stopped when she saw Mark and hesitated. Jack grinned at her, and Mark was left in no doubt of his future father-in-law's predilections as she flung herself into Jack's arms and kissed him passionately. Mark turned away and, feeling slightly nauseous, walked back into the house.

As he entered the kitchen, Mark looked around for Anastasia but saw only Fenella, who was making a start on dinner. He smiled at her. "You have some beautiful horses, Mrs. Lascelles, and such envious countryside in which to enjoy them."

Fenella stopped chopping onions and wiped her eyes on a tea towel. "Sorry, onions always cause this, no matter what I try. Yes, thank you; we love it here. Do you ride?"

Mark shook his head. "Unfortunately not. I'm a city boy; horses aren't really my thing. Where's Anastasia?" he asked as casually as he could, noticing Piers was also missing.

"She's with Johnny practicing for her birthday performance. It's supposed to be a surprise for her father."

"Oh." Mark frowned. "She hasn't mentioned it. Can I go along and listen, do you think?"

Fenella faced him. "She gets nervous, so it's probably best to leave her with Johnny. The set's only four songs, so they shouldn't be too long."

"What's she singing? Her dad's stuff?"

"Yes, Retribution songs," Fenella replied coldly. "Her dad may have sung them, but Johnny and Frankie were the geniuses behind them all." She was clearly stung by his innocent remark.

"Sorry." He had not missed the flicker of displeasure in her dark eyes. "I don't know much about the music world. Bit of a classical fan myself." He sat down and said, "I really ought to give them a try."

Regretting her tone, Fenella sat opposite him. "We have everything they've ever recorded here; just ask either Johnny or Rick. Frankie wrote some truly beautiful songs, and Johnny still writes for loads of others, Bryan Darnell included." She broke off to hold his eyes, curious to see how he would take the mention of Anastasia's ex-boyfriend.

Mark looked away and then back, the smile not reaching his eyes. "Another one I'm not familiar with." Hearing laughter approaching, he got up abruptly as Anastasia and Piers came back into the kitchen. "Hello, baby. Did the practice go well?" He pulled Anastasia into a hug and kissed her head.

She was surprised he knew. "Yes, not too bad, once *someone* stopped trying to join in." She threw a mischievous glance over her shoulder at Piers.

Piers grinned. "You can't honestly expect me not to join in with my favourite song. Not going to happen."

"You need to remember all the words in the right order, then," came a caustic comment as Johnny joined them. To Anastasia, he said, "You did great. I told you it would be fine. Just need to do it again tonight so Rick can hear. Are we finally agreed on the songs?" He raised a dark eyebrow and looked weary; this had been an ongoing argument.

Anastasia pulled free from Mark's grip and patted Johnny good-naturedly on the arm. "Yes, but be ready for the *Grease* song just in case."

Johnny made a derisive comment and asked Fenella, "Ricky not finished yet?"

"Soon," she replied, smiling knowingly at him.

"I need a drink." Johnny left the room shaking his head.

Piers wandered over to where Fenella had been preparing

dinner, and she asked with laughing eyes, "Does it meet with your approval?"

"Absolutely. You're an amazing cook. I love your cakes."

"Yes," Anastasia chipped in. "He's already eaten all the sponge."

"Honestly, Piers! That was for tonight! Why don't you get out of my hair and go to the ménage? I'm sure you could do with some exercise; work off all that food you make vanish." Fenella gave him a shove out of her way, but she loved how much he appreciated her food.

Resisting the urge to blame Anastasia for her part in the disappearing cake, Piers asked, "Are you coming, Stasia?"

"Yes, but I'll need to get changed first, though." She turned to Mark. "Do you want to come, too? Can you ride?"

He shook his head. "But I'll come and watch you both."

Piers grinned at him and said, "You might get lucky. Wouldn't be the first time I've taken a tumble." He let Anastasia leave first and then followed her towards the stairs.

"You'll be fine; we'll put you on Blaze. He's an angel," Mark heard Anastasia say as they disappeared from view.

Fenella picked up a jacket from a hook behind the back door and said to Mark, "You can come with me, if you like. She won't be long, and I'll start getting the horses ready."

Mark was curious and asked hopefully, "Do you have any bad-tempered ones?" He held the door open for her, and they were greeted by a chilly breeze.

"Oh, yes. I wouldn't expect Piers to cope with them, but I will put Stasia on one. She won't be happy, but it'll be good experience for her." She began to stride towards a stable block, calling out for her staff.

Mark was concerned. "She won't get hurt?"

Fenella laughed at him. "The amount of times this one's thrown her, and she's never had more than a few bruises. Stasia needs to learn how to handle him." Seeing he was unconvinced, she tried to reassure him. "It's ok, she'll be fine. She's really good, you know."

"I know. You taught her." Mark recalled what Anastasia had said. But his fears resurfaced as he watched Fenella lead out a huge dark horse that stamped his hooves and tossed his mane whilst looking down at them with disdain.

"Steady, Storm," Fenella murmured. "Steady. There's a good boy, and you'll get a canter." She fed him a Polo.

Mark was distracted by voices, and he saw the blonde groom from earlier come around a corner looking very pink-faced and now holding hands with Jack Travess. When she saw Fenella with Storm, she called out, "Are you sure, boss? He's been foul since Christmas."

Fenella looked at Jack and narrowed her eyes contemptuously before replying, "I think I know my animals best, thank you. Shouldn't you be mucking out the others by now?"

The girl flushed, and with a sideways apologetic look at Jack, she dropped her head and walked away.

Mark discreetly turned his back and tried very hard not to hear the low, obviously bitter exchange between Fenella and Jack Travess. He hoped very much that Anastasia would not see it as he knew this would upset her. Thankfully, the disagreement did not last long, and Jack fumed off towards the back garden and the conservatory whilst Fenella watched him go, a mildly triumphant look on her face.

Piers and Anastasia left the house together and saw Fenella saddling up Storm whilst one of her staff held his head.

"Oh, Jesus! She must be having a laugh," Anastasia said, stopping in her tracks.

"He can't be for me," Piers commented. "He must be for you." He took her hand. "You'll be fine. If she wasn't confident in you, she wouldn't risk it."

"I'll remind you of that when I'm flying through the air like last time."

Piers faced her and took her shoulders. "Didn't you tell me once not to panic? If you do, he'll know, and then you'll come off. Believe you can handle him, sweetheart, and you will."

She looked a little pale, but Piers could always instil confidence in her. She pulled herself together before walking towards her godmother.

Piers was relieved to see an old friend waiting for him; he had learned to ride on Blaze, who was a gentle giant, and he swung himself up onto the saddle with ease.

Mark watched Anastasia anxiously; she looked a little scared but determined, and he could not deny how sexy she looked in skin-tight jodhpurs. She steeled herself and then Fenella helped her up and into the saddle. Storm immediately tried to take off, but she had him swiftly under control with a sharp word, thankful for her strong grip.

"Lead the way, Piers," Fenella ordered, and they rode together towards the indoor ménage, Anastasia looking grim and Mark following nervously behind.

Piers encouraged Blaze, and soon they were trotting sedately; he had a good seat and light hands, but he knew he was out of practice and took things very steadily.

"Excellent, Piers!" Fenella called out. "You really have improved. Well done."

He was pleased; something about Fenella always made him want to earn her approval, a bit like a mother. He had lost his own at the age of thirteen and had gone completely off the rails, which made him very grateful to have Fenella in his corner now. He eased Blaze to a walk and watched over his shoulder as Anastasia trotted Storm out on a tight rein, preventing him from bolting and landing her in a heap on the floor again.

Mark suddenly found he was holding his breath, so worried was he for her safety, but as the minutes passed, he realised how good she was, and he wondered how long she had been riding for. Until now, he had assumed it was a recent interest.

As if reading his thoughts and seeing his concern, Fenella told him, "I taught her to ride when she was four. She could have gone to the Nationals, but her father disapproved; wouldn't let me take her."

Mark glanced at her, perhaps understanding more than she wanted. "I get the impression Jack Travess is a bit of a git."

Fenella's lips twitched but she forbore to reply, and they both carried on watching. Mark's heart skipped a beat when Storm suddenly lunged forward and seemed to go sideways, straight for the wall, until Anastasia wrenched him back under control. Feeling more confident, she was talking to him, soothing him, whereas previously she had been too scared to do anything but hang on and pray.

"That's much better," Fenella called out encouragingly. "Try to canter. Go on; you can do it."

Anastasia squeezed her heels into his dark flanks and he broke into a beautifully controlled canter, and now Mark could see what Fenella had meant; he could admire just how skilled Anastasia was atop a horse.

Piers watched with pride, knowing exactly how hard this was for her; Storm had been her *bête noir*, nearly causing her to give up riding altogether, and he was so pleased to see this. "Looking good, sweetheart," he called out as she came close to him.

Anastasia suddenly grinned, relaxing, and Storm came to a halt. "Want to try him?" she called back.

"I wouldn't want to show you up," Piers said mischievously.

Fenella was now confident they did not need her supervision anymore and so she said to Mark, "They'll be fine now if you want to come back to the kitchen for a snack?"

Mark wanted to stay, really hoping to see his brother make a fool of himself, but he could not see the point of watching someone ride a horse round and round in a circle. Deciding to try and ingratiate himself into Fenella's good books, he accompanied her.

As soon as they were back in the kitchen, Mark offered to help Fenella with dinner, to which she seemed pleasantly surprised. "That's sweet of you to offer, Mark, but I prefer to do it myself."

Trying to make conversation, Mark said, "You've made an excellent job of teaching Anastasia to ride. She looks at home up there."

Fenella smiled. "That's kind of you to say, but it wasn't all me. She has natural talent. Such a shame she wasn't allowed to pursue it."

They were silent for a few minutes, Mark watching Fenella as she worked.

Still making an effort to connect with someone so obviously important to Anastasia, Mark tried again. "Did you teach her to cook as well, by any chance? Lunch was excellent."

Fenella put down her knife and laughed. "No, I'm afraid. Anastasia has many skills, but domesticity is not one of them. The last time she tried to cook for us, we were all ill!"

"Ah." Mark smiled. "Guess she can't excel in everything," Now out of ideas, he picked up the newspaper and started to read.

About forty minutes later, he heard Fenella give a sharp intake of breath as she moved to the back door. "Oh, no! What happened?"

Mark rose swiftly to join her and saw Piers carrying Anastasia back towards the house. Panicked, he rushed outside, demanding, "What happened? Are you ok, baby?"

Anastasia looked a little pale but annoyed. "It's nothing; I'm fine. Just my ankle,"

Piers nodded towards the back door and said sharply, "Hold the door open, Mark." As his brother complied, he strode into the kitchen and put her down onto a chair.

"Did you come off?" Mark asked, hovering anxiously near her.

Piers lifted her left leg and placed it on another chair so that her ankle was raised. "She didn't come off. This happened after." He snapped, irritated by his brother's remarks.

"Just tell us, Anastasia." Fenella's words were a command which silenced the two brothers.

"We were walking the horses back and a bird came out of nowhere. You know what Storm's like about birds." Fenella nodded, well aware that he seemed to think all birds were out to attack him. "He reared and then pulled to one side, dragging me over on my ankle. But I'm fine. Piers overreacted, as usual."

She glanced at him, aware he was watching her intently.

Being practical, Fenella advised her, "Go and take those boots off and get changed. I'll get a cold compress for it." She broke off at the look on her goddaughter's face and said sharply, "Do as you're told, Anastasia Travess."

Smiling wryly, Anastasia tried to stand, but her ankle was tender and she buckled slightly. Piers was next to her instantly, but Mark put out his hand and said acidly, "I'll take care of my girlfriend, if you don't mind."

As Mark helped her out of the kitchen, Piers watched them go, an odd look on his face. He could hear Anastasia protesting. "Don't fuss, Mark! I'll be fine."

"Just let me help you in case it gives way again, baby," Mark replied.

Fenella shut the door and Piers faced her. In a voice tinged with pain, he said "Don't, Fenella. Please. Just don't say anything."

Fenella watched him stride back out into the yard, and her heart broke for him.

Chapter 15

JOHNNY AND RICK were talking at the top of the stairs when they saw Anastasia leaving her room supported by Mark, a look of frustration on her face.

"What's up?" Rick asked, moving towards them, slightly concerned.

"It's nothing." Anastasia began trying to brush the whole thing off; she hated fuss.

Mark's tone was stern. "She's twisted her ankle, but she's too stubborn to accept any help."

"Then let her manage," Johnny advised.

Anastasia threw him a grateful look. "I'm fine, honestly. It's very minor." Pushing Mark's hands away, she supported herself slowly down the stairs.

Mark was irritated; he wanted to look after her, to have her be reliant on him, for her to need him. He gave Johnny a sideways glance of resentment.

Johnny ignored him and said, "If she falls down the stairs, then it's her own damn fault."

Anastasia laughed and made it safely to the bottom, where she winced slightly and then hobbled back to the kitchen. Fenella was waiting, a cold compress on the draining board ready to go.

"Sit down and put your foot up," she ordered. Anastasia obeyed her, but she gave a gasp when she felt the ice-cold compress touch her skin.

"You ok?" Mark asked, putting his arm around her shoulders.

"Of course," Anastasia said impatiently. She looked around. "Where's Piers?"

"In the yard somewhere. He'll be back as soon as he smells food." Fenella handed Anastasia a cup of strong tea and two painkillers.

"Thanks." Anastasia relaxed back into her chair, sighing, before swallowing the tablets and making a face at the taste.

Johnny helped himself to a cold drink and asked suddenly, "Where's Jack?"

Rick's lips twitched. "Do you miss him?"

With a forced laugh, Johnny replied, "I just like to know where he is. He has a habit of appearing when he is least wanted."

"That would be 'always'," Anastasia added, and Fenella gave her a disapproving look. But Anastasia was feeling cross due to the pain in her ankle and continued remorselessly. "Someone should tell that little blonde he's off tomorrow to shag someone else. Keeping quiet isn't fair on her, really." She looked defiantly at her godmother.

Mark leant close to her ear and whispered, "Please, baby. Don't sink to his level."

Startled by his understanding, Anastasia said nothing further on the subject.

Fenella glanced around and decided that was enough. "If you want to eat at all later, then I suggest you all clear off and find something to do. Anastasia, you can stay there and rest your ankle, but everyone else has to go."

"Charming," remarked Johnny, laughing.

"You should be used to getting kicked out of places, Johnny. Three wives and how many girlfriends now?" Rick passed him another can of beer and then turned to Mark to ask, "Do you want to play snooker?"

That was something Mark could do. "Yes, thanks. Bit out of practice, though." He leant down to kiss Anastasia. "You rest up; do as you're told."

She smiled up at him. "Yes, all right. Go and have fun." As the men departed, she was left alone with Fenella. Anastasia glanced at her godmother, a little wary of the look on her face, and said remorsefully, "I'm sorry for what I said. I will try to behave."

Fenella dropped a hand onto her shoulder. "It's only you that gets hurt, darling. And you really should be a little more gracious when people are trying to help you." She smiled at Anastasia with understanding. "I know you hate fuss, but people only do it because they love you."

Anastasia shrugged a shoulder and looked uncomfortable. "But I feel like I'm being suffocated."

"If you mean Mark, then maybe he isn't right for you—and that's all I'm going to say." Fenella turned back to the worktop and continued with dinner.

Anastasia bit her lip and then said, "I have to give it a chance. It's only been a week."

Still with her back to her, Fenella replied, "Whatever you decide, darling. Just make sure it's what you want. Now, am I going to hear these songs later? What have you picked?"

Anastasia was grateful for the change in subject as Fenella had pricked a nerve. "Yes, as long as my father isn't around. But I expect he'll be otherwise engaged?" She shifted her position slightly so she could see Fenella's profile.

"I expect so, but I don't know why you want to keep it a surprise. You know how much he says he wants to hear you sing."

"Because every time I want to do something, he manages to mess it up. The only reason I left the manor for London was because you let me live in Belgravia and Rick employed me. He couldn't block that."

Fenella smiled ruefully. "I know, but you're nearly twenty-five. He can't hold back your trust fund after that."

Anastasia knew he would still try, but she did not want to deal with that now, so she answered Fenella's other question. "Well, Johnny and I have chosen *Retribution, Russian Lullaby, Twisted Kiss* and *Desolate Love*. In that order."

"Oh, *Russian Lullaby*'s beautiful! Frankie wrote that song for your Mama." Fenella sighed and wiped her eye.

"I know." Anastasia braced herself; now was as good a time as any to broach the subject. "There's something I've been meaning to ask you, about Frankie ..."

With a faraway look in her eyes, Fenella faced her. "Yes, Anastasia. He was in love with her."

That was not what she had expected to hear. "But wasn't he married then?"

"No, he was getting divorced when your Mama met Jack. He never should have hesitated ... but the rest is history. He was devastated when she died. Eileen didn't come into his life until you were about seven. Do you remember being a bridesmaid at their wedding?"

Anastasia recalled being made to wear a pink dress with lots of frills and having her hair all tied back, and she remembered being bored to death and pulling apart her posy in the church. "Just about." She grinned at Fenella.

"Such a shame. Eileen was good for him."

"And has Johnny seen her lately?" Anastasia was well aware that the band had a tangled set of relationships and Johnny had developed a very soft spot for Eileen Beaumont.

"You'll do well to stay out of that, if you know what's good for you. He gets very defensive if you hint at anything." Despite her warning, Fenella knew Anastasia was probably the only person who would come right out and ask him.

"I know. I just wish ... well, that's his business. I haven't seen Eileen for months, have you?"

"We met up for lunch just before Christmas. We're meeting again next week when Rick and you are back at work. I'm sure he'll let you extend your lunch break if you ask him nicely." Fenella smiled at her, knowing her husband doted on Anastasia. He had always loved her like a daughter; like the child they had never been able to have.

"I'd love to come along." Anastasia sat sipping her tea and

thinking about going back to work; she loved it at Original. She loved the freedom it had given her and all the friends she had made over the years.

"What's Mark going to do whilst you're at work? Does he have a job?"

"I have no idea, actually. He worked in PR in Paris and then he went to New Zealand for a while. I'll need to ask him because he's going to get bored pretty quickly with nothing to do." Anastasia had a sinking feeling he was going to expect her to spend all her time with him, and she had other commitments apart from work.

Fenella checked over her list—she could not function properly without one—and then asked suddenly, "What am I going to do for pudding now that Piers has eaten one of my cakes?"

Anastasia laughed. "We can eat the others and tell Piers he's already had his share."

A deep voice came from the doorway. "That's not exactly fair considering you helped me to eat it."

Both women looked up and laughed at the mock outrage on his face. "Don't worry. I'll make one just for you," Fenella reassured him.

Piers grinned at her and kissed her cheek as she poured him a cup of tea.

"How's the ankle? And I'm not *fussing*; I'm just asking." Piers sat down near Anastasia.

She changed colour briefly before replying, "It's fine. Do you want to help me with the crossword?"

Piers nodded and reached for the pen.

Chapter 16

AFTER AN EXCELLENT dinner, Anastasia's father sloped off without anyone really noticing and, Mark thought, without them caring. It was a strange setup which he could not work out. The only thing likely to keep everything friendly, he reasoned, would be financial reasons, because it was obvious that Fenella and Johnny both seemed to dislike Jack Travess intensely. He was not sure how Rick Lascelles felt about his bandmate and business partner; Rick was especially hard to read. He had been pleasant enough whilst they had played snooker, but Mark was conscious of being held at arm's length; that Rick did not seem to welcome anyone with open arms. Mark sat down in the huge living room, where everything was spotless and had its place, and he was soon joined by the others.

"Do you still feel up to a run-through after your accident, Stasia?" Rick asked as he followed Anastasia into the room.

"Yeah, of course. I need you to approve the setlist, otherwise I'm not doing it!" She kissed his cheek.

Johnny addressed Piers. "And no joining in, please! At least until she's done the four songs."

"You are so charming, Johnny." and Piers seated himself by Fenella.

"He can sing with me, come on Piers, it will be a laugh!" Anastasia gave Johnny a mischievous look.

"No way." Piers protested. "I need at least six pints before I'm prepared to make a fool of myself."

"But we do karaoke all the time," she wanted to wind Johnny up.

"Sweetheart, when we do karaoke no-one is listening to me; they're all too busy looking at you." Piers replied, effectively silencing her whilst Johnny laughed out loud.

Mark was not expecting to be impressed by Anastasia's voice; he half-believed that the others loved her so much, they would tell her whatever she wanted to hear. He, on the other hand, was quite prepared to give his true opinion if she was no good. The last thing he wanted was for her to embarrass him.

Rick stood by the enormous and obviously costly stereo system. "Ready?"

Anastasia nodded and glanced at Piers, who winked at her, and then, as the music sounded out, Mark was stunned; she really could sing. As she sang the haunting lyrics of *Russian Lullaby,* Mark noticed Fenella silently crying, and even Rick had to turn away; the track clearly resonated personally with them all, and he wondered why.

As Anastasia belted out the final words of *Desolate Love,* Johnny rose to his feet to applaud her and said with pride, "That's even better than earlier! And you made Fenella cry!"

She crossed the room to hug her godmother, who was hurriedly pulling herself together.

"These tears are a good thing, darling," she said. "It means you can do this." She held Anastasia tightly and whispered, "Your Mama would be so proud."

"Don't," Anastasia began. "You'll make me cry next."

Rick watched them and, smiling, he said, "We can try you in one of the studios next week at work. Johnny and I will play live with you. And if that doesn't help your confidence, you can practice anytime you want. But they're both right." He looked at his wife with a softened expression and then at his best friend, who was looking smug. "You can do this."

Anastasia gave him a warm look and then said brightly, "Can

we watch *Grease* now?"

Johnny groaned. "Please, no!"

"Don't be such a grump," Anastasia chided him. "We all know you are a closet fan."

Johnny tried to look annoyed, but he only laughed. "Ok, ok, but I'm *not* joining in with the bloody songs. Someone get me a large scotch to deaden the pain."

"I think I'll need one, too," Mark added. "Not my favourite film."

Anastasia moved to sit next to him whilst Fenella and Piers poured the drinks and Piers pulled out a box of shortbread that Fenella thought she had hidden out of his way. Mark put his arm around her and, whilst the others were busy, he said, "You were *brilliant*. What a voice! Can't we just go to bed?"

"No, it's far too early. And besides, I want to spend some time with my family."

Mark did not reply. With no intention of upsetting his hosts, he accepted his drink with a resigned sigh.

Chapter 17

THE NEXT MORNING, Mark sat on the bed and watched Anastasia getting ready. They were planning on taking a walk and getting some fresh air before breakfast. He had been trying to talk her into not going back to work; ideally, he did not want her to work at all, especially not in some insignificant office role.

"Can't you take some more time off? Surely you're not needed that badly?" Mark stood up and moved towards her, taking the hairbrush out of her hands and then holding her tightly. "And I'm sure you've probably got Rick Lascelles wrapped around your little finger." He kissed her cheek, missing the spark of annoyance in her eyes.

"No, I can't," she responded, pulling free of him. "Rick might be very generous, but he's also my boss. I need to be there to cover for others who have booked their time off. It's only fair." She resented his implication that what she did was not important.

Mark did not try to hide his disapproval. "Well, can't you shorten your hours? Finish early or go in late?" He did not see why he had to come second to an office job.

Anastasia held on to her patience. "I already finish early once a week. Rick lets me take regular time out to help out at a women's only self-defence class."

127

"Surely they have other volunteers? You must have already done your bit. We need to spend time together."

"Are you seriously objecting to me volunteering to help people?" Anastasia could not believe his attitude.

"If you were never around when he wanted, no wonder Bryan was at it behind your back!" Mark was stung into making an unwise reply.

Anastasia gasped and then managed, "That's neither fair nor true! It wasn't 'behind my back'. Never assume I'm stupid, I knew *everything* he was doing." She broke off to take a deep breath, suddenly aware of that glacial look in his eyes that scared her, then she plunged on regardless. "And Bryan was proud of me for helping others."

Mark gave her a filthy look before saying, "You are *my* girlfriend, and I will not tolerate anything or anyone getting in between us." He grasped her arms hard.

"You're hurting me! Get off!" Now scared, Anastasia froze.

Mark let her go, his face furious, and stormed out of the bedroom, leaving her white-faced and fearful. She sat down on the edge of the bed and realised that she was shaking.

Mark arrived at the breakfast table to find only Jack Travess sitting there and he faltered. Not really wanting to talk to him, he tried to make an exit.

Jack looked up from the newspaper. "Morning, Mark. How are you?"

Mark sat down. "Fine," he lied, doing a poor job of hiding his annoyance with Anastasia.

Jack observed him thoughtfully and then, showing insight, he asked, "What's my daughter done to upset you?"

Mark was taken aback; even though he was annoyed with Anastasia, he had no intention of telling Jack Travess anything. He shrugged. "Nothing. Nothing at all."

"Yes, she has; I know that look. Let me guess—she won't take time off and she won't give up her classes?"

Mark nodded and then Jack said, "Don't worry, I'll have a

word with her. Let her know where her priorities should be."

And in that moment, Mark knew he had made a terrible mistake.

LEAVING HER ROOM, Anastasia walked slowly down the stairs. She had misplaced her riding boots, and she needed to escape for a short while. Perhaps she should just tell Mark to get lost, but she feared causing a scene. As she reached the entrance hall, she saw her father walking towards her with a purposeful look on his face and she stopped in her tracks, wary.

"Ah, I was looking for you," Jack began, standing before her and folding his arms.

She was in no mood to be the dutiful daughter. "Well, you've found me. What do you want?"

Jack raised one eyebrow, and his eyes glittered with displeasure. "A little respect would be nice, but I've given up hope of that a long time ago."

Now annoyed, she responded hotly, "You have never done anything to *earn* my respect. Now, I want to go riding, so what do you want?"

Smiling unpleasantly, her father replied, "Just a few words." He brushed past her and held open a door. "In private, please, Anastasia."

Suspicious, she followed him in.

A short while later, Anastasia pulled on her riding boots with shaking hands. The argument with Mark had left her head in a mess, but the dreadful confrontation she had just had with her father had nearly broken her.

She heard the wind howl as she opened the door, and she sighed to herself. The weather was against her. Still, she would make do with seeing the horses and having a chat with the stable hands instead. As she strode across the courtyard, she heard Joanie, the head groom and yard boss, anxiously calling to her. Anastasia turned and headed in her direction. Tall, fair-haired and around twenty-nine, Joanie had worked for Fenella for a decade, making her way up the stable hierarchy.

"What's up?" Anastasia called out as she reached her.

"It's this weather. Bond is in the top field and I can't get him to come in." It cost Joanie something to admit that, but the horse's safety was more important than her feelings.

"Don't worry, I'll go fetch him. Is Mandragora ready to go?" Anastasia moved off to the stable office to grab a waterproof coat and a head collar, and she did up her riding helmet as she walked. Anastasia liked Joanie most of the time; she was excellent with the horses, but she could be prickly if she thought her authority was being challenged. She also had a massive crush on Piers.

After stuffing a handful of Polos and some carrots into her capacious pockets, Anastasia threw herself aboard a dappled grey mare and encouraged her to trot towards the fields. Mandragora was her favourite after Bond and the only horse he really got on with. Bond was special; he had been born during the summer she and Piers had spent together at Fenella's after her attack and she had named him. He was a handful and did not care for men; he tolerated Rick but was not above nipping him on the sly, and Piers was the only man he would willingly go to.

Mandragora covered the sodden ground with ease and jumped the corner hedge neatly. "Good girl," Anastasia encouraged her. "Let's go get our boy."

Piers came out of the house, hoping, like Anastasia, to get a gallop in before the weather turned. But as soon as he felt the wind buffet him, he knew there was little hope of that. He stopped to chat to Joanie, aware of and amused by the effect he seemed to have on her despite being totally disinterested romantically.

Joanie was feeling jittery, regretting not having sent someone to assist Anastasia due to Bond's cantankerous nature.

Sensing her anxiety, he asked, "Problem?"

Joanie blushed. "Bond wouldn't come to me. Anastasia's gone on Mandragora to fetch him in from the top field."

Piers cast a wary eye above at the great black clouds billowing across a threateningly purple sky. "Give me a bridle and I'll go up and help. Bond slipped a head collar last time. Stasia's probably forgotten."

Within minutes, he was grabbing a waterproof and jamming a helmet on. "We'll bring him in, don't worry."

Unable to help herself, Joanie replied, "Bond's just like you, you know."

Piers arched an eyebrow as she passed him the bridle.

"Handsome, stubborn, enigmatic and a diva." He grinned at her, and as he turned to go, she added in an undertone of bitterness, "And madly in love with Anastasia."

Piers did not hear Joanie as he ran up to join Anastasia. He was not a confident enough rider to tackle those muddy and slippery fields on horseback, but he was fit enough to make good time on foot. As he reached the top of the hill, ready to cut through a copse, however, he had to stop and catch his breath. As the wind increased, he swore. "Fuck! This is why the cigars have got to go."

A few seconds later, he picked his way through the undergrowth and came out near the top field. Anastasia had tethered Mandragora under some low-hanging trees to try and give her some shelter from the weather and was standing on the fence, calling to a light bay horse with a mahogany mane. Bond was recalcitrant.

Anastasia tried again, cajoling him. "Come on, you daft sod! Come to Stasia. I've got Polos." She waved a closed hand at him.

Piers grinned at her talking to the horse, but he stayed still, aware that even a breaking twig could spook him.

Bond pricked his ears and observed her.

Anastasia called out again. "Come on, handsome. Come and see Mandragora."

Bond trotted towards her, his eyes fixed on her handful of Polos. The horse reached her and pressed his velvet nose against her face, blowing at her with affection. She stroked him and offered him the sweets, speaking to him in a soft voice. "There's my handsome boy."

As Bond began chomping on the sweets, she started to put the head collar on him, slowly and carefully, conscious of him bolting just for the hell of it. With the Polos eaten, the horse jerked his head suddenly as he sensed someone else approaching and whinnied as he saw Piers moving out into the open.

"Nicely done, sweetheart." He held out the bridle. "I thought you might need this."

Together, they swapped the head collar for the bridle and led Bond out of the field, where he greeted Mandragora with fondness.

"How did you know I was here?" Anastasia asked, reaching up to brush leaves from Piers' shoulder.

"Joanie. I think she was concerned for you."

Anastasia laughed. "Hardly! You, maybe!" She looked slyly at him from under her lashes and then glanced back to Bond, who was now trying to extract a carrot from her pocket. "You really are just like your namesake."

Unsure if she was talking to him or the horse, Piers asked, "How?"

She smiled. "A bloody diva!"

"That's the second time I've been called a diva in the space of twenty minutes." He feigned annoyance, and she missed the laughter in his eyes.

Anastasia turned her back on him. "Help me up, would you? I'll ride him back."

"No, let me. He's too unpredictable." Piers spoke without thinking, her safety his only concern.

Anastasia was insulted, her nerves already at breaking point, and she rounded on him. "You can't ride as well as me; he'll have you off. And I can go cross-country. You take Mandragora back; she'll look after you."

He blinked at the anger he saw in her eyes and wondered if Mark had upset her already this morning.

She saw only annoyance on his face, annoyance at his brother, but Anastasia did not realise this.

He threw Anastasia up onto Bond's back and passed her the reins. "Be careful," he warned, letting the bridle go.

Bond took off, and Piers watched her go with disquiet. He really did not know what to do for the best. Sighing, he led Mandragora onto the road and pulled himself into the saddle with ease. It took him some time to adjust the stirrup length and then they trotted back to the stables.

Anastasia was waiting for him, her temper flaring at the unintended insult to her riding ability and her nerves grating from the morning's awful clashes. As she heard hooves approaching, she gave Bond his head and jumped him back and forth across the hedge on the diagonal.

Piers watched her, smiling. Even though he knew she was showing off for his benefit, defiantly proving him wrong, she was bloody good. He left her and rode into the stable yard.

Joanie came running forward, her face apprehensive. "Have you got him?"

"Anastasia's got him. They're hedge-jumping." He turned his head as Bond clattered into the yard, holding his head high and looking down his nose imperiously at them.

Piers leapt down from Mandragora, waiting to help Anastasia. He knew it would irritate her, but pushing her buttons was the only way he would get her to talk. As she swung a leg over, Piers reached up and grasped her waist, lifting her down with ease as the rain started.

She kept her back to him, patted Bond and said to Joanie, "He's in a good mood, actually. Didn't give me any problems." She faced Piers, who was staring down at her with concern. Anastasia struggled to unclip her riding hat, her hands starting to shake, and he did it for her. Taking her hand, he pulled her into an empty stable block.

As Piers took her by the shoulders, he saw tears begin to fall and suddenly she was in his arms, crying on his chest.

He tightened his grip on her, completely bemused. "What's wrong, sweetheart?"

Her sobs slowly subsided and she clung to him. "Bloody men." There was vehemence in her voice.

"Mark?"

He felt her nod.

No surprises there. Ironic, really, he thought bitterly. Just when he was going to tell her the truth, just when the strain of denying himself had taken him to breaking point, his bloody brother had to waltz back into her life and ruin everything.

"My utterly useless father, as well."

How was her father involved? "Two arguments before ten in the morning? That's going some."

"He's taking off again for the South of France this morning, to meet his latest tart." Now there was real anger in her voice. She pulled free from him, dashing the tears away and trying to regain control, but the bitterness was clear as she said, "How dare he make such a show of eternal grief for my Mama when he's off shagging some scrawny, gold-digging bimbo every five minutes! I wish he wasn't my father, I wish I had never been born,"

She gasped as he cut her words off, forcing her back round. "Never wish that, you are so loved, by so many people, never say that again!"

The intensity in his eyes scared her. She flung her arms around him. "Sorry, I'm sorry,"

He soothed her, "It's ok sweetheart, it's ok,"

She cut across him, "And you'll be disappearing again soon. Then what will I do?"

"You know the score; you'll cope. I'll be back soon, and we have Guy's party before then, anyway. It'll be fun. Guy and Lily are going to adore you, just like I do." That was the closest he would go, this time his blood was involved.

But she was not finished; other things had aggravated her, too. "And he says he may be back for my birthday, *if* he can make the fucking effort."

"Ah." Now Piers fully understood. "If he doesn't, are you and the lads still going to sing?"

"Absolutely." She was determined. "I've put so much effort into organising it. He's not going to spoil the first birthday party I've ever had."

She was still in his arms, even though the tears had stopped and the anger had kicked in, and in the warmth of his embrace, she was not stupid enough to tell him the rest.

"I'll do all I can to be there to support you."

He stroked her cheek, smiling at her now radiant face, and he remembered how he had watched her walk down the stairs for her eighteenth birthday dinner; another occasion her father had missed. She had been on Johnny Fielding's arm, nervous of the stairs in such high heels and wearing an ice blue silk gown that made her look like a Greek goddess. Johnny had clocked his expression and had caustically advised that he keep his mouth shut and put his eyes back in his head.

In that moment, Piers had known he had fallen in love, even though it had taken him eighteen months to admit it to himself. Now, almost seven years later, with various complications and with him being out of the country so much, he still did not know what to do. He was scared of losing her altogether by admitting his feelings, and although he cherished every time Anastasia called him her best friend, it was also like a knife through his heart.

They were still staring and smiling at each other when Fenella and Joanie came into the stables, leading some horses from the bottom field. They seemed to leap apart as Fenella spoke. "Well done on bringing Bond down so quickly."

"No problem." Anastasia did not smile.

Fenella looked from one to the other and cursed her timing, realising she had interrupted something.

"I hear Jack's about to bugger off again," Piers said, hoping to deflect Fenella's conjectures.

"Yes." Fenella's face darkened, and she said to Joanie, "It's ok now, love. Piers and Anastasia can help me."

Joanie reluctantly left, glancing over her shoulder and, for the millionth time, wondering why he was so besotted.

Piers moved forward to walk a flighty gelding into a stable as Fenella confirmed what he knew. "Yes, I think his car's just turned up. Rick was not impressed."

That was her way of telling them that her normally laid-back husband had exchanged angry words with his friend, although Anastasia knew it had been a bit more than that. Rick Lascelles was something of an enigma, easy-going and softly spoken but with the sharpest business mind, solely responsible for the continuing and enduring wealth of the rest of his Retribution bandmates.

They finished their tasks and left the stables together; the rain had eased, but the wind had increased and it whistled around like a banshee.

Joanie was waiting to intercept Piers. "We're all going to the pub at lunchtime. Want to join me?"

Piers took Anastasia's hand and asked her, much to Joanie's chagrin, "Shall we?"

Anastasia shook her head. "You go; someone should have fun today. I need to see where Mark is." She let go of his hand to struggle through the storm back to the main house.

"Thanks, but I'll give it a miss." Piers patted Joanie on the arm distractedly, still watching Anastasia.

Frustrated, Joanie said, "Can't you do anything without her?"

Piers heard Fenella gasp at her audacity and he gave Joanie a pitying look before replying, "I can but, I prefer not to."

Joanie bit her lip and glanced at Fenella as Piers walked away.

"Jealousy is no-one's friend," was her advice to her yard manager as she went to check on her horses.

Chapter 18

PIERS SAT ALONE in the huge kitchen, his head in his hands, wondering just how bad Anastasia's argument with her father had been. He was sure it had been much worse than she had indicated because he had never seen her behave like that after a clash with Jack Travess. Piers was pouring himself a scotch when Johnny Fielding strolled in.

"Ah, I was looking for you." He and Rick had decided to tell Piers what had happened to try and control his response.

"I've been helping with the horses." He downed his drink.

"Anastasia tell you about her row with Jack?" Johnny asked carefully.

Piers nodded. "Says he's gone off chasing women again and might come home for her birthday." As Johnny sat down opposite him, he became aware of a strange look in Johnny's eyes. "She didn't lie to me, did she?" It would not be the first time, usually to stop him from confronting her father.

Johnny held Piers' accusing blue eyes. "You just take it easy ..."

Now Piers was worried.

Taking a deep breath, Johnny relayed the salient points. "I don't know what started it, but amongst other things, he called her a whore. Sit down!" he said sharply as Piers made to spring from his seat. "She challenged him over his affairs and called him a murderer."

Piers stared at Johnny, not quite sure he had heard him

correctly. "A *murderer*?"

"She said she knew her mother had been leaving him when the car accident happened. That if he wasn't a deceitful, hypocritical bastard, her mother would not been driving that night." Johnny was not looking forward to telling him the rest.

"He cheated on Natalia?"

"Jack had been cheating on Natalia from the moment Anastasia was conceived. Natalia caught him at it, in their bed, the day she died."

Piers had somehow sensed what was coming. "He wasn't violent, was he? He never hit her?"

"Not Natalia, as far as I know, but Stasia was goading him, asking if he was going to try and shut her up like he used to; that he hadn't dared touch her since you came into her life. Jack said he wasn't scared of her tame stallion, and he slapped her."

Piers' grip on his empty glass tightened and it shattered, pieces of glass flying across the table, causing tiny cuts to his hand.

"He's already gone," said Johnny, reading his intent with ease. "Do you think I'd be telling you this if there was a chance you could get hold of him?"

"I hope she remembered what I taught her."

Johnny passed him a tea towel. "Wrap that around your hand. After that, Rick and I went in. I took her out, but Ricky was fizzing." Johnny smiled; crossing Rick Lascelles was not something you did lightly. "Rick punched him," he finished succinctly.

Piers got up to rinse his hand under the tap, shaking with anger.

"We thought you should know. We don't want her put under any more pressure; any more stress."

"What do you want me to do?" Piers asked, his back still to Johnny.

"Stop provoking your brother's jealousy, mate."

Piers spun around, stung. "I'm not doing anything!"

Johnny looked at him. "I know exactly what you're up to,

Piers Talbot. I've known you too long."

And with those enigmatic words, he got up and left Piers alone.

ANASTASIA HAD RETURNED to the house feeling miserable. She hated arguments, and she had lived through so many.

Her earliest and predominant memories were of a beautiful woman sobbing whilst her father shouted and raged. Anastasia had discovered the truth about her parents' relationship from Fenella when she was about sixteen; Fenella had drunk too much, and Anastasia had found her crying over a photograph. It had all come out: her father's endless infidelity; that her mother had wanted to leave him but had been scared of his temper; that Fenella had talked her into it and that she blamed herself for what had happened. Anastasia did not blame her at all; she loved Fenella and Rick and had so often wished they were her parents. And since Piers had arrived in her life, her father had not dared touch her. Until today.

She so desperately wanted peace in her life, and for now that meant peace with Mark. She found him, at last, in the conservatory, watching the wind demolishing the garden and bending the trees. He turned before Anastasia could say anything. "I'm so sorry about this morning, Anastasia; it won't happen again. I'm such a knob for behaving like that. I love you."

Anastasia was completely thrown by his genuine remorse and tears began to fall.

Mark gathered her into his arms. "I heard about your father; the row. I'm so sorry he upset you as well." He felt a stab of guilt, sure he had unintentionally triggered it.

She liked him holding her so gently; she could feel he really did care. "It was awful. He called me some horrible things, a whore, and he slapped me," she stammered.

Mark was outraged, but uncharacteristically he somehow knew she did not need that; she just needed some kindness. "Sit with me. It's up to you if you want to tell me anymore." He led her to the sofa. They sat down and he swung her legs over onto his lap, wiping her eyes with his sleeve. "How can anyone cry so much and still look so beautiful?" he asked, smiling at her.

She tried to smile back and then settled gratefully into his embrace, her head on his shoulder, wishing the pain would go away.

He stroked her hair, murmuring sweet nothings and nonsense to her which Anastasia appreciated and found soothing. She looked up at him, seeing him in a completely different light, and with a sudden need, she kissed him passionately.

Taken wholly by surprise, Mark responded nonetheless by sliding his arm around her waist to shift her closer.

Piers needed to be alone. As soon as some of the stable hands came in for tea and coffee, he walked out of the kitchen, the tea towel still wrapped around his hand. He sat outside on the wall, being battered by the wind, but at least the rain had stopped.

How had she been so normal after such a row? he asked himself. He knew that Anastasia had experienced a tormented childhood and he had even witnessed some of the arguments with her father first-hand, but he had never known that Jack Travess hit his daughter. Piers was not sure how he would ever face Jack Travess again. But that was not important right now; what mattered most was Anastasia, and he needed to check on her.

Getting up, he walked around the back of the house and stopped suddenly. He could see them clearly through the conservatory windows; Mark and Anastasia kissing like the world was going to end. He took a step back, a pain like nothing he had ever felt before spreading from the pit of his stomach to sit in his heart.

Well, he thought, *what did I expect?* But he had not expected it, and it hurt like hell. The only way he knew to deaden the feeling was to get hammered and do something stupid. Wondering whether Joanie would be down the pub that evening, he made his choice.

Chapter 19

ANASTASIA WAS JUST finishing putting on her mascara when she looked in the mirror and saw Piers in the doorway, a faraway look in his eyes.

"How long have you been drinking?" she asked, still watching his reflection.

"Since just before lunch. I was with Johnny; he was telling me Rick and Fenella's story. Quite the romance."

Anastasia could see he was already half-cut, but knowing that was probably down to her earlier outburst, she did not challenge him. "Yes, he followed her around the show jumping circuit for a year before she agreed to go out with him. Must have cost a fortune in roses and champagne."

Piers grinned suddenly. "She can't drink champagne."

She faced him as she sprayed Chanel over her cleavage. "Yeah, I know. Neither can I."

"You've got the hardest head for booze I know, but four glasses of champagne and I had to carry you to bed." His eyes looked her over appreciatively. "You look a bit too glamorous for the pub."

"That's because I'm not going to the pub. I'm going out to dinner with Mark."

His gaze made her feel slightly dizzy, not something she was used to, and she put it down to the fact he had been drinking for hours.

"Oh," was his unimpressed response.

Feeling she needed to defend Mark, she said, "He's gone to a lot of trouble. Asked Rick to recommend the place I'd like best." His constant intense stare was making her nervous.

"Oh," he said again. There was no denying the hunger in his eyes this time. "Have a good time, sweetheart." He hesitated, wanting to kiss her.

She put a hand on his upper arm. "Johnny told you the rest, didn't he?"

Piers nodded. "Why didn't you come to me?"

She could see he was hurting now; something she did not know quite how to deal with. "Because I really didn't want to think about it. All that turmoil and horrible memories."

He took her hand. "You could have told me."

"I know." She returned the pressure of his hold. "But just having you there was comfort enough." Anastasia stood on her toes and kissed his cheek. Wiping the lipstick off his face she said, "Try not to break too many hearts, hey handsome?" And she walked slowly away.

Mark and Anastasia had a very pleasant evening, with him showing an interest in the arrangements for her birthday party, her singing and her writing, and her asking many questions about his life in Paris, which ended with Mark promising to take her to Versailles.

Anastasia was beginning to feel she had been wrong about Mark, that maybe he was just insecure; that things could work out and be fun, for a while at least. As Mark drove them back to Rick and Fenella's home, she suggested, "Shall we call in at the village pub? I'd like to introduce you to some of my friends."

He considered for a moment and then, prepared to indulge her, he agreed.

As they got out of his Mercedes, she said, "If you want a drink, you can leave your car here and walk back in the morning. It's not far."

Taking her hand, Mark replied, "Good idea, baby."

Anastasia entered The Black Horse first and swiftly glanced around. The pub was small and already quite full, but she saw him straight away. Piers was sitting at a table with Joanie draped over him, and as Joanie saw Anastasia, she moved to sit on his lap, directing a triumphant look in her direction. Anastasia had no idea what expression was showing on her face, but she was sure it was not a pleasant one. Piers did not seem to have noticed her, and he put down his drink to whisper into Joanie's ear. She laughed loudly, and Anastasia forced herself to walk to the bar.

She was greeted warmly by the landlady, who she introduced to Mark, smiling perfunctorily as she complimented her luck in having such a handsome young man.

Anastasia took her drink and downed it straight away before turning her back on the now offending sight; much to the amusement of the rest of the pub, Piers was kissing Joanie. She put her arms around Mark in retaliation, moving to press her body against his. Mark was satisfied; she had ignored his brother and was now giving him her full and very affectionate attention. Anastasia reached up and kissed him, trying desperately to ignore the sick feeling in the pit of her stomach, telling herself that what Piers did was none of her business, however much she hated it.

Piers and Joanie soon left the pub, his arm around her waist, but Anastasia noticed he was very unsteady on his feet. Anastasia could not look at him as they disappeared into the night.

"Anastasia!"

Looking around, she saw her friend Sarah indicating two now free seats at her table.

Pulling Mark after her, Anastasia crossed the bar area to join the group sitting there; she knew them all. "Sarah," she said, smiling warmly. "Did you have a good Christmas?"

Her friend nodded, her streaked hair tied back in a sleek ponytail. "Yes, thanks; had a great time. But I missed this lot and the horses, so I came back a few days early. Which worked out well, because otherwise I might have missed you." She reached across the table to hug her.

"This is my boyfriend, Mark." Anastasia introduced him and sat down.

"Yes, we heard!" Sarah gave her a knowing look and then added, "It looks like Joanie has finally worn Piers down." She missed the flicker in Anastasia's eyes. "She was all over him! Couldn't have been more blatant if she'd stripped off and given him a lap dance!"

The whole table laughed.

Anastasia sat in silence, listening to the innuendo, and felt her nails begin to dig into her palms. Fearing that if she did not join in they would all suddenly guess the truth, she made a few caustic comments of her own that drew shouts of laughter from her friends. Within an hour, they were all very merry, Anastasia in particular, and once drunk, her affection for Mark increased rapidly. He was actually enjoying himself, finally the centre of Anastasia's attention, and he felt relief at no longer being in his brother's shadow.

They carried on drinking until time was called and then Mark had to help Anastasia walk home. She could barely talk for laughter at what her friends were saying, finding everything hilarious.

As they got to the front door, Sarah and the rest of the house staff drifted off to their rooms and Anastasia flung her arms around Mark's neck. "You're in for a good night," she said drunkenly. "Take me to bed."

Mark managed to get the door open without letting go of her and then he carried her into the conservatory, saying, "You stay here whilst I get you some water, otherwise you'll have one hell of a hangover tomorrow."

"I don't get hangovers," she protested. "But fresh orange juice always works." She sat on the sofa where he had put her as Mark went to the kitchen.

A moment later, unnoticed, Piers stood in the doorway. Anastasia was sitting on the sofa, taking off her stiletto boots which she discarded carelessly on the floor.

Piers observed her; she was obviously utterly smashed. "You must have been drinking champagne," he commented, leaning against the doorframe to stop himself from falling over.

She looked around but could not quite focus. "And you must be completely hammered to have shagged Joanie." She laughed at him, giving him such a sexy look that he was blown away. "I get it," she stated. "But you're a very naughty boy and should be spanked."

"Is that an offer?" he countered, intrigued by the heat in her blue eyes burning into his soul. He wanted her.

"One day, handsome." She swept those glorious eyes up at him. "One day."

Piers heard Mark returning and decided a retreat was in order before he did something completely stupid. He staggered away to try to find his bed, his head now totally confused.

Chapter 20

3rd January 1990

THE NEXT MORNING, Piers woke early. He remembered falling asleep in the bathroom where he had retreated so as not to hear the noises from Mark and Anastasia's room and made a mental note never to have a room near to them again. Champagne obviously affected her in more amorous ways.

As he got up, he knew he was on very dangerous ground. Never before had he cared so much that she was intimate with another man. Last night had been a real test; when she had looked at him, he felt scorched, and it had given him hope.

He also knew that if she heard about what he had said to Joanie, the reason for her slapping him, then he would not be able to deny the truth any longer. More importantly, if Joanie did what she had threatened and told Mark that Piers had called her Anastasia whilst having sex—and, even worse, called out her name as he climaxed—then all hell would break loose. He could not care less what Mark thought, but if Joanie did not stay silent, it would mean subjecting Anastasia to a bitter argument that could only end one way.

His thoughts were confused, and he kept going around in circles; if he told Anastasia how he felt and she rejected him, he did not think he could cope, but if he told her and then had to leave her because of his job, that would hurt just as much. Piers knew he could not expect her to start a relationship with him and then bugger off a week later for six months. This had been his problem for so long; he had given up so much and worked so hard to get what he wanted, and she had supported him all the way. Once he realised he loved her, his feelings had never wavered, but his way of life was not conducive to a real relationship. There was no choice; he would have to trust that this new Mark would not last, that he would revert to the jealous, spoilt brat he knew his brother truly was, and that in six months he would be back and could tell her the truth.

As he thought more clearly, he was confident that once Anastasia was back down The Star, then Mark's real nature would reassert itself. Piers knew exactly the sort of flirtatious banter she attracted when out. On the occasions where it sometimes got out of hand, all he had to do was look at the offender and that was usually enough, but he knew that Mark would throw a punch. Piers mused with certain evil pleasure that if Theo Cavendish was around, Mark would go loopy; after all, he had not liked finding out that he and Anastasia had previously dated. In fact, Theo Cavendish had been the only threat Piers had ever perceived for Anastasia's affections before she had rekindled things with Mark. The last time Theo tried to come back into her life, Piers had warned him off, under the pretence of Theo jeopardising his friendship with her. Thankfully, Theo was now married and a good friend to them both, but Piers knew it had been a close call.

He had decided he would not go back to Belgravia with them; instead, he would go to Guy's. That would give him a couple of days to clear his head and then enjoy the party without giving Anastasia any reason to be concerned or upset. He had not told her yet that he would be leaving the day after Guy's do, but he remembered he had promised to be at her birthday, something he was determined to do no matter what.

Acknowledging that he needed to face what he knew might be an unpleasant scene, he went downstairs to find Joanie, to make sure she would not cause Anastasia any problems; after all, she was all he really cared about.

As soon as Piers walked into the kitchen, there was a heartbeat of total silence before Fenella's staff started hurriedly talking about random subjects. He looked around, annoyed, and said in a dangerous voice, "At least if you're talking about my life, then you're not slating some other poor sod." He swept straight through and went out the back door.

Fenella was in the yard, and she spotted him heading towards the garden with a face like thunder. "Piers!" her voice carried, and he recognised the tone. Swearing under his breath, he stopped to face her. She pointed to the yard's office, and he obediently went there. Fenella joined him a few minutes later, and he eyed her with unaccustomed hostility.

She shook her head at him. "Joanie's very upset. What did you do?"

"What's she saying, because I was bluntly honest." He felt absurdly defensive, but then Fenella could have that effect on him.

"I asked *you*."

Piers sighed. "I was hammered. I asked her if she wanted sex. I made no promises of undying love; not a word about 'happily ever after'. I was quite clear about what I wanted. She could have said no." He was defiant now, still feeling slightly guilty but not enough to bother him for long.

"That's what I thought. You're an idiot, Piers Talbot. Joanie's hardly known for her discretion; you must have realised she would not keep quiet about it."

He sat down on her desk. "I didn't even stay the night." He shook his head. "I would never mislead any woman over my intentions."

"Don't worry, it'll be a five-minute wonder. Does Stasia know yet?"

Piers laughed ruefully. "She probably knew before it happened. That girl can read me like a book."

"Well, I hope Joanie doesn't say anything to her. God knows

how she'll react."

Fenella shooed him out of her office. "Go and take Bond for a canter in the ménage, will you? Do something useful for a change."

Piers gave her a warm smile and kissed her cheek.

ANASTASIA HAD WOKEN with a dreadful headache, courtesy of all the champagne she knew she should not have drunk. She left Mark in bed, and as she showered and dressed, she reflected on what had been a wonderful night—incredible, in fact—but she was not convinced that Mark had enjoyed that side of her at all. She was aware she had spoken to Piers before heading to bed and had a dreadful feeling she had made a verbal pass at him, which, given how drunk he was, she hoped he would not remember.

As she wandered downstairs and out through the back door, Anastasia was aware of people whispering and she knew that Joanie would have lost no time in broadcasting what had happened between her and Piers. She strode across the yard and put her head into the stable office, finding her godmother busy with the accounts book.

Fenella looked up. "Morning, Stasia. I hear you had fun last night."

"Tell that to my God-awful headache."

Fenella smiled. "Piers is in the ménage. I asked him to exercise Bond." She looked at Anastasia carefully, a worried crease between her brows.

Anastasia was chilly in her response. "I know what he did. I suppose she's telling everyone?"

"Joanie's been making out Piers lied to get her into bed. Don't look like that!" Fenella could clearly see outrage on Anastasia's face. "We all know he wouldn't have to. They're both as bad as each other on this one; her for wanting it, and him for entertaining it. She's made no secret of it, and from what I heard, she was quite explicit in her intentions down the pub."

But Anastasia was furious. How dare anyone cast aspersions

on Piers' character! The fire building within her, she stormed out of the office.

"Leave it alone, Stasia," Fenella called after her. "You'll only make things worse!"

Anastasia went to the ménage and found her anger immediately evaporating as she caught sight of Piers on horseback, cantering around with ease. She admired his improvement. "Keep your heels down!" she called out.

He rode towards her, smiling, and then dismounted to lean on the fence to talk to her.

"Been a bit of a prat, haven't you?" she commented. "You must have realised she wouldn't like being bonked and left."

Relieved she knew nothing more, he grinned sheepishly. "Yeah, well, I was drunk. We've all been there. Did you know champagne makes you outrageous, by the way? I heard you. Had to sleep in the bathroom in the end."

Anastasia coloured vividly. "Oh my God! I'm so sorry!" But what upset her was his obvious disinterest, reinforcing the words she had overheard from him on Christmas Eve.

"Stay away from champagne, sweetheart."

"Stay away from stable hands," she countered.

He grinned again. "I've learnt my lesson."

"Well, you should've known better than to dip your nib in the office ink," she joked, trying not to laugh at the expression on his face.

Piers struggled and then exclaimed, "You're a fine one to talk, Anastasia Travess! Theo? Bryan? That Danish showjumper?"

Anastasia bit her lip and then burst out laughing. "Well, if you put it like that …"

Piers reached out for her hand. "Maybe we should both practise what we preach. It'd make things a lot simpler." He winked at her. Then he looked up suddenly, hearing someone approaching.

Joanie was walking towards them.

Seeing his face harden, Anastasia looked around and called

out, "Morning."

Joanie hesitated and came over to them. "Having a good laugh about it, are we? I don't think the way *he* treated me is funny at all."

Piers frowned, but before he could say anything, Anastasia jumped in.

"Oh, shut up and quit moaning!" Anastasia snapped, her temper flaring. "You got what you wanted, but not what you hoped for. Life's a bitch; get used to it. And if I hear just one thing about Piers from anybody, you'll discover just what a vicious bitch *I* can be!"

Joanie stared at her, dumbfounded by the ferocity in her voice and the contempt in her eyes. Joanie opened her mouth and then changed her mind, walking away. She knew it really was not worth the row any revelations she made would cause.

Piers was stunned. "Anastasia?"

Anastasia whirled around to face him, fury still blazing in her blue eyes. "No-one is going to criticise you but me!"

Knowing he had to calm her down, Piers suggested cautiously, "Shall we go for a walk?"

She laughed suddenly, her temper gone. "Trying to put a lid on me?"

He grinned at her, reassured. "Remind me never to provoke you. And thank you for being such a good friend." As he said the words, he was conscious of the pang caused by longing for something more.

"I suppose I should see if Mark's up." She did not sound too keen on the idea. Their eyes met, and she added ruefully, "Your brother really isn't a fan of country life, is he?"

"Leave him where he is. Help me with Bond instead. We'll walk up to the top field and enjoy the view."

She hesitated.

"Come on, sweetheart. I'll be leaving again soon."

Her eyes flew to his face, holding his gaze for a moment, and then she moved to open the gate for him. In companionable silence, they walked the horse back to his stable, where one of the girls was happy to take him, and they set off together towards the lane. After the wild weather of yesterday, it was a lovely day; crisp air, blue skies and despite being chilly, the sunshine made everything feel good.

As they walked, Anastasia suddenly asked Piers, "Why was it so important to you that I gave Mark a chance? I don't understand; you're not exactly close to him. I don't even think you like him."

Caught completely off-guard, Piers did not know how to answer her. He stopped and stared at the view, with its glorious rolling countryside bathed in winter sunshine.

"Well?" Anastasia prompted him, not sure why he was avoiding the question.

Piers did not face her as he answered. "I wasn't sure how that summer had really affected you; if you'd ever got over him. I thought you needed to be sure." He paused and faced her, seeing disbelief in those blue eyes. "I know he was your first love. Your first ... encounter."

"Don't you know me at all?" Her words took him by surprise. "Theo was my first love."

She watched him carefully, see the disbelief build on his face.

"*Theo?*" he queried, trying not to show how this affected him; trying to deny he had made the biggest miscalculation of his life.

Anastasia could not believe this was news to him. "They put him in my office when I was just seventeen. We went out to do a shoot in London." She paused, Piers just staring at her uncomprehendingly. "We got caught in a massive downpour, and both of us were absolutely soaked. We were near the Savoy, so Theo flashed his smile and dropped his father's title and we got a suite. We ended up staying all weekend. When Rick found out, he did his nut, but as Theo quite rightly pointed out, Rick chose to put him in close proximity to me, so what did he expect?" She was smiling now. "We had such a good time. I often wonder if ... never mind, it was such a long time ago."

Piers ran his hand through his black hair.

"You didn't know?"

"You never told me." He broke off, knowing he had tried to do the right thing and realising he had only cocked it all up.

Anastasia thought for a moment. "Are you positive I didn't?"

"Oh, I think I'd remember that. When you pulled me out of the gutter, I knew you'd just dumped him, but no, I thought that was it."

"Firstly," she began patiently, unsure why he was reacting like this, "I did not pull you out of any gutter. I fetched you from a hotel and paid your bill."

"You gave me a home; made me believe I could make it. Even brought Eileen in to sort stuff out." As far as he was concerned, he owed her everything. She had turned up in a BMW with her driver, made him get in the car, paid his bill and told him he could stay with her for as long as he needed. They had stayed up most of the night while she listened to him, which she did without judgement. The next morning, Eileen, Frankie Beaumont's widow and a lawyer, had turned up and sorted out his money and reassured him that his family could not withhold what was rightfully his and she would have things settled in a few days. Anastasia had gone out to leave them to talk openly and she had returned laden down with a whole new wardrobe of designer clothes. Piers had been overwhelmed, and her explanation was simple; he had appalling taste in clothes. And then he had met Theo Cavendish, the ex-boyfriend, and tried desperately to hate him, but they had ended up finding common ground and had been friends ever since.

He put his hand over hers. "And that was the second time you gave me a wake-up call."

She was puzzled. "The second time?"

"That same summer, when all those girls turned up to the party and all hell broke loose. Don't you remember? You tore a strip off me."

"I never thought you'd listened, let alone that you'd still remember."

"I remember every word you said. That I was a disgrace; selfish; contemptible; no respect for the feelings of others. You asked me who I thought I was, treating people like that."

"I had no right speaking to you like that." Anastasia was astounded her words had stayed in his memory.

"You made me realise I was out of control. You made me look in the mirror, and I didn't like what I saw. You see, I really *do* owe you everything."

Anastasia put her arms around him to hold him close. "And you saved my life." She could feel tears gathering.

He held her, unable to speak. Daring not to speak.

Anastasia eventually pulled away, hurriedly wiping her eyes. "How did we get so deep? This is not who we are." She tried to laugh it off, but there was a look in his eyes she had not seen for over five years and she dare not misinterpret him again. Turning away, she walked down the hill. "We should get back. I'm hungry."

Piers watched her, knowing he had made a fundamental error in letting his head tell him what to do instead of listening to his heart. Cursing why he had not done as he had planned at Christmas, he followed her.

Chapter 21

THEY WALKED BACK to the house in silence, and Anastasia made her way to the kitchen whilst Piers went to make a couple of work-related calls. Anastasia could hear laughter as she neared the kitchen door and, as she entered, she was surprised to find Mark making omelettes and obviously charming Fenella. She stopped and stared; this, she had not expected.

He noticed her. "Hello, baby! I'm making brunch. Want some?"

"Yes, please. I'm starving. I've just been for a walk. The view this morning is glorious." She crossed over to see what he was doing, then sitting at the table, she told him, "You realise you should be honoured? Fenella never lets *anyone* use her kitchen."

HAVING CONTACTED HIS employer, Piers left Rick's office and spotted Johnny along the corridor. "Morning, Johnny," he called out.

Johnny stopped and waited for him to catch up. "I shouldn't go to the kitchen, if I were you. You might drown in an excess of charm."

Piers laughed ruefully, grasping exactly what he meant. "Mark being Mr. Wonderful?"

Johnny nodded. "Yep, but the boy can cook." He eyed Piers thoughtfully. "Come with me. I'd like you to take a look at some stuff I wrote before Christmas and give me your opinion."

Intrigued, Piers followed him to a small room filled with piles of paper, guitars and a desk. "So, Rick finally gave you some space?"

Johnny grinned. "Well, I practically live here, so fair do's really." He extracted a few pages from a pile in imminent danger of sliding onto the floor. "Here's my next hit for someone else."

Piers took them and looked for somewhere to sit. Johnny swept some more papers onto the floor and a chair suddenly appeared. Piers read the words before him and, as always, was amazed that anyone could write such beautiful lyrics. "Feeling romantic, were we?" he said once he had finished.

Johnny avoided his eye. "Well? Are they too much?"

Piers shook his head. "They're fabulous, Johnny; some great stuff. I wish I could talk like this, let alone write it down and then set it to music."

Johnny was flattered. "Tell you what. When you get married, I'll write a song just for you and your bride."

Piers laughed. "You'll be waiting a long time, mate. A *very* long time."

"Want to lay money on that?" Johnny asked mischievously.

"Do you have someone in mind, then?"

He turned to rummage in the desk drawer. "You know who just as well as I do."

Piers eyed him with displeasure and responded, "You go there with me and I'll go there with you and Eileen."

Johnny ignored him and held out a book. "Want to read the proof copy?"

Piers realised what he was being shown and took the book eagerly. "Yes. Is this the actual cover?" Then he noticed the author's name and, astounded, he said, "You did it, then. Does she know?"

Johnny was pleased by his reaction. "I haven't told her yet, but I thought you'd like to see it as you probably won't be around when it hits the shelves here."

Piers ran his finger along the bottom of the front cover and read aloud, "'Anastasia Alexashenko'. So, she's using her mother's name?"

"She wanted to and I agreed, but she still thinks she's just a ghost-writer. I want to tell her she's made the cover once I've got the real thing in my hands."

Piers turned over the book and read the blurb on the back. "I can't wait to read it. Have Rick and Fenella approved it?"

Johnny nodded. "Yeah, course. I wouldn't put anything in there that would upset them. Jack, on the other hand, is going to be pissed."

"I hope he can't sue you …"

"No way. My lawyer and the publishers' lawyers have been all over it with a fine toothcomb. I'd like to see him try."

"Thanks, then. In fact, I might go and start this now if my brother is flavour of the month."

"Don't worry, I've seen his type before. She'll be bored with him in under a month."

A few hours later, Piers could hear music coming from the lounge where Fenella had told him Anastasia was relaxing. He paused outside the door and listened to her singing along to the radio. He smiled and opened the door. Anastasia was sitting on the sofa, drumming her fingers on the arm in time to the music. She looked up as she heard the door and asked, "Are you ok? You missed lunch."

"Yes, I'm fine. I've just been with Johnny." He told her half the truth. "He's written some new stuff and wanted to know what I thought."

She smiled at him. "And what *did* you think?"

"It's great. I wish I could talk like he can write." There was a wistful smile playing around his lips.

Anastasia stood up and walked towards him, and he could not help his eyes flick up and down her body, lingering on those shoes. Then she was standing in front of him. "Just remember a few of his lines and use them next time you want to chat someone up," was her advice as she acknowledged the desire to have him say such words to her.

"I don't tend to chat women up," Piers commented ruefully.

She smiled slowly, like a caress, saying, "No, you don't need to. You just smile and suddenly they're on their knees."

"Is that all it takes?" He felt his heart begin to pound.

Anastasia put one hand to his cheek and said softly, "With you? Yes, that's all it takes." She held his eyes for a heartbeat and then started to walk away.

Just as she made it to the door, Piers said, "I'm going now, Stasia."

She stopped and half-turned, frowning at him over her shoulder. "Now? But we're going straight after dinner. How are you getting home?"

"I'm not going home. I'm going to Guy's. I'll see you at the party."

Her face fell and he could not pretend to be disappointed.

"Oh," was her only comment.

"One of the lads here is off to London, so he'll drop me to get my car and stuff. Guy's is a black tie do, so formal dress all round."

"Oh," she said again. "Thank you for letting me know."

Anastasia turned to walk out of the door, and Piers let her go. He always hated saying goodbye to her.

Chapter 22

4ᵗʰ January 1990

THE NEXT MORNING, Anastasia woke up in her own bed in Belgravia, Mark sprawled across her, and she tried to push him away without disturbing him. She needed to get up and go to work, and she would rather do that without any arguments. Anastasia sat up and heard him mutter in his sleep, then she made her way to the main bathroom, rubbing her eyes and yawning.

Dinner the previous night had been fun; Mark had been in an excellent mood and had even made Johnny laugh. But his words on the drive home left her in no doubt that he was not keen to repeat the experience.

Anastasia ate her breakfast in silence and then left the house, pulling her black raincoat tightly shut against the chilly rain. She was looking forward to being back in the office, seeing who was in and finding out what they had done over Christmas, but she was also a little apprehensive over the comments that were bound to be made about Bryan. As she sat on the Underground, she wondered if he would be in today, and whether Suzanna was still happy.

It was not long before she was seated at her desk and going through Rick's pile of messages; he was not due back until Monday. She heard a knock and looked up, surprised; people did not normally do that, knowing that they could just walk in. They knocked again.

"Come in," she called out, curious.

The door opened and in walked Bryan, an embarrassed look on his face. "Happy New Year, Stasia," he said. "How are you?"

"I'm fine." She paused to scrutinise his expression before asking, "How's Suzanna?"

He blushed. "She's good. We both are." He broke off and bit his lip. Anastasia knew he wanted to say something, but she did not prompt him. Eventually, he mumbled, "I'm sorry for my behaviour on New Year's Eve."

She smiled at him. "It doesn't matter. Drink can make a fool out of even the most sensible person."

He smiled back, relieved that she bore him no grudge. Then he took a deep breath, something else obviously on his mind.

"What is it, Bryan? Out with it."

"Suzanna and I are getting married!" He blurted it out whilst turning a very dark shade of red.

She sat absolutely still and stared at him. "Run that by me again?"

Bryan sat down opposite her and repeated himself. "We're getting married."

She still could not quite comprehend something so totally unexpected.

"Are you ok, Stasia?" He was concerned by her silence.

Anastasia nodded slowly, then finally spoke. "I did *not* see that coming. Jesus, Bryan! That's fast, even for you."

"I know, but it feels right, so why waste time? Venue should be confirmed this weekend."

"How soon are we talking for the ceremony?"

"Probably the weekend after your birthday, so any help you can offer us in making arrangements would be welcome." He was well aware of the extent of her connections.

"Yes." She looked at him again, wondering if this was a wise choice on her friend's part. "Yes, of course. Anything she needs, Suzanna only has to ask. Why didn't she tell me herself?" Anastasia was suddenly annoyed by that.

"Because she was worried how you'd react."

"She's my best friend, Bryan. Surely she knows I'd support her?" She held his eyes with a look of warning in her own. "Oh, and one thing, Bryan. If you hurt her, I'll hurt you."

He grinned. "That's fair enough! Is Rick in?"

She shook her head. "No, not until next week. And I'm not telling him!" That she would flatly refuse to do.

"It's ok, I want to tell him personally. Do you think it'd be ok to call him at home?"

"Yeah, why not? It's good news. I'm sure he'll be pleased for you." She could just imagine his face.

"Thanks, Stasia. Are you free this weekend to come out and celebrate with us?"

She shook her head, genuinely sorry. "No, it's Mark's brother's birthday party on Saturday." She thought for a moment. "But we could see you in The Star on Sunday evening for a catch-up?"

"That'd be good. I know Suzanna is dying to fill you in." He got up, saying, "See you soon," and with a wave, he left her alone with her thoughts.

Anastasia spent the rest of the day dealing with problems that had occurred over Christmas. Some of them were incredibly trivial, but she knew that was why Rick left them for her. At regular intervals, people popped their heads in to say hello, and a few wanted to know what had happened between her and Bryan, whom she deflected with ease. As she left the office, she was still trying to process what Bryan had told her, hoping very much that Suzanna was making the right call, but she knew she needed to see her friend's face to be the judge of that.

As she got home, she could smell something wonderful cooking and her hopes were raised that Mark was still in a good mood.

"Hi, baby!" he called out, coming to meet her at the door. "How was your day?"

She hung up her slightly damp coat and replied, "It was all right. Plenty of people in to talk to, and lots of ridiculous queries as usual." But Mark had already gone back into the kitchen.

She sighed and then prepared to tell him about Bryan and Suzanna. Hesitant as to where to start, she simply came out with it. "Bryan came to see me." As soon as she said his name, Mark whirled around to face her, ice back in his eyes.

"What did that loser want?"

"He and Suzanna are getting married."

"What? Really?"

"Yes, I was shocked, too." She braced herself. "I said we'd meet them in the pub on Sunday to celebrate."

His face took on an ugly expression. "No, we won't."

"Why? We'll be at Guy's on Saturday, but we're free Sunday."

He glared at her.

"I want to see Suzanna. She's my closest female friend, and I want to make sure she knows what she's doing; that she's genuinely happy." Anastasia began to feel her nails digging into her palms.

"You're not going near him because I say so." His voice was raised, and she flinched at his expression. He stood inches from her. "No means no." And then he turned his back on her to carry on with dinner as if nothing had happened.

"I'm going to get changed," she stammered, and she ran from the room.

For the rest of the evening, Mark behaved as if there had been no disagreement; that he had not shouted at her. Anastasia did not know what to do, and when he suggested what she should wear into work the next day, she agreed before she realised it. Anastasia went to bed first, as Mark wanted to watch a documentary, and, feeling trapped, she hoped very much to be asleep before he came up.

The next day, Mark was charming again. He got up early to make her a proper breakfast, just the way she liked it, and told her he would arrange the transport for Guy's party tomorrow so all she had to do was look gorgeous.

Even more surprisingly, as she was about to leave, he said, "I've been thinking. We'll meet Bryan and Suzanna on Sunday. I think it's probably for the best to get it over with. That way, we won't have to socialise with them again until the wedding—*if* they make it that far."

Taking that as a win for now, Anastasia found herself thanking him and feeling relieved. But at the back of her mind, she knew everything about her new relationship was beginning to look wrong.

Chapter 23

ON SATURDAY EVENING, Anastasia took a critical look at herself in the mirror and was pleased. Her red dress still fitted perfectly, its colour enhancing her dark hair, and she slid her feet into brand new red shoes—a Christmas present from Rick and Fenella—that sparkled as the light caught them. She had worn this dress to a party Piers had taken her to at the American Embassy last summer, and it had been a blast. She left her room and walked carefully down the stairs, hoping very much that Mark would approve.

At first, his eyes glowed when he saw her, then he noticed some finer points about the dress and scowled.

"Will I do?" she asked, twirling around.

He remained silent, then said furiously, "You're not going to my brother's in that dress."

Anastasia blinked, taken completely by surprise. "What's the problem?" she demanded, justifiably annoyed after all the effort she had made. "This dress was once good enough for the American Embassy, so it should be good enough for your brother!"

"It's too revealing, the amount of cleavage it shows and that slit up the side. I will not have you looking like some tart in front of my family!"

She flinched at his tone, her hands starting to shake, but this time she stood her ground. "Fine, I won't go, then. And when Piers is on the phone wondering where I am, you can tell him why I'm not there and see what you get." She knew that would push him to the edge, but if she did not fight back now, she would lose herself.

"Piers! Always bloody Piers!" His voice was raised. "And you both expect me to believe there has never been anything between you?" He slammed his fist on the table.

Anastasia was scared of the look in his eyes but dragged courage from somewhere to say, "I'm sick of you treating me like a possession, Mark Talbot. Now, either you trust me and we go to this party or we're finished, right here, right now."

Mark backed down quickly with bad grace. "Ok, ok, we're going. But I will *not* have you spending the night dancing with my brother. Can you at least try to act like you're *my* girlfriend?"

"Then try treating me like one," she sliced across him before slamming her way out of the house, barely able to believe she had finally stood up to him.

By the time they arrived at Guy's, it felt like a ceasefire had been silently agreed. Mark was at his most charming as he got out of the car and greeted some other late arrivals. He ushered Anastasia into the house, and they followed the sound of music and voices to a huge ballroom filled with people all dressed to impress.

"I'll find Guy and apologise for us being late." Mark eyed her warily. "You find a table over there." He indicated an area well away from the dance floor.

She was doing as Mark had asked when Anastasia saw Piers dancing; he looked good in his dark dinner suit. She walked over to him, all her anxiety slipping away.

"Sweetheart!" Piers called out. "Well, don't you look exquisite? Better late than never."

She shrugged. "Your brother objected to what I was wearing and we had a slight disagreement. I won."

He glanced over towards Mark and gave him a filthy look. Following his gaze, she tried to distract him. "I see your attempts at samba have not improved."

He grinned at her and suddenly produced some stunning samba moves she had never seen him pull off before. She stared open-mouthed, then managed, "What the …?"

"Just a little something I picked up in South America."

She folded her arms and stared at him for a moment before replying coolly, "What was her name?"

Piers blinked. Was that a spark of jealousy? Lips twitching, he said, "Don't remember, but she was brunette and nearly got me killed."

Anastasia raised one eyebrow, her arms still folded.

"She had brothers." Laughing, he left her standing on the dance floor, his heart suddenly soaring; he was now certain she was jealous.

Anastasia moved in the opposite direction, fearing she had let her true feelings show. She was not stupid; Piers was good-looking, charming, dangerous and she had lost count of the number of telephone numbers he had been given in clubs and thrown away. But Anastasia could not bear to think about him together with another woman. She felt her nails start to dig into her palms, and a wave of panic swept over her, then it was gone. She knew she was being grossly unfair, but that still did not mean she had to like it.

Anastasia glanced around and saw Mark at a table, obviously looking for her. Pulling herself together, she made her way to join him, forcing a smile back onto her face.

Mark gave her an appraising look and then said, "Can't you keep away from him for five minutes?"

"I was only saying hello. Where's Guy? I'm so looking forward to seeing him again; it's been years."

"He'll be over in a minute." Mark's voice trailed away as he saw his two brothers walking towards them, laughing at some shared joke and obviously comfortable in each other's company.

Anastasia turned her head to look. Guy was very similar in appearance to his brothers, albeit his black hair was run through with silver, which she thought gave him a very distinguished appearance.

He stopped as he saw her and raised his eyebrows in appreciation. "Wow, Anastasia! You look fabulous!" He leant down to kiss her cheek.

"Happy birthday, Guy." She returned his kiss. "You're looking very dashing tonight, but then you always did know how to dress with style." Her eyes flickered mischievously across at Piers, who winked at her.

Guy said to Mark, "You really don't deserve her!" and he strolled away.

Mark frowned and then tried to laugh it off, but he failed to sound convincing. Anastasia knew that Guy's words had stung. "Shall I get a bottle of wine for us?" he asked, still watching Guy walk away.

"Get two," Piers advised, and he sat down, making his intention clear; he was going to join them, whether Mark liked it or not.

Mark was soon back, begrudgingly including his brother in conversation, and they became engaged in spotting surrounding partygoers and not being able to remember many names. Piers glanced idly around, clearly becoming bored of the conversation, when he saw him strolling, without a care in the world, towards them. He stood up abruptly and dropped his hand onto Anastasia's shoulder to grasp it tightly.

"Piers!" she gasped. Her laughter died as she saw the look on his face. Fear, irrational fear, gripped her heart, and she followed that murderous gaze to where it was being directed.

"Courage, sweetheart," she heard him whisper, and as Giles descended upon them she felt a familiar wave of nausea sweeping over her.

"Piers. Anastasia." Giles nodded at them dismissively. "Mark, I need a word." He turned to move away, evidently expecting to be obeyed.

"Yeah, later," Mark replied loftily.

Giles stopped in his tracks; he did not appreciate being disobeyed. He turned back to speak again, but his eyes met Piers' and his words were left unsaid. Casting a hateful look at both Piers and Anastasia, he moved away.

Piers' grip on her shoulder suddenly slackened and Anastasia breathed again. He sat down next to her and, taking advantage of Mark being distracted by another passing acquaintance, said urgently, "You ok?"

She nodded. "Did you know he was going to be here?"

Piers checked Mark was still talking and leant in close to her ear. "I knew he was expected, but I didn't think he'd actually have the balls to turn up. Don't worry; he won't cause a scene."

"I know," she cut across him. "You're here."

Guy was now walking back towards them; he had been keeping a wary eye on Giles' movements, unsure of his intentions and regretting having invited him. He reached their table and leaned down to speak to Anastasia. "Come on, Stasia, salsa with me. I know you can."

Guy took her hand; no was not an option. He fixed his blue eyes, so like Piers', to hers, and she could not resist as Guy pulled her to the dance floor. "I may not be in Piers' league when it comes to dancing, but you cannot deny the birthday boy a dance. And I know for a fact I'm a damn sight better than Mark!" He laughed.

Guy was right, and Anastasia was soon enjoying herself.

Mark watched his brother with astonishment. "I didn't know he could dance like that. Am I the only Talbot with two left feet?"

"Dancing prowess obviously skipped you, little brother. He is good, though." Piers continued to watch for a short while, then, frustrated, he commented, "I'm going to cut in."

Anastasia suddenly felt herself being spun out of Guy's arms and facing Piers. "Let's show them how it's done, sweetheart."

She grinned at him. "No lifts, Piers. Not in this dress!"

The two of them owned the music after all those lessons

together, all those nights dancing together in clubs, and soon most of the other guests fell back from the dance floor to watch and admire.

Mark came to stand on the edge of the dance floor next to his brother and demanded, "Guy, why did you let him cut in?"

"They look so good together." Realising what he had just said, he tried to explain himself as he saw anger leaping into Mark's icy grey eyes. "I meant on the dance floor, Mark. Because they both know what they're doing."

Mark was still glaring at him; jealousy of Piers was never far away, and here was another reason for him to feel vindicated.

Piers and Anastasia left the dance floor to a round of applause, and as they reached the two brothers, she kissed Guy on the cheek. "Sorry, I told him off, but he doesn't care." She then turned to Mark, aware he was looking cross and feeling that she must placate him. "Don't worry; the slow dances are all yours."

He leant down to kiss her, and with a need to assert himself, he pulled her into his arms and kept her there. Exchanging glances, Guy and Piers left them to it.

Chapter 24

LILY TALBOT HAD been watching Anastasia from afar, a puzzled look on her face. "Guy, who is she?" she asked her husband. "I'm sure I recognise her. She really is a good dancer."

"That, my darling, is Anastasia Travess. I don't think the two of you have ever met, though."

Lily ran the name over her lips and replied, "Ah, so that's who Piers spends all his time talking about non-stop. But are you absolutely sure I haven't met her? She looks so familiar."

"Does the fact she's the daughter of Natalia Alexashenko make a difference?"

"Natalia Alexashenko! I adored her! She was a ballet icon. That's her daughter?"

"Did you know Natalia?" He was curious.

"Oh no, but she was a legend. So inspirational, to be that good so young."

"Well, I'll introduce you to Stasia properly, then." Guy moved through the crowd once again to the other side of the room.

Anastasia stood up as she saw him approaching. "Guy, what a fabulous party! Your taste in music is excellent!" she said affectionately.

Knowing it would annoy his little brother, he hugged her and kissed her cheek indulgently before saying, "My wife would like to meet you." Turning to address Mark, he teased, "I'll bring her back—eventually."

"Or I'll come and fetch her." He smiled at Guy, but there was no denying the edge to his voice.

Guy introduced Anastasia to a lithe, willowy woman whose auburn hair was swept back into a chignon and was wearing a beautiful jade gown which she suspected enviously was a designer original. The woman was smiling warmly at her as they shook hands and she said, "You look just like her!"

Anastasia was used to this and replied a little wearily, "Did you know my mother, Lily?"

"I never had the pleasure of knowing Natalia Alexashenko, but I always found her inspirational."

"My wife was a professional ballroom dancer and World Latin champion," Guy interjected, grinning at the look on her face.

Anastasia met Guy's laughing eyes. "So *that's* why you were so good out there; your wife taught you. That's cheating!"

"I never said I couldn't dance. I just said I was better than Mark," Guy pointed out.

"Mind you," Lilly added, "that's all he can do. We'll leave the rest of the experience in the corner where it belongs."

Guy rolled his eyes. "Always back to that bloody tango ..."

But Anastasia had warmed insensibly to his wife and laughed appreciatively at the look on his face.

"Did you ever try ballet?" Lily had to ask.

"No, I never did. My father forbade it; said it was too painful." She smiled ruefully. "In fact, I never had any lessons at all until Piers and I went as part of a dare from his mates. Best thing we ever did."

"Well, you're both very good." Lily looked at her appraisingly. "I'd like to see you both dance the rhumba; I think you'd be sensational."

Grinning as she remembered one lesson in particular, Anastasia let Lily down gently. "No, we tried that and got thrown out of class for laughing and taking the mick. We could do the steps, but our teacher kept banging on about a connection, making it real."

"Piers would have loved that," Guy remarked, imagining his

brother's reaction.

"But you *do* have a connection," Lily insisted. "It's obvious you adore each other. You were his main topic of conversation over Christmas."

"Don't all best friends adore each other?" Anastasia asked, trying to inject an air of innocence to avoid either Guy or Lily getting the wrong idea.

Guy tried to stop Lily from saying what he knew she was thinking, but he could not catch her eye. "I thought you were lovers."

Anastasia's laugh was brittle; she found the irony hurtful. "No, I'm with Mark."

"I shouldn't mention it to Mark, though, if I were you," Guy advised them both.

Anastasia held his eyes. "Mark needs to relax. There are some things in my life that are non-negotiable."

Lily gave Guy a gentle shove. "Go away, Guy! I want to talk to Anastasia without you interrupting."

He raised his eyebrows, but as he was obviously not wanted, he thought he had better do as he was told.

PIERS STOOD AT the bar, patiently waiting to be served, when he felt an icy chill run down his spine. Turning swiftly, he found himself face to face with his older brother Giles.

Giles was slightly shorter than him, his hair already grey, and his pale blue eyes showed contempt as he stared at his younger brother.

"What do you want?" Piers asked disdainfully.

"From *you*?" Giles glowered at him. "Nothing." Then, in a silky voice filled with animosity and calculated to get a reaction, Giles murmured, "When are you going to admit what you and that lying tart are up to behind Mark's back?"

Piers faced him squarely. "What did you call her?" He took a hasty step forwards, an intimidating act as Giles involuntarily took one step back.

"You heard me."

"Remember what I know." Piers' eyes were ablaze; he was trying very hard to keep control of his temper, a voice in his head telling him that this was deliberate provocation.

"Whatever she's said, she's a liar and a tart." Giles wanted to see how far he could push him. "You knew nothing then, and you know nothing now." Giles curled his lip, malicious intent in his eyes.

"You have a selective memory, Giles. I paid you a visit."

Giles did not reply; he did not need to.

Neither of them had noticed Guy a few feet away, hidden in the crowd at the bar. Sensing a problem through the noise of his party, he had watched with concern and then moved unobtrusively closer to them. He had heard enough.

Once Giles had moved away, a smug look on his face, and Piers had picked up his drinks, Guy stepped to intercept him. "Was that true?"

Piers started violently and sloshed some drink. "Was what true?"

Guy raised one eyebrow. "I heard what you said to Giles. Most interesting. Care to elaborate?"

He looked suspiciously at his older brother. "I don't know what you think you heard ..."

"Cut the crap; it's me you're talking to now. Cartagena ring any bells?"

Piers glared at him, aware he owed him but unwilling to tell him the truth.

"Was Anastasia the one Angela left him over?"

"No, Guy. You're way off," he scoffed.

"You said you paid him a visit. I'm sure it wasn't friendly," Guy persisted.

"Come outside—and keep your bloody voice down." Guy followed Piers over to the nearby conservatory doors and, glancing around, Piers stepped outside into the crisp night.

Guy followed him, watching his brother's face carefully and seeing an inner struggle taking place.

Once outside, Piers said matter-of-factly, "Giles attacked Anastasia."

Guy did not respond, dumbfounded.

"I don't know exactly what happened or why—Stasia would not tell me the whole story—but she ended up with a plate in her elbow and a scar on her back."

"When was this? Where were you?" Guy demanded.

"1984, while I was in West Germany for work. I'd heard a few things I didn't like, so I asked a couple of colleagues to keep an eye on her. They got suspicious one night, and they stopped him."

"Stopped what?" Guy pushed him.

"If I knew the truth, do you think he'd still be alive?" Piers was annoyed; he still blamed himself for not protecting her. "I assume you've worked out it was Giles who made Dad send Mark to Paris? It was him that lied to Mark about everything, and it's him that's turned our little brother into a twat. I've no idea why he went for her, or what his problem is, but he's scum!" Piers downed his drink.

"Why didn't you tell me this?" Guy knew Piers was balancing on the edge of his temper, but he also knew he would not lie to him.

"We were estranged, remember?" Piers replied scornfully. "Besides," he added unhappily, "I promised Anastasia."

Guy signalled to one of the security men stood nearby and ordered, "Fetch my brother Giles."

Piers stood in silence, wishing he had another drink and feeling twitchy; he had no idea what Guy was going to do.

Within a few minutes, Giles passed through the conservatory and out into the grounds. Piers felt Guy grip his upper arm and move him out of the way.

"You sent for me?" Giles suddenly saw Piers. "What is *he* doing here? There'll be no kissing and making up if that's what you want, Guy."

"I want you to leave." Guy had never been anything but direct.

Giles frowned. "What are you talking about? I don't understand."

Guy looked Giles over with an unmistakable threat behind his eyes but remained silent.

Giles tried again. "What lies has he been telling you?"

Guy shook his head. "Piers does not lie. No matter what we've all thought of him over the years, I believe that hasn't changed. In fact, it is *you* who has been lying. You've lied to Mark and you've lied to me, but worse of all, I now know you hurt Anastasia."

The three brothers stood in charged silence before Giles broke it. "I don't know what you're talking about."

"Just go, Giles. I know the truth. And if I ever get the proof, you'll pay."

Piers suddenly connected the dots. "Angela and Matthew? Is that why you asked that before?"

Giles suddenly leapt forward and grabbed Piers by the collar; a huge mistake. Piers swiftly broke free and pinned his brother to the wall, murder in his eyes. Intervening, Guy managed to separate them.

"Get out of my way, Guy!" Piers fixed those blue eyes on Giles, the need for revenge almost overwhelming. "Give me a reason, Giles."

Still holding Piers back, Guy spoke brusquely to Giles, "Leave *now*—and stay away from Anastasia and Mark."

Giles stared at them. "I'll go, but when you've calmed down, Guy, I'll expect an apology."

Feeling Piers still struggling and knowing he could not hold him back for long, Guy snarled at Giles, "Out!"

Giles sneered and walked away. After a few moments, Piers relaxed and Guy loosened his grip, saying with authority, "Don't even *think* about going after him."

Piers straightened his jacket and glared at Guy.

"What does Mark know?" Guy asked.

"He knows she was attacked, but he has no idea of the details. I promised her. If she wants him to know any more, she'll tell him."

"Will she?" Guy asked shrewdly, believing he knew why the incident had occurred.

"That's her business and no-one else's." Piers was still smouldering, and he met Guy's thoughtful gaze with a promise. "If he gives me a reason, I *will* finish it."

Guy sighed, foreseeing a minefield ahead. "I know."

Chapter 25

Guy left Piers to smoke a cigar and gradually calm down. All too aware of what Piers was capable of, he had an idea of who was best to help him and make sure he did nothing rash. Guy saw Mark talking with some second cousins he had not seen in years and homed in on his wife still laughing with Anastasia. He smiled; Lily did not make friends easily as she tended to say what she thought, something which many people did not appreciate.

"Anastasia," Guy called out as he approached them. She paused mid-sentence and raised her eyebrows. "Sorry to interrupt, but I think Piers needs you."

Her eyes widened and she felt panic rising, but she could not say what she feared. "Is he ok?"

"He's fine; he's just had words with someone, that's all." He gave her upper arm a squeeze to reassure her.

"Sorry, Lily,"Anastasia stammered. She impulsively kissed Lily's cheek. "I'll be back later. Where is he, Guy?"

"Outside, through the conservatory. He's smoking."

Anastasia nodded and hurried off.

"What was *that* about, Guy?" Lily demanded, worried.

Guy took her into his arms and kissed her auburn hair. "Brotherly love, darling," he said.

Anastasia had some difficulty getting out of the party, but she soon spotted Piers in the grounds. Smelling the cigar and sensing humour was the best approach, she called out,

"I thought you only smoked those at Christmas?"

Piers spun around as he heard her voice and, smiling ruefully, he walked over to her, putting the cigar out. "Guy told you, then?"

"He said you'd had words with someone. I'm assuming that someone was Giles." She felt a wave of nausea as she said his name.

"It's ok, sweetheart; Guy threw him out." He pulled her into his arms. "I'm sorry, but I told Guy. I think he's suspected something for a while." He felt her shudder and held her tightly. "Don't cry, Stasia. He isn't worth it."

Anastasia enjoyed being so close to him. She felt safe in his arms; the only place she ever really had. "Giles has always been jealous of you, you know."

"Jealous? What of?"

"Being the blue-eyed boy. You chose your own path and you stuck to it, no matter what. Your father never made any secret of how much he loves you, despite what went on. Giles has never had an easy relationship with any of you, has he? Except for Mark." Her voice trailed off. Was that where the personal animosity stemmed from?

Piers sighed. "You could be right. And it's no secret that Giles is something of a black sheep. He was never too thrilled about Guy inheriting the family business which he wants to legitimise."

"And?"

"I've been doing some digging. It seems Giles has been trying to engineer a takeover. I suppose you could equate it to a boardroom rebellion."

"Does Guy know what's going on?" But she knew the answer already.

Piers held her a little tighter. "Of course. Who do you think told me? No flies on my big brother." The satisfaction in his voice was evident.

Mark had managed to get away from his relatives and was looking for Anastasia. Seeing that the conservatory doors leading into the grounds of Guy's palatial estate were open, he wondered if she had stepped out for a breath of fresh air. A little way ahead, on the garden path, he saw two people; a tall man holding a brunette woman in a long red dress.

He knew it.

Striding out, he walked over and tapped his brother on the shoulder. "What the hell is going on?" he snapped.

Anastasia glanced up and saw the jealousy in her boyfriend's icy eyes. Thinking fast, she lied. "I wasn't feeling well."

Piers let her go. "It's stuffy in there, and she has had a fair bit to drink."

Mark looked from one to the other. "Why didn't you find me?" He was trying to control his temper, not wanting to chastise her in front of Piers.

"I was already outside. I think Anastasia's wellbeing is more important, don't you?" Piers was scathing.

Feeling wrong-footed, Mark apologised. "Sorry, yes, you're right; it is hot in there. You ok now, baby?"

"I am now." She took his hand, grateful there had been no outburst.

Piers held her gaze for a moment and said, "I'm going back in; Lily promised to dance with me. I'll leave you to it."

As Piers headed for the conservatory, Mark asked, "What's wrong, baby?"

"Nothing," she lied again. "I just felt a bit sick earlier. It's nice out here; I wish I could see Guy's grounds properly." She felt his grip tighten on her hand.

Now ashamed that he had shown his jealousy, Mark suggested, "We can go if you like? I don't mind an early night."

"No, that would be rude." She pulled her hand away and looked up into his eyes, glad to see the anger had vanished. "Besides, I want to see Lily dance. Did you know she was a professional?"

Putting his arm around her waist, Mark steered her back towards the main house and replied, "Probably, but I don't know her too well."

"I think she's lovely."

"Well, if you think so, she must be." Anastasia felt he was patronising her, something that annoyed her instantly, and she walked away from him to the edge of the dance floor to enjoy watching Lily and Piers dancing together.

Mark was right behind her. "She's better than him by miles," he remarked, and he could not deny that pleased him. He slid an arm back around her waist to hold her close.

Anastasia objected to being treated as property. She pulled away, saying over her shoulder, "It's still a bit warm in here."

Anastasia loved watching Piers and Lily dance, and she ignored Mark's muttered comments until he tapped her on the shoulder and said, "Come on, let's sit down. This is boring."

She looked crossly over her shoulder. "Do what you want. I'm enjoying it."

Mark scowled at the back of her head and stayed where he was.

As she watched, Anastasia's eye was caught by a man dressed immaculately in black trailing his way around the edge of the dance floor, his gaze focused on Lily. As the song ended, Piers kissed Lily's hand, but as he tried to lead her back to Guy, the man bowed and held his hands out to her. Piers blinked, then shrugged his shoulders and left her with her new partner. He crossed to join Anastasia, whose gaze was now riveted to Lily, her eyes wide with appreciation and envy. He stood next to her and did not acknowledge Mark. "Seems I've been supplanted."

"Who is he? He's bloody fantastic!" Anastasia unconsciously reached out for Piers' arm and gripped it.

"A friend of hers. An Italian dancer, I think." His voice trailed off as he watched, too.

Mark took hold of Anastasia's upper arm and hissed in her ear, "Come on, let's sit down," and he tried to pull her with him.

She let go of Piers and pushed Mark's hand away. "Don't! I want to watch."

Mark glared at her, his face suffused with anger, and then he glanced at Piers' face and stalked away.

Anastasia sighed and murmured without thinking, "Oh dear,

I'll pay for that later."

Piers glanced down at her, wondering if he had heard her correctly, but she was now re-focused on the dance floor.

They watched Lily and her friend for a while before Piers took her hand. "Come on, dance with me."

She laughed. "You want to compete with those two? No, thanks."

"Don't be daft. I want to dance, and there's no-one I love dancing with more than you."

His expression made her feel a little breathless, and she allowed him to lead her onto the floor.

Mark stood by the bar and watched, his eyes narrowing and his head full of suspicion.

After a while, Piers and Anastasia left the floor, laughing, and almost walked into Lily, who was waiting to intercept them. "Anastasia, this is my friend Alessandro. He's an Italian champion, and he's dying to meet you."

Alessandro smiled at her; he had long black hair tied back in a ponytail and the darkest brown eyes she had ever seen.

"*Ciao bella*," he said in a delectable voice, smooth and silky. He kissed her hand. "You dance divinely."

"Thank you, but that's nothing compared to you or Lily, though." She could not help feeling flattered by both his words and his gaze.

"Will you join me?" He indicated the dance floor and, glancing at Piers' annoyed face, he added, "If your boyfriend permits?"

Before she could deny the presumed relationship, Piers replied, "As long as you return her, that's fine." His eyes glinted with mischief.

"Of course. Come, *bella*." Alessandro's hand found her waist to guide her out onto the floor.

Lily tapped Piers on the hand and admonished him. "That was a very naughty thing to do. What are you up to?"

He grinned. "Teaching Mark a lesson. If he can't appreciate

her, he should bugger off back to Paris."

Lily eyed him speculatively. "Well, let's just hope it doesn't backfire and she spends the rest of the night dancing with him. Alessandro is very charming."

Piers simply shook his head and laughed at her.

Anastasia and Alessandro danced for a long time; his hands in places neither Mark nor Piers approved of to correct her movements. But Piers understood she had brought out the teacher in him; he had clearly recognised raw talent and was taking pleasure in guiding her.

Mark stayed at the bar, a scowl fixed to his face, annoyance and resentment building inside.

Guy was standing next to him. "Cheer up, little brother; it's supposed to be a party!"

Mark tore his gaze from Anastasia and in a brittle voice replied, "I'm fine."

"Tell your face that, then; you're starting to turn drinks sour."

Mark shrugged his words off and returned to watching the dance floor, brooding.

Eventually, Alessandro tucked Anastasia's hand into his arm and escorted her back to Piers and Lily. Anastasia was glowing, and she patted Piers' face indulgently before talking breathlessly to Lily.

"You see," Alessandro began, addressing Piers with a smile. "I have returned her. You are a very lucky man."

Knowing both Lily and Anastasia were too engrossed in comparing notes, Piers lowered his voice to reply, "Unfortunately she's not mine." There was rueful regret in his voice.

"Oh, my apologies." Alessandro looked bemused.

"No worries. You're not the first to make that mistake."

Piers walked off to the bar and found Mark sitting there, several empty glasses nearby. Mark glanced at his brother and asked, "What're you drinking? Finished watching her yet?"

"Guinness." Piers paused, then said sharply, "I was talking to Lily, actually."

Mark signalled to a bartender. "Yeah, right; course you were. Two pints of Guinness, when you're ready." Then he faced Piers to say, "If you have any real love for her, you'll let Anastasia make her own choices on how she wants to be happy."

Snapping back swiftly, Piers countered, "I would if I thought you could make her happy."

"Well, you won't know if you don't let me try." Mark took the outstretched glasses from the bartender and handed one to Piers.

"Well, tomorrow, you'll have your chance; I'm heading off. Just remember: make her unhappy and I'll be the one you'll explain it to."

He walked off before his brother realised his hands were shaking and his face gave everything away, because that was his greatest fear; that Mark would be able to make Anastasia happy, and he would lose everything.

AT THE END of the party Anastasia thanked Guy and Lily for a lovely night and promised she and Mark would come and stay with them very soon. She genuinely liked Lily; she was insightful and fun, and Anastasia appreciated the way that what Lily thought came right out of her mouth, making her unpretentious and open.

As she turned to wave goodbye, Anastasia saw Piers was waiting for her, and she paused to let Mark get into their car first.

"You were right. It was fun." She ran a hand up his arm; she knew he was leaving, and it hurt.

"I'll see you as soon as I can, I promise. Take care of yourself, sweetheart." He hesitated, then, unable to resist, he held her against him, breathing in Chanel and feeling the silk of her dark hair against his face. When he let her go, his eyes fixed on hers and he saw tears.

"You stay safe, handsome. I'll miss you." And then, before she showed how much her heart was breaking, Anastasia hurried into the waiting car.

Piers watched her drive away, and, as always, she had taken a little piece of his heart with her.

Chapter 26

7ʰ January 1990

THE TELEPHONE RANG out. Startled awake, Anastasia reached over to answer it, vaguely aware it must be around six in the morning and was unlikely to be good news. "Hello?" Her heart thumped, fear building that something had happened to Piers.

"I'm sorry to wake you, Stasia, but is Mark there?" Guy sounded distressed. "It's Dad."

She shook Mark, who was lying next to her. "Wake up, Mark." He groaned and then opened his eyes. "What?"

"Guy's on the phone. It's your dad," she said urgently.

He sat bolt upright and took the telephone.

Anastasia lay back down and listened to his side of the conversation. It seemed that Joseph Talbot had suffered another heart attack in the early hours and Guy had rushed him to the local hospital. He was now being transferred to his own doctors in London.

"Yes, I'll come straight away … no, I'm glad you told me. See you soon." Mark returned the telephone to her. "I've got to go. Dad's … Dad's …" He broke off, unable to say it because that would mean admitting the truth to himself.

"I know. Just go; don't worry about anything else." She reached up to caress his face, unsure how to offer any comfort.

Mark kissed her and then hurried to get dressed. As he left the bedroom, he said, "I don't know how long I'll be. You go ahead to The Star if I'm not back, and I'll join you if I can."

"Ok, but just concentrate on your father. Nothing else matters."

He managed a smile and then he was gone.

Anastasia lay back down and listened for the door to close. She felt his pain, just like she had when Piers had first told her that Joseph Talbot was dying, but she could not relate to it. If faced with the same information about her own father, she knew she would feel nothing. Did that make her a bad person? Probably, but at least she was honest with herself.

She tried to go back to sleep, but all she could do was worry about whether Piers had been told the news.

That evening, Anastasia walked into The Star alone and looked around, spotting Bryan and Suzanna straight away. Suzanna waved at her, using her left hand so Anastasia could not miss the sparkle on her finger. Smiling, she crossed the pub to join them.

"No Mark?" Bryan asked hopefully.

"He'll come down later. He's visiting his dad in hospital."

"Nothing serious?" Suzanna enquired kindly.

Anastasia made a non-committal face and replied in a bland tone, "A minor setback, but he really isn't a well man."

Bryan stood up. "What are you drinking, Stasia?"

"The usual, please," she replied, and she seated herself opposite her now anxious looking friend. "Show it to me properly, then. I know you're dying to."

Suzanna held out her left hand and Anastasia admired the round, brilliant cut diamond that reminded her of a flower about to bloom. "It's beautiful, darling. It really is you." She kissed her friend's cheek. "Congratulations."

Bryan passed her a scotch and sat back down, grinning as he held his fiancée's hand. Anastasia took a drink, suddenly feeling awkward but with no idea as to why. Trying to shake a feeling of envy at how happy they seemed, she asked, "And how are the arrangements coming along? Bryan said the ceremony would be soon."

Suzanna launched into a detailed recital of when and where, the dresses, the flowers, the cake and how her producer friend had already promised them a Rolls Royce. When she paused for breath, Anastasia managed to interject, "Have you got a photographer lined up?"

Suzanna exchanged glances with Bryan. "Well, we were wondering ... do you think Theo would be up for it?"

Anastasia considered for a moment; she was pretty sure he would be against the idea, not even for a friend. "I think he's in Italy around that time. Shall I ask him to recommend someone?"

Suzanna looked slightly disappointed, but she said gratefully, "Yes, please. Anyone Theo thinks is good must be."

"What's this hotel like, then?" Anastasia asked, interested, and as Suzanna answered, she could see Bryan's eyes starting to glaze over. He even seemed pleased when Mark arrived about ten minutes later.

Bryan got up and offered his hand, and Mark took it, saying, "Congratulations, you two. I hope you'll be very happy." Surprisingly, he sounded like he actually meant it.

Anastasia wondered if facing the reality that he would soon lose his father had changed his outlook, and she hoped he could now see the bigger picture. She took his hand. "How's your dad?"

"So-so. He was insisting on discharging himself, but Guy's talked him out of it for now."

"Good. Well, I hope he'll listen to his doctor and do as he's told." She made room for him next to her on the bench.

"Shall I get a round in?" Mark asked and then went to the bar with Bryan.

As soon as they had gone, Suzanna asked what was on her mind. "How's it going between you and Mark?" She remembered his mood on New Year's Eve.

"Up and down. More down than up," Anastasia replied without thinking. Seeing concern in her friend's eyes, she hastily made an excuse. "His father being so ill makes him moody."

"Really?" Suzanna did not believe her. "I thought that was his obsessive jealousy."

Anastasia did not respond.

"You've changed, Stasia. There's something different about you." Suzanna had genuine concerns.

Anastasia knew she had to shut this conversation down; she had no intention of discussing her relationships with anyone and had never been able to. "Are your nieces going to be bridesmaids?"

Knowing her friend well made Suzanna aware that there was definitely something wrong, but she was also not prepared to push. She told Anastasia how excited they were, that they were going to wear pink and what presents she was thinking of buying for them.

Mark and Bryan came back to the table and, seeing wedding plans were still being discussed, temporarily allied, they quietly went to play snooker.

THE NEXT DAY, Anastasia left for work after promising to meet Mark at the hospital. She could tell he was trying very hard not to admit anything was seriously wrong with his father, and although she could understand why and she sympathised, she did not think it was the right thing to do.

Around lunchtime, Theo Cavendish put his head around her door. "Hello, Anastasia! How's things?"

She looked up from Rick's now overflowing diary and smiled, happy to be distracted. "Same as usual. You?"

He came into her office and sat down. "I heard about Bryan and Suzanna. How long do you give it?"

"A lifetime, I hope. They've just got engaged," she replied, frowning at him.

Theo blinked. "Are you having me on?"

She shook her head. "Nope, Bryan told me himself—and I've seen the ring. Which reminds me"—she fixed her eyes to his face, which reflected shock and surprise—"they wanted you to do the photos, but I told them you'd be in Italy around the wedding date. If you want to do it, just tell them I got the dates mixed up."

Still not quite believing her, he replied, "You're probably right about Italy. And I don't like wedding commissions; not my forte. Can't stand having to be nice to people on their big day."

Anastasia did not disagree with him. "Well, can you recommend someone good? The wedding's the weekend after my birthday, so six weeks from now?"

"Six weeks?" Theo was dumbfounded before asking the obvious question. "Is she pregnant?"

Unable to stop herself, Anastasia laughed. "I wouldn't be surprised, but she hasn't said anything to me if she is. Come on, be a darling! Give me a name for her, but they have to be good."

Theo considered and then gave her a card. "Try Paula Whitelaw. She's been helping me for a while, and she is good with people. Very empathic personality."

"Unlike you." She took the card. "Thank you; I'll get this to Bryan today. He has a meeting with Rick this afternoon."

Theo showed no signs of being in a hurry. "Does Rick know?"

"Yes, Bryan called him and then Rick called me. He was blindsided by it, but he thinks it will be good for Bryan. I happen to agree."

"Gets him out of your hair, I suppose. Come out for lunch with me, Stasia; I haven't seen you in ages." Theo gave her that look she found hard to resist.

"I can't." She was tempted; she loved spending time with him.

He stood up. "Never mind. I'll see if Piers is free?" He raised his eyebrows.

"He's gone; left on Sunday. Not expected back before August, if I'm lucky." She gave him a sad little smile, then looked back down at her work.

Theo observed her thoughtfully. "Ok. Well, I'll see you soon, then. Take care." He smiled and swept from her office.

About an hour later, Bryan Darnell walked into her office, a big smile on his face on account of all the congratulations he had received on his way through the building. "Afternoon, Stasia." He smiled and sat down at her desk.

"Hi, Bryan." She picked up the card Theo had given her. "Here—before I forget, Theo's recommendation."

He took it. "Thanks, we appreciate it." Then Rick's door opened, and, giving her a wink, Bryan went into his office.

For the next three weeks, Anastasia's life followed a very regular pattern: work; practising whenever she could for her birthday performance; meeting Mark at the hospital to visit Joseph Talbot; and sleep. She had almost forgotten what it was like to go out and have fun, but she understood Mark needed her and she was glad not to endure any arguments. She was, however, extremely relieved when his father was finally allowed to go back to Guy's and hoped for a resumption of her usually active social life; she missed The Star and dancing at The Cathedral most of all.

When she got home on the Friday after a particularly trying day, Mark was looking annoyed. She sighed and wondered what she had done to upset him.

"You had a phone call. Just missed it." His manner was brusque.

"Oh, from who?" She hoped it had not been Theo; she guessed any contact from him would wind Mark up.

"Some bloke called Andrew. He wanted to know when you were going back to your class."

Andrew was her self-defence instructor. She felt guilty she had not been since just before Christmas. "Thanks for taking it. I need to call him back." She moved towards the telephone.

Mark put out a hand to stop her. "No need. I told him you wouldn't be going anymore."

She stared at him. "You did *what*?"

"And I've packed some suitable clothes for you. We're staying at Guy's for the weekend."

She continued to stare, unable to believe his audacity. Finally, she managed, "What the fuck, Mark? Who do you think you are? You cannot make decisions for me."

He grabbed hold of her and raised his voice to drown out her protests. "I am your boyfriend, and I have a right to decide how you spend your time. Now, get changed. We're going to Guy's."

She faltered under his arctic gaze and she unconsciously made excuses for him; he was tired, worried about his dad, and he needed her support. "Ok," she stammered, and she backed away from him, her hands shaking ever so slightly.

Chapter 27

LILY TALBOT WAS waiting to greet them, her smile incandescent, and she could barely wait to hug Anastasia, saying, "I'm so glad you were able to come. I've been looking forward to getting to know you better!"

Anastasia could not be cross after such a warm welcome, at least not with her hosts, and she kissed Guy on the cheek, murmuring, "How's your dad?"

Guy shrugged. "So, so. At least he's got his granddaughters to entertain him and stop him from wanting to leave."

Lily took her by the hand and led the way inside. "Come on, let me show you to your room. It's got a lovely view of the lake."

Guy noticed the glare Anastasia gave Mark over her shoulder as she went and he asked, "Have you done something to upset Stasia?"

"Her name is *Ana*stasia. I wish people would get that right," Mark replied roughly as he tried to brush past his older brother.

Guy stopped him. "I'm not Giles, Mark. I won't tolerate your moods."

Mark shrugged off his hand, but not wanting to upset him, he said contritely, "We had a few words; it was nothing. It's been a stressful few weeks."

"Well, you should be grateful you have her in your corner. From what I've seen, she's done nothing but run around after you. Let her enjoy herself whilst she's here; she's probably earnt it."

Mark did not appreciate his brother's advice and chose simply to ignore it. "Can I use your phone? Need to make a call. Anastasia's birthday present," Mark lied.

"Of course," Guy smiled, following him into the house.

Mark knew he would need to keep the call brief if he wanted to avoid any awkward questions. The last thing he needed was Guy getting arsy with him over wanting to check in with Giles.

Checking that no-one was in earshot, Mark dialled a number for Paris and waited.

"Giles Talbot speaking." His brother sounded weary.

"Hey, big brother. How're you keeping?" Mark was not sure how much to tell him.

"Not too bad. Glad I'm not flying back and forth to see Dad and avoiding Guy anymore." Giles' voice now had ice in it.

"Well, I'm at Guy's, so I can let you know how Dad's getting on. I promise to keep you updated."

"Thanks, that helps."

Mark hesitated, then asked, "When are you going to tell me why you've fallen out with him?"

"Why do you think?" Giles snapped back.

"Piers?"

"Got it in one. More lies from our esteemed brother." Giles switched subjects swiftly. "Did you ask her yet about Matthew?"

"Anastasia? No, I've not mentioned it. We're not exactly on speaking terms just now." Mark grimaced; he had not meant to admit that.

Giles remained silent, unsure if it would be simpler for their relationship to end and for him to deal with Anastasia himself or if he could still use Mark to get what he wanted.

"I'll call you on Monday, then."

"Yes, that'd be good." And without waiting for a reply, Giles put the telephone down.

Mark let Giles' behaviour wash over him; his brother had always been aloof. Deciding to try and smooth things over with Anastasia, he made his way upstairs to their room.

Anastasia looked up from unpacking the clothes he had chosen as he came in. He held out his arms, a sad look in his eyes. "I'm sorry, baby. I shouldn't have spoken to you like that before. I've been letting the stress of Dad's illness get to me."

Recognising it would make life so much easier, she stepped into his embrace, stifling the feeling of suffocation. "It's ok. I know it's tough on all of you."

"Thank you for understanding. Come on, let's go down for dinner. It smells good! And tomorrow, I'll show you around the grounds, just like you wanted the last time we were here."

She followed him because lying to herself was easier than facing the truth.

AFTER DINNER, DURING which Mark behaved impeccably, Lily took Anastasia into one of her living rooms whilst the two brothers went to check on their father. Anastasia felt a little overwhelmed by the elegance; she was used to big houses, but *this* was something else.

"Sit down, Stasia, and I'll get you a drink. What would you like?" Lily was eager to make her feel welcome.

"Scotch, please. You have a stunning home, Lily; really gorgeous."

Lily poured a drink from a bottle Anastasia did not recognise and passed her a glass, saying, "Thank you. It's been a labour of love transforming it."

Anastasia took a sip, and her eyes opened wide in appreciation. "Wow, this is *good*!"

Lily grinned at her and said mischievously, "It's Guy's favourite; the best, apparently. Enjoy!"

Anastasia took a larger drink and asked curiously, "Where did the two of you meet?"

"At a club in Acapulco, would you believe? He just swept me

off my feet! We were married six months later." Her face lit up from pleasant memories.

"How long ago was that?" Anastasia finished her first glass. She had missed her scotch; something else Mark did not approve of.

"Six years and two daughters ago." Lily laughed. "Speaking of which, I'm taking them to ballet tomorrow. You should come; it's too cute!"

Anastasia was not sure 'cute' was her thing, but she did want to meet Piers' nieces. "I would love to meet them. Joanna and Elizabeth, isn't it?"

Lily was touched she had gone to the trouble to learn their names. "Yes, Joanna for Guy's mother, and Elizabeth for his grandmother. Did Mark tell you?"

"I doubt Mark knows," she replied caustically; he had shown no interest in Guy's family whatsoever. "No, Piers mentioned it. I just about remember Joanna Talbot; she was very elegant." Anastasia had been eight when Piers had lost his mother, and she vaguely recalled a slightly aloof woman with the same black hair inherited by her sons.

"Yes, it affected them all deeply." She paused, then said, "You lost your mother so young, too, didn't you? Do you remember her?"

Noticing Anastasia's glass was empty, Lily re-filled it, this time leaving the bottle on the table in front of them.

"Thank you." Anastasia took another drink, unsure whether she wanted to reply. "Very little. I was four when she died, so I don't remember much of her." She had no intention of telling Lily about the arguments, the tears and the violence.

Sensing it was a difficult topic for Anastasia, Lily changed the subject. "How long have you known Guy and his family?" She really wanted to ask about her connection with Piers, and she re-filled both glasses generously.

Grateful not to be pushed, Anastasia replied, "Ages, since I was small. My father and Joseph are old friends."

Lily tipped more scotch into her glass, saying with a laugh,

"If I'm getting drunk, then so are you!"

Anastasia gave a rueful smile. "Lily, I can keep up with Piers. You've got no chance."

As Anastasia had mentioned his name again, Lily felt she could indulge her curiosity. "I only met Piers at Christmas, but I adore him. You and he are very close. How come?"

Now smiling happily, Anastasia replied, "We've always got along. Similar tastes and outlooks, I suppose. Most people think we're a bad influence on each other." Bryan had made that observation many times, and she was sure Mark would wholeheartedly agree.

Lily re-filled the glasses again, her head now slightly fuzzy, and, throwing caution to the wind, stated, "You love him, don't you?"

Anastasia blinked. She downed her drink in one and Lily tipped more in, waiting patiently for a response. "We're best friends. Of course I love him," she responded, twisting the truth. "I'd be lost without him." That much was true.

Lily eyed her carefully. "I think you belong together." She held Anastasia's blue eyes, seeing denial there, and then asked the question that intrigued her the most. "Have you two ever … Didn't you ever want to?"

Anastasia choked on her scotch, completely thrown by such a direct question.

Seeing her confusion, Lily took her hand. "You can tell me to back off; mind my own business. I'll understand."

"No, Lily, we've never been intimate." She paused. "But nearly, once, a long time ago."

She had never told anyone that before, and she blamed the scotch.

"What stopped you?" Lily asked, delighted her instinct at Guy's party had been right.

"Why are you asking?" Anastasia was wary.

"Because you two should be together! Surely you must see that?" Lily re-filled the glasses, the bottle emptying fast.

Anastasia looked horrified, and she resorted to dodging the

issue, which usually worked. "He rejected me. Not exactly a good indicator for belonging together." She downed her drink and re-filled it herself.

Despite her vision now being slightly blurry, Lily did not miss the telltale blush spreading across her guest's face and, for once, she made the decision not to say what was in her head. She merely commented, somewhat cryptically, "We'll see."

Desperate to divert Lily from further Piers-related questions, Anastasia asked, "Do you miss professional dancing at all?"

"Well, I still dance for pleasure and I teach children once a week in the village, but yes, the thrill of competition can never be replaced." Lily drank some more and confided, "But I do not miss the bitching from certain people one bit." She looked defiant.

"Glad to hear it, darling." Guy was standing in the doorway, looking amused, but his arrival caused consternation. Anastasia was looking particularly concerned, hoping he had not overheard much of their conversation. Guy gazed indulgently at his wife and noticed his favourite bottle of scotch was now almost empty. He raised an eyebrow but forbore to comment.

"Hello, my love." Lily tried to stand up but decided against it, her voice now slightly slurred. "I just *love* having Stasia here!"

Not affected by the alcohol at all, Anastasia smiled. "You're so lucky, Guy. A fantastic wife and such great taste in scotch," she added with a mischievous twinkle.

He picked up the bottle and emptied it into her glass. "I'm glad you approve. Although I can't say *I* approve of you getting her drunk." He was trying not to show how funny he thought this was.

"She did not!" Lily protested. "I poured my own drinks, thank you very much!"

"See, now you've made her belligerent." Laughing, Guy leant down to pick her up and said to Anastasia, "Mark's gone to bed, Stasia. You've been summoned."

"Don't forget you're coming out with me and the girls tomorrow," Lily said as Guy began to carry her away.

"I won't. And Lily—"

Guy stopped.

"I'll get you properly drunk at my birthday party, two weeks tomorrow."

"Excellent!" Lily blew her a kiss.

THE NEXT MORNING, Anastasia was up early and waiting downstairs for Lily; she was actually looking forward to the trip out, even though Mark had tried to dissuade her from going and was still in bed, sulking. She heard a clatter of feet and happy chattering advancing towards her and began to feel nervous; she had no experience with children. The kitchen door opened and two small versions of Lily, their auburn hair pulled up into buns, stood staring at her with wide open blue eyes.

"Hello. You two ballerinas must be Joanna and Elizabeth. I'm Anastasia." She smiled at them; they were adorable.

The youngest turned and hid behind her mother, but the eldest walked forward confidently and said, "Hello, I'm Jo. Mummy says your mummy was a great dancer. A *real* ballerina."

Charmed, Anastasia replied, "Yes, she was, but I'm not, so I'm hoping you two can show me how it's done."

Joanna held out her hand and led Anastasia towards the front door. "You can watch, but you're too big to join in."

Anastasia heard Lily laughing, but she agreed in a very serious tone as they left the house together, "Quite right, far too big."

When they returned, Mark and Guy were playing snooker, and the two girls ran off to tell their father what had happened in class. Anastasia turned to Lily. "Thank you, I had a great time. Your girls are just gorgeous."

"Well, we think they are, but it's nice when someone else agrees. Come on, we've just time to freshen up before I take you to lunch. There's a lovely pub in the village."

Anastasia hesitated, tempted.

"Don't worry about Mark; he doesn't own you." Lily could see the conflict in her new friend's eyes. She made her way towards the back of the house to find her husband, saying, "I'll just let them know they're in charge of the girls."

Wondering what Mark would make of being told he had to babysit his nieces, she followed Lily, catching up in time to hear, "I'm taking Stasia for lunch. You two can amuse the girls, but don't just let them have ice cream for lunch."

Guy kissed his wife and said with a smile, "My pleasure, and Uncle Mark can help." He glanced at his brother, not missing the look of fear that suddenly sparked in his icy eyes.

Mark scanned Anastasia crossly. "But I thought we were going to take a walk, spend some time together?"

Lily cut across him. "You can let her out of your sight occasionally, you know. I'll make sure she doesn't run off with the landlord." She caught hold of Anastasia's arm and gently pulled her away.

Anastasia smiled over her shoulder as they left.

Guy observed his youngest brother carefully, aware his daughters were still in the room. "If you try to control her, she'll run."

Mark glared at him. "I don't need your advice, thank you. I know her better than you, and once we're married—"

"*Married?*" Guy was shocked, unable to conceive an idea more ludicrous.

"Yes," Mark said insolently. "I'm going to marry her and take her back to Paris."

"And have you asked Stasia this?" Guy checked his daughters were busy pushing the snooker balls around the table before he added, "Do you actually love her or is this because you hate Piers?"

"My relationship has nothing to do with *bloody* Piers!" Mark erupted, storming off.

Guy smiled wryly; he had put his finger right on the point.

Throughout the next two weeks, despite the distractions of trying to keep Mark happy and balancing work, Anastasia felt the nerves beginning to take over as her party loomed ever closer. No matter how much Johnny tried to reassure her, she felt sick every time she thought about performing, and Mark did not help matters; he wanted to know why she had to spend so much time going over and over the same four songs, and why she even wanted to do it in the first place when it was making her so anxious. After one disagreement, he had even told her she would just make a fool out of herself and embarrass her father. *Embarrass* her father? That prospect did not bother her at all.

Anastasia felt miserable; she was missing her friends and her social life, and the closer her birthday got, the more she clung to Piers' promise that he would be there, but she dared not let herself believe he would. She could feel Mark chipping away at her confidence and she came close on a number of occasions to telling him it was over, but she feared the scene it would cause.

She was not yet strong enough to leave him, and the more she felt him trying to control her, the more she felt the walls closing in.

Chapter 28

THE NIGHT BEFORE her party, Fenella was waiting for Anastasia as she climbed out of Mark's Mercedes at Starbrook Manor. "Stasia, darling," she called out. "Come inside. I need to talk to you."

Anastasia glanced at Mark and shrugged at his questioning look. "No idea. I'll see you inside."

As she followed her godmother into the library, she asked, "Is there a problem, Fenella?" Anastasia was concerned; this was not her usual greeting.

Fenella hesitated; she tried so hard not to interfere, but she could remain silent no longer. "What is going on, Stasia? Why did you cancel your lunches with Eileen and me? Why have you stopped your classes? Is it *him*?"

Anastasia blinked, unsure how to answer.

"I know it's none of my business who you date, but we love you and we're worried he's changing you."

"I haven't changed," she protested. Had she? "His father's been seriously ill recently and visits backwards and forwards to the hospital were taking up much of our time. And amongst all that, I've been getting ready for tomorrow." She did not answer the third question.

"You haven't been down The Star for weeks; they haven't

seen you at The Cathedral or Retro since New Year; and you haven't even called Suzanna to see how she's getting on with the wedding, let alone returning mine or Eileen's calls. Mark Talbot is dominating your life, and it's not healthy!"

"Fenella, please, I don't want to get into it. I'm sorry I've been absent these past few weeks, but his dad is dying."

"You can pick up the phone, can't you? Rick says you've been almost silent in the office, not your usual self, and dressing like a different person." Fenella knew she could only push her so far before she would jump off at a tangent.

Anastasia moved towards the door.

"You are just like her." The words came out anguished and stopped Anastasia dead in her tracks. "Too much like your mother," Fenella continued, real pain in her heart.

Her hand on the door handle, Anastasia replied bitterly, "Rather that than like my father." She walked out, determined not to cry.

Fenella stood alone, her eyes filled with tears, as she remembered her beloved friend who had refused to see that something was wrong, that his behaviour was wrong, and for that, Natalia had paid the price.

Johnny was in the kitchen, rummaging in the fridge, when he felt Fenella's gaze on him. Johnny stood up and faced her, saying, "You want me to have a word with her, don't you? Maybe I should have words with *him*."

Distressed, Fenella had gone to look for Johnny in the hope that he could get through to Anastasia before she threw her life away on a copy of her father. "No, not him," she replied. "He'll turn the situation against us. Why does this feel like déjà vu?"

"Maybe we should stay out of it, Fenella. This is her business."

"I am not going to let history repeat itself, Johnny. She's been through enough."

Johnny knew that Fenella was referring to the attack. "Maybe she needs to see this is wrong for herself." He really did not want to get involved unless he absolutely had to; he knew

Anastasia would reject any advice he offered her because he was sure she knew the truth already. "Look"—he tried to offer a compromise—"why not ask Rick to speak to her? Maybe she'll listen to him? He never normally gets involved."

Fenella made a face. "I already have. He refused to broach the subject with her until after her performance. He's worried she'll be too stressed to go through with it."

"Well, there's your answer, then. He's right, and you know it."

Fenella nodded. "Ok, I'll leave it." Looking annoyed, she added ominously, "*For now.*"

Johnny watched her stalk away and gave a deep sigh of relief. He blamed Piers for this one. Picking up a book from the kitchen table and forgetting his food, he went off to give Anastasia what he hoped would be a pleasant surprise.

He found her sitting at the bottom of the main staircase, her head resting against the bannister, apparently deep in thought.

"You ok, *malyshka*?" he smiled as she looked up, startled.

"Are you going to lecture me, too?" she asked.

"Doesn't sound like me, does it? And Fenella is not 'lecturing' you; she just cares, that's all. We all do." He spoke sharply, not something he usually did to her.

"Sorry." She stood up. "I know you do. I love you all, too." She stepped into his arms for a hug, just as she had when she was little and scared.

"Trust your heart, *malyshka*. That's all I'm going to say." He let her go. As he pretended not to notice Anastasia dashing away a few tears, he held out the book. "Been meaning to give you this. It's ready."

Her eyes lit up as she realised what he was holding out to her, and she took it eagerly. As her eyes traced the cover, she gasped in disbelief. "Johnny …"

"You wrote it; it's your book."

She stared at him. "I never expected … I don't know what to say. Thank you so much." She burst into tears.

"I hope that's because you're happy?" Johnny asked.

Anastasia nodded, unable to speak, pride filling her heart; something she had not felt for a while.

Johnny put his arm around her. "Come on, we should fit a practice in. The stage is calling you."

Chapter 29

10ᵗʰ February 1990

"Happy birthday, baby!" Mark stood at the end of the bed holding a breakfast tray, evidently feeling pleased with himself.

Reluctantly, Anastasia opened her eyes. Seeing he had made an effort, she sat up and smiled at him. "Thank you."

"All ready for the big show tonight?" He placed the tray on her lap, unusually enthusiastic about something he had previously doubted her ability to carry off.

"Sort of." She looked at the tray and really did not feel that hungry, but she had no wish to upset his good mood. She started to eat.

Mark waited impatiently for her to finish. He had her birthday present ready, as he wanted to get in first before she saw the multitude of flowers and gifts he knew were downstairs already.

Anastasia pushed the tray away, feeling she had made an effort, but the thought of singing with a real band that night was starting to worry her again and the smell of food now made her nauseous.

Mark moved the tray out of the way and handed her a flat box wrapped in gold. "For you to wear at the party tonight."

She took the gift and ripped off the paper to reveal a black velvet box. She hesitated, knowing her reaction was hugely important, and then she opened it. Anastasia gasped and dropped the contents in surprise.

Mark smiled with satisfaction and lifted up a diamond starburst choker, an incredibly extravagant gift, and handed it to her, saying, "It will look perfect on you." He leaned forward to kiss her throat.

She tried to stay still, but since her attack she did not like anyone touching her neck or throat and she shuddered at the memory his lips stirred.

"How about I show you what you mean to me before you get up?" he whispered in her ear, taking her into his arms and kissing her hard.

Knowing that to refuse him would only cause problems for herself, Anastasia let him lay her down. She had been faking it for weeks now, so one more time was hardly a problem.

About thirty minutes later, Mark had gone back downstairs, and Anastasia was standing in the shower, asking herself why she was doing this; why she was letting him tell her what to do. The therapist her third boarding school had insisted on, just before she was expelled again, had told her she had a problem with needing constant approval due to losing her mother at such an early age and her dysfunctional relationship with her very absent father. Anastasia simply knew there was a hole in her life that needed to be filled and trying to fit Mark into that space was not working. She knew only one person would ever make her complete, just as she had always known it.

She dressed slowly, trying to get rid of thoughts that would do her no good, and then she took herself downstairs, ready to show enthusiasm for her birthday. As she got to the bottom of the stairs, the only thing Anastasia wanted was for Piers to keep his promise, and that was not something she felt he could do.

As she entered the dining room, she saw that the table was covered in presents and envelopes and there were flowers everywhere. "What the …?" she exclaimed, hardly able to believe her eyes.

Fenella hugged her. "See how popular you are? The door has

been going almost non-stop with flowers from all your admirers."

Her dig at Mark hit home, even though he did not immediately react.

Jack Travess surprised everyone and turned up about an hour before the party was due to begin bearing an enormous bouquet of flowers and holding a very tanned blonde woman by the hand. Johnny nodded at him and went to warn Anastasia he had arrived.

"Your dad's turned up," he said, eyeing her carefully as Suzanna was busy doing her make-up.

Anastasia rolled her eyes at him. "Did he bring me a present?" she asked, a wry twist to her lips. "And what else has tagged along with him?" Her voice was like ice.

"The usual, I'm afraid. He's bearing flowers and some woman on his arm."

Anastasia stood up abruptly, scattering Suzanna's brushes to the floor, but before she could say anything else, Mark walked in, accompanied by Jack Travess.

"Ah, here's my birthday girl!" Her father crossed to stand in front of her and kissed her cheek.

Anastasia felt his coldness, but she would not start the confrontation; she never liked to start them.

He glanced her up and down and said smoothly, "Looking lovely, as always! I'll see you in a bit."

Mark stared at him as he left the room, then said sarcastically, "How charming!"

Anastasia laughed. "It could have been worse. If you come back in fifteen minutes, I'll be ready and you can escort me downstairs." She blew him a kiss.

"That's her way of politely telling us both to bugger off until she's ready," Johnny told Mark. "See you in the ballroom, Stasia." They left her alone with Suzanna.

"Are you all right?" Suzanna asked anxiously, knowing the conflict now within her friend.

Anastasia considered, then replied, "Yes. In a way, I wanted him to be here, so I could show him what I'm capable of. I might even make him proud." She paused. "But, in all honesty, I wish he hadn't come."

Giving her a hug, Suzanna said, "I know, but he did. Guess he does care, in his own way."

Anastasia cut across her. "No, it's an opportunity to show the world what a devoted father he is. I know how he works even though I wish, I really wish he just loved me."

As she began to cry, Anastasia pulled away and said, "Sorry, I guess it's the nerves making me weepy." She paused and bit her lip. "That, and I'm missing something I need."

Suzanna completed her sentence and dabbed her face with a tissue. "You need Piers. Let me finish then I'll do a final touch up just before your guests arrive."

"I'm sorry, Suzanna, so sorry I've been absent. I have not been a good friend to you."

"It's ok; just make sure you are there next weekend. Don't let anything, or anyone, stop you. I'll need your cool, common sense when I freak out on Saturday!"

Anastasia smiled at her. "I will, and I know you're going to have an amazing day, I can't wait to see you as a bride."

Taking a final look at herself, Anastasia turned to Suzanna. "Well? Do I look like a rock star?"

"You look incredible; really stunning. God, I hate you sometimes!"

There was a knock at the door and, still looking critically in the mirror, Anastasia called out, "Come in."

Mark walked into the room and his eyes opened wide, but he remained silent.

"Well?" Anastasia asked, turning to face him. "Will I do?"

His eyes were glacial. Suzanna suddenly felt scared and wondered if she needed to get Bryan.

"What the hell do you think you're wearing?" he demanded, not impressed by her skin-tight leather trousers and sheer black top. "Have you any idea what you look like?" His voice was now raised and Suzanna flinched at his expression.

"Why don't you tell me?" She was in no mood for this; she was on edge about her imminent performance, let alone being subjected to another outburst.

"And you haven't even got your choker on!" He took its absence at her neckline as a personal insult.

"I didn't like how it felt. I won't be put on a lead!" she shouted back.

Suzanna managed to get to the door, and as she left, she called out, "Come on, Anastasia. You're going to be late."

Anastasia pushed past Mark, but he caught her arm and stopped her. "You're not going downstairs until you are properly dressed."

Suzanna hesitated, but then she heard heels clicking on the polished wooden floor behind her and knew that her friend must have pulled free from Mark's grip. As she hurried to find Bryan, she could hear the disagreement getting louder and more acrimonious. With a final glance behind her to check Anastasia was following, she walked straight into her fiancé.

"What the hell is all the noise about?" Bryan demanded.

"Mark and Stasia." She pulled him along behind her, knowing she needed to get to the ballroom to tell Johnny.

Bryan resisted and asked angrily, "Can I smack him?"

"Maybe later, but we need to get Johnny up here first."

Suzanna marched into the ballroom, a look of exasperation on her face, quickly followed by Bryan. Rick and Johnny were already onstage making their final checks for the performance, and both looked up as Suzanna said, "Johnny! Mark's lost it! You need to do something!"

Bryan held the doors open so they could hear the ongoing argument.

"You look like a tart!" Mark's voice was seething.

"What I wear is none of your fucking business!" Anastasia sounded upset, the argument taking its toll, and she came into the ballroom looking distressed.

Mark came after her, shouting, "Don't you turn your back

on me while I'm talking to you!" and he caught hold of her arm to stop her in her tracks.

Suzanna held up a hand to stop Bryan from rushing in; she knew he needed to stay out of this.

Johnny had heard more than enough, and he called out sharply, "Shout at her again, Talbot, and I'll flatten you."

Mark let Anastasia go, jealous anger suffused across his face, and he answered Johnny back. "Tell her she can't wear *that*! It's see-through, for Christ's sake!"

As Anastasia strode towards the stage, Johnny reached down a hand and hauled her up to stand between Rick and himself. "I suggest you leave this room and stop making a twat of yourself." Johnny held Mark's gaze; he was not impressed. "Anastasia looks just fine, and if you don't start showing some respect, we will throw you out of this house."

Suzanna glanced at Bryan, who was looking smug, and as Mark flounced away, Bryan slammed the doors shut.

Rick put an arm around his goddaughter and said soothingly, "Don't take any notice of that prick; you look great."

Suzanna knew Anastasia had been almost sick with nerves about performing that night, and Mark's words had not helped at all. "Surely you realise he only said those things because you look so good?"

Anastasia smiled at them, appreciative of their support. "Thank you, but his opinion should matter to me, shouldn't it?"

Suddenly, a deep voice called out, "Want my opinion, sweetheart? I think you look sensational."

They all looked around in surprise as Anastasia cried out, "Oh my God! Piers!" She vaulted down from the stage and flew across the dance floor to throw her arms around him.

Piers held her tightly, and he kissed her hair, relishing the feeling of having her so close to him again. "Happy Birthday, beautiful."

Anastasia clung to him, her heart racing, scarcely daring to believe he had kept his promise and hope firing in her heart.

He reluctantly let her go and gazed down into deep blue eyes that shone up at him with undisguised joy.

"Good to see you, mate," Johnny called out, causing Piers to glance up and break the spell.

"Good to be here. I need to change, though." He looked back down at her.

"Your stuff's in my wardrobe," she said. "Use my room; you know where it is."

"Be back soon." He kissed her hair again, and stopping only to pick up his bag, he left the room.

Suzanna came over to her friend and noted gladly how radiant she now was, her confidence suddenly soaring. "Let me re-touch your make-up. You've only got about ten minutes before people start to arrive."

Anastasia stood still, her heart still racing, as Suzanna completed her task, talking gently all the time, but Anastasia did not hear a single word.

Chapter 30

Piers made his way through the crush of people, exchanging greetings and trying to avoid Jack Travess. He did not want to spoil Anastasia's birthday by laying out her father, much as though she might have enjoyed seeing it. As he glanced around again, he saw Theo Cavendish waving at him and joined his friend.

"I didn't know you were coming. How did you swing that?" Theo demanded, shaking his hand.

Piers grinned at him. "I made a promise to a lady." He noticed the stage curtains were twitching and murmured in anticipation, "This should be good."

"Have you heard? There's a wedding next weekend." Theo deliberately did not say who.

Piers paled. "Who?"

Theo laughed wickedly. "Don't worry, it's not Stasia! Bryan and Suzanna." He waited for his words to sink in.

"You're joking?" Piers was shocked and relieved in equal measure.

"Nope. Next Saturday. No-one saw that coming." And then he was silent as the stage curtains swung open to reveal instruments and Anastasia standing alone, a microphone in her hand.

She glanced around and smiled as she caught Piers' eye. "Good evening, everyone." The room fell silent, and she felt a stab of panic as all eyes were on her. "I'd like to thank you all for coming, your kind birthday wishes and all the wonderful presents. Believe it or not, this is the first proper birthday party I've ever had." Anastasia paused and found Piers' face once again. "Now, many of you will also be aware that, for many years, my darling father has wanted me to sing for him without the support of a karaoke machine." She managed to keep the sarcasm out of her voice.

The crowd laughed appreciatively, and her father raised his glass in acknowledgement but did not smile.

"Well, for one night only, tonight, he is going to get his wish."

Amidst a throng of cheers, Anastasia carried on. "I'm not vain or stupid enough to attempt this alone, so I am very lucky to have two rising stars from Original joining me. Firstly, Bobby Lawson playing keyboard." She swept her hand to her left as a spotlight picked him out amid a wave of applause. Sweeping her hand to her right as another spotlight flicked on, she said, "And, on bass guitar, Julian Starling." Anastasia paused. "And I'm honoured to be joined by the King of Drummers, the legend that is Rick Lascelles!"

The crowd erupted into cheers, but she had not finished yet. "And because you can't have one without the other, on lead guitar, the God of Rock himself, Johnny Fielding!"

The crowd whooped and applauded for several minutes, astounded that Anastasia had managed to pull off such a coup for their entertainment. As the music began, they fell silent, and as she battled her nerves, Anastasia waited for her moment. Her voice rang out and Piers felt his heart soar; she had done it. The first note was always either make or break.

He smiled, pride filling his entire being, so thrilled that she had proved the doubters wrong. He watched, enraptured, and then his mind began to wander as he heard the haunting, tender lyrics of *Russian Lullaby*. His eyes slid down that sheer black shirt, down those legs clad in skin-tight leather and lingered on those shoes, sparkling red with metal, killer heels. He smiled indulgently, basking in his favourite fantasy: those legs wrapped around him; those heels digging in against the back of his thighs. He stopped and took a deep breath, banishing his inappropriate thoughts.

Forcing his focus back into the room, he suddenly realised Jack Travess was missing. He looked around and caught Fenella's eye. Looking furious, she mouthed one word: "Gone."

Piers felt his fists clench, and he breathed deeply. It was obvious why he had disappeared; she was just as good as her father had once been. Piers shook his head sadly. Anastasia deserved so much better.

Her performance was flawless, and, most importantly, she looked like she was having a blast up on that stage. When the final few notes of *Desolate Love* quivered into silence, the crowd cheered and called for an encore. Anastasia turned to face Johnny, who was glowing, and raised her eyebrows.

"Go on, kid—let them have it!" he called, and totally unexpected by her guests, the crowd were invited to join in with a Grease Megamix rendition which Johnny could not bear to deny her.

Anastasia was surrounded by friends as she left the stage, and Piers took the opportunity to speak to Johnny about something that had been worrying him for the past few weeks.

"Hey, Johnny." Piers beckoned him over.

"Did you enjoy the show? Wasn't she amazing?" Johnny was grinning from ear to ear.

Piers nodded. "It was fantastic. Stasia certainly looked like she enjoyed it." He was momentarily distracted by a fleeting image in his head. "I wanted to ask you something," he lowered his voice, "about the book."

"What?" Johnny glanced around to see who could overhear.

"It's a great read. I never knew Rick was so wild! But I can see why Jack will be pissed."

Johnny shrugged dismissively. "And?"

"Well, what's he going to say once he realises his own daughter wrote it?" Piers was genuinely concerned.

"Anything he wants to say to Anastasia, he can say to me. I'll deal with him." There was an evil gleam in Johnny's eye. "I've been waiting for the opportunity for years."

Piers lowered his voice even further. "When you do, give him a message from me." He held Johnny's eyes, malicious intent in his own. "If he upsets her in any way, if he so much as thinks of laying a finger on her, then I'll put him in hospital for a very, very long time."

And Johnny knew he meant it.

A short while later, Piers was standing at the bar. He had removed his Armani suit jacket and was feeling quite mellow after the live entertainment. As he waited to be served, he felt a hand on his back, small and cool through his shirt where her touch lingered. He made some room and Anastasia slid in front of him, standing on the rail around the bottom of the bar, as he put a hand on her waist to help her balance.

Laughing, she said, "They'll serve me quicker," and, sure enough, she immediately caught the eye of a bartender.

Across the floor, Rick and Guy were talking business. Lily was only half-listening, instead taking in the guests and trying to put names to faces. She spotted them at the bar and smiled indulgently; Anastasia was looking up adoringly at Piers over her shoulder and smiling. She watched as he leant down, speaking close to her ear, and Lily muttered, "For Christ's sake, just kiss her." But, of course, he did not and then they were moving around the bar towards the stage.

As they got there, Anastasia reached up and loosened his tie. He was gazing down at her, utterly oblivious to anything else as she removed it and placed it on the stage. Then Anastasia glanced up at the DJ, who gave her a small salute, and the music changed to blare out Rock and Roll. Lily's eyes widened as she realised they were going to jive, and she hurried forward to secure a good place to watch and enjoy. Just like at Guy's party, the other guests began to fall back and eventually they were the only two out there having a thoroughly fantastic time.

Lily smiled and waved at Fenella across the room and then looked back at the dance floor. The music had changed dramatically, having now slowed right down. "Oh, they can waltz as well," she murmured.

Lily continued to enjoy Piers and Anastasia dancing, trying to understand why they were not together, when someone disrupted her view to gain her attention.

"Hi, are you Lily Armitage, the Latin World Champion?" Theo Cavendish smiled at her, sure that he recognised this willowy woman with auburn hair.

Lily looked him over appraisingly and liked what she saw. "Yes—well, *former* World Champion. It's Lily Talbot these days."

He shook her hand. "I know, you're Piers' sister-in-law. I'm Theo Cavendish."

"The photographer! Wow! I loved your exhibition at the National last year. Just beautiful."

He was flattered by her reaction. "Thank you. Would you think it cheeky of me if I asked you to dance?" He had a charming smile and manner which Lily could not resist.

As he led her onto the dance floor, she asked, "Have you known Piers and Anastasia long?"

Theo took Lily in his arms. "I've known Stasia for years. I know Piers through her. The three of us used to go out a lot together, so yes, ages."

"I only met them around New Year, but I do adore them both." Lily glanced surreptitiously at the pair in question, still dancing beautifully and still seemingly oblivious to everyone else around them.

"Yes." Theo followed her gaze. "She is addictive." He was thoughtful for a moment and then said, "Dare we cut in?"

Lily laughed. "Do you think he'll let you?"

"Hardly, but he won't say no to you."

Still laughing, Lily replied appreciatively, "So *that's* why you asked me to dance! So you could cut in."

"No," he replied honestly. "That's just a bonus." They began to slowly dance their way over to them.

Anastasia was content in Piers' arms, resting her head on his shoulder as he held her in his powerful grip. She breathed in his aftershave, sighing unintentionally as she relished the feeling of absolute happiness. Piers leant down a little and she felt his breath on her neck. Her heart racing, she looked up and realised that he was smiling at her.

Piers felt her relaxing into his arms, and with blood pounding in his ears, he could no longer hear anything but his own heartbeat. As he smiled at her, he realised he was going to kiss her and he did not care what Mark thought or felt, but as he moved slightly, looking deep into those glorious eyes, he felt a tap on his shoulder. Swearing in his head, he looked around, the moment lost.

"You promised me a dance, Piers, and seeing you waltz so delectably …" Lily was smiling at him, totally unaware of what she had stopped.

Reluctantly, Anastasia stepped aside, cross that Piers had allowed someone to take her place, and found herself facing Theo. "Indulge me for old times' sake?" he asked.

She assented with bad grace, and as he held her close, he said mischievously, "I hope we didn't interrupt anything?"

She coloured and replied stiffly, "Just because you can be a knob doesn't mean you *should* be one."

He laughed. "When are you going to model for me?"

She pulled away from him, her desire to dance with anyone evaporating. "When you ask me properly. Come and talk to me."

Theo took her hand and guided her away from the dancing. As they moved away, neither of them noticed two brothers watching where Anastasia was going.

Once they stood a little way from the crowd so they could hear each other, Anastasia asked, "Where's Alice?"

"She's in New York at the moment, working on a project. She sends her love." Alice, his wife, worked for the British Museum, and they had been married for around eighteen months.

Anastasia grinned at him. "Marriage suits you, Theo. You've lost that annoying moody temperament."

"I'll have you know that 'moody temperament' is my professional persona," he responded, trying to look cross and failing.

"Oh? I thought your fake Cockney accent and wide-boy act was your professional persona."

He raised his hands in defeat, saying ruefully, "I have to adapt to my audience."

She looked him over and then asked, "So, tell me again about this modelling gig."

"I want to put you in my next exhibition."

"I am *not* posing nude," was her swift response.

He considered his answer. "I want you for a series of Burlesque-themed shots. I see you as my Mardi Gras Queen."

She blinked, flattered, and then replied, "I wouldn't want to be recognised."

He knew from her response she was actually considering it. "*Masked* Mardi Gras Queen. Exotic masks are commonly worn at carnivals."

Anastasia was seriously tempted; she knew Theo was well renowned in his field and that many girls would kill to work with him.

"It'll be fun. Which, let's face it, you look like you could do with."

"Why would you say that?"

"This is supposed to be your party, but the only time I have seen you smile properly all night was on that dance floor with Piers." He held her worried eyes and added, "I've known you a long time, remember? I hate to see you so unhappy."

"Please don't, Theo. Just *don't*." She felt tears pricking her eyes and a wave of unwanted panic starting to rise, and she dug her nails into her palms to keep control.

Seeing he had upset her, Theo tried to distract her. "So, how about it, then? Going to come to my Mardi Gras?"

Breathing deeply, Anastasia responded, "Ok, count me in."

His face lit up. "Thank you; it's going to be amazing, I promise." Then he added, "And one day, I will photograph you and Piers together."

That made her laugh. "I'd love to see you telling him he's got to do a photoshoot!"

"I think he would if the right person asked him." Theo held her eyes.

Anastasia considered this and replied, "It would be worth it just to see the look on his face." He had made her laugh and she was grateful. Anastasia saw Theo's eyes flick over her shoulder, and feeling a looming presence, she turned to see Mark standing behind her, glaring at them. She wondered how long he had been there and how much he had heard, and she feared another confrontation.

"I've been looking for you." His voice was tight and resentful. "I was hoping you might spare a few minutes for your boyfriend."

Theo vainly tried to hide his annoyance. Who the hell did he think he was talking to?

Without the energy for another argument, Anastasia did not answer him.

Resenting being ignored, he pushed her aside to stand before Theo. "And you can forget taking any pictures of my girl. *Ever.*" Mark took hold of Anastasia by the arm and dragged her away.

Theo stood alone and contemplated what he had just seen. Shaking his head, he turned and walked straight into Piers. Looking up to apologise, his voice was suspended by the livid blue eyes he saw.

"Sorry, Theo," Piers said. "You ok?" But his gaze was focused elsewhere.

"Yes, just chatting to Stasia," Theo replied warily, not sure if this politeness worried him more.

"Did you talk her into posing for you yet?" Piers was still looking over Theo's shoulder into the distance.

"Well, I thought I had, but then your bloody brother decided to spoil things. I'll ring her tomorrow; see if I can change her mind back."

"My brother has a habit of spoiling things," was Piers' response. Finally, he looked at Theo and said, "I wish she knew her own mind," before he walked off, lost deep in thought.

Chapter 31

BRYAN STOOD NEAR the doors leading into the ballroom and watched Piers unobtrusively. He knew what he was looking at; Mark and Anastasia were having words. Bryan walked over to him and said, "You're showing admirable restraint, Talbot."

Piers looked around, frowning. "It's her life. I can't interfere."

"Come off it, mate. If that was me, you'd be straight in there."

Piers shrugged. "It has to be Stasia's choice."

"He objected to her outfit earlier. What's his problem now?"

"Theo Cavendish." Piers could see Anastasia was looking troubled and every fibre of his being told him to march over and flatten his brother.

"Theo's just a flirt. If anyone can deal with him, Stasia can." Bryan could not deny he hoped Mark was riding for a fall. "What if he makes her cry at her own party?"

Piers looked around at him, his eyes filled with restrained anger. "*Then* I'll interfere."

"No need." Bryan pointed to the pair in question, and they watched for a short while as Johnny Fielding led Anastasia away from Mark onto the dance floor, where she was soon laughing again.

Piers smiled, relieved. "Looks like I have time for a drink. Care to join me? I'll have to be going soon." Piers started to walk towards the bar.

"Going?" Bryan questioned him. "Are you telling me you flew halfway across the world for a few hours?"

"How do you know where I've come from?"

"The driver said he'd met a flight from Asia."

Piers was annoyed. "Of course I'm here. I promised."

Bryan stared at him; he had always had his suspicions, but voicing them was a step too far. "Is it a scotch?" he asked as they stood together at the bar.

Piers nodded.

"What did Theo want? The usual?" Bryan waited to be served.

"I don't see the problem, if I'm honest. He only wants her to model for him, and he does loads of stuff for Original, doesn't he?"

Bryan agreed and grinned at him. "He is famous for his nudes, though."

"Theo doesn't want her to do that." Piers paused and took a swig of his drink. "Does he?" He raised his eyebrows.

Laughing, Bryan responded, "No, his next project is Burlesque." His eyes full of mischief, he watched in amusement as Piers' face coloured.

Piers finished his drink. "I think I need another one." A very intriguing image was now fixed in his mind. In the spirit of reconciliation, he said sheepishly, "Did I ever apologise for what I did to you back then?"

Feeling tranquil, Bryan replied, "No, but I did instigate it."

"That's no excuse; I could have walked away. I'm sorry." He held out his hand.

Taking it, Bryan commented wryly, "I was a bit thick, though. Not only did I poke the tiger, but I actually got in the bloody cage with it." He smiled, seeing more than Piers liked.

"Are you really going to marry Suzanna?" Piers was intrigued and a little sceptical of the match.

Bryan grinned. "Yep, sure am."

"Well, I wish you well. I'd love to be there, but, you know …"

"Thanks, I understand."

They both watched Anastasia again, now dancing with Lily and some other friends, and Piers glanced at his brother, sulking yet again. "I just want her to be sure. To be over the past." He was talking to himself.

"Better she realise now what he is than if she marries him," Bryan commented.

"Marries him?" Piers looked astonished.

"Stranger things have happened; look at me. This time next week, I'll be a married man. Scary thought, isn't it!"

"Yes," Piers agreed, thinking fast. Making a possibly rash decision, he pulled a business card from his pocket. "Do me a favour, Bryan?" He fixed his eyes on his newfound ally's face.

"Sure." Bryan took the card he was holding out to him.

"If anything happens you think I need to know about, call that number and leave a message. It'll find me."

Bryan was surprised and deeply curious. "Need to know?" His gaze fell on Anastasia.

Seeing he had grasped the point, Piers said, "Exactly." Then he strolled away, he needed to say good-bye to a friend.

Eventually locating Anastasia amongst a loud group, Piers leaned in close to her ear. "Meet me in the library in five minutes. I need to talk to you," he said, and he vanished back into the crowd.

Anastasia knew what was coming; he was leaving. She made her way through her guests smiling falsely as tears pricked her eyes.

He was waiting for her, leaning against the leather settee. "Hello, sweetheart."

"Hello, handsome." Anastasia closed the door and stood before him.

He noticed her nails starting to dig into her palms. "Hey, what's wrong?" He took her hands to stop her.

Anastasia wanted to tell him so much, wanted to spill her heart out to him, but she knew now was not the time; work came first, and she would never make him choose. She swallowed, struggling to keep back the tears, and managed, "I don't want you to go."

"I've got to go back. You know that."

She nodded. "I know; I'm sorry. I hate you going, but I'm so grateful you came tonight." Her eyes radiated anguish. "How long will you be gone?"

"Six months." His grip on her hands tightened as he heard her gasp. "It'll go by fast and I'll be back before you know it." There was a bitter smile on his face.

She pulled away. "You're breaking my heart. I'll miss you."

Piers knew he had to stay strong; he had to go. "My car's due any minute."

She was back before him. "Take care of yourself." She clutched his jacket.

He nodded, smiling down at her. "And you don't do anything rash."

Anastasia flung her arms around him, and knowing he had to go or he would stay forever, Piers gently removed himself from her hold and kissed her cheek. "Be good, sweetheart," he whispered, and he was gone.

Anastasia sat down on the settee facing the fireplace, feeling numb. She had come as close to the truth as she dared and there was no response; just that of a good friend saying goodbye. She felt bereft, her hopes stoked by his arrival now dashed. How long she stayed there, she did not know, and she did not care if people wondered where she had gone, but when Fenella came into the library looking for her, she felt guilty.

"Stasia? Are you all right?" Fenella sat next to her, concerned. Anastasia burst into tears, unable to speak, and sobbed in Fenella's arms. Remembering the little girl who had cried so often, she stroked her hair. "Is this because he's gone?" she asked Anastasia.

Between sobs, Anastasia said, "I wanted him to stay."

"Shall I get Mark?" Fenella said, against her better judgement.

"No, I don't want another argument. I'm tired of arguments; I just want to have fun." Anastasia rested her head against Fenella. "Is that so wrong?"

"No, darling; life should be fun. Why are you still trying to make this work?" She wanted to understand the hold Mark seemed to have over her goddaughter.

"Because … because … oh, God, I don't know anymore. It just isn't worth it."

"It's your life, your choice, and we will support you. You know how much Rick and I love you."

Fenella's words made her cry even more. "You two, and Johnny … and … and …" She could not say it.

"And Piers."

"You all mean the world to me. But I wish …" She broke off, real pain in her eyes as she admitted, finally, "All I want is for my father to love me. All these years, all I wanted was for him to care, but I didn't even mean enough to him for him to stay for the party." She sounded like her heart had broken.

Fenella held her, soothing her. "I'm so sorry, darling. I truly am."

There was a knock on the door and Anastasia pulled away from her godmother's comforting hold, worried it was Mark.

"Stay there." Fenella rose to answer the door. It was Johnny Fielding, and Anastasia breathed again.

"You found her, then." Johnny went quiet, taking in Anastasia's tear-stained face. He held Fenella's gaze for a moment. "I'll leave you to it." He shut the door.

Johnny stood for a minute, wondering if Mark had shouted at her again. Like Fenella, he was against the relationship, but he thought he understood why Anastasia persisted with it. Johnny had not spent the last eighteen months working with Anastasia on his book without realising where her head was; how it overruled her frightened heart. As far as he was concerned, Piers and Anastasia were made for each other, not her and Mark, but something in the shadows was keeping them apart. What that was, he had no clue, and he briefly considered having a serious word with Piers in an attempt to force his hand, but he was sure Anastasia would not thank him for it.

Needing a smoke, Johnny made his way to the front doors. When he got outside, he saw Piers looking at his watch, obviously annoyed. Johnny offered him a cigarette, which he refused, and asked, "What are you doing out here?"

"My car's late. I'm heading back to work." He ran his hand through his black hair.

Suddenly seeing a glimmer of light, Johnny asked casually, "Does Anastasia know you're off?"

Piers nodded. "I'll be gone for quite a while. You'll look out for her? Make sure no-one upsets her?" There was an edge to his voice.

"If you mean your brother, then yes. If I hear him shout at her again, I'll smack him myself."

Piers frowned. "He's shouted at her?"

Johnny nodded. "Obviously not in your hearing."

Piers held his eyes, wanting to say something, so close to confessing the truth, but his car pulled up before the words could form. He decided Anastasia had to make up her own mind about what she really wanted, even though he was scared of what her decision might be.

"See you around, Johnny."

MARK TRIED TO get past Fenella, but short of physically pushing her out of the way, he could not. Anastasia called out, sounding resigned. "Let him in, please. I need to talk to him."

Fenella moved very slightly, and as Mark brushed past her, she warned him, "Show some respect or you'll answer to me."

Mark frowned but did not reply.

Glaring at him, Fenella slammed the door behind her.

Mark sat down next to Anastasia, wondering why she looked so pale and her eyes were so red and instinctively realised she was going to finish it. Panicking, he took her hands and spoke rapidly. "Baby, please forgive me. I'm so sorry. I love you so much."

She took her hands away. "How can you say you love me when you keep treating me this way? You've shouted at me for the last time, Mark. I think we need to end this."

"*Please*." He was desperate. "Please give me one more chance. I've loved you for so long. Don't throw what we have away."

Every instinct told her to be strong, to say it was over, but she faltered, the pleading in his eyes making her hesitate.

"I swear to stop with the jealousy. To stop trying to change you."

She did not believe him. "Can you do that? Can you just accept me as I am? Accept my life as it is?"

He took her hands again. "I'll do whatever it takes to keep you in my life, Anastasia."

She needed to be honest with him. With recent history repeating itself, she said, "I don't love you."

His eyes widened; he had never even considered that as a possibility. What he and Anastasia had was special, solid. He got on his knees. "Give me one last chance. Please, I'm begging you! I'll make you love me again."

His last words were telling. Anastasia smiled sadly at him. "You cannot make me love you. I need some time to think."

"Take some time. I'll go to Guy's and then we can start afresh. I'll prove I trust you. I'll change." He was desperate now; he could not bear the thought of having wasted all this time on an unattainable dream. He could not bear the thought that Piers had won again.

And in that moment, her resolve crumbled. Needing someone to love her, she gave in. "Last chance."

He stood up, looking thankful.

"Give me some space for a few days, sleep in a guest room tonight, and then we'll try, one last time."

Unable to stop himself, Mark pulled her to her feet and flung his arms around her, kissing her hair. "Thank you. I promise I'll make this work. I promise."

She stayed passive in his arms, feeling utterly confused but convinced Mark was incapable of keeping his word.

Fenella waited until she saw Mark leaving the library, heading straight for the main staircase and looking pensive. She stepped in through the open door and asked, "Did you end it?"

"I said one last chance."

Fenella moved into the light. "Oh, Anastasia! Why?" Fenella

sat down beside her, her disappointment obvious.

Anastasia had a haunted look in her eyes. "He loves me."

Fenella dropped her head into her hands and sighed. "Promise me this is his last chance? Whatever he says, no matter how much he begs you the next time, you will not give him any more of you."

Fenella remembered the exact same conversation she had had with Natalia, and it made her feel sick.

Anastasia kissed Fenella on the cheek, avoiding her worried eyes, and walked slowly to her room. As she entered she found herself looking at a flat black box tied up with silver ribbon lying on her bed. Intrigued, Anastasia pulled on the ribbon, which undid smoothly, and lifted off the lid. A mountain of lilac tissue paper hid the contents, and a silver card rested on top. She extracted it and read it aloud. "Happy Birthday, sweetheart. Love always, Piers."

With her heart now pounding, Anastasia pulled aside the tissue wrapping to reveal something the colour of amethyst glinting with silver and she gasped as she shook out a long robe of silk worked over with silver embroidered lotus flowers.

"Oh, it's gorgeous!" she exclaimed. With care, Anastasia slid into the silken embrace; it fitted perfectly and was even the right length for her. "*Wow*," she murmured, admiring herself in the mirror.

She removed more of the tissue wrapping and lifted out a short nightdress with a fitted top. In the dim light, Anastasia blushed profusely, but she was absolutely delighted with her gifts, admiring their beautiful workmanship.

With a coquettish smile on her face but sorrow in her eyes, Anastasia commented to the empty room, "My favourite present of all, and I didn't even get a chance to thank you."

Chapter 32

11ᵗʰ February 1990

ANASTASIA WOKE THE next morning feeling exhausted and with an appalling headache. She knew she would receive no sympathy as everyone would assume it was a hangover, but alcohol was not responsible for her poor night's sleep; she had been awake all night, turning things over in her mind. She got out of bed and stood in the shower—the place she seemed to think most clearly of late—and considered what to do next. She knew—she had always known—that Mark could never be Piers, but with Piers closed off from her, his words on Christmas Eve still burning in her heart, she still needed to be loved.

After dressing and taking some painkillers, Anastasia hurried downstairs. She did not want any breakfast, but she did want to catch Mark, to try to establish some rules before he left. In luck, she found him just pulling on his coat and waiting with Guy for Lily to be ready. He looked up as he heard footsteps approaching and gave her a wistful smile. Anastasia felt guilty, he had a knack of doing that to her, even if he was in the wrong.

She greeted Guy and then said, "Can I have a minute please, Mark?"

He looked hopeful. "Of course." He followed her a short distance from the others.

Anastasia faced him, now unsure of what she wanted to say as his grey eyes held hers expectantly. "While we're apart, I want you to think very carefully if this relationship is what you want. I want you to be sure that you love me for me." She held up a hand to stop him, knowing he wanted to interrupt. "Please just think it through. It isn't me that needs to change, Mark. You have to stop with the jealousy, with telling me what I can and can't do and what to wear. If you can honestly do that, then be at Belgravia by three on Friday afternoon, and we can travel to Suzanna's wedding together."

"I don't need to think, Anastasia. I love you." He took her hands and held them tightly.

She pulled her hands away; she would not be deflected and she hoped he would miraculously see he could not comply. She was a coward for wishing it. "Just promise me you'll think it through?"

Seeing she was in earnest, he sighed. "Ok, I promise." He leant down to kiss her, but Anastasia moved her head and he only got her cheek.

"Bye," Anastasia spoke quietly.

"I'll see you soon." Mark walked slowly back to join Guy.

Fenella and Lily had witnessed the scene and glanced at each other. Fenella looked a little grim. "Do you want some breakfast, Anastasia?" she called out.

"No thanks, I'm not hungry."

Lily walked over to her, saying, "Take care, Stasia."

"You, too," Anastasia replied.

"Come and stay with us again soon. I'll miss you."

Hearing his wife, Guy added, "Yes, please do come and visit. We love having you."

Mark gave her one lingering look, and they were gone.

Fenella put an arm around her goddaughter. "Why don't you come home with us for a few days? We could go riding. Bond would love to see you."

Anastasia looked up gratefully. "Thank you, I'd really like that."

"Well, your father's off on another trip." Fenella tried to keep the disapproval out of her voice and failed.

"South Sea Islands, Johnny said. That's Tahiti, isn't it?" Anastasia was completely unconcerned; in fact, if she was honest, she could not care less where her father went. A part of her would never forgive him for walking out halfway through her performance last night.

"Go and pack, then, and we'll leave as soon as Rick is ready," Fenella advised her, hoping that she would get a chance to finally talk some sense into her.

Knowing her godmother too well, Anastasia simply smiled and went back upstairs.

A COUPLE OF days later, Theo tried calling Anastasia in Belgravia and got no response. When he tried her at Original, an irritatingly unhelpful woman told him Miss Travess was not available. He called Starbrook Manor to no avail and, now annoyed, finally tracked her down at Rick and Fenella's.

"Hey, Theo." She sounded relaxed, happy, and his annoyance melted away.

"Hey, angel. I've been trying to get hold of you."

"Oh, is something the matter?"

"No. Just wanted to make sure you're still up for my burlesque shoot? If so, I'll need you to fly up to Edinburgh on Sunday."

He was met with stunned silence. "Sunday? Are you kidding?" She sounded thrilled.

"Want me to book you a flight? We're staying at the Balmoral Hotel."

There was a heartbeat of absolute quiet before she exploded. "Oh God! The wedding!"

"That's Saturday." Theo was dismissive. "Just pack ready and then have your driver swing by Belgravia on the way to the airport."

"Yes, that's a great idea. What time's the flight?"

Theo told her all the details, adding, "And Alice says she can't wait to get drunk with you again. Which I think means she misses you." He heard Anastasia laugh. "I'll ring you on Friday with more details. See you soon." He hung up.

Anastasia turned to face Fenella, who was walking to the kitchen. "I'm going to Scotland!" she said excitedly.

"Have you got a decent winter coat?" Fenella was always practical.

Anastasia nodded, seemingly dancing on the spot.

"And Rick? You'll need some more time off."

Anastasia's face fell and she stopped jigging around, but then she brightened. "I'll work the weekend I come back to make up for it." She hugged her godmother impulsively. "I'm so excited!" She dashed off to tell Rick and Johnny.

Fenella watched her go with indulgence; this was how she should be, happy and enjoying life. She sighed; she always saw her dearest friend in her goddaughter's eyes and never more so than when they shone with joy.

Chapter 33

16ᵗʰ February 1990

ANASTASIA HAD ONLY been home from Rick and Fenella's for a couple of hours when she heard a car door slam shut and she looked anxiously at the clock; it was a quarter to three. It was probably him. She stood up and moved to the window to peer out as a taxi pulled away to find that she was right; there was Mark, carrying a sports bag and a suit carrier and struggling slightly up the stairs. She waited and let him knock.

Anastasia opened the door and smiled ruefully. "Made your decision, then."

Mark followed her back into the house, frowning slightly; this was not the welcome he had hoped for, but he would not be deterred. Piers was gone; this was his chance. He put down his luggage and turned her to face him. "I've thought it through, just like you asked." He paused, scanning her face; she looked apprehensive. "There's no question over what I want; I want you. If that means taking things very slowly, starting again, then that's what we'll do."

She gazed at him thoughtfully; that was more consideration than she had expected, and it would make what she had to tell him easier. "Thank you." She smiled. "The rooms at the hotel are booked, so I'll just get my things. My driver will be here any minute." She waited for him to realise what she had said.

"Rooms?" Displeasure flickered across his face.

"Yes, we've got separate rooms. Starting again is a good idea." She moved to collect her dresses and bags. She heard the horn of her car and told him, "You can get in. I'll lock up."

Scowling but accepting he had no choice if he really wanted this chance, Mark hauled his luggage back down the stairs and loaded it into the boot. A few seconds later, Anastasia followed him, carefully balancing two outfits in carriers. He took them from her, commenting, "Two?"

She grinned. "One really expensive one for the ceremony and then something I can have fun in for the party. Made perfect sense to me." She smiled at her driver and slid across the back seat.

Mark shrugged and got in next to her.

The journey to Suzanna and Bryan's wedding venue felt unnaturally calm and polite, but Anastasia knew this was the perfect opportunity to tell Mark about Theo and Edinburgh.

"Done anything exciting since your birthday?" Mark asked, determined to show her he cared; that what she did mattered to him.

"Yes," Anastasia smiled broadly. "Yes, very exciting!"

"Oh, really?" He returned her smile and hesitantly took her hand.

"I'm going to model for Theo." She broke off as his grip tightened suddenly. "Mark, you're hurting me!"

He let go, jealousy rising.

Anastasia was silent for a moment, holding his stare, then, determined, she carried on. "It gets better. The shoot's taking place in a partially restored art deco theatre in Edinburgh. How amazing is that?" Anastasia could not hide her joy.

Mark spoke in a brittle voice, desperately needing to control his anger. "Just the two of you?"

It was obvious he was not happy, but Anastasia laughed it off. Suddenly, she could see her way clear; she knew this was over, and she would not be told what to do by anyone anymore. "Don't be daft. There'll be Theo, his assistants, other models and Alice, his wife, will be joining us from New York. I haven't seen her in ages; I'm so looking forward to catching up."

Mark felt a disproportionate sense of relief that Theo had a wife, let alone that she would also be at the shoot. "When do you go?"

"The day after the wedding. We were so lucky to get the place to shoot in Edinburgh. I can't wait!" Her joy was palpable.

Not seeing he had already blown it, Mark took a deep breath and, with effort, managed, "That's great, baby. You'll have such a good time, but not *too* good, I hope!" He laughed.

Anastasia was not fooled; she had seen that look in his eye at the mention of Theo's name. Undeterred, she told Mark all about the old theatre Theo had secured, the many costumes she would be wearing, and how she longed for the new experience. Mark made sensible comments and managed to keep his jealousy under control, but he was only half-listening to her, planning the best way to propose. He had decided that once she returned from Scotland, once this photoshoot nonsense was out of her system, then he would tell her she was going to marry him.

Before they realised it, the car began to slow down and wind its way up a well-kept drive bordered with flowerbeds blooming with daffodils, crocus and snowdrops. Mark looked out with vague interest and then he heard Anastasia mutter in astonishment, "*Wow!*"

He leaned over her to see out of her window and stared; he had not expected to be confronted with a heavily restored castle, with turrets and drawbridge included. "Bloody hell! Where are we?"

They looked at each other, unable to believe what they were seeing.

"Suzanna did say this place was stunning. Guess she wasn't wrong!" Anastasia stared, open-mouthed, as they drove over the moat and towards the main entrance.

Liveried men were waiting to open the car doors and take their luggage into the Reception area. Anastasia and Mark were both stunned into silence by the opulence as they entered the hotel and looked around; Anastasia considered it way over the top, but Mark was impressed.

"Wow, this is amazing!" he said in hushed tones. "I love it."

Anastasia stared at him. "Really?" she queried. "Don't you think it would be better off looking like a castle and not a bordello?" She moved forward to the check-in desk.

Mark was still gazing up at the lavish ceiling when she returned with two keys and tapped him on the shoulder. "Room 303 for you." She handed him his key. "They'll take our stuff up. I need a drink." Glancing around with distaste, she walked to the bar.

Mark hurried after her and caught her up. "Which room are you in?" He hoped they were at least next to each other.

"I've got a suite in one of the towers called *Venus' Boudoir* or something equally ridiculous," she said dismissively. "Scotch, please," she asked as she reached the bar and then downed it gratefully.

Bryan came into the bar with a desperate look in his eyes, then he saw Anastasia and thought he had found salvation. He dashed over to her, saying with evident relief, "Thank God you're here! I need you." He proceeded to drag her away.

"Hang on a moment," Mark spoke in a loud, angry voice. "What do you think you are doing with my girlfriend?" He reached out to stop her.

Anastasia felt trapped between the two of them and knew Mark could well blow his top. Desperate to stop any aggravation and to stop Mark showing her up, she pushed both their hands away. "What the fuck, Bryan?" She raised her eyebrows at him.

Bryan glared at Mark and then, ignoring him, began to plead with her. "Stasia, I need to practice the first dance. I promised Suzanna I knew it backwards, but I have no idea. Help me!"

She laughed. "Typical. What song is it?"

He grinned shamefacedly at her. "*Lady in Red*."

Anastasia shook her head. "Honestly?"

"Not my choice. Bride's prerogative," he explained hastily, not wanting Suzanna to know he had not been exactly honest about it.

She looked to Mark, who was still fuming. "It's ok. I can't let him disappoint Suzanna. Tomorrow is her day."

"*Our* day," Bryan corrected her. "And I can't let my new wife down. Please, Stasia?"

"Come on, then. But the choreography had better not be too ambitious or you'll never get away with it," was her caustic comment as she followed him out of the bar and into the ballroom.

About an hour later, Mark looked up from his drink as he heard Anastasia laughing as she returned to the bar, obviously taking the mickey out of Bryan and his attempts at dancing.

"You'll get away with it if you do what I showed you. Remember to take the lead and she won't notice."

"Thanks, Stasia. You've been a godsend." He kissed her cheek.

She laughed at him again and walked over to join Mark, noticing he had been drinking steadily since she left him. "I think he'll manage," she smiled at him, taking the proffered glass. "Thanks. I'm hungry; has anyone mentioned dinner to you?"

"Why don't we have room service in your suite?" He took her hand and then stroked her arm.

She shook her head. "We can't. We're all supposed to be having dinner together." To her relief, she saw the doors open and another extravagantly liveried man announced that their tables were ready.

Mark downed his pint and reluctantly followed her.

The meal was excellent, and the wine flowed freely. Anastasia was feeling very happy and was looking forward to seeing her best friend getting married the next day, even if it was to her ex. Mark had been bored, but he had behaved impeccably and had been quite charming to the people near him, determined to show Anastasia he had changed.

As they left the dining room together, Mark holding her hand and hoping he might be invited to spend the night with her, Suzanna approached Anastasia.

"Stasia, feel like a drink with me in my room?" she asked.

Anastasia let go of Mark and said, "Do I get a preview of the dress?"

Suzanna laughed and blushed. "Of course. Come on, I've ordered champagne."

Anastasia turned to Mark. "I'll see you in the morning. Sleep well."

Suzanna challenged Anastasia almost as soon as they got to her impressive bridal suite.

"I wish you'd just tell me why you're with him. I really don't understand what you see in him."

Waiting for her friend to open the champagne and to finish pouring, Anastasia thought about what she wanted to say; there was so much going on in her head, but there was now light at the end of a very long tunnel.

"Well?" Suzanna prompted her.

Anastasia sipped her champagne. "I was going to end it last weekend."

"But?" Suzanna was pretty sure she knew what had happened.

Anastasia avoided her eyes. "He begged me for one last chance."

"But why did you give it to him, Stasia? Do you know?"

"Yes, I know." Anastasia sighed. "Piers doesn't want me the way I want him, and I think I've finally accepted my father truly doesn't give a fuck about me. It hurts, but there it is."

Suzanna smiled softly. "And where does Mark fit into that?"

"I needed to know I was loved. It was selfish of me, but I know now it has to end." She saw a flicker of apprehension in Suzanna's green eyes and added, "Don't worry, I won't do it here. I won't risk a scene at your wedding."

"Good. I'd like all eyes to be on me, not you having a lover's tiff," she said jokingly. "But what *do* you want from Piers?" It was a question that Suzanna had thought about often over the years.

Anastasia hesitated and then said, "*Everything*." She topped up her glass. "But all he's prepared to give is friendship."

"Are you sure that's all he's prepared to give?" Suzanna was convinced otherwise.

"Yes, I overheard him talking with his dad on Christmas Eve. And the way he said goodbye at my party … please, just leave it." She knew she would have to talk to him eventually, but she was not sure she had the courage yet to face losing him altogether. She put her glass down and, in an attempt to distract herself, asked brightly, "Where is this magnificent dress, then?"

Knowing Anastasia's confidences were at an end, Suzanna showed her, deep down craving her approval.

"It's gorgeous!" Anastasia exclaimed as Suzanna revealed her gown, genuinely impressed by its deceptive simplicity. She could see just how intricate the design really was, and she was thrilled for her friend. "I can't wait to see you in it tomorrow. You'll be the most beautiful bride." She felt tears in her eyes, overjoyed and yet somehow still deeply envious.

Suzanna embraced her, and both girls cried together. After a few moments, Anastasia wiped her eyes and demanded, "Why are *you* crying?"

Suzanna laughed. "Because I can't believe this is real. I'm so happy!" Then she surprised Anastasia with, "And did you manage to teach Bryan the dance?"

"Just about. Who blabbed?"

"No-one. I know him." Suzanna beamed at her. "I really do."

Anastasia gazed into those erudite green eyes and saw the truth. "Yes, you do. And you'll be happy to know I saw the way he feels about you in his eyes, too."

Tears of joy flowing, they embraced once more.

Chapter 34

17ᵗʰ February 1990

ANASTASIA WOKE EARLY the next morning. She wanted to keep her promise to drop in on Suzanna as she was getting dressed in case her nerves were getting too much. She did not know what to expect and she was sure that if Suzanna started crying, she would end up joining her.

Once she was clad in an ice blue wraparound dress and silver heels, Anastasia decided to check in with her friend. She knocked on the door to the Bridal Suite and waited, hearing lots of voices clashing and then children laughing and shouting. She did not want to go in.

The door was opened by Suzanna's older sister Jane, who looked harassed and had half her hair up in curlers and half hanging down. She also had a sobbing three-year-old bridesmaid clinging to her leg.

"Oh, Stasia, come in. Join the madhouse!" Distracted by her other daughter now pulling her sister's hair out of its French plait, Jane disappeared within.

Anastasia looked around her; the room was in utter chaos. She stepped over two bridesmaids who were fighting over who was going to hold whose hand and saw Jane telling her daughters off. She shuddered and went into the bedroom where, thankfully, the atmosphere was relatively peaceful.

"Anastasia!" Suzanna called out, sipping Bucks Fizz whilst having her long golden hair piled up into an elaborate bun. She offered her friend a glass.

"Already?" Anastasia queried, but she took it gratefully.

"Who's winning World War Three out there?"

"How many of the little hooligans have you got?" Anastasia knew that if she ever got married, there was no way she would tolerate so many children being involved.

Suzanna laughed. "Eight; my two nieces and six others belonging to various cousins. Alcohol helps." The hairdresser stood back and admired her work. Anastasia thought Suzanna was already looking gorgeous without her make-up, but once she put her dress on, she would be nothing short of stunning.

Being an expert, it did not take Suzanna long to apply the make-up she had decided on and then her sister shut the door on the children to enable her and Anastasia to help the bride into her gown.

Once Suzanna was dressed, they stood back to admire her and Anastasia could feel herself choking up, wishing she could be so happy and reminding her she was right; she had to end things with Mark. There was no point, and she was not being fair to either of them.

Slowly, Suzanna turned around so she could see herself in the mirror, and she gave a little gasp. "Well, I look better than I thought!"

"Amazing," her sister said, wiping her eyes.

Anastasia took Suzanna's hand and squeezed it and then managed, "You look incredible. I'll see you down there."

And she hurried away to finish getting ready, her heart conflicted by sorrow and joy.

Mark was waiting for her as Anastasia left her room for the second time, looking very smart in his dark grey suit. "You look sensational, baby," he said, leaning in to kiss her as she straightened his tie for him before hesitating and kissing her cheek instead. Taking her hand, he led her to the ceremony.

Listening to the string quartet as they waited, Anastasia considered how to end things with Mark. Whether Piers stayed in her life or not, their relationship was over. She glanced at Mark's profile; he had that glazed look she saw so often when he was bored, and as he turned his head to look at her, she suddenly saw a spectre of Giles in his eyes and her hand went automatically to her throat. She had never noticed that previously.

Afraid he would notice the fear in her eyes, Anastasia looked to the front, and as the bridal music began they all stood up, waiting expectantly. Anastasia caught Bryan's eye; he looked terrified, and she gave him an encouraging smile. Suzanna took her time walking to her groom, and when she was almost there, one of the bridesmaids cried out, protesting, "Melanie smells like poo!" Her voice echoed and Anastasia bit her lip, vainly trying to stop laughing. She could feel Mark shaking next to her as he, too, struggled with his laughter. Then she could see the people in front of her doing the same thing, and she knew if one person cracked, there would be uproar.

Suzanna carried on, serenely indifferent, and faced her future.

Once the ceremony was over, the guests were ushered outside for photographs and then eventually allowed into the pseudo Great Hall, complete with elaborate honeycombed ceiling, for the meal. Mark was drinking quite heavily, but Anastasia did not challenge him; she knew he was bored and trying not to show it and she had no wish to provoke him. If she was honest, she could not blame him; the amount of time it took the food to arrive was excessive, which Anastasia supposed was the penalty for having over three hundred guests.

The second round of photographs, however, pushed Mark's tolerance to the limit, and he took himself off to his room for a nap. Anastasia declined the offer to join him and stayed talking to people she knew until it was time to get ready for the party, determined not to give anyone a reason to whisper about her being the groom's very recent ex.

"Stasia!" Bryan came over to her, smiling broadly. She had never seen him look happier.

"Congratulations! I'll never forget that ceremony." Her lips twitched as she remembered the ad hoc bridesmaid's comment, and she kissed him.

He grinned. "Yeah, the little bugger! Still, least they won't be at the evening do." He glanced at his watch. "Which I need to get changed for." He dropped his voice. "I'm singing an original. Big surprise."

"That's so sweet!" She rested her hand on his arm momentarily. "You two look so happy together, Bryan. You've actually made me feel quite jealous."

"Well, he'll be home eventually," was Bryan's sly comment as he left her to contemplate his words in silence.

Anastasia had a huge amount of fun at the party. She had changed into a flirty halterneck dress reminiscent of the 1950s and spent several hours dancing with friends, colleagues and even people she had never met. Mark spent the night drinking, and she was astonished when she watched him seemingly chatting up one of the girls from Original; it did not bother her, but it did make her wonder.

Knowing she needed to go to bed soon as she was leaving for Edinburgh very early the next day, she approached him.

"Mark." She smiled at him. This was obviously not the time nor the place to tell him they were over; that would have to wait until she came back from the shoot. Only a few more days, she reasoned, and then they would both be free.

"Hello, baby. Having fun?" His words were slightly slurred, but he seemed in a good mood. Perhaps attention from another woman was what he needed; he certainly was not getting any from her.

"Yes, but I'm going to bed now. I need to be up at 5am to leave for my flight."

His eyes sparked, but he said nothing. When she came back, when she was over this particular quirk, then he would tell her about their wedding. Despite the picturesque setting, he had seen enough today to know this was not the style he wanted.

"Are you going to bed soon?" she tentatively asked, not wanting to tell him he was going to regret all the alcohol in the morning.

"Maybe." His eyes slid to the girl he had been talking to earlier and a lewd smile flickered across his face.

Anastasia was astonished; she had never seen him behave like this, and she considered if he was trying to make her jealous. She was not. In fact, she almost willed him to sleep with her. Infidelity on his part would strengthen her case for ending things between them.

"Well, whatever you decide, a car is coming for you at eleven, so don't oversleep. I'll see you in a few days and then we have to talk."

He returned his gaze to Anastasia and suddenly grabbed her, pulling her against him and kissing her hard. "Do behave with Theo. I don't want to be cross with you." He held her tightly and kissed her once more.

She pulled away, feeling uncomfortable, and again saw Giles in his eyes. Her hand went automatically to her throat and she stammered, "I'll see you soon."

As she hurried away, she knew it would take the courage she had to tell him the truth when she came back.

Chapter 35

ANASTASIA SAT IN the chair, trying to stay still, whilst the make-up artist fussed around her. This was their third day in Edinburgh, and after her nerves at the first shoot, she loved the whole experience.

Be that as it may, Anastasia had got into trouble with Theo the night before for defying his strict curfew to drink with his wife in their hotel's whiskey bar, but she had got off lightly. The other models were astonished when, instead of sending Anastasia straight home, Theo had given her a lecture about her behaviour and re-arranged his shooting schedule to accommodate the hangover he knew she would suffer. Anastasia had tried to dismiss his concerns, but Theo had been right; even at three o'clock that afternoon, she still felt rough.

"Oww," she said suddenly, as one of the stylists began to force a golden blonde wig onto her head. She had no recollection of agreeing to this, and she rightly suspected it was payback from Theo. She closed her eyes, making a mental note to stay away from certain whiskeys, and listened to Theo as he worked in the next room. Anastasia felt her eyes closing and decided to rest them for five minutes.

Suddenly, she jerked awake, hearing Theo calling out in a voice of mingled surprise and delight. "Where the hell did you come from?" She heard voices clashing, one of which had a distinctive Welsh lilt. Anastasia glanced at the clock and realised her five minutes had become half an hour.

Theo must have shut the doors again as she could no longer hear the conversation, and his assistant, Maddie, tapped her arm. "Showtime."

Anastasia stood up and gave her a look that showed just how much she was suffering.

Maddie laughed at her. "Don't worry about Theo; he'll forgive you as soon as he sees you. You look incredible." She held out a robe for Anastasia to shrug herself into to protect her costume. Maddie was right; the cerise and silver basque suited her curvaceous figure, and she had mastered walking in black platform stilettoes with ease. The black and silver spangled feathers fell from her waist to brush the floor like a closed peacock's tail, and her now blonde hair hung just like Veronica Lake's, leaving only one blue eye with its outrageously long eyelashes on view.

Maddie checked around the door. "He's got visitors. We'll have to wait until he's ready."

"Who is it?" Anastasia asked idly.

"Two very good-looking men; one dark, one fair. Come take a peek; they're lovely."

Anastasia leaned carefully around the door and gasped.

Misunderstanding, Maddie commented with satisfaction, "Told you so."

But Anastasia could not believe her eyes. What was Piers doing in Edinburgh?

Which was exactly what Theo was asking. "It's great to see you, but what the hell are you doing here?"

Piers grinned and glanced at his companion. "Matey boy here suggested I come on a forty-eight-hour liaison. He needed my charm."

His colleague coughed, and it sounded very much like "Bollocks!"

"Theo, this is Rhod." They shook hands.

Anastasia continued to listen as Piers asked about the local nightlife, the weather and Alice, and she wondered if he even knew she was there. Moving slightly, she positioned herself in the doorway, smoothing the robe down so it fell open. Piers' colleague looked over and saw her, she smiled at him and began to walk over, ignoring Maddie's hissed pleas to stop. Piers heard Rhod's sharp intake of breath and glanced over to see a stunningly sexy blonde sashaying her way towards them. He looked back to Theo and then did a double take.

"Hello, handsome. Isn't this a coincidence?" Anastasia stopped next to Theo, placed one hand on her hip and the other on Theo's shoulder and smiled. Piers gestured towards her golden hair, speechless, and she pouted, "Don't you like it?"

Seeing Piers was not going to introduce him, Rhod held out a hand and, in his musical voice, said, "I'm Rhod, and you are divine."

Anastasia looked appraisingly at him; he had liquid chocolate eyes and his smile was suggestive. "Anastasia." She took his hand.

"Jesus," he exclaimed and then addressed Piers "No wonder you've kept her under wraps!"

Forcing himself to speak, Piers managed, "Too late, Rhod. She's spoken for." He leant forward, unsure if he was allowed to kiss her and absolutely sure he dare not touch her.

"Make-up, sorry." She shrugged, and he moved away. "What's the matter, Piers? Aren't you talking to me?"

Rhod answered on his behalf. "He can't. You've obviously blown his mind."

Anastasia laughed. "Can we meet up later? Our hotel has the most amazing selection of scotch." She conveniently forgot her earlier resolve.

As pleased as he was to see his friend, Theo did not want Anastasia distracted. "Sorry lads, but we need to get on. *Someone's* already caused havoc with my schedule as it is." He glanced at Anastasia.

She put her hand up, saying contritely, "That would be me. You know how sorry I am, Theo."

"And you know I never could stay mad at you, which is probably why you did it. Let's take this off, shall we?" He helped her out of the robe.

She now had her back to Piers, and Anastasia glanced over her shoulder to ask, "See you later?"

"Yes. Of course." Piers still could not believe what he was seeing. "It's the hair; you threw me." He smiled at her, unable to prevent his eyes from flicking up and down her body, a pang of longing piercing his heart.

"We'll meet you at our hotel, probably around eight." Theo pushed them towards the door.

Rhod kept his eyes on Anastasia as he left. "Yeah, looking forward to it."

Once outside, Piers lit a cigar and, breathing deeply, enjoyed the weak winter sun on his face, trying to block the fantasies seeing Anastasia like that had just engendered.

"Bloody hell, Piers!" Rhod began. "You spend all your time talking about her, but not once did you mention she was absolutely stunning!"

"Whatever you're thinking, I suggest you don't."

Rhod held up his hands. "Definitely off limits. Besides," he grinned suddenly, unable to resist. "I don't think I could handle her."

"Can we be done in a few hours?" Piers did not want to acknowledge what she had just done to his mind and he needed to focus. Hopefully she would be fully dressed the next time he saw her, but that image would be forever lodged in his brain.

"With an evening of drinking and the company of models on offer, I'll make damn sure we're done." He slapped Piers on the back and set off up the street.

Pausing to throw the barely smoked cigar in a bin, Piers followed him.

Chapter 36

ANASTASIA HURRIED DOWN the stairs of her hotel and glanced at her watch. It was a quarter past eight, and she hoped the others already had a table. Anastasia took a deep breath and went into the bar. Looking around, she spotted them easily; it was early and the bar was only half-full, mostly her own party taking up several tables.

"Stasia!" Theo stood up and made space next to him and Alice.

Anastasia crossed to join them and greeted them both with a kiss.

"He wasn't cross with you for too long, was he?" Alice asked anxiously, trying to tie back her long black hair.

Anastasia grimaced. "No, he just read me the Riot Act and grumbled a lot."

She fixed her husband with reproachful dark eyes. "Hardly fair of you, Theo, especially after I told you last night's escapade was my idea."

Theo looked a little guilty and chose not to hear. He stood up again and waved. "Over here!" he called.

Anastasia watched Piers and Rhod approaching them. Piers was looking unusually casual in pale blue jeans and a checked shirt. She noticed he was also wearing trainers, which was not his usual footwear of choice.

Piers smiled as he reached their table and leant down to kiss Anastasia on each cheek before saying, "You look a bit different from earlier."

She held his eyes for a moment and, changing colour, said, "Thank you so much for the beautiful birthday presents. I love them."

He looked slightly uncomfortable, then, with his eyes averted, he responded, "My pleasure."

Trying to overcome the sudden awkwardness, she said, "Sit down. Are you hungry?"

He nodded. "Always." He grinned at her.

"I'll be back in a bit." She squeezed past him to go to the bar.

"Productive few days?" Piers asked Theo.

"Yes, it's been great. But are you going to tell me how you knew she was here?"

Piers held his curious gaze and confessed, "I always keep tabs on Anastasia, especially after …" He ran a hand through his black hair.

Theo did not respond; he knew something awful had happened to her years ago, but she had not chosen to confide in him about it.

"And I didn't want her disappearing anywhere with my bloody brother," Piers said as an afterthought.

Theo looked stunned. "You thought that was likely?"

Piers shrugged. "It was a risk I wasn't prepared to take."

"Finally going to make a move, then?" Theo commented shrewdly. Piers raised his eyebrows, but before he could speak, Theo seemed to read his mind. "Don't deny it. I'm not blind."

"I can't." Piers paused at Theo's sceptical look. "If I act now, Anastasia will have to go back to London and face Mark alone, and I'm not making a sacrifice of her for anything. If she told him she was leaving him for me, can you imagine his reaction?"

"Well," said Theo begrudgingly, "you might have a point."

A few minutes later, Anastasia returned, balancing several glasses of the hotel's whiskey taster selection on a tray. Rhod had taken her seat, and he reached up to take the tray from her. "Sorry," he said mischievously. "You'll have to climb over me to get in."

Anastasia gave him a withering glance and then did it.

Piers noticed and advised his friend, "Cut it out."

Rhod grinned. "Sorry, couldn't resist."

"Try these, but don't neck it," Anastasia warned Piers. "Believe me, they'll knock you for six." She chose a glass and took a long drink, commenting, "It's really good."

Piers joined her and heeded her advice. His eyes widened. "You're not wrong." He took another drink. "How was the wedding?"

"Suzanna looked gorgeous, of course. Very romantic." Her voice trailed away as she remembered the envy she had felt. "But far too many people and so much fussing about. Her sister needed a holiday afterwards."

He laughed at her. "You're such a cynic!"

"No, I'm not. If I ever get married, then I would probably only want twenty people there— and no bloody fairy castle and a herd of uncontrollable little bridesmaids. No way." She stopped, suddenly aware he was still laughing at her. "What's the matter? Would you want that?"

Piers stopped laughing; he had never considered it before, and he shook his head to reluctantly agree with her. "No, you're right." And as he held her eyes, he saw shades of that burlesque blonde from earlier that day.

A waitress was on her way over, carrying two enormous sub-sandwiches, a pile of French fries and a giant portion of onion rings.

Noting the expression on Piers' face, Anastasia said to him, "You said you were hungry."

Once the waitress had arranged the food on the table before him, Piers took a bite; it was delicious.

Anastasia looked at him with satisfaction. "I knew you'd love it. Want to try the duck?" He nodded, and she fed him a piece.

Rhod watched them with interest. Somehow, amongst all the chatter and noise at their tables, the two of them had effortlessly managed to isolate themselves. Nobody else mattered, and as an outside observer, Rhod could see that Piers was a lost cause, hopelessly enmeshed in that pair of blue eyes. He watched Anastasia carefully, obviously happy in his company, but Rhod could not be so certain she felt the same way about Piers as he knew his colleague felt about her.

The party drank steadily for over an hour before Alice wanted to move to the Old Town, find a club, and drink some more.

Rhod managed to detach Anastasia from Piers, and he tucked her arm into his to walk her down the street. "He talks about you all the time," was his opening salvo; he wanted to know if she was just good at hiding her feelings or if she was simply not into Piers.

Anastasia glanced up at him. "Does he? I've been accused of the same thing many times."

"Who by?"

"Old boyfriends and a soon-to-be ex." She gave him a glittering smile, knowing he had not expected that.

His face gave away his surprise. "But I thought …?"

"Piers did tell you I was spoken for. Mark's his youngest brother. He gets very jealous of Piers. Or any man, when it comes to me."

"Oh." Rhod was taken aback. "How come he's let you out of his sight if he's so jealous?"

"Hence the 'soon-to-be ex'." She recalled the look on Mark's face whenever she upset him, and she shivered. "And, of course, it didn't make things any easier that Theo was here."

Rhod raised his eyebrows quizzically.

"Theo and I have history. Before Alice, of course. We're just friends now, but Mark doesn't trust anyone around me." She sighed; these few days in Scotland, the fun, the freedom, had all reinforced what she already knew.

"That doesn't sound like a healthy relationship."

"You have no idea how right you are."

THEY ALL HAD a great time in the club, drinking and dancing without a care. Rhod managed to chat up one of Theo's models, and they disappeared back to the hotel a long time before the others left. Around midnight, they all made their way, in various stages of drunkenness, back to their hotel. Piers was feeling very mellow, his arm around Anastasia, and she was singing as they walked.

Alice was walking with them while Theo made sure Maddie was all right; she had thrown up just before they had left the club. "What are you singing, Stasia?" Alice asked, listening to words that made no sense to her.

"*Retribution*," Piers answered. "I think she's making up some of the words, but the tune is spot on."

Anastasia gave him a playful slap which he pretended had hurt and she carried on singing.

Once back at their hotel, Piers reluctantly stayed outside her door. "Another shoot again tomorrow?" he asked.

"Not till later in the morning, why?"

"Want to have breakfast?"

She smiled. "Sounds like fun. Knock on my door when you're up. Sweet dreams, handsome." She kissed his cheek.

Piers gave her a lingering look and went to his room.

Anastasia felt like a weight had been lifted; her decision to finish it with Mark had left her heart feeling light. No, she told herself, no more relationships because she was lonely; no more settling for second best.

She wanted Piers, and no-one else would do.

Anastasia had been dreaming about a lush green field full of wildflowers, a cerulean sky and being kissed by Piers when she heard a knocking sound. Turning over, she muttered, "Go away," but the noise got louder, more insistent.

She sat up, suddenly realising someone was knocking on her door, and slightly disorientated, Anastasia got out of bed. She squinted at the digital clock radio; it was half past four. Now concerned, she put the chain on and cautiously opened her door. She saw Piers standing outside.

"Hang on," she murmured and then she opened the door properly. "Come in. What's wrong?"

As Piers entered her room, she noticed he had a small suitcase with him and he looked annoyed. "Sorry to wake you, sweetheart," he began. "Something's kicked off, and we've got to leave now."

For a moment, Anastasia thought Piers meant the two of them before she realised he was talking about work. "Oh," she said. "That's a shame." She rubbed her eyes and yawned.

"I didn't want to just vanish." He hesitated, not sure how much to say.

"I wish you'd stay." Anastasia reached up to hug him.

As he let her go, Piers held her sleepy gaze; she was nowhere near awake. "When I get home, we need to talk."

She looked puzzled; she had used ominous words to that effect with Mark a few days ago.

"Nothing bad, I promise. We just need to talk."

As she watched him close the door behind him, Anastasia was completely bemused, and as she fell asleep, she was gripped by the unwanted and persistent fear he was going to tell her he was in love with someone else.

When she finally drifted off, her uneasy dreams were interspersed with images of a faceless girl wrapped in his arms.

Chapter 37

RHOD WAS WAITING for Piers by the taxi, looking disgruntled and dishevelled. They nodded to each other and allowed silence to dominate the ride to the airport. As they got out, Rhod remarked, "Absolutely typical. Best night I've had in ages—and then this shit happens." He passed Piers his suitcase and paid the taxi off, tipping him handsomely.

They checked in and, again, sat in silence, drinking coffee while they waited. Piers felt his mind begin to wander. He knew the way things were between him and Stasia was his fault; he had chosen to reject her that summer, even though he still believed he had done so for the right reasons. He knew she had been too vulnerable after the attack, he feared it had been far worse than he knew, and he could not take advantage of her. He recalled that look in those beautiful blue eyes just before she had kissed him, and it was a look he had never seen again.

It was a look he yearned for; a look that told him she wanted him.

ANASTASIA HAD A dreadful night's sleep. Her dreams had been fitful, and she woke up sweating and feeling sick. She was disorientated by the dark nature of her dreams, none of which she could remember but almost certainly involved Piers and Mark, and when she had a shower, she realised her nails had dug so hard into her palms overnight that they had bled. She also knew she was running late.

Theo was waiting for her. He tutted as she walked in, but his acid words about divas and timekeeping died on his lips once he saw her face. Instead, he elected for, "Everyone take a coffee break."

Anastasia paused and, puzzled, turned away.

"Not you, Stasia. I want to talk to you." He set a chair forward for her and pointed to it.

Reluctantly, she walked forward, not meeting his eyes, fearing he would shout at her and knowing it would break her.

Theo watched her walk towards him, wondering what on earth had happened to take away her good spirits from last night. When she still would not look at him, he grabbed another chair and sat beside her. "Stasia, has something happened?"

"Piers has gone."

"Gone? When?" Surely that was not enough to make her like this; he noted her hands were now shaking.

"About half four this morning. He woke me up." She hesitated. Theo was a dear friend; surely he would understand?

"What did he say?" He only wanted to help her.

"That we needed to talk." Her eyes filled with tears. "I think he's found someone."

Theo smiled ruefully. He knew differently, but perhaps thinking Piers was unavailable was what she needed for her to realise what he meant to her, what it could mean to lose him to someone else, and then perhaps she would sort this out for herself. "Well, if he has, then you know who to blame."

"Don't be cruel, Theo."

"Would you be that surprised if he had?" He wanted her to understand what she had taken for granted all these years. He would only push her so far; he just wanted her to think.

Anastasia glared at him. "No. No, I wouldn't."

"Well, lucky for you, he hasn't."

"How do you know?" Now she was suspicious.

"Because he told me as much last night. Anything else has

to come from him."

She did not reply.

"Come on, Stasia; use your brains if not your eyes. Surely you can see you're the only woman he has ever loved? And you should grab that with both hands."

She stared at him, her mouth slightly open.

Theo waited for his words to sink in before asking, "So, what are you going to do?"

Anastasia stared into the distance. "I'd already decided to end things with Mark."

"Maybe you should have considered that a bit earlier." Theo always talked straight.

"I know, but he ..." she hesitated, not wanting to admit her weakness.

"He scares you?" Theo finished her sentence for her.

"He does. But it's over, I don't think it ever really started."

Theo leant forward and put his forehead against hers. "Finally, you've seen sense."

Chapter 38

BACK IN LONDON, Theo and Anastasia were waiting for their luggage when he asked, "Still planning to do what we talked about in Edinburgh?"

She nodded, loading her suitcase onto a trolley and beginning to walk slowly towards the exit. "Yes. I'll end it as soon as I get to Belgravia."

She knew her decision was right, but there was still that fear of his reaction.

Their group passed through Security and walked into the Arrivals area. Theo faced her. "I'll call you tomorrow and check everything went ok." He kissed her cheek and moved to catch up with Alice. Suddenly, he stopped; Mark was waiting to meet Anastasia, and Theo knew it would not end well. He saw the shock and surprise flash across Anastasia's face as Mark crossed the concourse to greet her, throwing his arms around her and kissing her passionately.

"I hope you didn't have too much fun. I've missed you, baby." He started to push her trolley for her, leading her out of the airport. "I've got the car here, and I've got a surprise for you."

Against his better judgement, Theo watched him walk away. He had to trust that Anastasia knew how to handle him.

Anastasia was momentarily dumbstruck, then she followed him.

They got to the car and Mark loaded her suitcase into the boot. As he did so, she noted there were already two smaller suitcases inside the car. "Are we going somewhere?" Anastasia asked him, slightly confused.

He grinned at her. "It was supposed to be a surprise, but I've missed you so much." He paused and then took her into his arms. "I've booked a romantic break at a fabulously decadent hotel in the country, champagne included." He fixed his eyes, now tender, to hers and tried to kiss her.

This was not what she had expected or wanted, but, she reasoned as she pulled free, if he had to be told in an airport car park, then so be it. "Mark, I need to talk to you."

He opened her door for her. "Come on, it's a beautiful suite I've got waiting. Huge double bed." He grinned at her again.

"Listen to me. Please, it's important."

Her tone of voice told Mark that something was not right, but he ignored the look on her face he did not want to see. "Please come with me, baby. We can sort everything out away from any distractions."

She hesitated, then snapped as she got into the car, "Don't call me baby."

He shut the door, a frown on his face, but he thought that if he could get her to the hotel and show her how serious he was about marrying her, then he was sure she would say yes.

Anastasia sat in the Mercedes in silence, trying to think of the best way out. She dared not just come straight out and tell him, not while Mark was driving. She yawned suddenly and Mark said, "Why don't you sleep for a bit, baby? It'll do you some good."

"No." The word came out harshly. "Look, I've just got off a plane, I'm hungry and I'm tired. Can't we stop so at least I can get a coffee?" That was a good idea; the services on the motorway would do very nicely. "There." Anastasia pointed at a sign as they passed under it. "Services; seven miles. Come on, one coffee or

I'll just get to the hotel and pass out."

He gave in. "Ok, we'll stop."

The stream of vehicles pulling into the service station were a welcome sight, and Anastasia barely let Mark stop the engine before her seatbelt was off and the door was open.

"Get me a Coke and some crisps, please," he called after her as she strode away.

Anastasia held up her hand in acknowledgement of his request and practically ran across the car park.

Mark watched her go, wondering if maybe she was feeling ill, that perhaps the flight had been turbulent, and then he turned his attention to the post that had arrived just before he left Belgravia for the airport. He opened the large envelope and extracted the contents. His jaw dropped and his eyes froze over. This was not possible.

In his hands, he held pictures of Anastasia and Piers in Edinburgh, confirming all of his jealous suspicions. So that was it. The photoshoot with Theo had been a lie; a front to hide a sleazy liaison with his brother. He wondered how many times they had pulled a similar stunt over the years and the anger began to rise, humiliation and fury burning in his icy eyes as he watched for her coming back.

As Anastasia approached the car balancing drinks and snacks and trying to shut her bag properly, Mark flung himself out of the car in a blinding rage.

He came at her, his eyes now on fire. "You lying bitch!"

Anastasia took an involuntary step back and stared at him, totally thrown.

He grabbed her, sending her purchases to the floor and hot coffee splashing up and over her trousers, making her wince. "You are nothing but a lying bitch, Anastasia! You and him; I knew it all along!" He shook her roughly.

Out of the corner of her eye, she could see a car slowing, its two occupants eyeing the scene with concern.

"Let me go! Let me go *now*." She tensed, ready to floor him, afraid no longer.

Mark shoved her away and thrust the offending pictures in her face, snarling viciously. "Do the pair of you get off on it? Shagging in secret? Hurting other people? Your father was right; you are a whore!"

Anastasia took another step back and stared at him. Feeling unnaturally calm in the wake of his fury, she replied, "Four men in eight years is not a whore. And none of them was Piers."

Mark continued to glare at her, fighting his instinct to slap her until she admitted the truth. "Are you denying he was there?"

"No, Piers was there for twenty-four hours, but we didn't sleep together."

Mark reached out and grabbed her arm, and she watched his other hand rising in slow motion. "Do it, then. Prove the kind of man you are!" she goaded him.

Mark froze; his hand fell, and he let her go. "We're over." His face was inches from hers, and she could see the veins in his eyes. He threw the pictures on the floor, slammed back into his car and, revving the engine, screeched out of the car park without a backwards glance.

Anastasia took a deep breath. She felt a huge wave of relief wash over her and then she burst into tears. A few moments later, she pulled herself together as people were starting to stare, and she gathered up the photographs before dashing back to the shelter of the service station as the rain started in earnest.

As she hurried, she suddenly realised she was stranded there. Anastasia's first thought was Piers, but he was out of the country. She considered her options; if she called Rick or Johnny, they would go after Mark, but Bryan … Bryan would come for her. She could make him swear not to tell anyone the details.

Anastasia found a working payphone and then hesitated, not wanting to upset Suzanna and wondering if he was still in the studio. She dialled the number she knew so well and waited, and after a few minutes of being passed around, she resorted to telling the Original office staff exactly who she was and Bryan answered the phone. "Stasia! This is a surprise! How was Scotland?"

His voice threw her, and she could hear others in the background, and suddenly she did not know what to say.

Bryan spoke again. "Anastasia? You still there?"

"It's finished; Mark and I. We're finished."

"Stay there; don't hang up." She heard a door slam in the distance and then only Bryan's voice. "Did I hear you right? You've finally ended it?"

"Mark got there first."

"What?" Bryan could only think of one reason why he would do that, and it worried him. "Where are you? What happened? Are you ok?"

"I need a massive favour." She began to feel stressed, feeling people were watching her.

"Anything." He could feel the tension down the phoneline.

Gratefully, she told him where she was.

"Wait a minute." Bryan suddenly grasped what must have happened. "He just left you there?"

"Well, yes, but he had his reasons. Can you come?" She did not want to go into it over the telephone. "I'll explain more when I see you."

"Ok. I'll be there as soon as I can."

"Thanks." She hung up.

Chapter 39

BRYAN PULLED UP to the Services car park and saw her walking towards him through the rain. Anastasia looked for traffic and then ran across to the car. He leant over and opened the door, asking, "Are you all right?"

She nodded and got in gratefully, glad to see a friendly face, even if it was an ex.

"What happened, Stasia?"

As briefly as possible, she explained how Mark had met her at the airport and told her he was taking her on a surprise trip; that she had tried to stop him; that she needed to tell him it was over.

"So, you got him to stop here?" Bryan queried.

"Yes. I daren't tell him we were through whilst he was driving; I needed him to stop. Then I needed to get away for a few minutes to work out exactly what to say." She sighed. "I wanted to tell him why as well. I owed him the truth."

"Only an idiot wouldn't see that you love Piers. And I should know; I was that idiot once."

A single tear fell, which she dashed angrily away. "But as soon as I got back to the car, he got out and started yelling at me, asking me why Piers had been in Edinburgh. He accused us of being at it behind his back."

"Hang on." Bryan fastened onto one piece of information. "Piers was in Edinburgh as well?"

Anastasia nodded. "It was a work thing. He was there to help a colleague."

Bryan looked pointedly disbelieving.

"It was a coincidence," she insisted.

He laughed rudely. "Sure it was. Stasia, sometimes you are so thick!"

She shook her head, adamant. "No, honestly, it was."

"Ok, ok, I'm not going to argue with you. Carry on."

Anastasia sighed deeply and then told him about the photographs Mark had thrown at her and how he had driven off with her luggage and left her there. She also admitted she had been scared of him for a while.

"Anything else?" Bryan was sure she had left out plenty, and that Mark had no doubt said much more.

She shifted uncomfortably in her seat. "Nothing that matters." She shrugged it off, then finished with, "I'm so relieved, Bryan, despite all this. I can't tell you how lost I've felt. Like my identity was being gradually eroded."

"And now you're free."

"I guess so." She stopped, then, pre-empting Bryan's words, she said, "This isn't Piers' problem."

"We both know once he finds out, he'll make it his problem," Bryan said pragmatically.

Anastasia smiled. "The outcome is all that matters. It's over." She took his hand for a moment. "Thank you for fetching me, but please promise not to tell anyone else what went on. Mark and I are finished, and that's all anyone needs to know."

Bryan opened his mouth to argue, then he shrugged and agreed. "Fine, I promise. But what about Suzanna?" He had no intention of lying to his wife.

"You can tell her; she'll understand. Does she know you've come for me?"

"Yes, I rang her to let her know. She's been worried about you ever since the wedding, and that's the last thing she needs in her ..." he broke off, flushing.

Realisation dawned on Anastasia. "Ah, I knew it wouldn't be

long, but I wasn't expecting it to be this soon!" She smiled warmly at him. "Congratulations, I'm thrilled for you both!"

Pure joy spread over his face, and his hazel eyes shone. "I still can't believe it. Me, a dad!"

"When's it due?" Anastasia could not believe how fast Bryan had turned his life around, and although genuinely happy for him, she felt the pain of her own heart.

"September." He paused as her saw her expression. "I know, I know. It happened almost straight away."

"How is she?" Anastasia asked anxiously.

"She's fine; no sickness at all. Can you meet her on set tomorrow? Spend some time with her?"

"Yes, of course. I hope it's a girl, Bryan. In fact, I hope you have lots of daughters and then you'll know trouble!"

Bryan laughed. "You know, I think daughters would be good." Then he looked at her with a serious expression and asked, "What are you going to do now? About Piers?"

She looked away; she already knew the answer. "I can't do anything except wait for him to come home. That should be sometime in August. I'll talk to him then, but it'll feel like forever."

"But worth it." He smiled at her, then asked, "Shall we go?"

"Yes, please. I'd like to go home."

"Are you sure you wouldn't rather stay with us?"

"Thanks, but no. If I don't do this now, I might never go back at all."

He nodded and started the engine. "I get it. I'll take you home."

On the journey back, Bryan chatted happily about his new album, interspersed with his hopes for his baby and names he liked. Eventually, the car pulled up in Belgravia, and Bryan insisted on going in first. As he ran up the stairs, he looked over his shoulder, feeling like someone was watching, but he could not see anything out of the ordinary. He opened the door and then picked up a key that had obviously been shoved through the letterbox.

As he stood up, he felt Anastasia already pushing past behind him, saying, "Don't be daft. Mark wouldn't." Her voice trailed away as she looked around.

"Well he has." They both looked aghast at all of Anastasia's clothes and shoes from her luggage flung all over the room. She stepped forward, stooping to pick up a new pair of purple suede stilettoes she had not even worn that now had a heel snapped off.

"Vindictive bastard," she heard Bryan mutter.

She could not believe Mark would be so childish. "It doesn't matter," she said in a voice devoid of emotion. "They're only clothes, shoes … I can replace them." Then she spotted a photograph album half-hidden under her favourite, now ruined, leather jacket, and her heart screamed. Not that, surely.

Anastasia moved trancelike to retrieve it, and Bryan watched her face pale, her eyes suddenly huge with pain. He hurried forward to see what Mark had done.

He gently took the album out of her hands, and as he turned the pages, to his horror he saw every picture of Anastasia and Piers had been slashed. "Bloody hell, Stasia! The man's got issues."

Anastasia's knees begin to shake, and she felt faint. Noticing, Bryan grabbed her and made her sit down. "Shall I tidy up a bit? Get you a drink?" He had no idea what to do for the best, then he recalled the key he had picked up. Passing it to her and trying to offer some comfort, he said, "At least he can't get back in."

Anger was now replacing the shock. "If I ever see him again …" She dropped her head to her hand and sighed deeply. "Thank you collecting me, but you need to get back to Suzanna. I'll be fine."

"Come home with me; stay with us."

Anastasia did not reply.

"Please, Stasia. Don't stay here alone."

She stood up and faced him. "I really do appreciate the offer, but this is my home."

Bryan stared at her anxiously. "Promise you'll call the police if he comes back? Or call me. Promise me or I won't go."

"I promise." She held his gaze for a moment. "And remember, do not breathe a word about this to anyone."

"I agreed to that before he turned out to be a psycho!" Bryan protested.

Anastasia sighed and, turning away from him, said, "He isn't a psycho; he just likes his own way. I don't want anyone else to know. Please."

"Ok, ok." He gave in. "Do you still want to go on set with Suzanna tomorrow?"

"Yes, I'd like that. But you'd better not tell her about this. I don't want her worrying unnecessarily."

Bryan left her reluctantly, his only consolation that his wife would see her the next day and console her far better than he ever could.

All he could do now was to let Piers know exactly what had happened.

Anastasia watched Bryan drive away and then took another look at the devastation surrounding her. She did not have the will to start picking things up and she certainly did not want to cry. She thought about Piers, and Anastasia sat down abruptly, suddenly longing just to hear his voice. The answerphone; she always kept a message from him there just in case the need became too intense to bear.

Leaning over, she turned on the loudspeaker and pressed Play. There was nothing but silence. Frowning, Anastasia got up and peered closely at the display; it read zero. In his jealous temper, Mark must have deleted all her messages, not comprehending how much that would hurt. She breathed deeply. No, she would not crack or that would be it.

Anastasia hesitated. She had never tried to contact Piers through his work, but maybe, just maybe he had an answerphone, and maybe she could hear his voice. Her hand shook as she found the number in her bag and dialled carefully, her heart pounding so hard it hurt. The number rang out and then a male voice said, "Good evening. May I help you?"

Anastasia wavered; she had not really expected someone to answer. Then she heard herself speak in a clear, controlled voice she was sure did not belong to her. "Piers Talbot's office, please."

"Certainly, madam. Hold the line."

Anastasia had no idea what she was doing; she did not even know if he had an office. The phone continued to ring, a slightly different tone denoting an internal connection. She could feel beads of sweat building on her forehead and she was about to hang up when a female voice spoke. "Piers Talbot's phone." The voice was cultured, deep, and Anastasia felt intimidated.

"Is Piers available, please? This is Anastasia Travess." She had a mad hope her name might open a door.

The woman on the other end did not reply immediately. "I'm sorry, but he is temporarily unavailable." There was a pause as if she was considering something. "Can I take a message?"

Anastasia was stumped; she definitely had not expected that. "No, I just hoped ..." Her voice cracked a little, and dragging strength from somewhere, she spoke the truth. "I just wanted to tell him I love him."

Anastasia knew that was an utterly insane thing to say, but the woman now spoke in a softened tone. "I'll pass that on."

"Thank you." Anastasia felt her nails start to dig into her palm, and she knew that if she did not hang up now, she would shatter into a thousand pieces. The line went dead, and she was left standing with the feeling she may have just lost everything.

Choking back the tears and with her hands still shaking, she switched off the lights, leaving her clothes strewn about the room, and made her way to the stairs. She knew what she needed. As she opened his door, she paused to stare at the empty bed, a hollow feeling in the pit of her stomach. Anastasia walked forward and ran her hand over the covers, then opened his wardrobe and pulled out one of his tops. Holding it against herself, she imagined him taking her into his arms. She knew this was pointless, shallow, empty, but it helped.

Anastasia used his shower and stepped into his dressing

gown, wrapping it tightly around her. Then she noticed one of the photograph frames was missing from his bedside table, and her heart gave a little cry. He had taken her picture; a picture of the two of them together. She sat on his bed and picked up the matching frame; it showed him, her, Theo and Alice at a very posh party, and she kissed his face.

"Goodnight, handsome," she whispered, and Anastasia got into his bed.

Chapter 40

Once Mark had left Belgravia, he had driven aimlessly for what seemed like hours before he realised he was closing in on Guy's house in Surrey. Something had made him seek out his brother, and trying to concentrate, Mark carried on driving. He finally arrived, the Mercedes almost out of petrol, and rang the doorbell. Eventually, the door opened, and Mark realised he had no idea what the time was or how long he had been driving for.

"Mark?" Guy was surprised to see him, and then, scrutinising his face, he recognised something was terribly wrong. "Mark, is it Dad?" He pulled Mark, unresisting, into his home.

"No, Dad's fine as far as I know." Mark had a deadened look to his eyes.

"Thank God! But in that case, and don't think I'm not pleased to see you, but why are you here?" Guy watched his younger brother with growing concern.

Fighting tears of self-pity, Mark managed to say, "I've left Anastasia," before the enormity of his actions hit him hard.

Grasping Mark's upper arm, Guy steered him into a quiet room and made him sit down. "You've done what?"

"Left her, literally, at some motorway services."

"I don't understand. What's gone on?" Guy crouched next to Mark and tried to read his eyes.

"She's been cheating on me."

"What? No!" Guy was horrified. He stood up and paced up

and down the room, running a hand through his silver-streaked black hair. He did not believe it of her. Guy placed a strong hand on his brother's shoulder and felt his anger, his humiliation.

"And you know this for a fact?" Guy did not try to hide his scepticism.

Mark was struggling for control; he should have expected not to be believed. She had inveigled herself into Guy's good books and fooled him and his wife.

"Who with, Mark?"

"Who else would it be?" Mark was on his feet, rage in his icy eyes. "Fucking *Piers*!"

Unable to help himself, Guy laughed out loud. "That's bollocks, and you know it."

Before he knew it, Mark was nose-to-nose with his brother, but it was Piers he really wanted to hit.

Guy spoke very softly. "If Piers had been with her, do you think he'd ever let go?"

Mark was breathing fast, but then he sat down suddenly. "I need a drink."

Guy obliged.

A short while later, Guy took his brother to a bedroom and left him there, hoping to get the actual truth out of him in the morning. As he left, he heard the telephone click, he wondered who Mark was calling.

Mark could only think of one person who would truly sympathise with him; one person he could tell the whole story to. He dialled his home number in Paris and let it ring. Once he heard his brother's voice, he put the receiver down without speaking. He had no idea what he was going to tell him, but after taking some time to compose himself, Mark dialled again.

"Hello? Hello?" Giles was annoyed; this was the second silent call in the last fifteen minutes. He was about to slam the receiver down when he heard a voice.

"Giles? I've cocked everything up." A sob broke down the line.

"Mark?" Giles was now worried. "Mark, what's wrong?"

"I've left her. She cheated on me." Mark clung to the only thing he could understand; the only reason he could accept for her not loving him.

Giles considered; now he had split them up, he needed to keep them apart. "I'm so sorry, Mark. But at least you now know the truth. Who she really is." He listened to his brother's heart breaking, and he felt relieved; it had been far too dangerous to leave them together. "Mark, tell me, who was it? Come on, talk to me."

Mark's mind, blurred from drink and full of hate and anger, wanted only to blame them; not for one second was he going to admit the actual truth. "Piers. Fucking Piers. Her and Piers, all along, just like you tried to warn me. I'm sorry I didn't trust you." He trailed off, finding an alternative truth that made it easier to forget how much he was to blame.

Giles smiled and said gently, "Come home, Mark. Just come home." He wanted his youngest brother out of the way; he did not want or need him involved in what was about to come next.

"I need the truth. I want to hear her admit the truth about him." Mark was stubborn. "I want to hear her say Piers ruined everything for me." He was angry, his jealousy of Piers so long-standing it coloured his every thought.

Frustrated, Giles snapped, "Don't be a bloody idiot. Neither of them are worth it, least of all her."

But Mark's anger was now firmly rooted against Piers and he would not be deflected. "I will get the truth out of her. I want to hear her say she lied to me."

"Mark, please!" Giles tried to hide his annoyance. "Don't be so stubborn. Don't give them the satisfaction of knowing how hurt you are."

"I'll see you soon." Mark put the telephone down. He had to hear her say it; he needed her to take the blame.

Giles waited for the line to go dead and then made a call. He had waited too long.

Guy went to bed wondering what had really happened and refusing to accept Anastasia had cheated with anyone, let alone Piers. Lily had just come out of the bathroom, her auburn hair still damp, and he gave her a hug. He knew she was not going to be happy. "Mark's turned up. He's left Anastasia."

Lily pulled out of his hold. "Are you sure he's left her? She hasn't dumped him?"

Guy sighed. He relayed exactly what Mark had said and learned that he had been right; Lily was not happy.

"Your brother is a moron! How dare he accuse her of that!" Lily was outraged. "Doesn't he realise this is all his own fault? He's the one who's behaved appallingly."

"Anastasia should never have stayed with him if she didn't love him." Out of loyalty, Guy tried to defend his brother, even though he agreed with his wife.

"Well, I think he frightened her into staying so long. Mark's a bully, and he was clearly obsessed with her. Surely you saw that for yourself?"

Guy sighed again and ran his hand through his hair.

"What are you going to do?" Lily asked anxiously.

"Tomorrow, I want the truth."

Chapter 41

23rd February 1990

ANASTASIA WOKE IN Piers' bed feeling calm and refreshed; she had slept soundly without the nightmares she was prone to in times of distress. She glanced at the clock and calculated she had about an hour before her driver picked her up to join Suzanna. She thought she really needed to use her own shower, and as she got out of bed, a cold fear grasped her; she had not checked her bedroom.

She froze, suddenly terrified in case Mark had wrecked that, too. Her only concern as she ran down the corridor was her present from Piers. Anastasia tentatively opened her door, her heartbeat increasing rapidly, and to her immeasurable relief, everything looked untouched. She sighed and then dared to look more closely. No, her things seemed to be in the right place, but then she noticed one wardrobe door was not shut properly, a piece of shiny red material poking out.

Slowly opening the wardrobe, she saw it was her red dress, the one that had caused the argument before Guy's party. It was not hanging straight. Anastasia pulled out the hanger and the dress fell to the floor, as she picked it up, she realised it had been slashed right up to the shoulder; he really knew how to make a point. She was grateful Mark had done no other damage, and with one last look around, Anastasia went into her bathroom, knowing she had probably been lucky.

HER EXPERTISE AND popularity ensuring she was always in demand, Suzanna was working on the set of a horror production that day when Anastasia's driver dropped her off at a derelict castle in Kent. Anastasia waited with the security man until Suzanna was able to fetch her, and they walked a short distance to a Winnebago. Anastasia remained silent, unsure of what to say, but Suzanna spoke first.

"Bryan's told me what happened. Mark has a serious problem. Are you ok? Has he tried to contact you?"

With a sigh of relief, Anastasia sat down, shaking her head. "No, but I was a bit scared he might." She smiled at Suzanna. "I'm so relieved to be free." And she looked it. "But enough about my crap life! I'm so pleased for you both!"

Suzanna sat opposite her, delicately flushed. "Thank you. Bryan is so excited, he's already started decorating a room for the baby." Her green eyes were shining with happiness.

"I've told him he deserves daughters, then he'll understand what trouble is."

Suzanna laughed, then said, "Boy or girl, we want you to be godmother."

Anastasia nodded, speechless, and she felt tears fill her eyes as Suzanna embraced her. Slightly embarrassed, she asked, "Let's talk about something else before I blub. Is this for TV or film? The set looks really creepy."

"It's a horror serial for ITV. Some people stranded in a storm; the usual lurking presence picking them off one by one. It does have a really good cast, though." Suzanna smiled at her friend. "Have you heard of the actor Gary Buchannan?"

Anastasia thought for a moment. "Is he that pretty one from the sitcom we liked last year?"

Suzanna nodded. "Yes. He's the one I'm looking after. He's the villain, so not quite so pretty in this! Do you want to come and see some filming? I've got you a pass."

"Yes, please! Do you think I can meet him?" Anastasia stood up.

"I don't see why not. Gary is quite chilled, unlike the leading lady. What a cow!" Suzanna handed her a lanyard with a plastic tag attached and opened the door.

The two women made their way to the set, passing cameramen and lighting rigs galore. Eventually, Anastasia could see a small marquee and assumed this was the make-up and costume area. They showed their passes and went in. Two young women were having some grotesque prosthetics fitted.

"After the attack," Suzanna commented, noticing Anastasia's double-take. "Morning, Gary. Are you ready for me?" she called out, and a tall, peroxide blond man turned around to face them.

"Morning, Suzy." He leaned down to kiss her cheek. "I'm glad you were able to fit me in. I like only the best to look after me." He had a slightly crooked smile and cool blue eyes, which now flickered in Anastasia's direction and widened in appreciation as she removed her coat.

Suzanna would have bet on this reaction, and she introduced them. "Gary, this is my best friend, Anastasia Travess."

Gary took her hand and kissed it. "A pleasure. You're gorgeous, Miss Travess."

Anastasia burst out laughing and replied audaciously, "You're not so bad yourself."

Gary grinned at her as Suzanna carried on. "Stasia, this is Gary Buchannan, actor and champion bullshitter."

"Harsh, Suzanna, but true." Gary's eyes devoured Anastasia as he said, "I hope you're sticking around for a while? I do love to show off to a beautiful woman."

"I see what you mean, Suzanna." Anastasia took a vacant seat out of her friend's way where she could see the castle through the open marquee flap.

Gary used the mirror he was now sat before to watch Anastasia. He found her very alluring, that well-fitting pale pink cashmere jumper hugging her figure perfectly. He had not expected her to be so beautiful, and he acknowledged his luck was in as Suzanna had brought her along without the need for a prompt. This would be easy money. When Suzanna had finished, he winked at Anastasia and made his way to the set.

Anastasia rejoined her friend. "He's not as good-looking in person," she commented dispassionately.

"Perhaps not," Suzanna replied. "But he is a very good actor. I know he's off to New York soon; some serious spy thriller he's got a part in."

"Can I see the castle grounds?" Anastasia wanted to take a look around.

"Yes, of course, but stay away from the actual castle as they're filming in there. There's a nice kitchen garden to the south. I've got the leading lady to sort out now; she's a bit of a diva with the others, so I got lumbered with her. Come back when you're ready and we'll have some time to talk."

Anastasia impulsively kissed her friend's cheek. "Have fun with your diva." She waved as she left the marquee.

Anastasia passed the catering truck on her way south and took up the offer of a coffee, which she appreciated whilst sitting in the weak sunshine and enjoying the peace in a very run-down but somehow attractive walled garden. As she sat, her mind wandered, remembering that wildflower meadow, that summer when she had kissed him, and she smiled to herself, content with her own company, knowing she had made the right choice.

Gary's filming had finished in three takes, and he put his head back into the marquee. He saw Suzanna looking bored as his co-star droned on about how much she disliked the director, and he withdrew quickly. He wondered where Anastasia had gone—he saw no reason to delay—and he strolled to the catering truck. As he was served, he asked, "Have you seen a shaggable brunette?" His hands made a gesture mid-air to indicate her shape.

"Gary, you are a bugger!" mocked the man handing him his food. "She went that way." He pointed towards the garden, smirking.

Gary saw her sitting on a low wall, lost in thought, and he called out cheerfully, "Hello, gorgeous! Can I join you?"

Anastasia looked up, startled, then she smiled. "If you like. Have you finished for the day?"

"Not quite, but I thought I'd talk to someone more interesting than a bunch of self-obsessed actors." He sat next to her and offered her a sausage roll.

Anastasia shook her head. "No, thanks. And how do you know I'm more interesting?"

Still grinning, he replied, "You're a writer. Much more interesting."

Her eyes opened a little wider. "How do you know that?"

"I've just read Johnny Fielding's biography. I loved it."

"Thanks, but I was supposed to be ghost-writing. Johnny didn't tell me he was planning to put my name on the cover." She was still getting used to seeing her name in print.

"Well," he continued, "I'm glad he did. I always like putting faces to names. Perhaps we could discuss your book over dinner tonight?"

"Sorry." She held his gaze, his eyes a hard blue, their pupils dilated. "I'm already busy. Clubbing with some friends from work."

Gary looked disappointed. "Maybe tomorrow?" he persisted; he was not used to women turning him down.

Anastasia shook her head and tried a more direct approach. "Look, flattering though it is to be asked, I can't go to dinner with you. I'm waiting for my man to come home; he's abroad on business. I'm only interested in him." She stood up and walked away, knowing she had spoken the truth.

Gary sat alone for a moment, annoyed. That had not gone to plan. He got up hastily and called after her, "If I see you in a club sometime, will you at least let me buy you a drink?"

Anastasia stopped and looked at him over her shoulder. "There's no point."

Gary watched her go through narrowed eyes. Giles was *not* going to be pleased.

Chapter 42

MARK WOKE UP late. He had a headache and his mouth felt like an ashtray. He squinted at the clock and wondered if Lily would cook him some breakfast. As he stared at the wall, its rich copper hues making his eyes hurt, he knew she would refuse; she would no doubt be on Anastasia's side. With effort, he sat up, vowing never to drink again. That was Anastasia's fault, as well; her liking for alcohol had rubbed off on him. He reached out for the telephone, sure that Giles had been riled by his call last night; sure his brother needed placating. He waited, taking deep breaths, his eyes gradually closing.

"Hello?" a voice snapped down the line.

Mark jerked awake. "Giles?"

"Have you seen sense?" Giles was in no mood to take any more disobedience.

"I'm just ringing to apologise. I'll come back as soon as I have my apology. I need it from her. You can see that, can't you?" Mark willed him to understand; to be sympathetic.

"No, Mark, I can't. This is what you're going to do. You will get your stuff and go to Dad's place in St John's Wood. Tickets will be waiting for you for an afternoon flight."

Mark was silent; he had no intention of complying.

"And if you're not in Paris this evening," Giles continued in that same authoritarian tone, "God help you, I'll come and fetch you myself."

Lying, Mark replied in a sulky tone, "Ok, ok. I'll see you soon."

Giles was suspicious but merely said, "Thank you. I'll pick you up." He hung up, unsure but hopeful he would be obeyed.

Mark got out of bed, grimacing. Giles was *really* going to be pissed with him.

Piers had made a decision. He was already in deep shit over his absence for a birthday party, and once his bosses realised why he had volunteered so promptly to go to Scotland, he might very well be fired.

As he sat at his desk on the fiftieth floor, he opened a drawer and pulled out a handwritten envelope containing his resignation. As he pushed the drawer closed, he noticed a message lodged under his telephone. He picked it up and noted it was from his colleague in London, with whom he shared an office when he was home. He glanced idly at it, not really caring what they wanted; he had made up his mind. But he was startled as he saw her name, concerned that Anastasia had tried to contact him at work; she had never done so before.

Piers read the message carefully. Putting the paper down, he blinked several times, and then he read it again, not able to believe his eyes. He looked at the photograph he had brought with him; she loved him. Anastasia loved him.

And now there was no doubt what he had to do.

He snatched up his resignation. He had things to organise and a flight to catch.

Lily was just thinking about lunch when Mark walked into her kitchen, looking pale and moody. He always reminded her of a spoilt child, denied for the first time. "Morning." She said as little as possible to remain polite.

Mark felt her hostility. "Any chance of something to eat, please?"

Lily regarded him carefully, then replied as she stalked away,

"Help yourself. There's plenty in the fridge."

Mark sat down, dropping his pounding head into his hands. He had really wanted someone else to make his breakfast for him. He lifted the coffee pot and thankfully poured himself a cup as Guy came into the kitchen.

Guy stood and watched his brother and then jumped straight to the point. "Tell me the truth, Mark. What really happened yesterday?"

Mark did not look at him. "I told you. She cheated and I dumped her."

"How did you leave things when you drove away?"

"That is none of your concern. I want an apology from *her* and then I'll be going home."

From behind Guy, Lily burst out angrily, "*You* want an apology? What about Stasia? *You* should be apologising to *her*!"

Guy placed a warning hand on his wife's arm.

She shrugged it off. "You know full well this is all in your obsessed head. Why don't you take a good look in the mirror and admit this was all you!"

"Why don't you mind your own business?" was Mark's aggressive reply.

"Do not speak to my wife like that." Guy stepped hastily forward.

"Why not? She should show some respect." Mark stood up, knocking the chair over, his anger at Piers blinding him.

Guy was inches from him, his lips white at the edges as he held himself in check. "How about you get dressed and get out until you learn some manners, little brother?"

Seeing Piers in Guy's eyes, he took an unwise swing at the wrong person.

Guy moved swiftly, caught Mark's arm and swung it down, slamming him onto the table.

"Guy, don't! The girls …" Lily cried out, suddenly hearing her daughters running towards them.

"Stay away from Anastasia." Guy's voice was so quiet Mark

could barely hear him, but he did not need to. Guy had made himself perfectly plain.

Mark left as soon as he was dressed, but he was still determined to track her down. He wanted what he perceived was the truth, and he did not care what he had to do to get it. After dumping his stuff at his dad's London house, he began to seek her out.

He had no luck when he rang the doorbell in Belgravia and a quick stop at The Star resulted in him being blanked. He eventually decided that the place to find her was The Cathedral and, knowing it was useless to arrive there too early, he waited till around 10pm. As he queued to get in, he considered what he needed her to say. About ten minutes later, Mark strode into the club to the pulsing sound of salsa music assaulting his ears. He made his way across to a bar.

As he stood waiting to be served, he did not notice that he had attracted the attention of a solid, fair man. Rhod had spoken to Bryan Darnell, taken his message for Piers, and what he had heard concerned him. With his friend's interests at heart, he had also tracked Anastasia down, wanting to see for himself that she was all right; he dared not contact Piers unless he knew for sure.

Rhod had been about to leave when he saw him. He opened his mouth to call out Piers' name when he realised it had to be his brother. He was shorter and there was a coldness to his expression, but the similarity was striking. He watched, refusing to interfere unless he had to.

Searching anxiously for any sign of her, Mark asked the girl who served him, "Is Anastasia Travess in tonight?"

She nodded and pointed to the dance floor.

Mark's jaw dropped as he spotted her. She was wearing the shortest skirt he had ever seen combined with a halter top and knee-high boots. She looked stunning, and he felt a pang of longing that conflicted with his utter disapproval of her outfit. She did not notice him, which was hardly surprising in the crowd, and he debated whether to try to speak to her now or intercept her on the way out.

As he watched, Mark saw a vaguely familiar peroxide blond man with angular features slide an arm around her waist. He stood frozen as the man pulled her close and kissed her, his hands everywhere. Mark hastily looked away, horrified, and now absolutely convinced he had been right all along, he marched out of the club without a second glance.

Watching him go, Rhod still hesitated, waiting in case Anastasia needed assistance. He grinned as he watched her shove the blond away, and he guessed she had just told him to get lost. But the man did not look deterred, and Rhod stayed where he was.

Anastasia was used to feeling eyes on her whenever she was in a club, but Gary's eyes made her uncomfortable. She turned her back on him and carried on dancing, trying to ignore the prickly feeling running down her spine. She gave a gasp as Gary slid an arm firmly around her waist. Slapping his hand away, she shouted over the music, "Let me go!"

Gary looked across the room towards the bar. "Come on, have a drink with me." He tried to kiss her for a second time, hunger written all over his face.

Anastasia pushed him away. She thought she had made herself clear a moment ago. "Get off me. I told you, I'm not interested."

Refusing to give up, Gary moved closer to her. "Come on— you know I want you. Have some fun. I won't tell if you don't."

"Why don't you just fuck off!" she yelled, and thanks to a slight lull in the noise, everyone in the vicinity heard her.

Gary was livid; even if she had struck him, he could not have been more humiliated. He tried to take hold of her arm to play down the situation, but a shadow loomed over him and he found himself facing a bouncer.

"Is this gentleman annoying you, Miss Travess?"

With satisfaction, she replied, "Yes. Time to throw him out, he's barred."

Chapter 43

As ANASTASIA SAT on the Underground the next day, she felt jumpy; her encounter with Gary the night before had stirred up unwanted memories and given her nightmares. Giles' face, twisted and angry, feeling his fingers around her throat, and then his face had morphed into Mark's and she had pleaded with him to no avail until she woke up, drenched in cold sweat. She kept looking around at her fellow travellers, her nails digging into one palm, her other hand at her throat, trying to breath and telling herself she was safe.

As she walked to the office, she could not help looking behind her, hearing footsteps and feeling chills up and down her spine, and she was glad to reach the Original building. As she passed the main reception, she hesitated, requesting that they not send any visitors up to her without her permission. *Ridiculous*, she told herself as she climbed the stairs, but it had made her feel safer.

She went through the same worries on the way home, and she was relieved to make it to her front door without suffering a full blown panic attack. She breathed deeply and then started violently as the telephone rang out. Anastasia took a couple more deep breaths and answered it. "Hello?"

"Stasia? It's me, Guy. I need you to do something for me,

please." His voice was anxious and he spoke rapidly.

"Anything. What's wrong?" She was conscious of a desire to help, her irrational fears pushed to one side.

"My dad, he's …" Guy broke off; saying it would make it real. "Dad's in hospital. He's dying."

"I'm so sorry. What do you need?"

"Piers is on his way. He'll need you here."

"Tell me where and I'll be there." She wrote down the directions. "See you as soon as I can."

Pausing only to grab her handbag, Anastasia hurried to the front door, wondering if a taxi or the Underground would be quicker. As she opened it, she felt the door being shoved towards her, and she watched, terrified, as Gary forced his way into her home.

Anastasia turned and ran for the telephone, and she had just started to dial 999 when the handset was ripped from her grip and slammed down.

"Lovely to see you, Anastasia. We need to talk."

Gary pulled her to face him and hit her hard. She cried out in pain, her hand flying to her cheek, but Gary did not care about her anguish as he forced her across the room and made her sit down.

"I have nothing to say to you. Leave now." She managed to speak calmly despite her heart trying to escape her chest as he leered over her.

Gary sat down, close enough to grab her if she tried to run and close enough to watch her face, enjoying her agony. His eyes were slightly unfocused, and she feared his intentions.

"You refusing my advances was unkind, Anastasia. Giles is most displeased."

His words took her completely by surprise and she simply stared at him. She could feel nausea building, and she dared not ask what Giles had to do with this sudden invasion into her home.

"Don't you want to know what trouble you've got me into?" He tipped his head to one side, relishing her fear.

"Get out!" Suddenly, she was on her feet and snatching up a lamp to use as a weapon.

They briefly struggled before he managed to disarm her, but Anastasia knew from the effort it took him that she could hurt him.

Gary forced her back down onto the sofa and, with his face close to hers, snarled, "Giles paid me a small fortune to seduce you." His expression betrayed that his fear of Giles was almost as great as her own.

"Why did he pay you?" She wanted to get him talking as she looked for a way out.

He eyed her lecherously. "He wants what you have on him, and I owe him." His voice trailed away, and as his focus on her slipped, she edged closer to the end of the sofa.

"What do you owe him?" Her hand now rested on the little table, the vase close.

He seemed lost for a moment. "My sister, Angela. I killed her."

She gasped; she had not expected that.

"Giles gave me the drugs for her and her prick of a new boyfriend, but I miscalculated and gave them too much." He looked into her eyes. "It wasn't intentional." His face showed his anguish.

She stayed silent, letting him talk, her fingers were almost there.

"Giles covered up. He sorted everything, and for that, I owe him. You are the price."

Suddenly he was back, his eyes locked onto hers with vicious intent, and Anastasia grabbed the vase, smashing it across his face. Gary was knocked sideways by the force she put into her swing, and in that moment, she ran for the door. He was up fast but unsteady on his feet, and he gave a roar of anger as he chased after her.

She slammed the door in his face, and she was running for her life, from the past, to Piers.

Chapter 44

RHOD WAS WAITING for Piers as he exited the airport.

Piers stopped and looked at him, surprised but pleased. "I knew they'd send someone to chastise me; glad it's you! How are you, mate?" He shook his hand and then saw the look in his friend's eyes. "What's happened?"

"Get in and I'll tell you."

Piers slung his small case onto the back seat and got into the black BMW. "Well?" he asked impatiently; if this was work-related, they could stick it.

"I took a call from Bryan Darnell."

"Is she all right?" Piers demanded, paling a little.

"Yes, don't worry, she's fine, but it's over between her and your brother. He abandoned her at some motorway service station. Bryan went and fetched her."

"He did what? Did he hurt her?" Piers felt his fists clench.

"No, I told you, she's fine. There's more." He wanted him to know it all before he would break the worst news, just before they arrived at the hospital.

Piers sighed. "Go on."

"I found her last night. I wanted to see she was ok for myself as I knew you'd go off at the deep end if I didn't. She was in The Cathedral with a load of friends and this blond bloke kept pestering her. I thought you should know in case someone tried to shit stir."

"She left with her friends, though? He didn't try to follow her?"

"No, he seemed to get the message after a bouncer threw him out."

Piers smiled and relaxed back in his seat. He looked out at the streets, lights reflecting in the rain, the cars, the people, and was insensibly glad to be home. After a while, he suddenly asked. "Where are you taking me?"

"Your dad's in hospital," Rhod said in a gentle tone. "He's in a bad way."

"How bad? Is this it?" Piers felt a cold knife slip into his heart.

"Guy thinks so." Rhod stopped the car. As Piers got out, he called after him, "I'll take your stuff back to the office."

THE NURSE WALKED over to the group waiting anxiously in the corridor outside of Joseph Talbot's hospital room. "Mr. Talbot?" Three men looked up. "Sorry, Guy Talbot?"

Guy stepped forward. "Yes?"

"I have a message for you."

Guy let go of Lily's hand. "Hopefully it's news of Piers," he said to her. He was soon back and Lily stood up as he approached her. "He's downstairs, I don't understand how he got here so fast, it's as if he knew." He felt his wife take his hand again and looking down into her green eyes he confessed "I rang someone else earlier, she'll be here." Lily squeezed his hand, she knew he meant Anastasia.

Guy turned to his two other brothers, and announced, "Piers will be here imminently, I don't want any problems or you'll answer to me." He wanted it clear; he would tolerate no disrespect at his father's deathbed.

As Guy finished speaking they could hear swift footsteps approaching and Piers was with them. Guy gave him a one-armed hug and said, "I don't know how you got home this quick, but I'm glad you made it."

Piers distractedly ran a hand through his black hair and replied honestly, "I was already on my way back." His eyes involuntarily found Mark's, and they stared at one another, their mutual animosity making the air crackle.

Unable to control the vitriol and jealousy within him, Mark spat at him, "You're too late; she's already shagging someone else!"

Piers hesitated. He knew that was not true; even without talking to Rhod, he knew that was bullshit.

Mark wanted a reaction; he wanted the chance to take out his frustration on the person he blamed for it all. "Never mind. I suppose you can continue screwing her in secret."

Piers made an odd face and flew at his brother.

Guy and Giles both watched in horror as Piers floored Mark with ease. He leant over his younger brother and said in a very quiet voice, "Watch your mouth." He turned away.

Mark struggled to his feet and lunged at Piers to no avail; he heard him coming and swung around, pinning Mark to the wall.

"Not here!" Guy spoke urgently.

Piers let Mark go, and Lily managed to get near him, moving him gently towards a seat furthest away from Giles and Mark. With their backs turned to the others, she lowered her voice. "Anastasia will be here soon. Guy sent for her."

His eyes flickered, but his expression was unfathomable.

After a few tense minutes, they heard heels clicking along the corridor, and Anastasia arrived wearing an England rugby top and looking for Piers.

Guy moved to meet her. He hugged her, murmuring, "Thank you. This is going to be hard on him."

Anastasia greeted Lily with a kiss and a look and then sat down next to Piers, Mark watching her in brooding silence.

Anastasia simply took Piers into her arms, whispering, "I'm so sorry." He began to cry silently, his head resting gratefully on her shoulder. They sat that way for a while and then, shifting his position, Piers grasped her hands. As he held them, he felt the cuts on her palms.

He pulled away and held her eyes, seeing past her concern for him to the fear lurking behind. "What's happened?"

She swallowed hard and lied. "Nothing."

Anastasia fought the panic beginning to rise as she felt him seeing the truth. Piers turned her hands over and glanced at her palms, noting the tell-tale signs of her method to fight her panic attacks. Then he suddenly tilted her chin up to examine her face closely.

Guy and Lily watched, astonished, as Piers wiped away some make-up to reveal a livid purple bruise across her right cheek and under her eye.

He felt her tremble under his touch. "He hit you." Piers stated the fact in a clear, loud voice, murder in his eyes as he sought out Mark. "He *fucking* hit you."

Realising the misapprehension and afraid of what Piers might do, Anastasia stammered, "It wasn't Mark."

Lily pulled away from Guy's arms. "Stasia, what happened?"

Anastasia shook her head. "This is not the time."

In the distance they could hear raised voices, a nurse calling out desperately, "Please, no, you can't go down there!" Gary Buchanan was striding towards them.

Giles was utterly horrified; this was not what he ordered and certainly not what he needed.

Terrified, Anastasia glanced at Piers and stood up to block him as Gary got nearer, shouting, "How dare you run out on me!"

Guy moved quickly to stand next to Piers, ready to intervene if needed.

Then Gary was before her, his eyes glittering unnaturally under the corridor's harsh lights.

Finding her voice, Anastasia replied calmly, "I told you to fuck off last night." She could feel Piers' breath on the back of her neck as his breathing quickened, and she knew he was poised.

Gary scanned her up and down with contempt. "Who do you think you're talking to?" He reached for her throat.

As Guy restrained Piers, Anastasia demonstrated her flexibility by bending back and out of Gary's reach as her boot rose in one swift motion to kick him in the torso, winding him. Guy was so taken by surprise that Piers slipped his hold and slammed Gary to the floor, choking him.

All Piers could hear was white noise as the blood pounded in his ears, and his eyes, full of wrath, focused on a face he wanted to destroy.

Anastasia stood near him. "Let him go."

He heard her voice clearly, the only one that could reach through his rage.

This time, her voice was a command. "*Now*, Piers." He released him.

She stepped in front of him, looking down at Gary. "Stay away from me and my house."

Gary glared at her from the floor. "This isn't over."

Piers' voice sliced through the air, so deadly calm that it was more frightening than his rage. "If you touch her again, I'll kill you."

Giles watched, disgruntled, as Gary struggled to his feet and retreated. He had told Gary to drug Anastasia, not take them himself, and as he re-shuffled his plans, he smiled. How kind of Piers to provide a solution.

Anastasia turned contritely to Guy, "I am so sorry, I thought I lost him on the way here."

Guy regarded her face carefully. "What happened between you?"

Anastasia could feel Piers' eyes fixed on her. This was not the time or the place to pour out the truth.

Lily intervened, "Leave her, Guy."

Anastasia flicked grateful eyes in Lily's direction and then she felt Piers' hand grip her shoulder, turning her to face him. She did not want to see the look in his eyes, and she was thankful when the doctor leaving Joseph Talbot's room distracted him.

The doctor cleared his throat. "Your father is ready to see you. I'm sorry, but there isn't much time."

Anastasia involuntarily looked up into Piers' face and saw

only anguish there. Wishing there was something better she could do, she hugged him, whispering, "Don't waste this time. I'll be here if you need me."

She felt his arms tighten suddenly around her, and he did something he had not done for over five years; he kissed her neck. Then he was gone, with his brothers, to say goodbye to their father.

Lily tentatively held her arms out to Anastasia. "Who was that guy?"

Fighting the urge to break down and sob, Anastasia sat down, saying harshly, "It's not important now. He's just someone who wouldn't take no for an answer."

Lily sat next to her. "Are you ok?"

She put a hand to her bruise, wincing slightly, and commented, "I thought I'd covered it up well."

"He saw it in your eyes," Lily replied shrewdly. "He knows you better than anyone."

Anastasia sighed; Lily was right. "This shouldn't be about me. I shouldn't have come." Anastasia focused on the reason she came. "Did the doctor say how long?"

"They've brought him round so they can say their farewells. You know doctors, won't give a straight answer to anything."

Wanting to do something practical, Anastasia suggested, "Shall we get some coffee for when they come out?"

"It will probably go cold." Lily broke off as the door opened.

Guy beckoned and Lily leapt up and dashed to her husband's side.

Chapter 45

ANASTASIA SAT ALONE. Feeling as though she was intruding on the Talbot family's grief, her hand went to her neck where he had kissed her. All these years, she had been so monumentally stupid. She had been so afraid of losing the most important person in her life that she had missed the signs. But deep down, she supposed she had known the truth. She hoped Piers had got her message, though this was hardly the place to discuss their feelings for each other; only his father mattered now.

Anastasia had completely lost track of time, but she guessed at least an hour or more had passed. She crossed to one of the windows and gazed out over the street, the streetlights flickering, and she rested her head against the cold glass. She heard a door open behind her, and she saw Guy and Lily leaving the room, Guy being supported by his wife. Anastasia hesitated as she saw Giles and Mark walking slowly in her direction. They all looked devastated.

She moved past Guy and Lily, touching Lily gently on the arm, and as she passed Giles, she braved meeting his eyes, murmuring, "I'd ask for my money back."

His eyes widened at her words, and he knew that she and Gary were liabilities that must be dealt with.

As she reached Mark, she stopped. "I'm so sorry."

He nodded, his jaw clenched, unable to deal with the fact his father had just died.

Piers was leaning against the doorframe, looking lost, and her heart broke for him. Unsure if he wanted sympathy, she halted. He turned his head and gazed at her, those blue eyes showing his pain, and she knew there could not be a more inappropriate moment to tell him she had experienced an epiphany.

Anastasia held out her hand. "You don't have to say anything; just sit with me."

He gratefully reached out and interlocked his fingers with hers, allowing her to lead him to a seat.

They sat together, him gripping her hand, and the silence became a balm.

After a while, Guy came to stand before them. "Can I have a word with Piers, please?"

Anastasia looked up. "Of course." Standing up, she slid an arm along Piers' back, saying, "I'm going to get some fresh air. Do you want anything from the shop?"

He still had hold of her other hand, reluctant to let her go. "Chocolate, please, and cheese and onion crisps."

"I won't be long. Guy?"

He shook his head. "No, thanks. Lily's gone to the café for me."

Anastasia nodded and gently tried to pull her hand out of Piers' grip. "I won't be long."

"Please don't be." He finally let her go.

Anastasia hurried to the staircase and made her way to the ground floor. She felt drained and her head was beginning to ache. She paused at the bottom of the stairs, suddenly feeling like she was being watched. Looking around, she saw nothing to worry her, and she reached the exit. As she pressed the button to open the doors, Gary Buchanan walked back in. Anastasia backed up quickly, glancing around for a security guard; for *anyone*.

"Hello." His voice was ever so slightly slurred. "I told you this wasn't finished." Before Anastasia could react, he backhanded her across the face with a speed she did not know he possessed.

Anastasia staggered backwards, crying out in shock. She heard footsteps as a security guard ran towards them.

Knowing this was his only chance, Gary made a grab for her hair. This time, she was ready for him, and dodging his outstretched hand, Anastasia brought one foot swiftly up to connect with his face. Gary swore at her as blood spattered onto the floor, but with the security guard reaching them, he abandoned his need to hurt her and ran.

"Are you ok, miss?"

She nodded. "Yes, just don't let him back in."

The guard got out his radio and locked the front door.

Anastasia took a seat near the main reception desk and took a few deep breaths. She recognised she had not panicked, so that was something. She felt her other cheek and realised she was bleeding very slightly; he must have scratched her. Getting up, she made her way to the ladies to clean herself up. Anastasia observed her face dispassionately in the mirror; she looked appalling, and she rummaged in her handbag for her make-up to try to repair the damage. The last thing she wanted was Piers to notice, but she knew he would.

Sighing, she made her way to the small shop near the main reception. The many benefits of a private hospital like this were its excellent, always open, facilities. She bought crisps and the largest bar of chocolate they had, then made her way back upstairs, fearing Piers' reaction if he noticed the new mark on her face.

Guy was still sitting with Piers, and Anastasia suddenly realised both Giles and Mark had left. As she got closer, Guy stood up and smiled at her, but as he moved out of his brother's line of sight, Piers' eyes widened and he ran towards her. She stopped, unsure what he was doing.

As he reached her, he demanded, "Where did that blood come from? Where is he?"

Looking down, Anastasia saw blood spattered across her white rugby top. Her eyes stayed down, her heart racing. "He was downstairs. But it's his blood, not mine."

"His?" Piers' lips twitched into a fleeting smile.

She held his blue eyes. "I had a good teacher."

He breathed deeply and then suddenly jerked her into his arms.

"You two are coming home with me." Guy was now standing near to them, a curious expression on his face. "There's nothing more we can do until they release ..." He could not say it.

Piers suddenly let her go and, with his hands now either side of her face, made her look at him. Anastasia saw such passion there that she gasped as he said in a voice of anguish, "I love you."

She opened her eyes wide, unable to believe her ears, not daring to hope she had actually heard those words from him.

Suddenly terrified, Piers panicked and blurted out, "Have I just cocked everything up?"

Radiant joy shone from her eyes as she slid one hand up his stomach and across his chest. "No, you've just made everything perfect."

Piers was elated. He let go of her face to pull her against him and then he kissed her; kissed her like she had never been kissed before. Anastasia felt her knees give way and she totally forgot where they were, what had just happened, never wanting this moment to end.

Guy cleared his throat loudly, but they were oblivious. Loath though he was to interrupt, he knew Lily would be waiting and he moved forward to tap Piers on the shoulder. Piers looked around at his brother, refusing to let her go, not daring to in case this was not real.

"Come on, let's go home." Guy smiled at them, so pleased to find a spark of joy after such a destroying day.

"Have you got any of that really expensive scotch left?" Anastasia was starting to feel breathless as Piers crushed her in his arms.

Guy grinned briefly at her, remembering the last time she had decimated his whiskey. "I've restocked." He tried again. "Come on, Piers, let's go home."

Still not prepared to let her go, Piers led Anastasia towards the lift. As the doors opened, she put her hand to Piers' cheek, whispering so only he could hear, "I love you, too."

Piers grinned down at her, and they followed Guy into the lift.

"Where's Lily?" she asked, looking around.

"She's gone to get the car," Guy replied as the lift doors closed behind them.

Chapter 46

THE JOURNEY TO Guy's palatial home passed in silence. Piers did not trust himself to say anything, and Anastasia did not want to share her feelings with him in front of other people. When they arrived, Lily's daughters were asleep; their nanny had thought it best to leave breaking the sad news until the next morning.

They sat in the kitchen, and Guy poured out drinks.

Piers downed his scotch in one, to which Guy said, "Steady on. I'll get the cheap stuff out if you're just planning on getting hammered."

"That's probably a good idea." Anastasia sipped hers and savoured the taste.

Lily watched both Piers and Anastasia curiously; they were looking furtive, stealing glances at each other as if they dared not make eye contact. She wondered very much if she had missed something.

Guy removed the bottle that cost a small fortune and replaced it with a bottle of Johnny Walker. "Knock yourself out," he said, and downed his own.

Taking charge, Lily tucked her arm into her husband's, saying gently, "I think you need to go to bed. Come on, try to sleep."

Guy sighed, suddenly realising that he really wanted his bed and some peace. "You two can help yourselves. There's plenty of food in the fridge, as well."

"You know where the rooms are," Lily added. "I'll have

two made ready and put some stuff in there for you." She held Anastasia's eyes and saw her blush.

As Guy passed his brother, he gripped his shoulder. "Don't stay up drinking all night; you need some sleep."

Piers saluted him. "The jetlag will kick in soon. I won't be long."

Curious, Guy paused to ask. "Where were you?"

"Hong Kong. Great food; rubbish scotch." He downed another glass.

Lily watched him anxiously, and seeing her concern, Anastasia tried to reassure her. "I'll look after him."

Lily smiled with sudden understanding. "I know you will." She and Guy left them alone in the kitchen.

Pouring himself another, Piers said, "You up for an all-nighter, sweetheart?"

She removed the glass from his hand. "Slow down and we'll see."

He regarded her carefully, his smile growing larger; he still could not believe she had said it.

Anastasia drank the scotch herself. "Give me a chance to keep up at least."

Piers grinned, distracted, remembering many happy times drinking with her. "You know if it's scotch we're drinking, then I'll be under the table before you."

"Oh yes! That Kentucky bourbon!" she exclaimed.

He reached out for her hand. "Thank you for your message."

She blushed. "I meant what I said; I do love you. I always have."

His grip on her hand tightened. "I love you more than life itself, but I was too scared to tell you."

Anastasia changed colour again. "I think I've always known, but I was too stupid to admit it. I was too scared I'd lose you after … you know." She broke off and bit her lip; she did not want to bring unhappy memories into this moment. Later, they would talk, but now was not the time.

"I know. I'm sorry I didn't make myself clear that day." He stroked her hair, and she felt his hand tremble ever so slightly as it brushed her skin. "I should have told you how I felt then, but I thought it was too soon. You were too vulnerable after the attack."

Anastasia took his hand and held it against her face. "No, that was me being a moron." She turned her head slightly and pressed a kiss into his palm, then, raising blue eyes with the look he had longed to see, said, "Please kiss me."

And he did.

As he eventually let her go, Anastasia could see Piers was going to fall asleep at the table, which would do him no good at all. "Time for bed."

He nodded. "Good idea. Do you know where Lily put us?"

"Come on." She opened the kitchen door. "This way."

Piers followed her, his head starting to swim, and he needed to grip the handrail to assist him safely up the stairs. Lily had left two doors open with the lights on.

Anastasia stood outside one of the doors. "Come on, in here."

He stood in the doorway and then faced her, unsure of what to say. "Stay with me, please. No pressure—I just want to be with you."

She could not resist. "I'll be with you soon. I really want a shower."

He grinned. "Me, too; might clear my head a bit." He kissed her hair, whispering, "Love you, sweetheart." He went into the bedroom.

A short while later, Anastasia retuned to Piers, feeling nervous and suddenly incredibly shy. He was already in bed, just one lamp casting his shadow across the walls. She got in beside him, leaning over to switch off the lamp.

He surprised her by asking, "Are you nervous, too?"

She laughed. "Yes, it does feel a little strange, but this is what I want." She ran a hand across his chest and, as she felt his lips connect with her neck, she shivered with pleasure.

Feeling her response, Piers let his hands wander over her body, her silken skin, and he felt the hairs on his arms stand up. "Just how naughty do I have to be to get spanked?" he murmured into her ear.

She gasped.

"I wasn't as drunk as you thought, when you made that offer." He kissed her.

She moved closer to him and replied, "Very."

"*Good*, that was my intention."

And Anastasia was lost in the moment, completely forgetting she needed to tell him what Gary had said about Giles.

Chapter 47

LILY WIPED HER eyes. She had just broken the news of their grandfather's death to her daughters and now she had left them with their father. Making her way to the kitchen, she thought she would make everyone breakfast—something to keep her occupied—and she passed by the two rooms she had got ready for Piers and Anastasia. One door was wide open, and as she looked inside, Lily could see the bed had not been slept in. Despite her sadness, she was pleased to anticipate a gleam of happiness, and she knocked gently on the door to the other room. Lily waited, listening carefully, and then Piers opened the door. He looked half asleep still, but he smiled at her. "Morning, Lily."

"Do you want to come down for breakfast?"

He rubbed his eyes and, nodding, replied, "Yeah, I'm starving. Stasia's still asleep." Then, realising what he had just implied, he blushed profusely.

A smile spread across Lily's face. Seeing his confusion, she patted his arm. "It's none of my business. Come down when you're ready." Lily moved away, satisfaction in her eyes.

Piers looked around the room, and spotting a dressing gown that had slid onto the floor, he pulled it on. He stood for a moment and gazed down at Anastasia, deeply asleep and, as always, the most beautiful sight he had ever seen. He stared at her bruises and his face shadowed, he would give anything for five minutes alone with the bastard who had given them to her. She moved slightly, sighing; Piers could see she was smiling, and he wondered what she was dreaming about. Taking great care not to disturb her, he kissed her forehead and crept out of the room. As he made his way downstairs, he knew he had never been happier.

When he got to the kitchen, he was greeted by a volley of delicious smells, bacon in particular making his mouth water. "That smells good, Lily," he announced, sitting at the table expectantly.

Lily wanted to ask so many things, but she merely smiled, saying, "I hope you're hungry; I think I've gone a bit mad." She dished up a huge plate of bacon, scrambled eggs and sausages. "There's toast on the table. Help yourself."

Piers breathed in deeply, enjoying the aroma of a really good cooked breakfast. Lily watched him indulgently and ate toast. As he was finishing his second plate, Guy joined them. He had obviously been crying.

"How are the girls?" Lily asked anxiously, putting fresh bread in the toaster.

Piers watched his brother's face, wondering how a father told his children their granddad was gone.

"They're still upset, but they'll be ok. I promised to take them for pizza and ice cream later. *Lots* of ice cream."

Lily gave him a hug. "I'll check on them in a bit. Do you want two sausages or four?" Her instinct was to feed him.

"I'm not hungry," he replied, but the smell was tempting. "I'll make myself a bacon sandwich." He held his wife for a moment, relishing her.

As he ate, Guy addressed Piers. "Shall we pay Belgravia a visit? Check he isn't hanging around?"

"I do hope he is." That murderous look suddenly reappeared for a brief moment.

"You could bring Anastasia a load of clothes back," Lily

interjected practically. "I've nothing for her to wear that would fit."

Piers grinned. Yes, Anastasia was far too voluptuous for Lily's clothes, and he dwelled momentarily on last night.

"Shouldn't you ask her?" Guy had seen Piers' expression and guessed exactly what he was thinking.

His brother shook his head. "Don't disturb her; she's still asleep. I'll just fill a suitcase."

As Guy went to the sink to rinse his hands, he exchanged glances with Lily, who simply looked pleased, and he was unsure what he had missed. "Get dressed, then, and we'll go straight away."

Piers stood up and stretched. "I'll be ready in five."

ANASTASIA WOKE SUDDENLY; she thought she had heard Piers' voice and then she panicked in case last night had just been a dream. She gazed around the room looking for a sign he had been there and eventually spotted a flower from the vase on the windowsill on the pillow next to her.

Spotting a discarded dressing gown, she made her way to the shower, wondering where he was. A short while later, and feeling much more awake, Anastasia went downstairs, following the smell of a cooked breakfast, and she found Lily loading the dishwasher.

"Stasia!" she looked up, startled. "Piers said you were still asleep."

"Have I missed breakfast?" she asked anxiously, not having eaten properly for days.

"No, of course not. What can I get you?"

"Anything will do. I'm really hungry. Where's Piers?"

Lily poured her a large glass of orange juice and said, "He's gone with Guy to Belgravia."

Anastasia choked on her drink. "What?" There was fear in her eyes.

"It's ok," Lily reassured her. "They're going to check that man's not hanging around and get your clothes. Don't worry,

Guy's with him."

Anastasia did not look reassured and she seemed to have lost her appetite as she ate very little of the food Lily placed before her.

Unable to sit in silence, Lily asked, "Did you sleep ok?" She glanced covertly at Anastasia's face.

"Sort of." She held Lily's curious gaze. "Yes, Lily, I did spend the night with him."

Lily blushed and protested. "It's none of my business."

Anastasia eyed her before caving in. "Yes, we did." She grinned, feeling like a teenager in the throes of first passion, adding, "It was *amazing!*"

Lily got up and hugged her. "I'm so pleased. I knew the first time I saw you together that you were crazy about each other!"

"I was blind, Lily. He's loved me for such a long time, and I was too self-absorbed to notice."

IN THE CAR on the way to Belgravia, Guy eyed his brother curiously. "So, how are you going to know what to pack for Anastasia?"

Piers grinned at him. "Wouldn't you be able to fill a suitcase of clothes and shoes for Lily?"

"Whatever I put in she'd say was wrong, and we've been married for six years."

Piers simply replied, "I know my girl."

"Is that what she is? Your girl?"

Piers sat in silence, then said, "I love her. I always have." He was more than happy to admit the truth, but he did not want a lecture from his big brother about wasted time. Instead, Guy just smiled.

A short while later, they pulled up in Belgravia. "Are you ready?" Guy asked.

Piers had a nasty look in his eyes as he got out of the car. "Please let him be hanging around."

Guy followed him to the front door. "Don't do anything rash," he warned, placing a restraining hand on his shoulder.

Piers shrugged the hand off and opened the front door.

The two brothers were greeted by absolute silence; everything looked normal except for a smashed vase and a lamp lying on the floor.

"You take down here; I'll check upstairs." Piers set off climbing the stairs, knowing he was going to be disappointed.

Guy eventually joined him on the first floor. Piers had a bag of his own clothes already packed and a half full suitcase on Anastasia's bed.

Looking up, Piers said, "No sign of any intruders."

Guy could not help feeling relieved and then he had to know. "Didn't it ever bother you?"

"What?" Piers stood up, knowing exactly what he was asking.

"The others." His voice trailed away, not sure he should have asked.

Piers suddenly sat down on the bed and ran a hand distractedly through his hair. "I knew she never loved them, and I was out of the country so much. I didn't own her; what right did I have to mind?"

"And Anastasia was always there when you came home," Guy remarked shrewdly.

Piers nodded. "She always made it clear I was her best friend, and she always chose me over them." He laughed coldly, adding, "And I was too stupid to see the truth."

Guy sat next to him and braved his anger. "And Mark?"

A shadow passed through his eyes as he replied bitterly, "That was my fault, I pushed her into it, thinking I was doing the right thing. Moral high ground is a cold place if you cock it all up."

Guy watched him, puzzled, but he did not interrupt.

"Mark made it abundantly clear he wanted to push me out of her life and if she really did love him ..." Piers broke off.

"She'd let him," Guy finished.

"That was hard to accept. But what could I do? Stasia had to make up her own mind. Of course, I didn't realise what he was capable of."

Guy looked concerned. "What did he do?"

"Come off it! You must have seen him try to control her? Must have realised it was obsession, not love?"

Guy sighed. "Actually, I think it was all because he hates you. Anastasia was a bonus."

Piers glared at him. "If I could get hold of him …"

"Stop it. Enjoy what you've finally got, and never let a day go by without showing her how much you care."

Piers stared at Guy, then he smiled slowly. "Thanks, you're right, as always." He stood up, shivered and added, "It feels wrong here. Let's get out."

As they left the house, Piers asked his brother, "Do me a favour? Can you drop me near Lambeth Bridge?"

"Why?"

"I need to go into the office. Leaving Hong Kong would have caused quite a stir."

"Can't you do that by phone?"

Piers shook his head. "Better to go in and face the music. I'll pick my car up and then drive back myself." He grinned at Guy. "I want to take my girl out for dinner. We've never been on a date before."

Chapter 48

GUY RETURNED HOME, bringing with him Anastasia's suitcase and the bag containing his brother's clothes. He left the luggage in the entrance hall and went to the kitchen to find his wife. Lily was looking pleased, and she smiled broadly as if trying to tell him something.

"Hello, darling." Guy held her, kissing her hair.

Anastasia got up from the table. "Where's Piers?"

"He's still in London." He saw her face blanch. "No, it's ok," he began, realising he seemed to have a knack of alarming her. "No-one was hanging around Belgravia."

She sat back down, a hand at her throat, her eyes still wary.

"Piers had to call into work. He's driving himself back. Something about taking you out on a date?" He grinned as she changed colour.

Anastasia breathed a sigh of relief and smiled gratefully at him. "Did you get me anything to wear?"

"Yes, Piers packed a suitcase. It's by the front door."

"Cheers." She left the kitchen.

Guy looked at Lily, pre-empting her words. "I know, he told me."

They smiled, hopeful for the happy conclusion they both wanted.

ANASTASIA TRIED TO relax, but she was beginning to get twitchy as Piers had still not returned by lunchtime. Lily and Guy had asked her to join them and the girls for pizza and she did not like to say no.

Guy looked at his watch. "We could go now before it gets too busy?"

Lily rose. "Yes, I'll get the girls and we'll go."

Left alone with Guy, Anastasia asked, "Did he wreck my house?"

Knowing she meant Gary, he replied, "No, everything looked fine. There was a smashed vase and a broken lamp, though."

"Yes." She paused and then met his eyes. "The lamp was my first attempt to escape, then I hit him with the vase. It was Meissen, so not an ideal choice really."

Guy put his arm around her and hugged her, saying, "I couldn't help noticing you said something to Giles at the hospital."

She remained completely silent, absolutely still.

"I saw his face. He was shocked." Guy waited.

Still she did not speak.

"Please, Stasia." He let her go. "I need to know." There was anxiety in his voice.

She answered in a level tone, "I told him he should ask for his money back."

Guy was still in the dark and tried to get more. "Please, Stasia, this is really important."

Anastasia capitulated and briefly told him the facts.

Guy's jaw dropped.

"I don't know what your brother"—she never said his name unless she absolutely had to—"thinks I've got on him, but I never knew Matthew."

"Did Matthew ever give or send you anything?" Guy could feel he was so close.

"Well." Her brow furrowed. "A book. A beautiful first edition for my collection—but that was just a book."

He smiled; all this time, she had been the key, and he had never even considered it. Clever. He grasped her arms. "I need to see it."

"Piers can take me to the manor tomorrow to collect it." Surely this could not all have been because of a book?

Seeing her face, Guy gripped her arms harder. "I think—no, I *know*"—this was difficult to admit—"Giles was responsible for Matthew and Angela's deaths."

Her eyes flew wide open and she shook her head. "No. His own brother?"

Guy let go of her and lowered his voice. "Yes, not only did Matthew steal his fiancée a week before the wedding, he also stumbled upon what Giles was up to. That's why he wanted Piers, and that's why he sent you what I hope he sent you."

"But not his own brother?" She really could not believe that, not even of Giles.

"We both know what he's capable of." Guy paused, watching her face pale significantly. "He was beyond furious when Angela dumped him for Matthew. I think that alone would have been enough, regardless of any other transgressions."

Anastasia faltered slightly as she accepted the truth; *that* was why he had attacked her. That was why he had been prepared to do anything to intimidate her.

Guy put out a hand to steady her. "It's ok, Stasia. You're safe with us."

She nodded, seeing blurred visions in her head that still terrified her, and if Piers' colleagues had not burst through the door, she knew now she would have died that day. Her hand went to her throat; she could feel his fingers, just like it was happening again. "I need some air."

She hurried away, leaving Guy to make her excuses to Lily.

Anastasia had been walking around Guy's grounds. Extensive and beautiful, their appearance was not scenic enough to block the painful memories he had stirred up. She tried not to dwell— she had survived—but realising just how desperate Giles must have been made her feel sick. She accepted that when Piers got back, they needed to discuss things; she owed him the whole truth and then, hopefully, she could truly move on.

She had no idea how long she was outside, but once it started to drizzle, Anastasia made her way back to the house, in need of a cup of tea. No-one was around, and she helped herself to biscuits whilst the kettle boiled. In the centre of the kitchen table was a piece of folded paper with her name on it, which included a message from Piers in writing she did not recognise. He was delayed in London, but he was sending a car at two to bring her to him.

Looking at the clock, she had about twenty minutes before the car arrived, and she rummaged in her handbag for a pen. Crossing out her name, she wrote Lily's in its place and then added inside "Gone to London to meet Piers" in her bold script. She propped it up against the teapot, knowing Lily would find it, and then Anastasia fetched her leather jacket and waited for her lift by the front door. A black BMW pulled up on time and she was on her way to London through the fine drizzle of the afternoon, happily anticipating a reunion with her man.

And starting to drive through that same drizzle was Piers, on his way back to his brother's, unaware things had all gone terribly wrong.

Chapter 49

THE CAR DROVE up a carriage driveway in St John's Wood and stopped outside a large house set well back from the road, it was up for sale. Anastasia was puzzled why Piers wanted to meet her here, but after thanking the taciturn driver, she walked towards the front door and hesitated. It was open. She paused on the doorstep, calling out, "Piers?"

The house felt vaguely familiar and she was sure she had been here before, a very long time ago. She walked forward and stopped, her heart pounding so hard it hurt. She could see him lying face down on the floor, one hand stretched out at an odd angle.

She moved carefully forward, wary after their last encounter. "Gary," her voice trembled. There was no response. "Gary." this time, her voice was loud and clear, but still there was no response. She wavered and then moved closer, leaving the front door open in case she needed to run.

Anastasia stood over the recumbent form; she could not hear him breathing or see any movement. She put down a hand to shake him and gasped as he felt cold to the touch. Then she noticed the syringe which had rolled across the floor. Unsure what to do, she dropped to her knees to check for a pulse.

Nothing. He was dead.

Her head reeled, and she looked for a telephone. There was no ringtone. She began to feel the waves of panic rolling up her body and she breathed deeply, forcing herself to think logically. A phone box? Or maybe she could run to the next house and ask for help?

She turned and fled for the door, but she did not hear him until it was far too late. Giles grabbed her from behind, his fingers digging into her throat.

She tried to scream, but his grip was firm. She struggled, rapidly forgetting all her classes, her mind cast back to the fear she had felt all those years ago.

His voice was deeply poisonous, hissing into her ear from behind. "Were you expecting someone else? So sorry, Anastasia."

Anastasia began to feel unsteady on her feet; he was choking her without remorse. Then his hand moved and he was forcing her mouth open; she could taste blood as his nails sliced her lips and liquid trickled past her teeth. She choked again; she felt dizzy and swallowed involuntarily. He let her go, and she fell to her knees coughing violently.

She turned and saw him staring at her with a look that made her feel sick. Still she could not speak. Anastasia was lightheaded, and her last conscious thought was for Piers as her face made contact with the hard wooden floor.

Chapter 50

PIERS PARKED HIS Jaguar some distance from Guy's house and ran up the driveway through the now heavy rain. He opened the front doors and listened, but there was no sound; the place felt deserted. Closing the doors, he felt a sense of anti-climax and disappointment; he had imagined her waiting for him, throwing her arms around him as he kissed her for a very long time. Piers called out, "Guy? Lily? Anyone home?"

He heard footsteps hurriedly approaching and the housekeeper appeared, looking flustered. "Oh, Mr. Talbot, they've all gone out. We weren't expecting you."

"No matter," he said, realising it would have been a good idea to call first. "Where are they?"

"They all went for lunch before your brother's appointment at the funeral directors." She paused to express her sympathy.

"Ah, yes, that makes sense." Piers had not even considered that arrangements needed to be made, and he felt slightly guilty he was not helping Guy. "Lily isn't back yet?"

"Mrs. Talbot planned to take the girls to visit a friend after."

"What about Anastasia?"

"I think Miss Travess must have gone with them as she's not in the house." Seeing his frown, the housekeeper ventured, "Do you want a cup of tea while you wait? There's plenty of cake made just this morning."

That made him smile. "Yes, please; I love your cakes." He

followed her into the kitchen. As he sat down, he noticed the note with Lily's name on it and recognised Anastasia's flourishing script. Why would she have left Lily a note if she had gone with her?

There was a second script on the paper. "Is this your writing?" he asked the housekeeper, pointing to Anastasia's name which had been crossed out.

She squinted at it. "No, but it looks like Louise's, the nanny."

Giving in to his curiosity he opened the note as the housekeeper busied herself pouring him tea. Choking on his cake, he felt his blood turning to ice. He half-rose from the table, knocking his cup to the floor, but he did not hear it smash. In his head, Piers could only hear Anastasia screaming and, suddenly, he was paralysed with terror.

The housekeeper watched him, scared by his reaction, and as she heard the front door, she ran to see who it was.

Guy stood in the doorway, shaking the rain off his coat and feeling melancholy. He started as the housekeeper addressed him breathlessly. "Mr. Talbot, come quickly!"

"What?" he began to ask, but she had run back towards the kitchen and he went after her, alarmed by her words. What he saw worried him more; Piers still half-standing, frozen, clutching a piece of crumpled paper in his fist. Guy put a hand on his shoulder and forced him to sit down. "Piers, what's going on?"

Piers grasped his brother's jacket and pulled him face to face. "Someone's got Anastasia!" The words tumbled unchecked.

Guy spoke as calmly as he could. "How do you know this?"

Piers handed him the crumpled paper and Guy suddenly understood. "This is Louise's writing. Mrs. Patterdale," he addressed his housekeeper, "please send Louise to me immediately."

Nodding, Mrs. Patterdale rushed off, leaving Guy to think. She reached the entrance hall where Louise was helping Joanna and Elizabeth off with their coats. She spoke rapidly, "Louise, Mr. Talbot would like to speak with you in the kitchen. *Now*."

Looking surprised but feeling the anxiety in her voice, Lily said, "Go, Louise, straight away," and the nanny, now puzzled, did as she was told.

"What's happened, Mrs. Patterdale?" Lily asked, struggling with her own coat and trying to stop the girls from rushing to their father.

"Miss Travess is missing."

Lily did not know how to respond to that, but she did know what to do. "Please take the girls upstairs and I'll send Louise up as soon as I can. Is Guy in the kitchen?"

Mrs. Patterdale nodded, taking the children by the hand. "And Mr. Piers, too," she added over her shoulder as she ushered them up the stairs.

Lily did not understand; how could Anastasia have gone missing? Lily arrived in her kitchen to find Piers interrogating her nanny over a telephone call and a message taken. Guy had stepped back to allow his brother to handle the questions.

"At first I thought it was Mr. Talbot." Louise indicated Guy. "But he then gave your name." She was looking straight at Piers.

The two brothers exchanged glances. "Cheers, Louise. You can go back to the girls now." Guy thanked her, and she left the room with a curious backwards glance.

Noticing his wife, Guy handed her the note with an expressionless look. Catching on, Lily said, "Dear God, why would he do this?"

"Who?" Piers asked sharply.

"Mark, of course." She remembered his obsession and shuddered.

"Mark?" Piers scoffed, and stated what he now knew must be the truth. "No, not his style. This has Giles' fingerprints all over it, but why?"

"Giles?" Lily gasped and looked to her husband, seeing confirmation and apprehension in his eyes.

"Security cameras!" Piers jumped to his feet. "Where's your footage? We can get the car's plates and then I can trace it."

Lily wanted to ask how, but she saw the murder and anguish in Piers' eyes and she dared not ask anything at all.

Within minutes, Guy had the information Piers needed and he left him in the hall to make telephone calls to his colleagues. Now alone with his wife, Guy tried to reassure her. "Don't worry, I promise she'll be safe. We'll find her."

Lily did not look convinced. "Why didn't she just come with us?"

"There's something Piers needs to know." Guy was thinking about his earlier conversation with Anastasia, now wishing he had waited.

"Needs to know what?" Piers walked back into the kitchen.

"Any leads?" Guy was not keen on telling him anything Anastasia had said.

"Give them ten minutes and I'll know. No point haring off to Belgravia yet."

"Why Belgravia?"

"Seems the obvious place to lure her." Piers held his brother's eyes. "What aren't you telling me, Guy?"

"Sit down." Guy told him about Gary and Giles, that Anastasia might inadvertently have proof that their brother was implicated in fratricide.

Piers ran his hand through his hair; he was calmer than Guy had expected, but losing his temper was a luxury Piers could not yet afford. "A book? All this aggravation over a *book*?"

"Piers, you're supposed to be the expert here." Guy stood up and said, "I need to make a call, maybe pull in a favour."

Piers looked at Lily anxiously. "I don't know what I'd do if ..."

Lily could see the pain in his blue eyes. "Anastasia loves you. Hang on to that."

Piers dropped his head into his hands, knowing she was facing this alone; that he could lose all that ever mattered.

Guy came back into the kitchen, wary of his brother's reaction. Piers pulled himself together and looked up. "Any news?"

The telephone rang; Lily jumped and then answered it. She

held out the receiver to Piers. After a very brief conversation, Piers said, "Didn't expect that." He looked puzzled.

"What?" Guy prompted him.

"The car went to St John's Wood."

The two brothers stared at each other and suddenly they knew.

"Dad's place." Piers moved towards the door.

"Let's just wait for my contact to come back to me." Guy spoke with authority, and a few minutes later, the telephone rang again. Guy picked it up and Piers listened intently. Guy was silent and his face changed dramatically. "Yes, yes, I understand." He put the telephone down.

"Any sign of Anastasia?"

"I need someone else to check in." Guy knew Piers was ready to fly at him; that he needed an outlet soon. "I've been having Giles tailed." He hoped that would be enough to keep Piers in check.

"Bugger that, I'm going." Piers tried to shove past his brother.

"No!" Guy stopped him. "The last thing we need is to rush off and cock this up. Just wait."

Piers lowered his voice. "Get out of my way." The threat was explicit.

"No." Guy knew he had to keep control of his brother.

Piers recognised he would have to punch Guy to get past him, and as he clenched his fist, the telephone rang again.

Lily grabbed it. "Guy, quickly."

Still holding Piers' murderous gaze, Guy took the call. "Yes, I see. Are you sure? Yes, thank you, I owe you big time. Send them there; I think I'll need them." He put the telephone down, pulled Lily into his arms and kissed her. "We'll bring Anastasia back safely, I promise."

"Please do." She was desperately trying not to cry, fearing she might never see Anastasia again.

"He's there and so is she. Are you coming?" Guy knew what he had to do.

Piers said simply, "He's mine."

Chapter 51

As GILES CAME back around to the front of the house from the garden, he saw the door was not closed properly and he approached it with caution. Surely they could not be on to him that quickly? He slid himself inside and listened.

He watched through malicious eyes as Mark was crouched down beside a drugged Anastasia, shaking her in an attempt to rouse her.

"Anastasia? Anastasia? I don't understand what's going on …" He trailed off abruptly upon hearing a derisive laugh from close by and he jumped to his feet. "Giles? Quick, something's wrong with Ana …" He stopped, the look of ire in his face making Mark take a step back.

"What are you doing here, Mark? I told you to get on a plane to Paris. I didn't want you to be a part of this. Why must you constantly disobey?" Giles moved towards him, picking up the poker from the fireplace, disappointment in his cold eyes.

"I forgot my passport; I had to come back." Mark took another step away from his advancing brother and glanced involuntarily at Anastasia, unconscious on the sofa.

"Sorry, little brother." Giles struck him hard, and as Mark hit the floor, he sighed; he really had not wanted to do that. Now he was really annoyed.

"MARK? MARK!" ANASTASIA shook him, desperate to revive him

from what she assumed must be a drug induced stupor. He groaned and attempted to push her hand away. She tried again.

Mark managed to open his eyes, his head thumping. He groaned again, trying to sit up and failing.

Anastasia helped him. "Are you ok?"

"I feel bloody awful," he managed, holding onto her as his head swam unpleasantly. "Where am I?"

"A cellar. I think we're at your dad's old place." She glanced uneasily around, the multitude of wine bottles casting odd shadows across the walls.

"What's going on?" He was starting to feel sick, and Mark leant back gratefully against the cold brick wall.

"What do you remember?" she asked, dropping to her knees in front of him.

Mark thought hard, trying to grasp the pieces of memory that slipped through his fingers like smoke. "I shouldn't have been here. My passport ..." He looked very pale, the pain behind his eyes agonizing. "My passport. I forgot it, but when I came back, you were there, asleep on the sofa. I knew that was wrong." He was not sure about the next bit, the unpleasant memory hazy.

"And?" Anastasia prompted him.

"Giles ... he was furious. He hit me, and I blacked out. Then, nothing until now." He put his hand to the back of his head and felt the lump there.

Anastasia took a deep breath; she was pretty sure he was not going to believe her. "Giles was the one who attacked me all those years ago. He thinks I have something on him. He paid that guy at the hospital, Gary, to seduce me, and when it didn't work, Gary flipped out and tried to hurt me. He's here. Oh God, I think Giles killed him." She took another breath and finished hurriedly, "Giles lured me here. I think I was next."

Mark stared at her, aghast. "No! No, you're mistaken! Lying ..." She had to be!

Anastasia held his eyes. "I'm not, Mark. Guy thinks Giles was responsible for Matthew and Angela."

He blanched, fighting to stop the nausea from winning.

"I'm sorry, little brother." Giles was leaning against the doorframe, his shadow draped across the concrete floor. "But she is actually telling the truth."

Mark reeled. "That's not possible! Giles, why would you do this?"

Giles moved towards them, holding something small in his left hand. "Why? How can you ask that when you know what losing Angela did to me?"

"But ... but ..." Mark tried to stand, but his legs would not work. Now he really wanted to throw up.

"The only woman I've ever loved, taken from me by my own brother. You know what that feels like, don't you, Mark? It's no different to how Piers has treated you. History repeating itself. And that brother could not keep his nose out of my side of the business. He was going to destroy *everything*." He was looming over them now. Anastasia glanced around, ready to run.

"Don't," Giles advised her. "Don't try it or Mark will pay for your mistakes."

She sat down on the floor; she believed him.

"Where do I come into this?" she demanded.

"Matthew sent you a copy of all my"—he paused and considered his words—"*little innovations,* and he needed Piers to decode it. You never even looked at it, did you?"

"What? That old book?" She thought she heard something; the minutest sound.

"I thought, after all these years, that I was safe. But then you had to ensnare Mark again, and I *knew* it was only a matter of time."

Giles shoved her aside and took hold of Mark's lifeless arm. He tried to resist, but his head was swimming now and he could barely focus.

"Don't hurt him, Giles," Anastasia begged.

Astonished by the fear in her voice, Giles responded, "How sweet. You see, Mark? She does care after all." And then he plunged the needle into the back of his brother's hand. "It's ok, Mark; when you wake up, this will all be over. And this bitch will be gone forever."

Mark tried to protest, the words clogging his mouth, and then he slipped silently into oblivion.

Anastasia froze as Giles turned to face her. "Well, it's just the two of us now. I should have dealt with you all those years ago, Anastasia; it would have been so much easier." He grabbed her by the hair and wrist and dragged her away from Mark.

Anastasia screamed; if she stood any chance of someone finding her, she needed to make as much noise as possible.

"Shut up! No-one is coming for you." He heaved her to her feet and took hold of her throat. "No-one will see you ever again."

She stared into his unfathomable eyes and saw nothing but hatred. Then she heard it again, only the slightest of noises, but this time, she was sure.

"Once I've dealt with you, I'm going after Piers."

Suddenly a voice rang out. "Why don't you deal with me now?"

Keeping his grip on Anastasia, Giles took his time in facing his brother. "I knew you wouldn't let me down. Now you can watch what I'm going to do to her."

Piers stood rooted to the spot; he knew he had to do something, but he was terrified anything he did would trigger Giles into drastic action. Giles had Anastasia directly in front of him, like a shield, with one hand gripping her throat and the other pinning her to him. Piers' eyes flickered anxiously over her, noting her scared face and that she was holding one wrist at an awkward angle.

Anastasia ached all over, her panic making her want to scream; but she knew she had to remain silent, absolutely still; she had to be passive.

Giles moved his hand across her throat, taunting Piers. "Such a beautiful neck, so fragile. How often have you dreamt of kissing this neck? This throat?" He saw Piers flinch and knew just what this was doing to him. "And how often have you longed to have her lie underneath you?" Giles fixed eyes with malicious intent on his brother's face. "I really hope you've tasted heaven before I send you both to hell."

Anastasia could see Piers' dread, and she wanted to tell him how much she loved him, one last time. She took a risk, needing to say the words. "Piers—"

Giles tightened his grip and cut her off. "No, he's getting nothing from you. *Nothing.*" He sneered at his brother. "Come on then, Piers. What are you going to do?" He applied more pressure to Anastasia's throat, and she began to choke. She knew Giles was fixated on Piers, and she had just caught sight of another shadow overlaying theirs—Guy—and he was close.

"Let her go!" Piers cried out, unable to stay silent any longer.

Anastasia took her chance as she felt Giles' grip slacken in response to his brother's torment; she brought her right leg up in a high kick, and her shin connected hard with his head, hurting them both. Giles staggered backwards, knocked off balance, and she staggered forwards, desperate to reach Piers. But as Guy broke cover, Giles caught her wrist and pulled it so hard she screamed. Giles spotted Guy and, suddenly, he let her go. Anastasia fell to the floor, her head spinning, her wrist now in agony. Guy moved to drag her away, but as she looked back at her tormentor, she could see he now had a gun pointing straight at Piers.

Giles moved his hand until the gun was covering Guy. "Get away from her." Guy took a reluctant step backwards.

"Stop this, Giles. Just let her go and we can sort this between us. Between brothers." Piers wanted Giles' attention on him, hoping Guy had a plan.

Anastasia struggled to her feet, stranded between them all, too petrified to move.

"I am going to end this my way!" Giles had a haunted look to his eyes.

"What have you done with Mark?" Guy's voice was agonised; he could see his little brother in a heap at the back of the cellar.

Giles moved slightly, the gun now aimed at Anastasia's heart; he knew they would not dare rush him and risk him shooting her. "Safely drugged." Giles then grinned at her, a maniacal gleam in his cold eyes. "If I shoot you, then I will have the pleasure of taking you away from him forever. And that is going to make everything worthwhile."

There was silence, the sound of breathing all she could hear.

Guy suddenly spoke, trying to talk reason. "It's me you've got the issues with, Giles. It is me who can expose you. I've got the book," he lied, anything to distract Giles.

"You're just trying to stall." Giles was contemptuous. "I know it's over, but I will take one of you with me. Question is, which one?" Giles swung his pistol randomly, his eyes wild, disappointed dreams now controlling him.

Anastasia stood in between his two brothers, absolutely terrified, desperately trying to defeat her panic and control her pain. Then she knew. Giles' hatred for Piers was always going to win, and the split second she saw confirmation in Giles' pale, haunted eyes, she moved like lightning to shove Piers out of the way. The bullet hit her in the stomach and, gasping, she staggered backwards. Her blue eyes held Giles', cold and malevolent, and she fell to the ground.

All she could hear were voices phasing in and out. Then anger. Voices and anger. Her sight was blurred, figures moving above her, then shouting and then silence. Her head felt fuzzy, like being really drunk, the most drunk she had ever been. Someone was kneeling beside her, and she was aware of pressure, a hand pressed firmly against her stomach. He was speaking urgently, calling her back from the blackness she longed for. Her eyes closed.

He seemed to need her, and Anastasia tried to focus on his words. "Please, don't leave me. Stay with me, Anastasia." He needed reassurance, but she could not speak.

She heard him again, now crying. "Please, Anastasia. Hold on, sweetheart."

With monumental effort, Anastasia forced her eyes open, but

speaking was still too much. She saw Piers, agony and anguish on his face and terror like she had never seen before in his blue eyes. "Don't leave me. Please! I love you!"

She tried to reach out for his hand, but she was tired now, and sleeping seemed a good idea. She could still feel the pressure of his hand, and Piers' face was close to hers, his eyes begging her. "Stay with me. I want to marry you."

She smiled up at him, and then there was only blackness.

Chapter 52

PIERS SAT IN the hospital corridor, his head spinning and fear in his heart. Everything was confused in his head; he had no idea how Guy had arranged things so fast, why a private ambulance had been waiting and how they had got Anastasia to a hospital so rapidly. The only thing he knew for sure was that he could not live without her.

A nurse handed him a cup of strong tea and tried to offer him some comfort. "Your wife will be out of surgery soon. It's all going to plan."

"Thanks." He took the tea, and as she walked away, Piers realised what she had called Anastasia; his wife. He frowned and then it came to him: next of kin. He had signed paperwork, and only a next of kin could do that.

He sipped his tea and wondered how long Rick and Fenella would take to get there. This was the second time he had done this to them; sent for them because Anastasia was in hospital. He did not have long to wait. He soon heard the same nurse's voice as she escorted a pale faced Fenella and a stoic Rick Lascelles towards him.

Rick reached him first. "What the fuck happened, Piers?"

Piers faltered under his furious gaze, and he looked to Fenella for support.

She patted her husband's arm and told him, "Sit down and let him tell us." Fenella held Piers' blue eyes, and what she saw there dismayed her. "Take a deep breath and tell us."

Piers was not sure where to begin and plunged on without thinking. "She took a bullet meant for me. She's in surgery."

Fenella's hand went to her heart, and she blinked rapidly. "A bullet? Is she … oh dear God …"

Piers took a deep breath and then told them everything about the first time Giles attacked her, about his involvement with Gary and him luring Anastasia away to cover up his misdemeanours.

Rick and Fenella sat open-mouthed, forlornly trying to comprehend what they were hearing. As Piers came to the end of his explanation, he wavered and then finally broke down, his voice raw with emotion. "I should've protected her. And now I might lose her …" He began to cry.

Rick spotted a doctor walking towards them and went to intercept him whilst Fenella put an arm around the distraught man sitting beside her.

"You can't blame yourself, Piers. Your brother caused this, not you."

"I should have finished it the first time." His head was in his hands.

"Come on, you need to be strong." Fenella tried to encourage him; she flatly refused to accept that Anastasia might not make it. "I know how much you love Anastasia." She lowered her voice, wanting him to understand that now was not the time to fall apart. "And I know how much she loves you. Don't give up now."

"Has it been that obvious?"

"To me, yes, ever since that summer …" Fenella broke off as Rick came back to them.

Piers stood up, his heart in pieces, but Rick was smiling at them. "She's out of surgery. The doctor wants to talk to her husband, apparently." Rick raised his eyebrows at Piers. "Forget to tell us something?"

"A misunderstanding. They needed next of kin to operate, and I have no idea where her father is."

Rick narrowed his eyes. "Probably for the best; he wouldn't

be any bloody use anyway." He put a hand on Piers' shoulder and said in a gentle voice, "Go speak to the doctor."

Piers impulsively turned and embraced Fenella. "Thank you."

Rick looked at his wife as Piers left in search of the doctor. "It's ok, darling. She's going to be ok. She's strong; she's a fighter."

Fenella stepped into his arms and a sob escaped her. "I couldn't bear it if anything happened to that girl. She's the daughter we always wanted."

Rick held her. "I know, and Anastasia knows that, too."

Within a few minutes, Piers was back with them, his relief palpable. "She's in recovery and then they'll move her into a room. We can see her soon."

"And everything's ok? No complications or concerns?" Fenella asked anxiously.

Piers shook his head. "Anastasia lost a lot of blood, but there was no major damage. She was lucky."

Fenella took his hands and smiled at him. "There. Perhaps now you can get cleaned up? We'll wait here."

He frowned at her, puzzled. "What do you mean?"

"Look in a mirror," Rick advised him. "I presume that's her blood in your hair, on your face?"

Piers ran a hand through his hair and gazed at his hand. "I was trying to staunch the blood. I didn't realise."

"She won't want to see you looking like that. Go on, we won't go anywhere." Fenella gave him an encouraging smile.

He turned to go, calling back as he ran, "I won't be long."

Rick and Fenella sat down. "What about Johnny?" Rick asked. "He'll be livid if we don't let him know about this."

Fenella knew he was right, but she advised, "Let's wait until she's in her own room and then he can come and see for himself. They won't want loads of people here now."

The nurse approached them. "Has Mr. Talbot gone?" she asked, sounding surprised.

"Just to get freshen up; he had blood all over him," Rick explained.

"Good idea; we don't want to alarm his wife when she comes round. You must be her parents? The doctor said you were here." She waited for confirmation.

Fenella hesitated and then said, "That's us." Well, she reasoned to herself, Anastasia was their goddaughter, and she had no-one else to act in that capacity.

"You can come and sit with her, if you like. She's still sedated but comfortable and doing well."

Fenella and Rick followed her and stood in the doorway, staring at the bed. Fenella felt tears begin to fall. Anastasia was laid on her back in a most unnatural position, and Fenella was uncomfortably reminded of a body laid out for burial. Rick took his wife's hand and, together, they moved to stand next to their goddaughter. Her breathing was laboured, and they noticed her wrist was heavily strapped.

Fenella stroked Anastasia's cheek and whispered, "Everything's going to be all right now, my darling girl. I promise."

Chapter 53

PIERS HURRIED BACK along the corridors and saw a pale and dejected Guy waiting for him. He faltered, anxious in case something had gone wrong in his absence.

"It's ok, she's fine." Guy put a hand on his brother's shoulder. "Rick and Fenella are in with her. She's just woken up."

Piers dropped into a vacant chair and breathed deeply. "I'll give them some time. It's only fair after what I've put them through."

Guy sat next to him. "This wasn't your fault, you know."

Piers shrugged; he wanted to take the blame.

Guy regarded Piers and smiled. "I'm glad we got the chance to put things right. My only regret is that I wasn't there for you all those years ago."

Piers looked uncomfortable. "It doesn't matter. We all have to walk our own paths, and ours didn't cross that often."

"It *does* matter. I'm your big brother; I should have tried harder."

"Well, I didn't exactly make things easy, did I?" Piers suddenly grinned, remembering many altercations over the years, usually at his instigation.

"You know how proud I am of you."

"If you tell me you love me, you're going."

"I understand if you blame me for this whole mess." Guy stood up and walked to the window to gaze out, unseeing, over the streets below.

Piers took a few seconds to reply. "Why would I blame you?"

Not able to face him, Guy continued to stare blankly ahead. "I should have stopped him, but I could not bring myself to believe Giles was capable of all this."

Silence hung over them as Piers thought over his words. "Anastasia is safe, and that is all that matters to me. I don't blame you at all. If anything, your quick thinking meant she survived, and I am profoundly grateful for that. She's the love of my life."

Guy now faced him, his eyes glistening. "I know, little brother. I know."

Piers stood up and crossed towards him, hesitated and then hugged Guy, trying to put his gratitude into that brief gesture. Guy clung to him, wanting to break down but knowing he did not yet have that luxury; there were still things he had to do.

As Piers broke away, he heard a door open, and a voice he loved called his name.

Piers rushed towards the room to see Anastasia sitting up in bed, several pillows supporting her. He let Rick and Fenella leave, and he stood just inside the doorway, smiling at her. She was smiling back, her blue eyes inviting. He shut the door and crossed to the bed. "What did the doctor say?"

She waved an impatient hand at him. "I'm ok. I want to talk to you."

He looked a little wary, unsure what she was going to say.

She took his hand, and now those blue eyes were huge with trepidation. Anastasia breathed in deeply, winced slightly and said, "Piers, I need to tell you everything that happened."

He kissed her forehead. "When you get out of here, you can tell me anything. Just concentrate on getting better first."

She hesitated, and he knew she wanted to ask what had happened to Giles. "And don't worry, he will never hurt anybody ever again." His eyes told her that was the truth.

"Mark? Is he ok?"

Piers smiled and replied, "Yes, one hell of a headache, but he'll be fine. He's going back to Paris in a few days, to sort things out for Guy on that side."

She relaxed back against her pillows; now she could say something much more pleasant. "I don't remember much after I was shot, but I do know you were with me, talking to me."

Piers nodded as he sat on the bed beside her and ventured, "Did you hear what I said to you?"

Her hand grasped his tightly, her eyes like stars. "Oh, yes, I heard."

He held her rapturous gaze, hope in his heart.

She reached up to caress his face and said, "I thought that was it, my time, and what more could I have wanted at that last moment than to see your face." She looked radiant. "And yes, I'd love to marry you."

Piers leant in towards her, hardly daring to believe. "I love you, sweetheart."

"Then kiss me." Her smile was joyous.

Piers hesitated, a mere breath between their lips, and then he kissed her with such gentleness and so tenderly that she sighed with content. They parted, and Piers felt his heart racing. There were no words to express how he happy he was.

She grinned at him. "Do that again, please." And he obliged.

Chapter 54

RICK AND FENELLA were waiting outside in the corridor, ready to take Anastasia and Piers back to their country home. "Why did he need to speak to the doctor? I thought we'd been given our instructions." Rick sounded annoyed.

"I'm sure Piers just wants to make absolutely sure before we leave," Fenella soothed him, hoping her instinct was correct.

Piers came along the corridor—he had not stopped smiling for days—and he called out, "Sorry, just one last thing to do." He walked straight past them to enter Anastasia's room and shut the door.

She looked up, startled out of her thoughts but very pleased to see him. "Hello, handsome."

Piers sat next to her and kissed her before saying, "I have something to tell you." He paused then stated, "I've organised the wedding for Chelsea Register Office on the 6th of April, with a handful of people we actually care about. You don't have to do anything except decide what to wear. I want do everything."

She blinked, completely thrown, then laughing, she replied, "Ok, you're on."

"They're watching, aren't they?" Piers asked.

Anastasia nodded in confirmation.

"Well then, I'd better do this properly or Fenella will slap me." Piers dropped down onto one knee. "Anastasia Travess, will you marry me?"

"Yes, oh yes!" And leaning down, she kissed him.

Within seconds, Fenella and Rick had burst into the room; Fenella was crying with joy and Rick was hurriedly wiping his eyes.

Piers stood back up as Rick reached him and shook his hand. "We're thrilled! Absolutely thrilled! But bloody hell! I owe Johnny a thousand pounds."

Anastasia rolled her eyes. "You bet Johnny?"

Rick exchanged glances with his wife, who obviously disapproved and declined to respond.

Fenella ignored him and took Piers' place next to Anastasia to hug her, still crying. "Stasia, this is what I've always wanted for you; for both of you. This will be the wedding of the century. So much to plan!"

"Sorry, Fenella, but it's all in hand." Piers said, beaming.

Anastasia tried to explain. "That's not what we want, all that fuss …"

"I'm organising it all." Piers grinned at the look of horror on Fenella's face. "All I want Anastasia to do is get well and choose her dress. That's it. Trust me, I've already got this."

Fenella looked at Anastasia, open-mouthed.

"It's ok, I trust him." Anastasia kissed Fenella's cheek. "I trust him with my life."

"Well, come on then," said Rick ever practical. "You can both stay with us for as long as you like."

Piers held his hand out to Anastasia and led her away.

30th March 2015...

PIERS LEANT AGAINST the veranda and gazed out over the Caribbean Sea. The sun was setting, and it really was breathtaking; the colours, the sound of the waves, the smell of flowers in the evening air. And then he saw her. His wife. Nearly twenty-five years of marriage, and he loved her more with each passing day.

Anastasia was sitting by their pool on her mobile, and from the joy on her face, he knew she must be talking to one of their children. He could see she was saying "Daddy," so it must be Elena rather than her twin brother James. He strolled down towards her, so proud of all they had achieved, and he could not wait to get back to London for the huge surprise Silver Wedding celebration he and Fenella had planned. It was to be a double celebration now, following Elena recently becoming engaged to Theo Cavendish's eldest son. Who would have guessed all those years ago? Certainly not him.

As he got closer, he knew that wedding plans were already in full swing. Elena was not like her mother; she loved the fuss and show and it would cost him a fortune, but she was worth every penny.

He heard Anastasia say, "Yes, put James on," and Piers knew they would be discussing football. Fancy his son playing for West Ham; he could barely look the rugby lads in the eye, but when James wore those three lions, Piers did nothing but boast for weeks.

Piers continued to watch the sun setting and then she was next to him, her hand small and cool on his back, her touch lingering.

"Hey, handsome. James has got us tickets for the match, and

Elena's already stressed over wedding details." Anastasia moved to be in front of him and stepped into his arms, looking up into his face and clearly seeing their twins, who both took after their father. She felt his heart beating against her and sighed; how she got so lucky, she would never know, but she was deeply grateful.

He held her close. "Elena worries too much. We'll be in London in forty-eight hours." Then he kissed her hair, breathing in Chanel, and murmured, "Come on, sweetheart. Let's have an early night."

She laughed and kissed him, happiness engulfing them both as the sun set in the distance

Coming next....

Desert Rose

Conaria 1964...

Leaving the nightlife of London far behind Victoria Barrington embarks on the archaeological trip of a lifetime, relishing her chance to explore the previously closed desert kingdom of Conaria.

Tadejah, the spoilt and favourite son of the Sultan, anything he has ever wanted has been his for the taking. Passionately patriotic, when he spots a stolen piece of Conarian history on Victoria's wrist his rage engenders an outrageous plan for its return.

Lured into the desert, far from civilisation, their guide vanishes leaving Victoria and her friends to face the machinations of a man who has never been denied…

Caught by the Moon

London 1817...

FINALLY FREE FROM her abusive marriage Alexievna, Countess Trischolvak, has vowed never again to be in the power of a man. But whilst experiencing her first taste of London society Alexievna finds her resolve tested to the limit.

Dangerously charming Hugh, Viscount Marchwood, has enjoyed making his reputation as a heart breaker, but never in his chequered career has he encountered a woman as unconventional as himself.

When Vladimir Ragenovitch arrives from St. Petersburg, Hugh perceives him as a rival for the Countess' affections and is forced to face the fact he has finally fallen in love...

FOR UPDATES AND release notifications please follow on Facebook at https://www.facebook.com/C-L-Tustin-Author-109346397535473.

About the Author...

C L TUSTIN was born and raised in the East Midlands but spent her teenage years in Sydney, Australia. Returning to the UK in 1989 via Singapore and the Middle East the travel bug has never left her and she has explored countries and cities across the world.

C L Tustin began writing at the age of 11 when she didn't see why James Bond had to be a man and created her own female version. Her first published novel "Escaping from the Shadows" is a romance with an undertone of threat set in the social media free world of 1990. She is currently working on editing and completing her second romance "Desert Rose".

C L Tustin has worked for two major banks, a tool company, the MOD and the NHS. She volunteers for Butterfly Conservation and passionately supports rescue dogs. C L Tustin lives currently with her rescued 15 year old Jack Russell Terrier and a diverse collection of books and sci-fi memorabilia.

Printed in Great Britain
by Amazon

54490888R00213